THE ANATOMY OF FEAR

Written by

Trudie Skies, Tim Hardie, LL MacRae,
Bjørn Larssen, Lee C Conley,
Jacob Sannox, Krystle Matar,
BA Bellec, Sean Crow, HL Tinsley,
Ryan Howse, and Zamil Akhtar

Jacob Sannox

[signatures]

The Anatomy of Fear

What do you fear?

Acknowledgments

The authors would like to thank the following people for their generous backing and continued support. Thank you!

Lana @IndieAccords, NC Koussis, Varsha, Jen Jarvis-Schroeder, Ashley Brennan, Thomas J Devens, Root, Seba Tellechea, Michael Delaney, Andrew Wainwright, Sylvia L Foil, Pierce A. Erickson, Phil Howard, Michael H. Sugarman, Paul & Laura Trinies, MyScorpian, Raymond B, Carly S, Dylan Humphreys, Sheri Hoyte, Señor Neo, Mark MacRae, Josh Bye, Jack Roots, Carrie Chi Lough and Mihir Wanchoo.

The Anatomy of Fear combines horror and dark fantasy - stories in this anthology contain adult content, including gore and violence. Some authors have elected to offer their readers story-specific trigger warnings which can be found on the 'Our Authors' page at the back of this book.

CONTENTS

FOREWORD

It's a universal truth that we are all afraid of something. Some fears we experience are rational and reasonable. Others are perhaps not so rational. Most are learned or inborn of our protective instincts to protect us from danger because danger lurks all around. We have a right to be afraid of certain things. Even if they are unlikely to harm us, the fear can remain. Not every predator will attack, not every fall from a height will maim or kill, nor will every venomous snake or insect bite us.

But what about the fears that we can't necessarily touch, smell, or quantify? Our fear of the strange, fantastical, and unknown? The stories designed to provide the adrenaline rush that makes us feel so alive - the heady surge that charges our sense of fight or flight.

I am eminently confident that you'll love The Anatomy of Fear. A gripping multi-genre fantasy horror anthology where fear and fantasy converge, this amazing collection of stories explores, among other questions, 'What do we fear, and why do we fear it?'

Featuring award-winning, highly lauded writers, The Anatomy of Fear fuses horror, fantasy, grimdark, Gaslamp, and modern gothic influences to create twelve unique stories. These tales will creep you out, get under your skin, and make the hair on the back of your neck stand up, and you'll adore every minute of it.

Krystle Matar, Sean Crow, Tim Hardie, Zamil Akhtar, Bjørn Larssen, L.L. MacRae, B.A. Bellec, Lee C. Conley, Trudie Skies, Jacob Sannox, H.L. Tinsley, and Ryan Howse are all writers at the top of their game. The Anatomy of Fear is one of the most gifted assemblies of fantasy, science fiction, and horror authors I've seen come together for one anthology (edited by the venerable Sarah Chorn). You will never look at your eyes, mouth, liver, and other organs and appendages the same way after you read this stunning, haunting, and unforgettable anthology.

Enjoy!
PL Stuart

PL Stuart is a fantasy author and blogger, and an avid consumer of fantasy, historical fiction, science fiction, and horror stories. He is the creator of The Drowned Kingdom Saga.

BLOOD

By

Trudie Skies

There were many appropriate responses when one came across a corpse. The human heart, as feeble as it may be, was designed to protect its sensibilities. Fright was a survival instinct to prepare the body to either fight or flee — or in some cases, to freeze entirely, which in this autumnal climate was perfectly understandable.

My instinct was none of those things. It was to observe. To understand. Even if my sensibilities argued otherwise.

This unfortunate fellow bobbed beside my feet. He'd been dragged to shore by the encroaching tide, his unceremonious demise hidden by the mist now blanketing the horizon. Waves lapped over him, claiming him as their own. If not for the blood moon casting her light, I may well have missed him. Though no, wherever I wandered, death wasn't far behind.

Footsteps thumped across the sand. I tightened the scarf around my neck — my only defence against the biting cold winds of the North Sea — and turned to Officer Sterling waddling between the dunes. His rotund silhouette was lit by the quaint coastal town behind him, and the lantern dangling by his side.

'Oh, it's you, Mr Westworth. You gave me a fright, sir.' He lowered his lantern to the fellow at my feet, angling the light to get a better look. 'Good heavens! Another one?'

'I'm afraid so, officer.' I nudged the body over with my boot, and it turned onto its back with a wet squelch. The body appeared fresh, yet the skin was deathly pale and taut. 'See there?' I pointed to its neck. 'Two puncture marks. The calling card of a fiendish devil.'

Sterling staggered, his black boots kicking up sand. 'A rat could have done that.'

'What kind of rat would leave such a mark? Face the facts, officer: since I've arrived in Radcliff, I've discovered three bodies washed up on the shore. All have been found in similar circumstances — pale, their blood drained. And all have been found at night.'

'Begging your pardon, sir, but what you're talking about is impossible. It doesn't exist! These vampires, or whatever you call them —'

'They're real. I've fought them. And they're becoming bolder as the days draw on.'

Someone — or some*thing* — preyed upon the good townsfolk of Radcliff, and I was determined to find them.

Sterling rubbed his neck. 'There's an explanation for everything, even your vampires. Would you accompany me to the station, sir? Help me write a report of this one.'

'I can't tonight, officer. I've been invited to a dinner party at the castle.' Which was the purpose of my visitation to this grim part of the country. 'What can you tell me about Baroness Radcliff?'

'The baroness? Well, she's a quiet lady. Bit of a recluse. Keeps to herself since Baron Radcliff passed away some years back.'

'A recluse, you say? I hear she creates art using rather… unique materials —'

'She may be peculiar at times, but what rich widows aren't? You're surely not implicating her ladyship in these murders, are you, Mr Westworth?' His gaze shifted to the western coast and the island visible from the shoreline.

The castle loomed over Radcliff like a spectre in the mist.

A solitary woman living alone on an abandoned island; it certainly painted a picture, didn't it? When the invitation came to my office, I simply couldn't refuse. And that was why my curiosity had pulled me to the northern coast. An eccentric woman by all accounts. Twice widowed, the baroness spent her days creating art of an unseemly medium.

She painted in blood.

'Do you fear the creatures of the night, officer? Because you should.' I adjusted the scarf around my neck. Criminals or justice didn't concern me. Leave that nonsense to the bureaucrats.

I hunted monsters, and Radcliff was riddled with them.

Though I believed I may have found their lair.

***

At almost six o'clock in the evening, I found myself riding in a rickety carriage under a cloak of darkness to the castle of Baroness Radcliff.

My carriage rattled across the causeway, splashing through puddles of mud and seaweed. I peered through the window and was rewarded with a salty spray. The North Sea sloshed against the wooden wheels — high tide was fast approaching.

Across the horizon, the ocean writhed like a sea of bats. Clouds obscured the blood moon that graced this most unholy of evenings, for tonight was All Hallows Eve, an open invitation for all that was foul and wicked in the world.

I came prepared for a long night.

Once the carriage cleared the causeway, we made our ascent to Radcliff Castle.

'We're here,' called the driver. 'Best wrap up warm, sir. We're in for a cold one.'

I heeded his advice and rewrapped the scarf around my neck. Upon opening the carriage door, I was beset by a rush of cold wind that almost made me stagger. The baroness's island had little to shelter it from the elements. Indeed, the few trees dotted about were stripped of leaves, their bony branches creaking with the groans of the dearly departed, their gnarled arms reaching out from beyond.

Only faint lamplight highlighted the castle before me. A well-known landmark to the locals and often spoken of in hushed tones, this old stone estate had passed through generations of barons and courted royal guests, though now its walls were chipped and moss-ridden. The windows were smeared with soot and hidden by thick curtains. Men had died behind those walls, banished to the history records. Though now, it resembled little more than a dilapidated tomb.

One other carriage remained parked in the driveway. I wasn't one for being fashionably late. It was time to make my entrance.

'Thank you for the ride, my good man.' I dug a few coins from my pocket and handed them to the driver. 'For your trouble. Will you make it back?'

'Oh aye, Mr Westworth. I best get going now to beat the tide. You sure you want to spend the night 'ere? I've heard all sorts of tales, I have. The baroness... They say she isn't quite right, if you take my meaning.' He shuddered and turned up the collar of his jacket.

'That is precisely why I'm here. To assess such

rumours myself.'

For that was my plan: infiltrate the castle and find evidence of the supernatural.

After that? God only knew.

'I meant no offence, sir. I'll be back in the morn when the tide's out, but I won't linger too long, if that's all the same to you.'

I patted him on the shoulder. 'Safe travels.'

The driver left my luggage at my feet and abandoned me to the whims of the wind. I crunched my way across the gravel and reached the castle's main door.

Three heavy swings of the rusty door knocker, and the door groaned open like a corpse rising from the dead. I was greeted by an older man dressed as impeccably as I, though he sported a moustache far grander.

'Mr Westworth, I presume?' he said with the careful manners of trained staff. 'We've been expecting you.'

I lingered by the threshold. There was no salt cast across the ground. No garlic dangling from the archway. No wards or protections. Nothing to keep away the wicked or foul… Nor to keep it locked inside. 'May I?'

The butler gestured for me to enter. 'Please, leave your luggage and come in. On behalf of her ladyship, Baroness Ruby Radcliff, welcome.'

I entered the vestibule and handed over my jacket, patting my waistcoat to check that the wooden stake I'd brought for such an auspicious occasion remained hidden within my inner pocket.

Oil lamps and carved pumpkins glowed with sporadic pools of light, highlighting the various dark oak furnishings. Dust swirled in the air and gathered upon the many cobwebs hanging from the rafters. Gaudy mauve wallpaper lined the hallway, almost blood red in this light. It appeared as neglected as the outside, yet I couldn't fathom if this was the castle's natural state, or if it had been decorated this way for show.

'You won't mind if I keep my scarf, will you?' I asked.

'There's an awful draft.'

'If it suits you, sir.' The butler lifted a candlestick from the wall. 'This way.'

I followed the fellow down a corridor where stern portraits of long-dead aristocrats stared in judgement as I passed. These halls were ancient, their floorboards screeching with history. I was a stranger to their home. A usurper encroaching on the peace of these hallowed halls.

'Her ladyship is currently entertaining her other honoured guests within the drawing room,' the butler said as he explained the itinerary for the eve. 'With your arrival, she will be pleased to host the unveiling of her latest art pieces. We will then adjourn to the dining hall for supper and wine tasting. Once you are ready to retire, I will escort you to your lodgings.'

'Sounds delightful. Are there many other guests?'

'A handful. Her ladyship likes to keep her dinner parties intimate.'

'Does she host these parties often?'

He glanced over his shoulder, his eyebrows raised. 'Once a full moon.'

Intriguing. There were all manner of cursed creatures haunting this world. Perhaps the baroness was of a lycanthropic variety.

We reached a set of double doors. The butler opened them with dramatic flair, allowing warm light to spill across my face. 'Mr Westworth has arrived, my lady.'

What I stepped into was less of a drawing room and more of an art gallery. Abstract portraits and landscapes covered every inch of the walls between decorative vases and marble statues. Four of Radcliff's gentry sat on couches within the centre of the room — three men, one woman — dressed in their most extravagant finery, their faces already flush from wine. Though it was the woman in red standing beside a collection of covered canvasses who caught my attention.

The ravishing Ruby Radcliff.

An older woman in her late forties, the baroness's beauty shone beyond mortal means. Pale, delicate skin, sleek black hair, ruby-red lips. Vampires who fed off the lifeblood of others were able to retain an unnatural youthfulness despite age. Innocent men such as I were warned of the seductive wiles of evil's temptresses. That is how they operated – they charmed their victims into their lair and devoured them.

Having now witnessed the wicked temptations for myself, I could deduce that such men were not so innocent.

'Mr Westworth.' She swaggered toward me, those thick hips swaying with the suggestive allure common to powerful women. 'So glad you could make it. I hope the journey didn't prove too trying? Travelling at this time of year can present so many… dangers.'

I took her hand and placed a lingering kiss above an onyx ring. Her scent washed over me with the force of the incoming tide, and I breathed in its salt and sweetness. 'I may be a stranger to these parts, my lady, but I know danger.'

'Oh, Mr Westworth, your hands are freezing! Make yourself comfortable and warm up with a glass of wine. Keegan, if you will?'

I took my place on a couch beside an elderly gentleman as the butler – Keegan – poured me a full glass of a dark red vintage.

The gentleman looked me over above the rim of his spectacles. 'Ah, so you must be Ruby's secret guest.' He offered his hand. 'Professor Rothwell – or Clancy, if you'd prefer. I'm a haematologist with a PhD in pathology and phlebology. How nice to make your acquaintance, Mr Westworth.'

A doctor of blood? Interesting. I shook his hand. 'Please, call me Morgan. I'm a freelance investigative reporter with the Antiquarian Society –'

'The *what* society?' one of the baroness's other guests

called out. 'I've never heard of you.'

'You wouldn't,' the baroness said as she leaned on the arm of the couch.

One by one, she introduced me to her other guests. The well-dressed couple in black were Mr and Mrs Harkin, the owners of a thriving funeral directors whose business I was vaguely aware of from researching obituaries. They looked to be in their mid-forties, though a life of wealth kept their skin and teeth in marvellous condition.

Beside them was a younger man about my age, early-thirties, named Jasper Flanagan. Another doctor, but of the psychiatric kind. He worked with the Harkins as a grief counsellor for their customers and had apprenticed with Rothwell. It seemed the baroness's guests were well acquainted with one another, which left me as the odd man out.

'And this strapping young gentleman —' The baroness rested a possessive hand on my shoulder. 'Is the author of many a ghost story. Those he claims to be true.'

'My work for the Antiquarian Society involves investigating incidents of a supernatural origin,' I explained. 'Which most of my colleagues find quite unbelievable.'

'Supernatural?' Mr Harkin jeered. 'What, ghosts and ghouls?'

'Occasionally.'

Mrs Harkin peered over her wine glass. 'Do you believe in ghosts, Mr Westworth?'

'The jury's out on that, but what I aim to uncover is the truth. I often work with the local constabulary to help investigate murders of an unusual nature. That is what brought me to Radcliff — a spate of unusual murders that I believe to be of a supernatural origin.' I met the baroness's eyes and raised my glass in a toast. 'And of course, her ladyship's generous invitation.'

The baroness chuckled. 'I invited Mr Westworth here after reading a fascinating article penned by his own hand. In fact, I was rather inspired by his account of monsters in the night, which led me to create my latest pieces.' She approached the covered canvasses on display before us, a collection of portraits and landscape shapes. 'You know me, my loves. I enjoy exploring the supernatural with my ink.' She ran her crimson nails across the covering of the nearest canvass. 'What I show you tonight came from the very depths of my soul.'

She gripped the covering in a tight fist and pulled it free, revealing the art beneath.

A smattering of gasps, shocked delight, and applause filled the room as the baroness uncovered each of her art pieces.

The paintings were artistically done, if somewhat tasteless. Many were of anatomically accurate organs oozing with blood, including a human heart — ventricles, veins, and all. Others were of naked women drowning in an ocean of blood. The most fascinating was of a male vampire biting into the neck of a female victim, her face an exquisite depiction of pleasure caught in the throes of pain.

Each painting was red on a white background. To the unaware, it seemed like a collection of various shades, from a bright red to a darker crimson and black. But my trained eye could see the truth. The splotches and veins that stretched across the canvas were inked with blood.

It was disgusting. Depraved.

Delightful.

'How macabre!' Mrs Harkin shrieked with excitement. 'Truly, you are an artist without peer.'

'Indeed, Ruby,' said Rothwell. 'You've outdone yourself this time.'

'I concur!' Flanagan added. 'May we take a closer look?'

The baroness drank in their praise. 'Why of course.'

Her guests meandered to the various art pieces on display, exchanging comments. Members of the aristocracy who delighted in the macabre were typically one of three breeds: those who indulged in the dark arts as entertainment befitting the socially maladjusted upper classes, those who had experienced such supernatural horrors for themselves and sought to understand their brush against darkness, and those who were born from the darkness itself and bathed in it.

Where did the baroness fit in my assumptions?

I approached the portrait of the vampire and his victim and examined it with a critical eye. Each brushstroke had been applied with laborious care. This close, the paint glistened. I pressed the tip of my finger into a red splotch and pulled back a smear. The paint was fresh.

I licked my finger and almost swooned at the flavour. It was blood, all right.

Human blood.

These pieces had been painted earlier today, which meant the source could still reside within the castle grounds. Could the baroness have bought pig blood from the butchers in Radcliff town? Or perhaps Rothwell provided donations from his patients?

There could be a reasonable explanation. But there could also be a supernatural one.

The baroness stood beside me. 'What do you think? Did I achieve the correct likeness? I based him off your expert description.'

'Oh, what is it meant to be?' Mrs Harkin asked with eagerness, as the others gathered to admire the painting.

'A vampire,' I said. 'A creature of the night. They stalk human prey and use fangs to drain the blood of their victims.'

'You don't say! Have you ever encountered one?'

'They're a child's tale,' Mr Harkin said. 'You don't actually believe in such nonsense, do you?'

'Don't be rude, Adam!' his wife chided. '*I* believe in it. Go on, Mr Westworth.'

The rest of the baroness's guests waited for my

account.

I swirled my glass, forcing the blood-red wine to slosh on a tide of my own making. 'I understand your scepticism all too well. I'm an educated man, Mr Harkin. A graduate of linguistic cynicism. I didn't believe in the supernatural until one fateful night when I encountered a creature of the night myself. It leapt upon me with such inhuman strength, I feared for my life.'

'That could have been any old drunk caught out after hours,' Mr Harkin said. 'What made you believe it to be a — what did you call it — vampire?'

'Because it went straight for my jugular.' I tugged at the scarf around my neck. 'And when I'd scared the beast off, I came across its first victim. The chap had been drained completely dry of his blood. I had a coroner confirm it.'

'A monster that drinks blood?' Mrs Harkin exclaimed. 'Whatever for?'

'During my investigation, I discovered tales of such creatures throughout history. Vampires were once human. They stalk their prey at night and sustain themselves by drinking blood.'

'Why night?' asked Flanagan.

'Sunlight is deadly to them.'

'Sounds like madmen to me,' Mr Harkin muttered. 'Have you ever heard such nonsense, Clancy?'

Rothwell lowered his spectacles and leaned closer to the painting. 'Certainly. I've read accounts of men who suffer from blood-related diseases that force them to consume the blood of others. It's a strange phenomenon. Such men suffered an adverse reaction to sunlight, as you describe, Mr Westworth —'

'Preposterous! Listen, man. I've worked in the funeral service for years and never come across a corpse drained of its blood.'

'Pray that you don't.' I smiled. 'Vampires are charming creatures. They integrate into society and make fools of us all.'

'You sound like you admire them.'

'How could he not?' the baroness said. 'To be desired for one's blood and not for one's estate makes for a romantic tale, doesn't it?'

'Indeed,' I said. 'You've captured their likeness well. Where did you source your paint?

'From anyone foolish enough to visit my castle.' She flashed a wicked grin. 'Each of us have brushed against death in one way or another. Though I'm unfamiliar with your history, Mr Westworth. Would you regale us with tales of your exploits?'

'Yes, go on,' Mr Harkin urged. 'I'd love to hear what drives a man to hunt blood-hungry creatures. Is it the thrill of adventure? Danger? Of uncovering the unknown? Or a paycheque with your name in print?'

I took a polite sip from my wine. 'It could be all those things and none at all. But I'll say this; it's a hunger of its own.'

'Would catching a vampire sate your hunger, Mr Westworth?' the baroness asked. She encircled the rim of her wine glass with the tip of her painted nail and watched me.

'I'd rather like to find out.'

The drawing room door creaked open. 'Dinner is ready to be served, my lady,' the butler announced.

'Thank you, Keegan,' the baroness said. 'Well, this has been a fascinating conversation. Shall we continue it over dinner?'

The butler escorted us through to the dining hall. We entered a dark room intimately lit with brass candles and a blazing hearth. Thick crimson curtains kept any natural light from reaching us, and more bloodied paintings decorated the wall.

The baroness took her place at the head of the table and gestured for me to sit at her right. Rothwell sat on my left as the Harkins sat opposite and Flanagan took the other end beside Mrs Harkin. Bowls of steaming red soup accompanied by a side of ryebread were already placed and waiting for us. A fitting starter. I caught a whiff of pork rising with the steam, though the soup contained the colour and consistency of beets.

'To the creatures of the night, the true artists of our fears!' The baroness raised her glass. 'And to you, my dear friends, for once again joining me on this darkest of nights. It wouldn't be All Hallows Eve without a good ghost story, but tonight I ask; what do you fear?'

'I fear the health of the living!' Mr Harkin grabbed his wine glass with vigour, letting a drop of red spill across his waistcoat. 'Eat, drink, and die young, I say! Though I for one am grateful if Mr Westworth's vampires would like to speed the process along. Don't get me wrong, I still don't believe they exist, but my business is with the dead. It matters not if the corpses who come through my door died in their sleep or met their end at the hands of another. Business has never been better.' He raised his glass. 'To death! Long may he ply his trade. I'm saving up for a new Benz.' He laughed and tilted his glass at Flanagan. 'How is your new practice going, by the by? Can you afford a motorcar yet?'

Flanagan sat up and straightened his necktie. 'I'm not ready to open my doors. Not without more investment. It takes time to establish a reputation—'

'You're too afraid to grab life by the balls, man.'

'It's not about fear—'

'There's no shame in fearing the unknown,' the baroness said. 'What about you, Amber? What do you fear?'

'Dying alone in my sleep!' Mrs Harkin whooped. 'Can you imagine? How dull!'

'Would you rather be ravished by a vampire?' Flanagan asked, his smirk partially hidden by a sip of wine.

'Depends on if he was a handsome vampire. I wouldn't bear my neck for just anyone.'

Rothwell choked on his soup. 'Excuse me.' He patted

his lips with a napkin, leaving a red stain.

'And you, Clancy?' the baroness asked. 'You've seen enough death in your time. Is there anything left for you to fear?'

'Only retirement, my dear. But even I must face my fears. Would you allow me a few words? I wouldn't want to hijack your evening.'

The baroness smiled. 'Go ahead.'

Rothwell pulled a handkerchief from his inner coat pocket and cleaned his spectacles. 'My dear friends. Attending these parties with you has been the highlight of my twilight years. If it wasn't for Ruby bringing us together, I wouldn't have made these wonderful connections.' He pushed his spectacles up the bridge of his nose. 'Working with you, Adam, has allowed me to expand my medical knowledge.' He nodded at Mr Harkin. 'As has working with you, Jasper, allowed me to understand the psychological aspect of my work.' He nodded at Flanagan. 'But now it's time for me to retire.'

'No!' Mrs Harkin gasped with mock shock. 'I can't imagine you resting on your laurels! Whatever will you do?'

'Enjoy my pipe and library, I expect.' Rothwell chortled. 'Though no, I'm planning on writing my memoirs. I have… much to write about. Things I'd like to get off my chest before I end up in your mortuary. Perhaps I'll take some inspiration from your accounts, Mr Westworth.'

Silence hung in the dining hall. Mr Harkin cleared his throat as Flanagan fidgeted in his chair.

'May we all live long enough to retire like Clancy.' The baroness once again raised her glass in toast. 'And you, Mr Westworth. What do you fear?'

'I fear the sun will rise without the answers I seek.'

'How poetic. You don't fear that death awaits you?' The way her dark eyes held mine captive was like that of a predator marking their prey. And I, against my own sensibilities, welcomed it.

I'd offer myself on a platter if it meant luring my

monster. 'Do you?'

Something tapped on the window.

Mrs Harkin dropped her wine glass. Dark crimson spilled across the table. 'Something's out there!'

'It's all right, my dear.' Mr Harkin patted her thigh. 'It's only a tree.'

'What is it you said earlier, Mr Westworth?' Mrs Harkin asked. 'That you had uncovered murders in town?'

'That's right. Three bodies have appeared on the beach just outside Radcliff in the past few days. Would you happen to know anything about this, your ladyship?'

The baroness tore into her ryebread, ripping it to shreds that fell into her bloodied soup bowl. 'I gave up my administrative duties a long time ago, but it's not uncommon for sailors to wash ashore. The North Sea is an unforgiving mistress. Those same waves took my poor husband. I still have nightmares of him walking out of the sea and entering my chambers at night. Odd, isn't it, how a dead man can invoke my greatest fears.'

'Apologies for broaching such an uncomfortable subject —'

'Keegan?' she called. 'The main.'

My stomach growled as the main dish was served. Investigating whetted my appetite, and the bloodied mess on my plate did nothing to dissuade me.

'Is this liver?' asked Flanagan.

'These are the hearts of my dear ex-lovers. Pickled and kept for such a special occasion.'

'If this was the baron's heart, surely it would be more shrivelled?' said Mrs Harkin.

'It's lamb's heart,' Rothwell said. 'Quite nutritious.'

'Don't ruin my secrets, Clancy.' The baroness dug into her dinner with too much eagerness befitting a lady of her status and made a show of relishing her meal. Her dark eyes met mine as she licked a dribble of blood from her lips.

Another tap thwacked against the window, this time with vigour.

Mrs Harkin squealed with fright.

Flanagan laughed. 'Did you invite your late husband for dinner, Ruby?'

'Oh, don't say that!' Mrs Harkin whined.

I needed an excuse to search the castle grounds without arousing suspicion. 'If it would put your mind at ease, Mrs Harkin, I'll take a look outside.'

'Would you, Mr Westworth?' she pleaded.

'Really now!' Mr Harkin rose from his seat with a groan. 'Let the professionals handle this. What say you, Clancy? Jasper? Care to stretch your legs and have a smoke?'

Flanagan topped up his wine. 'Not for me, thank you.'

Mr Harkin huffed. 'Suit yourself.'

'Will you join us for a cigar, Mr Westworth?' Rothwell asked.

'I'd be delighted to.'

I followed Mr Harkin and the professor outside to the castle's front porch, where they huddled together in the cold. Thick fog hid the town of Radcliff across the sea. The tide had risen, completely submerging the causeway.

Mr Harkin handed out a round of cigars and lit each with a faint spark that was quickly sucked into the void of night. 'A memoir?' A thick puff of smoke escaped his lips. 'What are you going to put in it? No one wants to read about our line of work. Hardly savoury, is it, Mr Westworth?'

'Didn't the unsavoury bring you here, Mr Harkin?' I inquired.

'Good company brought me here, not flights of fancy. Amber enjoys tea parties and ghost stories. I relish an opportunity to discuss business. Not going to be much of that if you're retiring, old boy.' He gave Rothwell a nudge.

The professor took a drag from his cigar. 'I've done

enough. Wasted years with a lifetime of regrets. Sometimes a man has to wonder if it was all worth it, just to fill
his pockets.'

'You've got a nice house, haven't you? What is there
to complain about? We've provided a public service. Advanced medical science.' Mr Harkin pointed his cigar at
the professor. 'What's the point in resting on your laurels
now? Retirement won't suit you. It's already boring you,
making you ruminate on the past, and what good is that?
Keep yourself busy, I say. Regrets are like the dead; better
off buried.'

'There's more to life than work. You ought to realise
that before your wife does. She doesn't just attend these
parties for ghost stories.'

'You don't know what you're talking about.' Mr
Harkin flicked his cigar from the porch and stomped back
into the hallway, letting the door slam behind him.

Rothwell shook his head. 'I do apologise for bringing
up our personal business. Are you well? You look a tad
pale. I understand Ruby's evenings can be, ah, unconven-
tional.'

'Thank you for your concern. My line of work keeps
me up late. You all seem to know each other intimately.
How did you and Mr Harkin come to work together?'

'Through Ruby's late husband. The baron advocated
my work. Thanks to his backing, I've gained a greater understanding on diseases of the blood. My journals have
saved lives.'

'How fortunate that these recent murders are keeping
you and Mr Harkin in business.'

The professor gave me a sly look. 'If you don't mind
my asking, is there an older Mr Westworth at the Antiquarian Society? I used to read copies of their journals
when I was a lad, you know, and the name rings a bell.'

'Not that I recall, though the Society has been around
for some time.'

'Indeed.' He eyed me over the edge of his spectacles,

his gaze dipping to the scarf around my neck. 'Do you truly believe vampires to be real?'

'Don't you?'

He hummed, as though confirming something, and then pulled a golden pocket watch from his waistcoat. 'Excuse me. I best attend to Ruby.' He snuffed his cigar out and hurried back inside, glancing over his shoulder as he did so.

A man with regrets could be desperate enough to dabble in the dark arts. The professor likely knew of vampiric practices from his research — he'd alluded to such before dinner. At his age, immortality was certainly tempting. Alas, my visit to Radcliff Castle had proven fruitless thus far.

In my search for a monster, I had unwittingly stumbled into a nest of the bloodiest kind: capitalist bureaucrats.

I tossed my cigar into the wind and headed back inside. The scent of blood overpowered my sensibilities, and I found myself wandering back to the drawing room.

A new piece had been added to the baroness's art gallery.

There, in the centre of the room, stood a large frame. In the dim candlelight, the details were hard to interpret, but the painting was of a life-size figure — a man — with their arms spread in an unholy crucifix. Crimson paint ran down the figure's neck and dripped to the floor.

Voices and laughter echoed behind me. I turned as the baroness, Mrs Harkin, and Flanagan entered the drawing room.

'Good gods!' Flanagan exclaimed. 'Is this another of your paintings, Ruby?'

The baroness's face paled. 'This isn't one of mine.'

I grabbed the nearest candlestick and examined the painting.

Mrs Harkin screamed.

The body spread across the frame, held up only by

rough rope and the leather of his belt. The collar of his jacket had been pulled away, and his head lolled to one side, revealing a trail of blood running down his neck.

Wide eyes stared back at me, but there was no life in them.

Professor Rothwell was dead.

***

On my insistence, the baroness and her guests retreated to the dining hall where I ordered them to remain. Summoned by his wife's screams, Mr Harkin found me in the drawing room, and together we carried the body of Rothwell to the castle's disused chapel. It was a modest space with no decoration or religious paraphernalia, save a few lit candles. Silence and dust permeated the air, making me feel ill at ease.

Carefully, we spread the body across the altar. I watched as Mr Harkin performed his examination. In the light, Rothwell's pained features were clear, as was the blood congealing about his neck.

'Cold, waxy skin,' Mr Harkin murmured. He turned the head to one side, exposing the wound on his neck. 'Two puncture marks. Death by blood loss.'

Both marks were the shape of one's jaw. There was only one conclusion. 'A vampire bite.'

'Nonsense!' Mr Harkin scoffed.

'There are all manner of beasts in this world, Mr Harkin. Beasts with fangs and claws. What makes a vampire so hard to believe?'

'Men don't become beasts.'

'You've buried numerous bodies -- you surely don't believe that?'

'Look, man, I've buried enough bodies to recognise stab wounds when I see them. You're an investigator, aren't you? There's a goddamn murderer on the loose. Whoever did this wanted us to find him. It's a message.'

I pulled a notepad and pen from my pocket. 'Why would one of the baroness's guests wish the professor harm?'

'Don't ask *me* —'

'You seemed rather perturbed by the news of Professor Rothwell's retirement.' Most of the baroness's guests did, in fact. 'Angry, I could say.'

Mr Harkin crossed his arms. 'Are you accusing me?'

'You were absent when I discovered his body —'

'God forbid a man should attend to his gentlemanly needs! You're new to our circle, Mr Westworth. Ought we to suspect *you*?'

'What motive would I have to murder a man I'd just met? Though you don't seem too upset by the loss of a dear friend and former colleague.' I flipped my notepad to a clean page and raised an eyebrow.

'Don't mistake my demeanour for complacency.' His voice came out in a low growl. 'While you're prattling on, the murderer could still be out there — my *wife* could be in danger. So why don't you take that smug face of yours and do what you're here to do? I'd like time to prepare Clancy's body for the morn.' He turned his back to me, his dismissal clear.

A foul deed had been committed this eve. Whether by a supernatural hand, or that of a betrayer, this meant none of the baroness's guests were safe. With the tide now in, I was trapped on this island with a formidable killer.

Exactly as I'd planned my evening's entertainment.

But of all the baroness's guests, which were capable of murder?

I returned to the dining hall. The plates and cutlery had been cleared away, leaving only half-empty wine glasses and freshly brewed cups of tea. Flanagan sat with his arm around Mrs Harkin as she quietly dabbed her eyes with a handkerchief. Opposite them sat Keegan the Butler and a young red-headed girl in a pinafore.

The baroness herself stood by a bay window, staring

out into the darkness as fresh rain lashed against the glass. She turned at my approach, her brow furrowed. 'Is Clancy…?'

'Dead.'

Mrs Harkin let out a mournful wail and buried her face into Flanagan's shoulder.

'But… How?' The baroness staggered to a chair and half-collapsed into it. 'How could this have happened?'

'Mr Harkin is still performing an examination. However, the evidence seems to suggest death from blood loss. In short, Professor Rothwell was murdered by a vampire.'

'Now, see here, Mr Westworth,' Flanagan said. 'Clancy is — *was* — a good friend of mine. A mentor and a colleague. And I don't appreciate you spouting such nonsense — '

'Are we in danger?' Mrs Harkin glanced up, her mascara smudged from tears. 'Is there a vampire here? On the island?'

Flanagan pulled her against his chest. 'Of course there isn't, sweetheart.' He shot me another scowl. 'Look what you're doing, sending her into hysterics. This is no game. There are no such things as vampires or demons or what have you. Please keep such drivel to yourself.'

Sceptics were always difficult to handle. 'Face facts, doctor. A man has been murdered. Either the killer remains in hiding on this island, or he hides within this very room.' I scanned the faces of the baroness's guests and staff.

'Absurd!' snapped Flanagan. 'Who are you to accuse one of us?'

'I'm an investigative reporter, doctor. This island is now a crime scene.' I turned to the baroness. 'Is this all of your staff?'

'All that I require to run my estate, yes. Keegan, you've met. Poppy helps maintain the kitchen and my chambers.'

Given the dilapidated nature of Castle Radcliff, I was inclined to believe she kept a short staff. 'With your permission, your ladyship, I would like to launch an investigation into Professor Rothwell's death while the blood is still warm. My concern is for your safety, and that of your guests. Are you able to arrange travel to the mainland? I must contact the local constabulary while I question your guests—'

'Question us?' Flanagan's head shot up. 'No. I'm sorry, Ruby, but I won't tolerate being interrogated like this! By all means, send for the constabulary. Mr Westworth has no authority here, and you ought not listen to the fancies of some lunatic.' He stood, lifting Mrs Harkin with him. 'Will you come back with me to town? At least we'll be safe there—'

'You can't,' the baroness said. 'The causeway is out during high tide. But... we do have a boat for emergencies. If you feel unsafe and wish to leave, then we shall arrange transport. Keegan can row you ashore.'

'That would be appreciated, thank you—'

'I'm afraid I can't let you leave.' I stepped in front of the doctor.

Flanagan's nostrils flared. '*Sir*—'

'*If* there is a monster afoot, be it man or beast, then it is my duty to investigate. Not only to protect the baroness and her estate, but also to discover whoever is responsible for Professor Rothwell's death. The killer could be lurking in a disused room or cellar.'

'You think you can take this beast, do you?'

'Hunting monsters is what I do.'

Mrs Harkin hung off Flanagan's arm, her eyes wide as they darted between us.

'Please Jasper, do as he says,' the baroness said. 'This is my home. I cannot fathom what manner of evil would hurt Clancy. You're welcome to investigate, Mr Westworth. I'll help however I can. I and my staff have nothing to hide.'

Flanagan sat back down with a sigh. 'Very well. I, too, have nothing to hide. I'll answer your damn questions, but as soon as it's safe to do so, we're getting on that boat.'

'Then it's settled,' I said. 'Keegan, if you'd prepare the boat for departure. The rest of you should remain together for your own safety while I secure the castle's exits.'

I began my investigation in earnest by taking possession of a lit candlestick and using the opportunity to explore the castle unabated. There'd be time to question the baroness's guests later, but I couldn't afford to let a monster escape me. Regardless of Doctor Flanagan's 'professional' opinion, I was determined to find evidence of vampirism in this castle. Though, was it safe to leave them with the baroness? Her remorse had appeared genuine, though I was not convinced. Acting was merely another art perfected by the undead.

The more time I spent in the baroness's company, the more certain I felt that she was hiding something. A dark and deadly secret that I intended to unravel. All the bodies I'd found had washed up on Radcliff's beach, and what better method to remove the evidence than to lure her victims to the open sea?

Her guests were also intriguing. They knew her and this manor intimately. They could be her allies, or perhaps unwitting victims. It was clear that each had a working relationship with Rothwell that became all the more complex via his retirement. By all accounts, the baroness's guests acted with the decorum of the upper classes.

It wasn't paranoia that drove me to uncover the truth, but dogged experience.

First, I returned to the scene of the crime. As per my instruction, the baroness had left the drawing room untouched. Blood still glistened in a collection of droplets from where I'd unceremoniously cut down Rothwell's body. The fastenings that had held him across the frame were still attached, now frayed. The frame itself was made from sturdy wood and iron. A vampire would be strong enough to subdue and then display the professor's body in such a fashion. They certainly held a penchant for dramatics.

I carefully examined the rest of the room. Unfortunately, the blood splatters and dust had been disturbed by various footprints, destroying any residual evidence. Nor did I find any sharp items which could have been used as a murder weapon. No knife or other tools. Only paint brushes streaked in dried red flakes. Whatever answers I sought weren't to be found here, nor was my quarry likely to return.

Slowly, I retraced my steps along the hall, careful to avoid spots within the floorboards that creaked. Learning to adapt to an environment and sneak throughout was a much-needed skill in my line of work, one that I'd perfected over the years. I wouldn't be discovered unless I wished to be.

I made my way through the castle and confirmed my earlier suspicions. During my stay here, I'd not come across a single mirror. Vampirism was little known outside of academic circles. Through my research, I'd learned their weaknesses: an aversion to sunlight, holy imagery, mirrors, and for some reason, garlic. They also enjoyed the darker, danker parts of their hovels. I'd once come across an abandoned lair within a basement and felt sure that is where I'd find evidence of foul doing.

In short, I needed to find the castle's cellar.

Rain continued to tap out a staccato on the windows, muffled by the closed curtains and the whistle of wind. I stalked across dust-laden carpets and passed locked doors. The further I ventured, the thicker the air hung with oppressive shadow. These halls hadn't been disturbed in some time and only the eyes of angry portraits kept me company. It gave the distinct impression of being watched.

I eventually came back to the kitchen. In a darkened

corner hidden by crates of potatoes, I found a hatch. Presumably it led underground. The dust here *had* been disturbed, and recently. Unfortunately, the hatch was locked, which made it all the more suspicious.

Damn it. I needed that key.

A floorboard creaked behind me.

I snuffed out my candle and pressed into the shadows. My eyes adjusted to the dark as two familiar figures sneaked into the kitchen.

'You don't think it could have been Adam?' spoke the hushed and frantic voice of Flanagan. 'You heard what Clancy had said — that he'd tell all in his memoirs —'

'Adam isn't creative enough to stage a murder,' Mrs Harkin replied. The two of them were huddled by the main kitchen doors, their silhouettes bent so close their breath clouded the air around them. 'And why kill him like that? In front of that investigator? If Adam thought Clancy would reveal any of our secrets, then he would have asked me to slip something into his wine, for god's sake! Why the show? The spectacle?'

'Because he's a damned fool. Three murders in town, so Westworth claimed. Was Adam responsible for those?'

'You know that's not our style. There're always enough bodies to collect at this time of year. The weather brings the dead.'

Flanagan paced. He paused by a table and lifted a chef's knife, examining the blade. 'What about Ruby? She must have known Clancy planned for his retirement. This is exactly her sort of spectacle.'

'She's done us a favour, hasn't she?'

'Has she? Then why invite that reporter here? On tonight of all nights?' Flanagan set the knife back down. 'We can't very well toss his body into the sea if he's known to the local constabulary.'

Mrs Harkin rested a hand on his chest. 'Don't worry about him.' She pressed a tender kiss to Flanagan's lips.

The doctor grabbed her chin, holding her still. 'Clancy

knew about us—who knew what he told Adam. He might suspect.'

'Let me handle my husband.'

The two embraced and then slunk out of the kitchen.

I waited in silence. The conspiracy regarding the baroness and her guests only grew more tangible. Flanagan likely had his own reasons for wishing Rothwell dead. Mrs Harkin, however, intrigued me far more. This was a woman who'd wailed and cried in fear and grief only an hour ago.

I found Mrs Harkin wandering the hall outside the kitchen. Alone.

'My goodness!' she gasped. 'Oh, it's you, Mr Westworth!'

'I told you to remain inside the dining hall. Your husband will be worried.'

'I was just on my way to find him. He's been gone for an awful long time. Would you mind escorting me? I'd feel much safer in your company.' She slid her hand around my arm.

I tensed at her touch. 'You'd not be afraid to witness Professor Rothwell's body? He won't be in a pretty state.'

'Bodies don't scare me, Mr Westworth. I'm a mortician. I have an affinity for all things dead. It's my desire to make them beautiful in their rest. I perform my best work at night. Do you ever rest, Mr Westworth?'

'Truth be told, I'm not accustomed to sleeping at night either, Mrs Harkin.'

'Please, call me Amber.' She smiled, her perfect white teeth flashing in the dim lamplight. With her beauty and charms, she was the perfect portrait of a vampire. Working as a mortician would give her cover and an opportunity to feed as her dear husband carried on his work oblivious, and oh, did poor Mr Harkin seem oblivious.

Mrs Harkin hung off my arm as we made our way to the chapel.

I knocked on the wooden door. 'Mr Harkin? Are you

still in here?'

There was no reply. I pushed the door open.

A streak of crimson led to the empty altar where Mr Harkin leaned, his head resting on the stone. The body — Professor Rothwell — was gone.

'Is he asleep?' Mrs Harkin tutted. 'I know it's late, but that's no excu—'

'Wait by the door. Mr Harkin?' I approached and placed a hand on his shoulder.

My fingers grazed his neck. His skin was cold, though my fingertips pressed into warm, sticky blood. The flesh was a mangled, pulpy mess, as though a wild animal had sunk their teeth deep.

Mr Harkin was dead.

I stepped back. There was no sign of struggle. Nothing to suggest he'd fought for his life. Only a golden watch half-hung out of his pocket. Rothwell's watch.

'Adam?' Mrs Harkin's face paled, though not with the deathly pallor of the undead. 'No!'

I grabbed her shoulders. 'Stay back. Your husband has been bitten by a vampire. He may turn.'

She shook in my grip. 'I don't understand—'

'Professor Rothwell has risen and fed off your husband.' Given the state of Mr Harkin's neck, I wasn't just dealing with one vampire, but perhaps another feral one. New-born vampires were driven by a blood-hungry lust, which made them all the more deadly.

'What are you saying? That my Adam may turn into one of them?'

'Unfortunately. But I can prevent that from happening.' I reached into my waistcoat pocket and produced a wooden stake. 'Step away, Mrs Harkin. What I'm about to do will not be pleasant.'

Mrs Harkin hid behind the chapel's pew and covered her mouth, suppressing her rasping sobs.

With one hand, I rolled Mr Harkin onto his back. Blood clung to his front, still damp and pungent with that strong, heady aroma. I tore open his waistcoat, then his shirt, and angled my stake above his heart.

His wife screamed as I plunged it deep into her husband's chest.

Blood, shards of broken bone, and other fleshy bits of viscera splattered across my waistcoat and chin. The latter I wiped away with a handkerchief.

Mr Harkin was not the vampire I sought. Nor would he ever rise again. But now I knew for sure that a vampire stalked this castle, including Professor Rothwell himself.

Perhaps if I could find him before he preyed on any others, I'd wrap my investigation up by dawn.

I took Mrs Harkin's hand and hurried her back to the dining hall. Only Flanagan and the red-headed girl — Poppy — remained.

'Where's the baroness?' I demanded.

Flanagan rushed to Mrs Harkin's side, his eyes bulging at the state of my waistcoat. 'Oh my god, what happened?'

'It's Adam!' She ran into Flanagan's arms and sobbed. 'He's dead!'

'What? How?'

'The same way as Professor Rothwell,' I said. 'Where is the baroness? How long ago did she leave?'

'She left not long after you to check in on Amber when she hadn't returned —'

'How long have you both known the baroness?'

Flanagan sat Mrs Harkin down and shoved a teacup into her shaking hands before addressing me. 'The baroness has been a family friend to me and the Harkins for years. I don't know what you're trying to insinuate —'

'Two men have died in her castle, doctor. More have washed ashore. Do you not find it odd that her ladyship paints in blood? That she lives alone in this grand castle after her husbands have passed on?'

'I prepared Baron Radcliff's body,' Mrs Harkin said with a sniff. 'For the funeral.'

'Was there anything odd about it? Puncture marks, for instance?'

'I don't—I don't remember—'

'Think, Mrs Harkin!'

'That's enough,' the doctor snapped. 'You are a guest in this castle, but you are no gentleman, Mr Westworth-'

'Poppy, is it?' I turned to the red-headed girl who started out of her seat. 'Apologies, but I require your assistance. Do you have a key to the kitchen cellar?'

Her brown eyes opened wide. 'I—I do—'

'Would you mind opening it for me?' I offered her my hand, which she took with tentative apprehension. 'It's vital to my investigation. You'll be quite safe. I promise.'

'Just what are you planning?' Flanagan called after me.

'To find the baroness. She may be in grave danger.' Or the source of it.

***

Instinct drove me to return to the cellar's hatch with Poppy in tow. She produced the key necessary to continue my investigation.

'Do you need me to wait here, Mr Westworth, sir?' She fidgeted with the strings of her apron, not quite meeting my eye.

I hadn't spent much time in her company, but observing her now, her skin had an unusually pale pallor, and her neck was covered by the frilly collar of her uniform. If she worked for the baroness, then she could be a potential thrall, or worse—a kept meal. Even the dead needed unholy servants to do their bidding during the day. What better servant than one who served as a midnight snack?

I reached toward her collar. She hurried back and pressed herself against the kitchen wall.

'Apologies. I didn't mean to spook you.'

'It's—it's okay, sir. My lady, she—she taught me to be

wary of strange men, sir. Except for Keegan. He looks after us.'

'That's wise. It's just the three of you?'

'Yes sir. Has been ever since the baron passed, sir.'

'Is the baron buried here on the island? Did you ever see the body?'

She gave me an odd look. 'I didn't attend the funeral, sir.'

I turned the key and the hatch lock clicked open, revealing a set of stone stairs leading down. 'Do you have any garlic?'

Poppy shook her head. 'We don't stock it, sir. Her ladyship doesn't like the taste.'

Of course not. I took my candlestick and made my way down into the dusty, underground musk.

This part of the castle remained as grey stone and not the wallpapered disorder upstairs. I passed by barrels and racks of wine. Cobwebs stretched across the ceiling, and spiders scurried away from my candlelight. Footprints marred the dust and I followed them to what appeared to be a stone door, carved with intricate patterns belonging to the Radcliff family crest.

The entrance to a crypt.

It was time to discover the truth.

I pushed open the heavy stone door. An intoxicating aroma hit me once more, stirring a primal instinct to follow it and obey. I blinked, soaking in the lamplight and the sight of Baroness Ruby Radcliff in a slim gossamer gown, her black hair straggling down her back.

She spun around, clearly startled, her eyes opening wide.

Blood stained the front of her gown. Human blood.

'Mr Westworth! I can explain—'

I grabbed her wrist, yanking her close. Her scent overwhelmed me—I could taste it amongst the dead. 'What beast are you?'

'It's *my* blood!'

I stared at her. At the throb of her throat, the beating pulse that marked her as human — alive. Those eyes fluttered in my hold, yet she did not struggle, nor cower. 'Yours?'

'Women bleed, Mr Westworth. Are you not married? Or has your pursuit of the supernatural taken over your life?'

I released her arm. 'I'm sorry, I… Your paintings?'

'Are painted with my own blood, yes. My flow is heavy each month. It provides me with an ample amount to paint with. Is there anything else you wish to know, or may I change in peace?'

I blinked and took in the room. Yes, we stood in a crypt. The walls held various caskets that had been marked with the passage of time. But the crypt had also been repurposed into a bedroom of sorts. There were no windows, but a four-poster bed, a dressing cabinet, and a closet which was open to a selection of gowns and… 'You have a literal skeleton in your closet.'

'It's my late husband.'

Well. I could scratch off the old baron from my list of suspects. 'Dare I ask why you keep your husband's skeleton in a closet?' It was in remarkably good condition.

'My art, of course. I place him in various poses to aid my composition. Honestly, Mr Westworth, do you assume me to be a killer? Do you believe I invite guests to my home so I may eat them?'

'Let's see, now. You sleep in your family crypt —'

'So I may keep an eye on them. Read enough ghost stories of family members rising from the dead and you'd be inclined to watch them, too.'

I raised my eyebrow. 'You served us heart for supper.'

'Lamb heart, by god! So I enjoy the macabre. Why else would I invite you here? If I wanted you dead, you'd be dead by now.'

'You're twice widowed.'

'Lucky me.'

'Two men have died in your estate.'

'Two? Who else…?'

'Mr Harkin. I found his body in the chapel, and Professor Rothwell's is now missing. I'm afraid to say he's turned.'

'Turned?'

'Become a vampire.'

A whining sound caught in her throat. 'God, I… Who could have done this? Why?'

'Do you believe in the supernatural?'

She looked me in the eye. 'Yes. But… Where could a vampire have come from? Examine my crypt if you must, but I assure you that my family remain where they are. Who would want Clancy dead? Or Adam?'

'Someone who did not wish for Professor Rothwell to pen his memoirs. Be honest with me. What secrets lay buried in this castle?'

She sighed and strode to her closet. 'If you must know… This began because of me. My anaemia. I've always struggled with getting enough iron in my diet, and with my monthly bleed… Clancy was researching diseases of the blood, and my husband thought if he introduced Clancy to Adam, they could form a partnership that would ultimately benefit me.'

'What sort of partnership?'

'You know Adam runs a funeral business. He often took in bodies with no identification. No history. Those he donated to Clancy.'

Ah. Grave robbing before the grave was dug. Illegal in this part of the country, but naturally the aristocracy would ignore such depravity if the results benefitted them. 'And then Professor Rothwell developed a guilty conscience?'

'No. My late husband did.'

'He wasn't lost at sea, was he, my lady?'

The baroness cupped her late husband's cheek bone. 'The locals were growing suspicious. My husband confessed to Jasper, during one of their psychiatric sessions. Jasper threatened to reveal the truth, unless we funded his new practice.'

'Sounds like you killed the wrong man.'

'Do you believe Jasper to be the vampire?'

Flanagan certainly had the motive and inclination to kill both Rothwell and Mr Harkin. Was he the vampire I sought? 'If he is, then I aim to find out. You should remain here where it's safe —'

'No. This is my castle. My home. Only I may desecrate it.' She allowed her gown to drop unceremoniously, revealing her bare flesh, her curves.

I couldn't keep myself from approaching. From placing my hands upon her hips.

From breathing her in.

'Your hands are so cold, Mr Westworth.' Her skin rippled with gooseflesh at my touch.

'Call me Morgan.'

'Your hands are so cold, Morgan.' She drew from my touch and slipped on a fresh gown. While she changed, I made a point to examine the caskets around the crypt. The lids lifted easily, allowing me to deduce that the contents inside were quite dead.

Once Ruby was ready, we made our way out of the cellar. The scent of fresh blood hit me before we emerged into the kitchen.

Poppy's body lay slumped against the sack of potatoes. Her throat a mangled mess, in a worse state than Mr Harkin's. The poor girl's head lolled to one side and was barely hanging on.

Only a feral vampire would leave a corpse in such a state.

I blocked Ruby's ascent. 'Don't look —'

'Who is it? Who —' She pushed past me. 'No! Not Poppy!'

'Stay back. She may turn —'

'Then stake her! That's how you kill vampires,

correct?'

I grasped my wooden stake—still sticky with Mr Harkin's blood—and put Poppy's soul to rest. Her blood pooled upon the kitchen's pristine tiles. Another unnecessary victim.

'If Jasper did this…' Ruby wiped a tear from her cheek. 'Poppy deserved better.'

We returned to the dining hall. Mrs Harkin sat alone, nursing a glass of wine.

She sat up at our arrival. 'Oh, thank god you're both safe—'

'Where's Jasper?' Ruby demanded.

Mrs Harkin blinked. 'He went to check in on Keegan. He's taking ever so long with the boat—'

'Oh god, Keegan.' Ruby slumped against the chair.

'I'll go find him,' I offered. 'Remain here where it's safe.'

Ruby nodded, and then reached for the wine.

I docked my candlestick by the main entrance and welcomed the cold deluge of autumn rain. The sky was a mass of mourning black, though I could make out the driveway well enough. Only the dead and desperate would be out in this storm. Muddy prints left a trail heading towards the causeway. I elected to follow.

There was little shelter between the castle and the causeway. No places to hide. Yet I picked my way across the sodden land with careful precision.

A silhouette shrouded by mist waited down by the shore. The butler. He remained still, anchored to a small wooden jetty as the boat writhed against the ferocious waves. Choppy was too light a word to describe the raging sea.

'Keegan!' I called out.

There was no answer.

I staggered down the dunes. The butler was sat hunched against a sea bollard within a puddle of red that sloshed beneath him. His eyes reflected the blood moon.

Open. Vacant.

Not even the rain could wash away the evidence of his demise — the torn flesh that flapped within the wind.

Something caught my eye, and I turned to face the castle. A shadowy figure watched from the clifftop.

I reached for my wooden stake.

And waited.

The rain and mist reduced visibility, but a figure was indeed making its way toward me. As it came closer, I tightened the damp scarf around my neck.

'Ruby invites a stranger to her home on All Hallows Eve,' came the voice of Doctor Flanagan. 'And then her guests fall to their fate, one by one. Quite a coincidence, isn't it, Mr Westworth?'

'The baroness —'

'Doesn't suspect you, but I do.' He came to a stop only a foot away and glanced past my shoulder. 'Is that the butler? Is he dead, too?'

'I trust you believe in the supernatural now?'

He huffed. 'Hardly. I've counselled men like you. Serial killers. They think themselves as heroes performing a public service.' He held up the chef's knife taken from the kitchen. 'A public service would be ridding the world of such filth.'

'Put the knife down, doctor. If you turn yourself in, the judges may be lenient —'

'You think *I'm* the killer? Clancy was my mentor. Adam, a dear friend. Even Ruby and her husband have helped invest in my practice —'

'Through blackmail. Professor Rothwell knew you and Mrs Harkin were having an affair. And I'd expect Mr Harkin wouldn't be too pleased. What would your lover think if she knew you played a part in her husband's death?'

'Amber delights at becoming a widow. It's part of her aesthetic. As for you, Mr Westworth, you're a sorry excuse for an investigator. Or perhaps this guise you put on is merely for show. I see through you.' He laughed.

And then he thrust his knife at my chest.

I leapt to one side, kicking up sand. Flanagan thrust again and again with the vigour of a madman.

His knife sliced through my jacket sleeve, narrowly missing my skin.

Despite his eagerness to stab me, he lacked the physical prowess of a vampire, and his efforts soon became slow and sloppy.

The doctor was mortal after all. A pity.

On his next thrust, I grabbed his wrist. He dropped the knife.

I pulled him close, as though about to embrace.

And thrust my stake into his heart.

He gasped; his dying words lost in the wind.

I let him fall backward and land with a soft thud.

Doctor Jasper Flanagan's dead eyes stared up at me, his mouth open in shock. I placed my boot on his abdomen and yanked my stake out. Blood and pulpy lumps of flesh dripped from the wood and onto the sand. I'd left a gaping hole in his chest. His ribs were caved in, shattered into his heart.

In hindsight, the doctor had needed his own therapy.

I wiped rain from my face and turned to the dock. The boat—our only means of escape—had become untethered and now was carried toward the sea.

We were trapped here.

And Rothwell was still loose.

I trudged back up the bank to the castle and dragged muddied boots into the hallway. My clothes were drenched through and covered in sand and blood. I shrugged off my waistcoat, which had borne the brunt, and untangled my scarf, allowing the sodden mess to squelch to the floor.

Screaming echoed along the corridor.

I ran for the dining hall. The doors were wide open with neither Ruby nor Mrs Harkin inside. Chairs were scattered about the room, and wine marked the carpet from where it had been tossed. An argument turned deadly? Or the arrival of a vampire?

The screaming continued. They'd retreated to the drawing room.

I readied my stake and charged inside.

Professor Rothwell — the vampire — advanced on Ruby, who wielded a paintbrush as a makeshift stake. She truly had read my articles. How touching.

Behind her, Mrs Harkin cowered behind a barricade made from Ruby's paintings. The useless woman cried hysterically.

'Please!' Mrs Harkin screamed. 'Do something!'

Professor Rothwell turned.

Blood soaked the professor's shirt, as though he'd spilled an entire bowl of Ruby's beet soup down his front. It clung to his lips, which cracked into a wide smile, exposing the sharp lift of his newly transformed fangs, and the torn shreds of flesh between his teeth.

'You!' he rasped with the croaking voice of the dead. '*You* are Morgan Westworth —'

I thrust the stake into his heart.

The beast blinked for a moment.

And then his body collapsed into a pile of dust.

'Is — Is he dead?' Mrs Harkin whimpered. She took a few shaky steps forward before her legs buckled.

I tossed my stake aside and caught her as she fell unconscious. 'Help me carry her!'

Ruby lifted Mrs Harkin's legs and we placed her onto a couch. 'Is it over?'

'Yes. Doctor Flanagan is dead.'

'And… Keegan?'

'I'm sorry.'

Ruby bit back a moan.

I wrapped a comforting arm around her waist and breathed her in. That scent had long teased me from the very first letter that arrived at my office — an invitation written in blood.

Her delightful blood.

She stiffened in my arms and glanced up. 'Have you been bitten?'

I absentmindedly rubbed the scar on my neck — two puncture marks. 'I told you — I was once attacked by a vampire. Fortunately, I am no easy target.'

'How were you saved?'

'I wasn't.' I smiled, allowing my fangs to show.

My beautiful baroness didn't scream or cry as my fangs sank into her flesh. I lapped her blood with my tongue, savouring the very taste of her. It sent my shrivelled veins aflame.

'Why?' she groaned as I lowered her down onto the spare couch.

'Because I'm a vampire hunter, my dear.' I sat beside her and smoothed a lock of her hair. 'I've searched far and wide for others of my kind. To find a kindred soul. And you *did* invite me for dinner. I was only too happy to accept.'

Tonight, my search would end.

Why continue the hunt when I'd found the perfect vessel?

It had only been necessary to kill Rothwell — by a stroke of bad luck, he'd recognised my name from the Antiquarian Society — yet turning and unleashing him on Ruby's guests had proven far more amusing than I'd anticipated. I'd hoped the threat of a vampire would reveal a nest, though alas. It hadn't been a wasted evening.

I sat and waited as Baroness Ruby Radcliff awakened into something new. Something pure.

Her hungry eyes settled on the unconscious form of Mrs Harkin.

Births were always messy affairs. My new wife ripped into Mrs Harkin's throat with gusto. Once she was satisfied, I'd take my fill, and then Keegan would arise to help clean up the mess. I hadn't bothered staking his heart for that very reason. It was hard finding good staff these days.

Blood dripped from the baroness's lips, leaving splotches of red paint across a new canvas.

We'd have ample time to paint together.

EARS
THE WHISPERERS

By
Tim Hardie

*O*nce, in happier times, the Principality of Perund was the jewel of the Amrilt coast. Thousands flocked to attend the annual regattas, some parading on the marina, others lounging on their pleasure yachts. They would bask in the admiration of their peers, dressed in the season's latest fashions, bedecked in rich silks and intricate high-necked gowns, sparkling with gold and jewels. Vessels came into port from all four corners of Assanda, the crews resplendent in their uniforms as they stood on deck, enjoying the adulation of the crowds.

That was before the Harrowing forced us to lock our gates and hide behind our walls. Before we were cut off from the rest of the world. Before we became afraid of the dark and knew the terror brought to our land by the Whisperers…

***

Amira Ducat found the quiet hum of the church of Saint Marcus comforting, the decorative vaulted ceiling and the bright banners of the Holy Mother bathed in white light, which poured through the high windows into the grand space. She joined the long queue of people, her ten-year-old daughter Clarissa holding tightly onto her gloved hand as she stared at the building with wide eyes. Clarissa carried a leather suitcase, scuffed and battered at the corners. The queue shuffled forwards inch by inch as they drew closer to Brother Percival.

'I'm so *bored*,' whispered Clarissa after about five minutes.

Amira looked down with an indulgent smile. 'There are lots of people here to offer their prayers to the Holy Mother. We have to wait our turn.'

The child thought on that for a moment. 'She's going to be very busy.'

'The Holy Mother has time for each one of us and lovingly cares for all our souls,' Amira recited.

'But how does she find the time? Is that why she has people like Brother Percival and Sister Agatha to help her?'

The person behind them in the queue stifled a laugh as Amira replied. 'Yes, that's right. The church's brothers and sisters do the work of the Holy Mother here on Assanda, ministering to the poor, the needy and the sick.'

'Everyone's so sad.'

Clarissa's words caught Amira by surprise, her throat tightening. Not trusting herself to answer, she squeezed her hand tighter as the queue shuffled forward.

Ahead, Brother Percival stood in his long black robes, praying with a soldier whose crisp blue uniform denoted he was a member of the Silent Division. The young man's head was bowed, eyes closed as Percival placed his hands on the soldier's shoulders. Amira supposed Percival's whispered prayers directed at the Holy Mother must be effective, even if the deaf soldier was unable to hear them.

grandfather, had grown rich after securing the contract to provide passenger services across the principality and beyond. After the Harrowing, Perund's economy collapsed virtually overnight. The Perund government sequestered the railway business to maintain vital supplies to the capital, whilst the ravages of rampant inflation quickly eroded the value of the meagre compensation paid to the Ducat family. Soon they were only surviving on Max's salary, since Amira's husband was appointed by the government to manage the company, repurposing their engines and carriages to carry goods rather than people.

A few of the railway workers recognised her and the station master doffed his cap, carrying her case as he walked her towards the armoured train. Ahead, Amira saw three men waiting for her, two of them wearing the blue uniform of the Silent Division. The third man was wearing a brown three-piece suit, wire-rimmed spectacles perched on the end of a long nose. One of the soldiers stepped forward, the yellow star on his chest marking him out as a captain as he offered his hand to Amira.

'Mrs Ducat. I'm Captain Amad Hamtha of the Silent Division. I had the honour of serving with your son Sebastian in the Perund Cavalry during his period of conscription, before I swapped my cavalry greys for the blue. I'm very sorry to hear of his illness and I pray for his speedy recovery.'

Amira was careful to ensure she faced him directly so he could read her lips. 'It's a pleasure to meet you, Captain Hamtha. The circumstances of my visit to Dornos are grave but I pray you're right and my son will soon recover. You have my thanks for accompanying me on this journey.'

'The Principality of Perund owes the Ducat family a great debt and the Silent Division is happy to assist. This is Sergeant Brasco,' Hamtha added, gesturing at the second soldier, who was a broad man with a flattened nose, which appeared to have been broken several times. 'And this is Mr Stevens, notary of the Ducat Company, who is also travelling to Dornos.'

Mr Stevens reached out with a nervous smile, his palms clammy and cold as Amira shook his hand. 'Please, call me Arthur, Mrs Ducat.'

'I'm pleased to meet you, Arthur. Is this your first journey beyond the city walls?'

Arthur cleared his throat. 'Is it that obvious, Mrs Ducat?' he replied, staring at the armoured train with trepidation.

Amira followed his gaze as they looked at the train, tendrils of steam drifting from the funnel as the driver and fireman readied for her departure. The steam engine was the only part of the train to have windows, and those were tiny. The glass was not only bulletproof but, far more importantly, soundproof. Once the doors were closed, the heat in the engine cabin would be unbearable. Behind it stretched a dozen grey goods cars and Amira swallowed as she saw the great gouges raked in the steel of several of them. The metal was spotted with rust and other brown stains that Amira didn't want to inspect too closely. One car was peppered with the unmistakeable marks of bullet holes. There was a single windowless carriage for passengers, shrouded in thick steel plate. Amira noticed more claw marks running along the side of the carriage, made by the savage hounds now roaming the beautiful countryside.

'The driver tells me they're ready to depart,' said the station master. 'May the Holy Mother protect you all.'

Hamtha offered Amira his arm. 'Come, Mrs Ducat. I know it's a fearful prospect but I have made the journey to Dornos several times. The armoured car is quite impervious to the sound of the Whisperers, I can assure you.'

'I'm not sure I want to take your word for it,' muttered Arthur, pushing his glasses further up the bridge of his nose. He forgot to face Captain Hamtha as he spoke but Brasco was able to read his lips and he quickly signed the notary's concerns to his superior. Until then, Amira hadn't realised it was possible for a hand gesture to be sarcastic.

Captain Hamtha turned to Arthur. 'Sergeant Brasco tells me you're nervous. I understand – I was too when I made my first train crossing. Just remember, we're dealing with little more than wild animals. They're no match for this technological marvel or,' he patted the revolver at his hip, 'a bullet through the brain.'

***

The dark carriage was hot and claustrophobic and Amira quickly shed her jacket, stowing this with her sunhat on the wire rack above her head. Opposite, Sergeant Brasco placed his rifle and sabre in his own rack and brought out a small book from his backpack. He settled down to read in the light from the softly hissing gas lamps as the train shuddered and began to move out of Saint Luke's Station.

Brasco noticed Amira staring and with a smile he leaned forwards and passed the book to her. It was titled, *The Anatomy of Fear: a collection of fantastical short stories designed to chill the blood*. Amira idly flicked through the first few pages, reflecting that she'd never heard of any of the contributing authors. Fantastic tales weren't her favourite form of reading material. She preferred to remain grounded in reality – frankly, that was fanciful enough without encouraging an over-excited imagination.

'It looks intriguing,' Amira remarked as she returned the book. Brasco crossed his legs and started reading the first story as the carriage gently swayed as the steam train built up speed.

Arthur was already sweating, wiping his forehead as he removed his jacket and undid the buttons on his waistcoat. 'Goodness,' he complained, taking some papers out of his briefcase and fanning himself. 'How far is it to Dornos?'

'Three hours,' Hamtha replied. 'Plenty of time to reach our destination with the protection of sunlight. If I were you, Mr Stevens, I would dispense with the tie as well. You look like you're going to melt.' The notary followed his advice, rolling up his tie and placing it with the rest of his clothes.

Amira closed her eyes, dozing as she succumbed to the warmth inside the passenger car and the rhythmic clack as the train hurtled along the rails, gaining speed. Once, there had been several stations along the way to Dornos and the journey to the edge of the principality had taken much longer. One by one, those had closed as people fled for the safety of the ancient city of Perund. However, people needed to eat and Dornos was situated in the most fertile region of their country. The army had fought several bloody battles at terrible cost to protect the town and its surrounding farmland. *'Save Dornos or the principality starves'* had been a common saying. Max had been obsessed with how to keep the railway lines open, the government investing a fortune into building the armoured trains that kept Perund provisioned. Once Sebastian had finished his military service and, praise the Holy Mother, survived his tour, he had joined his father and helped him run the railway business from Dornos.

Amira fretted, thinking of the short note from Max in her jacket pocket, the words hastily scribbled, so unlike his normal handwriting.

> *Ducat Railway Company Headquarters*
> *The Old Corn Exchange*
> *High Street*
> *Dornos*
> *The Principality of Perund*
>
> *7th July 1877*
>
> *My dearest Amira*

THE ANATOMY OF FEAR

It grieves me greatly to put pen to paper and send you such terrible news. I regret to inform you that our dearest son has been taken seriously ill. The doctors fear for him, my love, and in his more lucid moments he's asking for you. He's too sick to travel to the hospital in Perund, so I must beg you to come with all haste to Dornos to be at his side.

The company will arrange transport and you will be accompanied by officers of the Silent Division for your own protection. However, I urge you not to mention any of this to Clarissa. The Holy Sisters of Saint Marcus will ably care for her during your absence and if you speak to Brother Percival, I have every confidence he will make all the necessary arrangements.

Travel safely and I hope to see you tomorrow.

All my love

Maximillian

Amira's insides squirmed, the words burned into her memory. Max must have been beside himself at the time but she cursed him all the same for sending a letter that prompted so many questions. What had happened to Sebastian? He was a fit, healthy young man who had completed his military service less than a year ago. She prayed fervently to the Holy Mother that the Whisperers or their hounds had not found her son, who should have been safe within the ancient walled city of Dornos. Surely Max would have mentioned if that was what had happened? She kneaded her hands with worry, remembering the knock on the door last night and the bitter shock of reading those words. She had stayed calm for Clarissa's sake, helping the young girl pack her things, making it sound like a grand adventure. Clarissa doted on her elder brother, who behaved more like a benevolent uncle towards her due to the age gap between them, always spoiling her with sweets and toys.

'Mrs Ducat, are you alright?' Arthur asked, peering at her through those round, wire-rimmed spectacles.

'Please forgive me. I think I must have been having a bad dream –'

There was a dull bang as something crashed against the outside of the carriage and Arthur sprang to his feet with a cry. Amira remained in her seat, heart pounding, whilst Brasco continued reading his book, flicking the page with a look of concentration. The seconds passed and then there was another muffled thud, followed by three more in quick succession.

'What kind of bestial mentality causes such a creature to throw itself at a moving train, only to claw futilely at six inches of steel plate?' mused Arthur, his voice shaking.

'The hounds are hungry,' Captain Hamtha told him. 'If one of them manages to find some purchase, others can sometimes cling to their fellows long enough to try and prise open the door. It's an advantage of having six limbs.'

Arthur paled. 'And have they ever *succeeded*?'

'You mean in gaining access to the passenger car? No, not so far. The security door is very strong, I can assure you. However, there was an unfortunate incident at the cannery last year when one of the hounds managed to find its way into a goods container. Several workers died before the Silent Division was able to put down the fell beast.'

Arthur dropped into his seat, lost for words. Amira shuddered as more of the evil creatures battered the carriage. Closing her eyes, she tried to ignore the muffled thuds and the scrape of their claws. Now she wished she'd had the presence of mind to bring a book like Sergeant Brasco, or some other pastime – anything to distract herself from what was on the other side of those carriage doors.

***

The Whisperers' hounds gave up their efforts to attack the train, which thundered down the tracks at full speed until they approached Dornos Station. As the train began to slow everyone hurried to retrieve their clothes and other possessions, no one wanting to linger longer on the platform than absolutely necessary.

When the train came to a stop, brakes squealing, Sergeant Brasco quickly opened the door, rifle at the ready as he stepped off the carriage. He glanced around, gun following his line of sight as he surveyed the platform, taking his time as Amira, Arthur, and Captain Hamtha waited by the open door. Amira noticed the captain was holding his revolver in his hand.

'Just a precaution, Mrs Ducat,' he told her with a confident smile when he saw her looking at him, although his eyes remained wary.

Brasco turned to them, lowering his gun a fraction, as he signed to Hamtha with his free hand, the movements swift and precise.

'The platform's clear,' the captain announced, jumping down before turning and offering his hand to take Amira and Arthur's luggage.

Amira gasped as she climbed down the steps and saw the state of the carriage. Fresh claw marks had been gouged in the metal, concentrated around the single door, and the lower part of the carriage was splattered with blood, particularly towards the rear of the car. The hounds had thrown themselves at the armoured train and clearly many of them had met their deaths under its wheels. Amira looked down at her leather boots and when she shifted her foot it left behind a sticky, dark bloodstain on the platform, where the carriage steps had been spattered.

'They're determined creatures,' said Captain Hamtha, taking hold of Amira's arm to steer her away. 'We cannot linger, Mrs Ducat. Mr Ducat will have sent a carriage to bring us to your son. We must go and find them.'

The sun was bright and hot, Amira grateful for the protection afforded by her sunhat. Dornos Station was completely deserted and the train's whistle sounded, the driver anxious to be on his way to their final stop at the cannery. The armoured train slowly began to draw out of the station, smoke billowing from its funnel. Amira allowed Captain Hamtha to lead her away, Sergeant Brasco keeping his rifle ready as Mr Stevens uttered either a prayer or a curse under his breath before hurrying to follow them.

Outside, on the main road, a single horse-drawn carriage was waiting. Humans were unique in their susceptibility to a Whisperer's power, causing considerable debate amongst scholars and academics. Were humans vulnerable for physiological or psychological reasons? Regardless, humanity had only begun to fight back once Professor Laurent perfected his technique at the university. Deliberately rendering a person permanently deaf posed some serious ethical questions, quickly brushed aside by the principality's rulers once they realised it made the creation of the Silent Division possible.

The carriage's driver was a woman, wearing tweed trousers and a jacket despite the summer heat. She looked up, gauging the progress of the sun. They would need to be within the confines of Dornos' city walls before sundown. The station had been built in more innocent times, when people travelled to this region to enjoy the rich, rolling countryside and explore picturesque villages nearby – all now abandoned, of course. There was talk of building a branch line into the centre of Dornos but, so far, the bankrupt government had been unable to raise the funds for the venture.

It was only as they drew closer that Amira realised with a jolt that she knew this woman. The driver looked at her uncertainly, offering a thin smile as she greeted them.

'Welcome to Dornos, Mrs Ducat. You'll forgive me if I hurry you along but the fell creatures are growing bolder and I don't want to waste the sunlight's protection.'

'Then surely we should be on our way?' said Arthur, looking up and down the deserted road in alarm.

'It's Maria, isn't it?' asked Amira. 'Maria Toussan? You served in my household until three years ago.'

Maria nodded, watching as Brasco and Hamtha loaded their luggage into the carriage. 'I'm surprised you remember me, Mrs Ducat.'

'Of course I remember you. I'm glad you've found work elsewhere.' Amira felt herself flush as she uttered those words. A carriage driver was one of the most dangerous occupations, and although Maria moved with confidence and she spied the barrel of a rifle next to her seat, Amira was quite certain this wasn't a job Maria did willingly.

Maria merely acknowledged her with a nod. 'We must all make a living somehow, Mrs Ducat. Your husband hired me to fetch company employees to and from the station.'

'Perhaps now would be a good time to fulfil your duties and take us to Mr Ducat,' said Captain Hamtha with a forced smile. 'Time waits for no one.'

'Indeed, and time is short for we need to ride out into the countryside.'

Captain Hamtha stiffened at her words. 'I'm sorry, I think I misunderstood. We ride for Dornos and the Old Corn Exchange with all due haste, Miss Toussan.'

Maria shook her head. 'No, you read my lips correctly. Mr Ducat and his son are not residing in Dornos.'

Amira exchanged a look with the captain and his sergeant. 'Maria, this makes no sense. Whatever is Mr Ducat doing in the countryside?'

'He's doing exactly what the principality requires of all its farm labourers, Mrs Ducat,' Maria replied. 'Crops do not harvest themselves and your son has volunteered to help the common folk. Mr Ducat is… I'm afraid there is no way I can put this delicately, so please forgive me. Mr Ducat is concerned that your son has taken leave of his senses. He's tried every means of persuasion and is out there even now, trying to reason with your son. He's hoping a visit from his mother and sister might break through the… malady afflicting him, although I see young Miss Clarissa is not with you.'

'No, she's not, Miss Toussan. My husband was quite explicit in his letter on that point,' Amira replied, her mind reeling. 'Are you saying my Sebastian… Holy Mother protect us, you're telling me he's gone mad, aren't you?'

Arthur cleared his throat and pushed his glasses back with his thumb. 'Mrs Ducat, I'm so very sorry to learn of your son's unfortunate circumstances but is this plan wise? I have business to attend to in Dornos and I can ill-afford a delay.'

'You're welcome to walk,' Maria replied, sneering at the look of horror on Arthur's face. 'No? I didn't think so. I'm very sorry Mrs Ducat, your husband was most insistent. We have some distance to travel and very little time -- there's a fortified farmhouse a few miles down the road. That's where Mr Ducat and your son will be waiting.'

Captain Hamtha's face exuded disapproval, although he elected not to argue as the carriage bounced over the uneven track, Maria driving their horse hard. Brasco stared out of one window, whilst the captain gazed at the other side of the road, eyes narrowed and alert for any sign of movement. No doubt Maria would be keeping a careful watch on the road ahead.

'Sacred Holy Mother, it's not even soundproofed,'

gasped Arthur, clutching his briefcase to his chest as if to ward off evil.

Amira sighed. 'Unfortunately, Mr Stevens, they have yet to breed a horse capable of pulling a carriage made of steel plate. Maria's right, if we expect the farm workers to make their living this way, we shouldn't shirk from such things ourselves. We've grown soft, hiding behind the thick walls of Perund. In some ways, I admire the stance Sebastian is making.'

Arthur shook his head, muttering something under his breath that Amira was unable to catch. Brasco looked up and rapidly signed to his captain.

'You'll apologise to Mrs Ducat for that remark,' Captain Hamtha told Arthur with a glare, 'and then I don't want another word to leave your lips. Do you understand me, Mr Stevens?'

Arthur mumbled an apology whilst looking at his polished leather shoes. After that altercation a sullen silence fell over the four of them, while outside, Maria continued to drive their horse as fast as she dared towards their destination.

Amira looked out the dirty glass window, trying to ignore the anxious feeling in the pit of her stomach as the sun lowered and the sky, by slow degrees, began to darken. What was Max thinking, taking them so far out of town? She might have stood up for her son in front of that irritating notary but privately, part of Amira wanted to strangle Sebastian. The corn in the fields was already bright yellow, swaying gently in the breeze, tinged now with the first hint of a pink sunset. Amira swallowed, trying to appear braver than she felt until eventually she could stand it no longer. As the carriage swayed from side to side, she clambered to her feet and knocked hard on the roof.

'Maria. Maria, how much farther do we have to go?' When Maria didn't answer Amira contemplated opening the door and leaning out the window, deciding against it when she saw how fast they were travelling. She pounded on the roof once more, to no avail.

'Sweet Holy Mother, is she deaf?' Arthur complained, looking horror struck as he caught Brasco's eye and realised what he'd said.

'No,' Hamtha replied. 'She's ignoring us. This was a mistake. We should never have let her persuade us to travel away from the city.' He drew his revolver from its holster, raising an eyebrow as he saw Amira's expression. 'I'm not going to shoot her while she's driving the carriage, but we'd best be prepared. I don't trust this woman, Mrs Ducat, and neither should you.'

***

Eventually the carriage slowed and came to a halt, surrounded by wheat fields with a green hill rising in the distance. There was no sign of the fortified farmhouse Maria had mentioned and the sun was low to the horizon, dusk creeping across the land.

Arthur looked around wildly as they heard Maria getting down from her seat on top of the carriage. 'The woman's lost her mind. She's kidnapped us and brought us out into the wilderness.'

'This is hardly the wilderness,' said Hamtha, 'but you're right. We're in danger out here.' He signalled to Brasco, who already had his rifle pointing at the door as Maria opened it. She, too, was carrying a rifle and the pair glared at each other as they considered their options.

In the distance, a creature howled. Unlike the Whisperers they served, the hounds did not fear the sunshine, although they became bolder at night. Maria took a couple of paces backwards, keeping her rifle levelled at Amira and her companions.

'Did you hear that?' Amira said, trying to keep her voice steady. 'Maria, I don't know what's going on but we're all in terrible danger out here, yourself included.

We need to turn this carriage around and make for Dornos with all possible haste, whilst we still have the light.'

'No.' Maria's lip was curled with disdain as she took another step backwards.

'Miss Toussan,' began Captain Hamtha, 'I'm going to exit this carriage. If you attempt to harm me or my companions, we will not hesitate to fire upon you. Do you understand?'

'You've no idea what it was like,' Maria replied as the captain put his foot on the carriage steps and began, slowly, to climb down. 'I was destitute after your husband gave me the sack, Mrs Ducat. Do you know what it's like to live in Perund with no means to support yourself? The authorities are quick to clear the streets of people like me, people who, until recently, led respectable lives and had prospects. They dressed it up nicely, of course. A wonderful opportunity to serve the principality, growing food for everyone, keeping us fit and strong as we fight this war. Except it's not a war, is it? It's an occupation and we're already conquered.'

One of the hounds howled to its fellows. The beasts were drawing closer and their horse stamped nervously. A sick feeling was spreading through Amira as she listened to Maria's tale. Sacking their domestic staff had been a necessary economy and Max had returned to Perund to tell them personally. Amira could still picture Maria's shocked face and remembered feeling terrible at the time. However, she'd put those painful memories aside afterwards as she took charge of their household in Perund. Holy Mother, she'd never given the poor woman a second thought. They'd written her a glowing letter of recommendation and cast her out onto the street, until Maria's path crossed Max's once more.

Hamtha was now standing on the road, his gun levelled at Maria. 'Sergeant Brasco is going to leave the carriage, Miss Toussan, and then you're going to lay your rifle on the ground and step away from the weapon. Do I make myself clear?'

'You don't hold the advantage here, Captain. You'll do exactly as I say if you want to find Mr Ducat and his son.'

'What have you done to them?' Amira cried, feeling trapped inside the carriage as Brasco made his cautious exit. 'How do we know they're still alive?'

'Because they're waiting for you, Mrs Ducat. You'll find them over there, on that hill.'

Something in Maria's words chilled Amira's blood and when she glanced in the direction of the hill she felt a sense of dread. Part of her wanted to flee, yet at the same time she needed to know what had happened. She *had* to find Sebastian and Max.

'But for the twists and turns of fate, my life could have been yours,' Maria told them. 'The rich of Perund have always been careless with the lives of ordinary folk. Now, the Whisperers have given me a chance to settle the score.'

'She's in *league* with them,' squeaked Arthur. 'It's not your son who's lost all reason, Mrs Ducat, it's this woman. We have to secure the carriage and flee before it's too late.'

'No. Not without my son and husband.'

By now, Sergeant Brasco was also out of the carriage and had taken several paces away from the door, making it more difficult for Maria to keep her rifle trained on both soldiers as Captain Hamtha spoke. 'The time for discussion is over, Miss Toussan. Surrender your weapon or we will fire upon you. You will not receive another warning.'

With a snarl, a pack of hounds burst from the field, battering the carriage as they flung themselves against it. The windows broke and as Arthur recoiled in panic Amira found herself staring into the wild eyes of the savage beast. Six-limbed, like the Whisperers, they were not of Assanda, although their thick furry hide enabled them to endure the sun's rays, unlike their masters. The nearest hound planted four of its clawed arms around the broken window, standing on its remaining two limbs as it strained against the frame. The horse screamed as it made a futile attempt to bolt, as more hounds descended on the terrified animal. They brought it down, sinking their fangs into its flesh as the carriage door shattered and the hound burst inside and dove for Amira. She closed her eyes, bringing her arms up as a shot rang out, quickly followed by two more. Amira tumbled out of the broken carriage and landed on the hard ground.

'Get up.' It was Arthur, dragging her to her feet as more shots rang out. 'If you want to live, run.'

Amira staggered away from the shattered remains of the carriage, the monster that had tried to kill her lying in a pool of spreading blood as Captain Hamtha put a final round in the beast's head. Most of the remaining pack were rending the horse to pieces, although two were circling round, having noticed that Maria was separated from the rest of the group. One of them growled, crouching on its six powerful legs, getting ready to pounce.

'No, I did what you wanted. I did everything you asked me to do!' screamed Maria as the two hounds leapt towards her. 'Call them off! Call them off!'

Maria had time to fire her rifle once, the bullet hitting the side of one hound as it sprang into the air. The creature cried in pain, the noise mingling with Maria's shrieks of fear as she was dragged to the ground by its front claws. Its companion dived straight for her throat, its razor-sharp jaws cutting off her terrified screams as she died, legs thrashing on the floor.

'Move,' Captain Hamtha told them, pushing Amira in the small of her back.

Together, the four of them fled the scene, running through the wheatfields. Amira led the way, making for the green hill Maria had indicated earlier. Max and Sebastian were there, she was sure of it. Eventually, her lungs burning, she could run no further and they stopped next to a small brook at the edge of one of the fields. Arthur cast a frightened look back the way they had come, no doubt expecting the hounds to be in hot pursuit. Their tracks were all too easy to follow but, of the hounds, there was no sign.

'Perhaps… perhaps they've had… their fill,' Arthur gasped, still holding firmly to his briefcase as if it were the most precious object in the world.

'Unfortunately, those fell beasts move far more quickly on six legs than we can on two,' Hamtha remarked, taking the opportunity to put another six rounds into his revolver, Brasco also reloading his rifle. 'They have our scent and they will hunt us down. I just wish I knew whether Miss Toussan was telling the truth when she mentioned a fortified farmhouse nearby. Our only chance is to find it.'

The sky was still light but Amira felt a chill, sensing rather than seeing the last sliver of sun sinking below the horizon of the Dornos countryside. Although Hamtha and Brasco were oblivious, she and Arthur both froze, petrified, at the thin, keening wail that drifted out over the fields.

***

The four of them ran on, making for the hill in the absence of any other plan. Amira wiped sweat from her eyes, cursing under her breath when Arthur stumbled and spent what felt like forever looking for his glasses. He almost sobbed with relief when he found them, brushing off the dirt with his fingertips before placing them back on his nose.

'I don't understand,' Arthur breathed. 'Those hounds should be on us by now.'

Hamtha pursed his lips. 'They're coming, you can be sure of that. However, now that the Whisperers are abroad, they'll hold back and defer to their masters. They're stalking us.'

'We need –' Amira gasped, unable to finish her sentence as the Whisperer's Wail struck, closer and more powerful. The sound raked at her ears, pulsating through her body, tendrils of pain spiderwebbing through her organs, a dozen hot pins driven into each and every bone.

She slumped against Captain Hamtha as Arthur leant on Brasco for support, moaning. The sound faded, although Amira was sure she could still hear it, echoing somewhere. She blinked, watching as the crops began to sway on the far side of the wheatfield. She swallowed, unable to find her voice as she grabbed Hamtha's arm and frantically pointed. When Hamtha spotted the motion he swiftly signed to Brasco, who nodded and hauled Arthur forwards.

'It would be a great help, Mrs Ducat, if you could try and walk a little faster,' Captain Hamtha told her, voice calm.

Amira moaned, trying to find her strength and quell her rising fear. Enough had been feverishly reported in the press over the years since the Whisperers first appeared to make her aware of just how much danger they were in. The Wail was used to disorientate and disable their prey, incapacitating them until they were close enough for the Embrace. She prayed to the Holy Mother that it wouldn't end like this. With an effort, Amira broke into a run and she could hear Arthur's ragged breaths right behind her. There was another noise as well, coming through the wheatfields. A low growl, drawing closer.

'The hounds,' Arthur called. 'They're coming!'

Amira looked over her shoulder and saw that Sergeant Brasco had dropped back, rifle ready, as the wheatfield behind him erupted and the hounds closed him down. He growled, planting his feet and raising his rifle, discharging a shot straight through the head of the nearest hound.

'Captain Hamtha, they're upon us,' Amira screamed.

Brasco fired again, felling a second beast. A shadow rose up from behind the baying hounds and Amira's voice failed as Brasco backed slowly away, making every shot count. The Whisperers were six limbed like their hounds, although their skin was a mottled grey, spotted in places where, no doubt, the monster had been exposed to the sun. Although they ran on all six legs, they were able to stand on two and as the Whisperer raised itself up it towered over Brasco, measuring at least eight feet. It was the sightless, earless head that was most alien, unlike the fanged visage of the hounds. The creature's head was entirely comprised of a drooling mouth tapering at the end of a flexible neck, its jaws opened unfeasibly wide as it emitted a piercing Dagger Shriek, the sound focussed entirely on Brasco.

Amira felt the impact wash over her, feeling nauseous but not as debilitated as when the beast used the Wail. Were it not for his deafness, the Dagger Shriek would have rendered Brasco unconscious. Raising his rifle, three shots rang out in quick succession as they punched into the torso and one of the Whisperer's shoulders. The monster howled in pain and the hounds leapt to its defence. A deaf man couldn't be touched by the Wail or the Embrace but the Whisperer's hounds were still deadly. They charged Brasco as he tried to escape, one dying from a gunshot to the heart moments before the pack brought him down. Brasco growled, ramming the muzzle of his rifle into the maw of one hound, its head exploding as he pulled the trigger. The beast's body slumped away but its fellows pinned Brasco's arms and legs, tearing at his flesh. Brasco looked up, face covered in blood, his eyes meeting those of his captain and he gave a single, short nod.

Captain Hamtha swallowed hard and took careful aim, a single bullet striking his comrade in the heart, and Brasco's struggles ceased as the hounds descended on him. Amira sobbed as they turned and fled the scene, trying to ignore the noise of the hounds feasting.

***

'I'm sorry, I was too slow,' Arthur said yet again as they scrambled over a barbed wire fence and found themselves at the foot of the hill. 'It's my fault. It's my fault Brasco's dead.'

'It was my shot that took his life. If the positions were reversed, he'd have done the same for me,' Hamtha replied, looking exhausted. There was no sign of their pursuers and the captain reached into his belt, slipping a bullet into the empty chamber of his revolver so it carried its full complement of six rounds.

'I don't understand,' Amira gasped, looking down at the ripped sleeve of her blouse, which she'd torn on the wire fence. 'They were right behind us. Why didn't they finish us? Why let us escape?'

'We haven't escaped,' muttered Hamtha. 'They wanted us to come here. Remember what Maria said?'

'They're waiting for us,' said Amira. 'She said Max and Sebastian were waiting for us on the hill...' She trailed off as she saw a figure standing where the hill was crowned by a dozen standing stones. She gasped. 'There! You see? That's Max!'

Hamtha shook his head. 'Mrs Ducat, please. We can't trust anything Miss Toussan said. We don't know who or what that is.'

The person was waving them forwards, urging them to climb the hill. The light was fading quickly and it was impossible to distinguish his features but something in the way he was moving gave Amira's heart a jolt of hope. It was *Max*.

'Captain Hamtha, please listen to me. I *know* that's my husband. Wouldn't it make sense to go to him? Isn't it easier to defend ourselves if we have higher ground? We might be able to spot the fortified farmhouse from up there, as long as we reach the summit before darkness falls.'

Her voice died in her throat as the Whisperer

appeared on the edge of the neighbouring field, limping from the wounds Brasco had inflicted, its surviving hounds crawling along in its wake. Arthur cowered, all of them expecting the debilitating Wail that would leave them helpless. It didn't come.

'What are they waiting for?' mused Hamtha, looking torn as he glanced back towards the summit.

In the dimming light, Amira saw the man waving at them, more urgently this time. She made her decision. 'I'm going to him. You two can follow me or face those monsters, but my husband is calling to me and I'm not going to leave him out there alone.'

**

Amira struggled up the steep hill, Arthur and Hamtha reluctantly following in her wake. Darkness crept across the Dornos countryside as she drew near the summit, but the faint light was enough to reveal the outline of Max's square jaw and his handsome features. Amira was sobbing with relief as she ran into his arms.

'It's you, it's really you. We've found you.'

'Amira', Max whispered in her ear, holding her tight. 'My love, I'm so sorry.'

'Mr Ducat,' Captain Hamtha said, drawing in a deep breath as Arthur crouched, looking like he was about to be sick. 'We're pleased to have found you but I regret that we are in some distress and, unless you know something that would aid us, I fear we're trapped up here by this Whisperer and its foul hounds.'

Max looked at the soldier, glancing at his revolver. 'You came alone? No other soldiers?'

Hamtha shook his head, moving closer to Max to be able to read his lips in the gathering shadows. 'I regret not, Mr Ducat. We did not anticipate setting out into the open countryside. We were misled by your own employee, Miss Toussan, who used a ruse to drive us out here. My sergeant lost his life defending us.'

Max sighed, rubbing Amira's shoulders as she stood next to him. 'The Whisperers have no love for the Silent Division, I'm afraid. You offer poor sport for their malignant appetites.'

'Yet they hold back,' said Arthur. 'Why is that Mr Ducat? What are they waiting for?'

A shadow passed across Max's face as he moved his jacket, drawing out his firearm from the holster at his side. It was a heavy revolver, a common weapon carried by the gentry when travelling beyond the confines of Perund and not dissimilar to Captain Hamtha's gun. People wanted something relatively discreet but powerful enough to bring down a hound, if they had no other option except to fight.

Captain Hamtha sighed. 'I'm afraid we're lacking firepower, Mr Ducat, although any weapon is welcome –'

Max pointed the gun at Hamtha, whose eyes widened in shock the instant before Max pulled the trigger. The sound of the gunshot ricocheted around the standing stones as Hamtha staggered backwards, dropping his revolver to the ground. Arthur cried out in fright and Amira rushed to Hamtha's side, frantically trying to stem the flow of blood gushing from the neat hole in his chest, an ugly, dark stain spreading across the pale captain's star on his uniform.

'Max! Maximillian! What have you done? Oh, sweet Holy Mother, Captain Hamtha. Hold on, Captain. Arthur, help me.'

Captain Hamtha stared up at her and as the last of the light was leached from the sky and darkness fell, Amira realised the poor man couldn't understand a word she was saying. She grasped his hand tightly in hers, aware it was slick with blood, choking back tears as she felt his strength failing.

'Mrs Ducat...' he gasped, 'you... must... run...' His hand went limp and Amira sobbed as his breathing stilled.

'Captain Hamtha,' she whispered.

Nearby, Max calmly struck a match, lighting a lantern which illuminated the circle of standing stones. Arthur was staring at him in disbelief and at the foot of the hill, one of the hounds bayed, perhaps picking up the scent of freshly spilled blood.

'I'm sorry, Amira.'

She stared at the man who looked, moved, and talked like her husband, the man who might as well have been a complete stranger. 'You're sorry? You've just *murdered* a man, Maximillian. You've murdered a captain of the Silent Division in cold blood. They'll hang you for this.'

'Oh Amira, you don't understand. I'm already dead. I tried to fight but Maria Toussan betrayed us. All this time, we thought we were dealing with murderous beasts but we're not. They're creatures of rare intelligence. This is a deliberate attack on our family, as they know we run the railway company. They know how vital the rail links are to Perund's continued existence. They can't stop the armoured trains, but they can still go after those who work for the company.'

'People are *dead*, Max,' said Amira, rising on shaking legs. 'All I'm hearing are the words of a madman. What could these monsters possibly know about such things? What have you done? Where's Sebastian?'

Max gestured with his lantern in the direction of a jumble of stones halfway down the other side of the hill. 'He's not far. He's waiting for you down there. You'll need the lantern, so you don't turn an ankle going to find him.'

'Max…' Amira's words trailed off. She didn't want to ask the question. Couldn't ask it, even though her heart was breaking from not knowing if her son was living or dead.

Max turned to look at her, his face a mask of misery in the lantern light. 'I tried to fight them, after the Embrace.

Maria made me write to you. She wanted…' He sobbed, pausing to wipe his eyes with the back of his hand, still holding the revolver. 'She wanted you to bring Clarissa, so the whole family would be here. My hands were shaking so much when I wrote the letter – I couldn't stop her from bringing you here, but I managed to seal the envelope without her realising I'd not followed her instructions perfectly.'

'Did you say… Did you say, the *Embrace*?' whispered Arthur, voice trembling.

'Tell me it's not true,' Amira cried.

Max shook his head. 'They've whispered to me and their words can't be forgotten. They're in league with some of the people out here. People who've given up the struggle to fight the Whisperers and rid our lands of their foul presence. I had no idea, but some of the townsfolk are working with them, trying to bargain in order to spare their own lives. All this time, after all the fighting, we never understood what the Whisperers actually wanted.' Max gave a bitter laugh, which he choked off in a half-sob. 'You need to go to Sebastian. Go to him and all of this will be over, I promise you.'

'Max, you need to come with us. We can bring you back to the university and they can find a way to help you. There has to be a way!'

'It's too late for me. Tell me, is Clarissa safe?'

Amira nodded. 'She's with the sisters back in Perund.'

Max smiled, a broken thing that spoke of sorrow, pain, and relief. 'That's good. Well done, Amira. I love you so, so much and I'll miss you terribly.'

Max set the lantern on a stone and placed the barrel of the revolver in his mouth. Amira didn't even have time to scream before her husband's head disintegrated into a bloody pulp as a second gunshot rang out around the standing stones.

***

'Mrs Ducat,' Arthur called out, stumbling behind her as Amira headed down the hillside towards the stones, lantern held aloft to light their way.

'Mrs Ducat, please. Please stop and listen to me.'

Amira halted and spun on her heel, the lantern revealing the thin notary, who had finally dispensed with his briefcase, Captain Hamtha's loaded revolver an unfamiliar weight in his right hand. Neither of them could bring themselves to touch Max's weapon.

'I have to know, Arthur. You can leave if you want but don't try and stop me. You'll have to shoot me before I'll turn aside from my own son.'

'Mrs Ducat, this is clearly a trap. Your husband told us as much. The Whisperers want you to find your son, don't you see? No good can come of this, I know it. Please, Mrs Ducat, I beg you to listen to me.'

'Those hounds and that foul Whisperer are still out there. If we flee they'll hunt us down, so I choose to learn the truth, Mr Stevens. If I'm to die, I'll not go to my grave without knowing the fate of my son.'

Arthur's face twisted as he made one last, desperate appeal. 'Amira, stop and think. What about your daughter? Who'll take care of her if you die?'

Amira's resolve wavered in the face of Arthur's logic. 'Mother!'

Arthur gave a strangled cry as Amira turned towards the stones. 'No, Mrs Ducat, please. It's a trap. Don't be fooled. Think of Clarissa!'

'Sebastian!' Amira called and her heart leapt into her throat as she heard his muffled voice once more.

She scrambled over the rocks, ignoring Arthur's protests as she followed the sound and discovered the entrance to a shallow cave. Her lantern cast its light over a figure, crouched at the very back, huddled against the wall, arms wrapped around his head as if to ward off an invisible enemy. She approached, boots slipping over the jumble of sharp stones, Arthur next to her, holding the gun in both hands.

'Put that thing away. That's my son.'

'Mother,' said Sebastian in a thick, wet, broken voice, turning to look at her.

Amira screamed as she saw the sharp stone held in one of his hands, slick with blood. His own blood. Her precious boy had taken the sharp flint and carved open one side of his face, cutting away the flesh, putting out his own eye.

'They've whispered to him,' Arthur groaned. 'They have him in their power now, Mrs Ducat. There's nothing you can do to help him.'

'Sebastian,' Amira wept, dropping to her knees next to her son. She screamed as he drew the flint across his face once more in a slow, deliberate motion, his remaining eye wide with pain and fear. He was losing a lot of blood and Amira realised he was already beyond help.

'Mother,' Sebastian spluttered through the remaining half of his mouth.

Amira could hear soft footfalls growing closer. She turned to see the pack of hounds had surrounded the cave and the shadowy form of the Whisperer was standing behind them. It took a step forwards, sniffing the air, glistening tongue licking the rows of teeth that filled its giant mouth.

Arthur rose, pointing the revolver at the Whisperer. 'By the sacred heart of the Holy Mother, you'll not come a foot closer. Haven't you hurt enough people already? Stand back, spawn of the underworld, or I'll put a bullet through that putrid mouth of yours.'

The Whisperer cocked its head to one side, emitting an odd, husky sound. Amira's insides slowly turn to ice as she realised it was laughing. 'Arthur, in the name of the Holy Mother, get back.'

The Whisperer took a step forward and with a cry Arthur pulled the trigger. Nothing happened and he stared at the gun in confusion, unsure how to release the safety catch. The Whisperer rose up above him and unleashed another Dagger Shriek, the sound tearing through Arthur and driving him to the ground, senseless. The Whisperer stepped over Arthur's inert body and approached Amira as the hounds circled, hoping their master would grant permission for them to begin their feast.

Amira closed her eyes, knowing it was over as the Whisperer wrapped its arms around her in the Embrace, tenderly as a lover. In those final moments she drew strength from the Holy Mother herself, feeling her presence and drawing comfort from all that was holy and good. Whatever sorrows she experienced in this life, the Holy Mother was waiting for her and she would be reunited with Max.

The drooling, fetid stench of the Whisperer's breath washed over Amira and she felt its lips against her ear, surprisingly gentle as it whispered to her. It wasn't language as Amira understood it, the soft noises emitted by the Whisperer were strange and unfamiliar as they passed through her skull, needles of sound sliding into her brain. She gasped in horror as she felt their minds connect, their thoughts entwine, the two beings becoming one. In that terrible, terrifying moment, she understood why killing her hadn't been enough.

She felt naked, exposed, and unable to hide as the Whisperer sifted through her thoughts, peeling back her memories, seeking out those concerning the ones she loved. She could feel the creature's desires and its giddy rush of delight when it found what it sought.

The Whisperer feasted on the exquisite misery it had inflicted upon her, savouring those raw, painful emotions as it devoured them. This wasn't some wild beast. Max was right – the Whisperers were diabolical and evil but it took intelligence to devise this plan and, more importantly, intelligence to understand and feast upon the depths of her sorrow, the anguish of losing her family.

The pain of Max's death filled her mind, only to be stripped away as the memory faded, vanishing into the invading creature's mind. Losing something so precious of herself in this way felt like a part of Amira had died. Their minds intractably locked together in this deadly dance, the Whisperer imposed its will on Amira and she cried as the monster revealed its plans for her.

'Holy Mother, forgive me,' Amira prayed as the insidious compulsion took hold. She walked past the hounds and picked up Hamtha's abandoned gun. She took off the safety catch with shaking fingers, just as Max had shown her all those years ago when they were first married.

'Mama,' Sebastian muttered, half-conscious and slumped against the cave wall in a pool of his own blood. 'I can't... finish it.' Her son was dying. He was slipping away and, as he drifted in and out of consciousness, there was nothing for the Whisperer to feed upon. No reason to keep him alive.

'I love you,' she whispered, the power of the compulsion was so strong it was as if she was watching someone else raise the gun and place it against her son's temple. The single shot was enough to end Sebastian's misery and compound her own. Their minds joined together, she felt the Whisperer's rush of pleasure as it enjoyed her torment, despair washing over her as she realised she was utterly alone. Moments later, the pain of losing her son faded, the memory consumed by the Whisperer, another part of Amira gone forever.

'Holy Mother, help me,' prayed Amira as she turned back to the Whisperer, trying with all her strength to make one final effort to raise the revolver and kill the beast. Her arm wouldn't move, limp at her side. The creature mocked her, sifting through her thoughts. It had already gorged itself on the agony of losing her husband and son, leaving Amira with nothing except a hollow absence, aching dully in her heart, yet still it would not be sated. It touched on another thought, pulling at that thread. Clarissa would miss Max and Sebastian so much. *Clarissa.*

Fuelled by the Embrace, a terrible idea began to take root in Amira's mind. What better way to pervert and twist a mother's love than to take the life of her own daughter? Max had tried to thwart their evil plan but the sisters at the abbey would never suspect a thing, until it was too late.

No.

Despair warred with a sense of calm as Amira committed her spirit into the care of the Holy Mother, knowing she was but a few moments away from being reunited with Max and Sebastian. Using every ounce of willpower, Amira placed the gun barrel into her mouth. She sobbed and closed her eyes. The Whisperer howled in frustration, the last thing she heard before squeezing the trigger.

***

Clarissa's high heels clacked on the tiled floor of Saint Marcus' church, drawing several disapproving looks and at least one well-articulated *tut*. She raised her head high and ignored them all, walking towards the altar. If the height of her heels didn't cause a scandal, the length of her black skirt certainly would.

Bishop Percival, standing in his purple robes, recognised her immediately. 'Miss Ducat. A pleasure to see you, although I know this day is one that brings us all sorrow.'

Clarissa nodded, unsure what to say, holding out the four red tealights clutched in her hands. 'Please, would you help me light these, Bishop Percival?'

Clarissa watched as the flames grew from the taper, as Percival lit each candle in turn. She'd done this every year for the past decade, offering her prayers for the souls of her parents and brother on the day she'd last seen her mother, on this very spot in the church. The fourth candle was for Arthur Stevens. Clarissa had been to see him twice in the asylum, visiting him more out of duty and morbid curiosity than anything else. She'd decided she wouldn't be going a third time.

Bishop Percival didn't try and say anything, knowing she didn't need his words. Together, the pair of them prayed in silence for those four souls. When Clarissa was finished she walked away, looking back once, and noticing how those four flickering candles had become indistinguishable from the host of others surrounding them. Row upon row of candles, all representing a loved one, someone who only the Holy Mother was able to help now.

People had once talked about how the church was in decline, as science and reason found answers to various questions and fuelled the progress of society. Clarissa's lip curled in a wry smile as she walked out of the main church doors into the bright sunshine of the plaza.

That was before the Harrowing forced us to lock our gates and hide behind our walls. Before we were cut off from the rest of the world. Before we became afraid of the dark and knew the terror brought to our land by the Whisperers.

BONE
THE BONE COLLECTOR

By

LL MacRae

'Would it kill ya to show me some fucking affection for once?'

Lena cowered as her father's voice shook the cabin, sending ash and sawdust tumbling to the floor. Her bare toes scrunched against the rough wood. She counted to nine. Her age. A safe number. Something she could focus on.

Anything to distract her from the cold fear that snaked through her belly.

One. Two. Three. One. Two. Three. One. Two —

Something loud smashed into the wall, breaking her concentration. Lena flinched as if she'd been struck, her breathing quickening. She hoped it had been one of the clay mugs that had been flung against the wall. She'd seen all those beautiful pots and bowls in pieces the morning after one of her father's rages. Alcohol made it worse — the smell of wine turned her stomach, knowing what it did to him — but he never needed the bottle for violence. The dark red around his lips was all-too-reminiscent of the blood he drew from her mother, and the bones he broke.

The tinkling of a bell sounded. Faint for a moment, almost distant, then loud as shattered glass.

It wasn't bright, like the bell in the temple spire summoning villagers for service, nor was it delicate, like the sing-song bells on the back of the merchant's cart when he came to trade.

This sound was hollow. Empty. As if darkness swallowed it before it could fly free.

It meant clay hadn't been broken. The realisation stole her breath.

Lena knew *it* was coming. Her gaze was drawn to the far wall before the bell's toll faded. Even from across the room she could see the swirling, writhing mass of darkness as *it* manifested.

It always appeared when a bone broke.

She'd seen *it* when the neighbour boy fell from a low stone wall and broke his wrist.

When two young girls had been thrown from their horse as *it* reared up at a snake. They'd broken more than their wrists, and *it* had manifested again, bigger than before. Lena never looked at *it* for too long, had always been too scared of what might happen if *it* caught her looking.

No one else paid *it* any attention, and Lena had long wondered whether she'd been imagining things. Whenever she was unable to sleep through the noise of her father's rampages and stayed awake until first light, she'd see things that weren't there. Animals and colours and strange faces that only appeared when she was too tired to think. Living dreams that faded quickly.

But *it* wasn't a dream. She was sure of that.

Lena huddled under the table in the cabin's main room, pulling her thin nightshirt over her knees as if the rough spun could provide comfort from the fear that

81

permeated the air like smoke. She watched *it* writhe around the bottom of the door to her parent's room, along the floor, a creeping shadow that moved spider-like up the wall, looking for a way in. She focussed on *it* and not on the screams beyond the door. Focussed on the darkness and tried to keep her breathing even, though each ragged gasp hurt.

It paused and faced her, the skull of some small, indeterminate creature clutched in one clawed hand, missing its lower jaw and shaped into a bell. Empty eye sockets set deep in the bone watched her, silent, a tiny blue flame flickering within.

Lena shivered, covering her face with her hands. She didn't *want* to look, but she couldn't help herself — and peeked through the gaps between her fingers.

Something cracked in the other room, followed by a shriek that set Lena's teeth on edge. She clamped both hands over her ears, drowning out the noise. *It* responded with a violent pulse, turning the entire wall dark for a heartbeat.

The bell rang again, high and sweet.

Another bone had broken.

'Now look what you've done!' her father bellowed.

The door burst open and slammed into the wall. It sent more sawdust trickling from the ceiling and snatched Lena's attention away from the dark creature. Pipe smoke followed her father out of the room, settling in place of the falling dust and adding another layer of grime to the floor.

She made herself as small as possible underneath the table. Didn't look at him, didn't dare attract attention, not when he was like this. Instead, she resettled her attention on *it* as *it* stared at her through sightless onyx eyes. *It* terrified her. But *it* terrified her less than her father.

Then, as if responding to an invisible signal, *it* slunk through the door her father had left open. *It* had business in that room. Lena wasn't sure what that business entailed, and though curiosity gnawed at her, she didn't move from her spot.

Feet marched past, completely ignoring both her and *it*, as her father grabbed something from the kitchen. A moment later and he was gone, shutting the door behind him with a crack.

It was in that bedroom now, and a faint whimper escaped Lena's throat.

She wanted to get away from the nauseating stench of pipe smoke, wine, and the violent rages of her parents. Away from constant uncertainty, how a calm day could turn into a maelstrom if someone said the wrong thing. Away from knowing safety could be snatched away in an instant.

And away from *it*, now that *it* had seen her.

Lena promised herself that as soon as she was old enough, she'd get away and never look back.

She was afraid, and she didn't want to be any more.

Lena hurried across the main room to the red timber door. Beyond it lay the world outside, and things even her parents feared. Roving packs of fellwolves salivated for human flesh; bandits who prowled the roads, as like to snatch unwary travellers as the coin they carried; old magic that billowed out of the ground in fetid pools, poisoning plants and turning animals into demonic aberrations.

She strained, reaching for the brass handle, but the latch wouldn't open. A metal bolt kept the door locked in place, but she wasn't tall enough to reach it.

Turning away, heart in her throat, she scrambled up the stacks of boxes to the wide sill, where the window was open a crack. It was dark beyond the thick glass, her only company the moonlight. Further beyond the boundaries of the cabin was the rest of the village, each stone and wood building a silhouette in the rainy gloom.

And just beyond the nearest lodges, the white tree shone like a beacon.

She pushed on the heavy frame, trying to widen the opening. The window gave way with a loud, grating screech.

Lena paused, breath held, but no further noises came from her parents' room. They hadn't heard.

A breeze drifted inside, heavy with moisture. There was already a fine sheen of sweat on Lena's hairline, and the rain outside would be a welcome coolness. Night birds called to her, distant owls swooping over fields like grey ghosts. Toads croaked a chorus, probably fighting over the best rocks in the narrow stream that ran alongside their cabin.

She hunched down, clutching the sides of the window frame. She was certainly small enough to fit through the gap.

Yet she remained crouched on the sill, only her fingers tasting freedom.

Her chest tightened.

Lena inched forward and pushed her head through the open window. Another wave of terror overwhelmed her. What would happen when her parents realised she'd run away? Would anyone in the village help her, or would they bring her right back to where this all started? No one ever seemed as afraid as she did. Most didn't know there was a problem.

Her heart pounded fiercely and her fingers trembled where the humid wind brushed them.

She didn't see anyone anymore. No one came to the house and she never left. Hadn't in… how long had it been?

Lena pushed forward again. Stopped. Pressure thickened the air—a barrier she couldn't pass. Tears welled in her eyes at the resistance.

She couldn't leave.

Lena pulled away from the window and faced the dark room. It was quiet now. No shouting. No screams. Nothing being smashed or broken. She let out a breath, every muscle tense and aching.

Filled with shame and sorrow, she hid in her corner and pulled a blanket over her face, exhausted. She hoped sleep would grant her temporary escape, although she knew it was fruitless.

***

In her dream, Lena crouched on the floor. Sunlight streamed into the room, banishing the heavy clouds that she knew were there now. Her small fist was wrapped around a long nail she'd found. The coarse metal dug into her palm, but she didn't mind. Her fist was now bigger than she saw it, but she slipped into the dream-memory as clearly as the day it had happened.

She used the nail like a stick in the mud, carving into the wooden floorboards and bringing what she saw in her mind's eye to life. She was a terrible artist, of course, but she and the other village children spent weeks during the rainy seasons down by the muddy stream bank to see who could come up with the most elaborate pieces.

She'd practise hard this summer and show Elissa.

Lena and Elissa had been friends since as long as she could remember, but they had grown apart recently. Elissa used to visit Lena in the garden, but she didn't come over much anymore.

Lena had chosen her favourite corner of the cabin — which always enjoyed the most sunlight — and worked on the wood, using the nail to gouge great chips in the floor. She smiled as she worked, lost in the world she imagined, ideas forming faster than she could dig them in.

She'd picked the white tree as her subject because it was the thing that fascinated her most, and she'd seen it every day of her life from her window. Having committed its vision to memory, she carefully scratched out the curling roots as they twisted about themselves.

'Lena!'

Her father's roar froze her for a moment, then panic pushed her to her feet.

He strode in through the main door — she'd been so caught up in playing that she hadn't heard it open — sweat on his brow from the burning sun, arms full of logs he'd been splitting in preparation for the coming rains. He dumped them on the floor with a loud thud and she flinched, her concentration broken. 'Look at what you've done!'

She dropped her gaze to the floor. A moment ago, she'd seen the picture she was practising. Now, she saw what her father saw. Deep scratches had shredded several wooden panels, holes forming where the wood was thinner, wood chips and sawdust smudged against the nearby wall.

'How am I supposed to fix that?' He jabbed a finger at the mess.

Her throat tightened as he yelled at her, scared of what could follow. The guilt of what she'd done, and what someone else would have to do to fix it, flooded her. She didn't look at him, leaning back as he snatched the nail out of her clenched fist. His knuckles were rough, pale scars crossing them.

'Have you even bothered to sweep the kitchen?'

'I… I did.' Lena's voice was as small as she felt. She'd *started* to clean, but she'd found the nail by the trapdoor at the back of the kitchen. Become distracted. Hadn't realised so much time had passed. She swallowed with difficulty.

He dragged a hand through his hair and the muscles in his cheeks tensed as he ground his teeth. 'What's the village chief going to say when he visits and sees the floor in that state?'

'I don't know… I didn't think —'

'You never think about what you're doing!' His voice rose along with his anger. 'I'm trying to get us ready for the rains. Why are you making everything so difficult?'

Lena shuffled back, her throat stinging. She was going to cry and it would make him angrier. She didn't know what to say, what would stop him being upset, so she didn't say anything.

'Get out the way!' He shoved her to one side as he took a better look at the floor.

Tears streamed down her cheeks and her body twisted, caught between desperation to flee, and desperation to run to her father for comfort from her fear. Caught between two instincts, her panic rooted her to the spot. Her breathing became quick and painful, each shallow gasp a knife down her throat.

'What you crying for?' His voice filled her, sent a fresh wave of tears streaming down her cheeks. Lena clutched her nightgown. Her panic grew from a ball of terror into something all-encompassing. It filled her head to toe, every finger shaking as her sobs grew. Her fear became something heavy, squeezing her chest, rooting her in place. She fought, desperate, to stop her tears, to prevent his anger from billowing over. Even as she tried, his gaze darkened.

His voice softened to a whisper. The last warning before he exploded. A great stillness before the whirlwind of violence. 'What are you fucking crying for?'

She opened her mouth, fumbled her words. She knew what was going to happen. Had seen it happen too many times. Had hidden from it whenever she could.

He loomed over her, filling her vision with his presence. The world shrank down to nothing, darkness edging what she could see.

Lena swallowed, took a breath, but couldn't speak through her short, sharp gasps. 'I... I...'

'How do you think it makes *me* feel when you're like this?'

'Sorry.'

'Why don't you ever think?'

'Sorry.'

'Stop fucking apologising!' He lashed out, upending a wicker basket and scattering the contents across the floor. Cups and trinkets cracked, pools of darkness opening up under them like everything else in the world. The floor swallowed them slowly. The room twisted, her dream-memory giving way to the nightmare.

The skull bell tolled, but only Lena heard it. Her skin burned. The room tilted, her father's form taking up more space than was possible as his anger erupted.

A knock rattled the door, insistent, and he turned to face it.

Lena didn't wait a second longer. She took the opportunity and bolted to the kitchen, straight into the low cupboard, and wedged herself in beside sacks of grain.

There, in the cool darkness, she breathed in and out, as slowly as she could. She counted the whorls in the wood, her gaze tracing an all-too familiar pattern, until the panic ebbed.

Lena kept counting just to be on the safe side, and only when the voices in the main room quietened, and the heavy thud of the front door echoed faintly, did she stop.

It was long dark outside before she exited the cupboard again.

***

Lena woke with a start, heart racing, sweat making her skin clammy. Murky dawn light drifted in through the window and rain pattered gently on the glass panes. Her toes were cold. She shivered and pushed away the memory.

She hunkered into herself, wishing she could have a dreamless sleep. Awake or asleep, her terror permeated everything. Had that memory been from last summer or the one before that? It was impossible to tell. Harder still to ignore when it, and countless others, were always on the edge of her mind.

Useless.

She was useless.

Too stupid. Too scared. Too useless!

Lena hit her face. Cheeks. Forehead. Scratched along her arms.

If she wasn't so useless, she'd have been able to *fix* this! She'd never have been in this situation in the first place.

She *hated* herself. Hated what she was. Hated what she could never be.

And she couldn't get away. There wasn't any escape.

All she could do was endure until she was old enough to leave. She stared at the open window and wished she was stronger. Wished desperately she wasn't afraid anymore.

Lena drew her knees up to her chest, wrapped her arms around them, and nestled her face to hide her sobs.

It was some time before there was movement elsewhere in the cabin, and she remembered what had happened the night before. *It* had visited again. There'd been another bone broken. She remembered hiding under the table and seeing *it* slither into her parent's room.

Lena looked up as loud voices carried through the walls and the door to her parents' room opened. Her mother staggered out, a shawl draped across her shoulders, her left hand clutched in her right. Two fingers stuck out at odd angles, and Lena understood they were the cause of *its* manifestation the night before.

Despite everything, her mother held her chin high, though her eyes were red.

Lena kept her head low as her parents crossed the main room of the cabin to the front door. Neither looked at the window or at her, and as much as she disliked being forgotten, she preferred it to having their attention.

Her father was supposed to join the village hunt, but instead he had to drag her mother to the healer three villages away. He was furious about the loss of venison he could have caught, blaming her for causing it. Her mother snarled back, pain fuelling her words. The bone tree could fix her, but he was too superstitious to use it.

Their fury rolled around the cabin and Lena moved from corner to corner, trying to block it out, palms flat against her ears, waiting for them to go and stillness to settle upon the place.

It wouldn't be peaceful.

It was simply the absence of them.

Peace meant there was nothing to fear.

They continued to ignore her as they argued and left, and Lena watched from her spot on the sill as they made their way down the muddy path, shrouded in mist from the falling rain. Wet, overgrown grass brushed their knees, birds calling out in warning as they passed.

Lena half-wished they'd never come back.

It was a dark thought. She'd told Elissa that, once, and Elissa had looked at her so aghast that Lena had immediately laughed and said she'd been playing pretend. That she didn't *really* mean it.

She didn't see Elissa anymore.

But it wasn't all bad. It was *good*, some of the time. Her father was one of the most experienced hunters in the village. He'd travel far and wide, bringing back enough money through trade to keep them comfortable. They'd trade a lot, actually. People were always coming to their lodge to ask for this or that.

He feared nothing, fought bandits and animals alike when the need arose, and their station in the village was high. He'd always be in a good mood following those successes. Would let her stay up late while he told stories. Would share gossip and news from other villages, talking to her as if she wasn't a child. He even made her mother laugh.

There'd often be a group of villagers in their lodge during the worst of the rains, eating, drinking, smoking, and playing dice. Or in summer, they'd go on outings and she'd sit atop his shoulders to get the best view of the flowers. Even the chief visited, and whenever a decision needed to be made, he always asked her father's thoughts.

That was when things were pleasant.

And that was what made him so terrifying — she never knew when his mood would switch to something darker. When something she'd do — perfectly acceptable the day before — suddenly was not permitted.

And once his mood switched, it was near impossible to stop.

She hated the uncertainty. Hated how one day could be fine and fun and silly, and the next it could explode into an inescapable nightmare.

Hated how others only saw the good times, couldn't fathom the fear.

She stared out the window, at the spot where they'd vanished around the corner. And then her gaze was invariably drawn to the ghostly pale shape in the centre of the village.

The white tree had always captured Lena's attention. It was a willow, a twisted thing of pale bark that grew alone. Nothing, not even grass, grew beneath the tree's drooping leaves and white branches. The village chief had always claimed it had powers due to sorcerers who'd lived centuries before. They'd touched the land with their magic, and now people could receive the tree's blessings. A safe birth. Good hunting. The strength of an ox for a day.

The stories claimed sorcery was also responsible for the dangerous creatures that roved the land, making travel unsafe. Some remnants of their magic, uncontrolled and misunderstood, that still held sway.

Lena didn't know if all those stories were true, but the tree was real enough. She'd seen it cure fevers, remove the weeping sickness, and once, it reversed death for one lucky soul.

The tree had always reminded her of the standing

stones far to the north, made by some ancient and powerful people who left no clear reasoning for their structures.
She loved playing among the gnarled roots, so thick
they'd take ten hands to fit around. The roots popped out
of the dark soil like a sea monster from the old tales. Pale
and dull, they reminded her of carcasses picked clean by
crows.

She'd watched the long leaves that draped along the
ground and wondered what it would be like to sit and
flow and be so carefree. To have a power that people cov-
eted, to choose whether or not to bestow that.

Lena had once stared at a hole in the trunk so hard that
she could have sworn a pair of eyes stared right back at
her.

She'd kept away from the tree for a while after that.

Lena adjusted her position on the wooden windowsill,
worn from sitting there so often over the years. She'd
fallen from it once, landing hard enough to graze her shin
and bleed, darkening the wood. She'd been yelled at for
making a mess, so she'd tried to be more careful.

Carefully, she pushed her arm through the open window. Cold rain splattered onto her hand, but the same
pressure from the night before remained. Her chest tightened. She *couldn't* leave. Something was stopping her. It
was both a physical barrier and some instinctual fear.

Lena let out a shaky breath and willed the bubbling
panic to settle. She took what solace she could in the quiet
morning that spilled into the cabin through murky windows.

Even on the edge of the village, she could see the outline of the tree, a faint glow in the gloom.

The rain might be unpleasant, making her cold to her
bones, but demons and night creatures avoided hunting
during the rainy season. There'd been talk that the summer droughts pushed the creatures to be bolder, to hunt
people and attack in the dead of night.

If her parents were travelling to another village, there

was little chance of them being taken by one of the fell beasts while it rained.

Lena wasn't sure how much time had passed, because when she next blinked, the sun had burned away most of the mist, the heavy rain slowing to a light drizzle, and several of the local children were playing in the grass outside the cabin.

Most were her age, some a few years younger.

She scanned the group, then slumped back, disappointed. Elissa wasn't there. For a moment, she'd hoped her friend might have come to see her.

The children were playing roughly — wrestling and jabbing each other with sticks — while laughing in delight as mud splattered their skin and clothes. Lena longed to join them, and again tried to leave through the open window. But that pressure held her back, forcing the breath from her.

It was a barrier she could not cross.

Not wishing to see anything more, Lena clambered down from the sill.

The bell tolled again, so high and faint she wasn't sure whether she'd imagined it. She froze, well-practised in keeping still, and listened.

As she was about to dismiss it as an errant daydream, a shadow darted across the open doorway to her parents' room.

Swallowing a lump in her throat, Lena shuffled towards the door. Past the corner where she'd damaged the floor several summers ago, past the hole in the wall her father had made the previous rainy season, and to the room's doorway.

Lena peered in, unwilling to walk into a room that was often out of bounds, and looked for the shadow.

There, in the motes of pale light streaming in through the window, she saw *it*.

She didn't know what *it* was. A shadow made alive? A remnant of the sorcerers' magic from the village chief's stories? Something hideous and unspeakable?

She wondered why she'd never seen anything else like *it* before. No other manifestation of sickness, death, or blood — gods, there was always so much blood — ever appeared.

It only manifested from bones.

And only where they broke.

It lingered, half-in, half-out of the light, watching her expectantly. *It* held the skull bell, as before, the fire within wavering as if caught in a breeze.

They regarded each other for long seconds, the distant, muffled laughter of the children outside the only sound. She gathered her courage, ready to bolt at the tiniest sign of movement.

Eventually, Lena said in a small voice, 'What are you?'

It did not reply for some time, and Lena took a hesitant step closer, crossing the threshold into the room, though she kept one hand on the doorframe for comfort.

It stepped towards her, bird-like in *its* movements and colouring — a raven or magpie perhaps — with a twisted beak and a cloak of black feathers around its hunched shoulders. About the size of a large dog, barely tall enough to reach her shoulders, its limbs appeared covered not in skin or fur, but the scales of a lizard. Each scale was black as night, though the creature's pale grey head was in contrast to its body.

There were two round, oozing blobs where its eyes should be, dark like logs burned too long. Lena didn't think *it* could see out of those, yet her skin prickled. She was definitely being watched.

'Just as there are carrion feeders in this world, picking clean corpses, there are vultures in the world beyond. I am one such entity.'

Lena wanted to flinch at its voice, thick with rust. She hesitated where she stood. Was *it* a dream? *It* had to be. What *it* said didn't make any sense. 'Why can I see you?'

It tilted its head. 'You seek my power.'

Lena frowned, her eyebrows furrowing as she thought. 'I don't understand. I don't know what you are.'

Its feathers rustled. 'You are curious.'

Lena didn't know how to react. She was so used to second-guessing what her father expected that she found herself utterly at a loss for how to speak with this creature. What did *it* want? What was the right thing to say?

It spoke of power. Could *it* hurt her if she made a mistake?

Lena stumbled backwards, wanting to get away from this unknown. If her parents returned, if they caught her where she wasn't supposed to be, doing what she wasn't supposed to do —

It spread its arms, feathers erupting from its scales, and engulfed the room in shadow.

Lena yelped in fright and squeezed her eyes shut. She didn't want this.

She kept them closed as long as she could. Until the light patter of rain on the window disappeared, replaced by a gentle warmth.

Carefully, slowly, Lena peered out of one eye. Her mouth fell open in unrestrained shock.

They stood outside, warm sun chasing away any thought of rain. Lena was still barefoot and in her nightgown, and the grass between her toes tickled. She giggled, crouching and picking at a few blades. Dandelions blew away in the breeze, pulled free by her fingers.

Her heart was full of the simple joy of watching dandelion fluff soar in the wind, and she wondered where it would go, what it would see before it landed somewhere new.

There were more dandelions in the grass, and she happily bounded between them, picking them and throwing them to the wind.

When she spun around to look for more, her laughter abruptly stopped. *It* was there, sitting on one of the exposed roots under the white tree, watching her. She stumbled back and looked around. The white tree was in the heart of the village, but there were no buildings here. Only fields and fields of grass and flowers in all directions.

'Where are we?'

'You don't recognise this place?' *It* tilted its head this way and that.

'I know the tree, but —'

'Then you know where you stand.'

'Is this a dream?'

The flame in the skull bell blazed, shifting from orange to blue. 'Far from it.'

Lena pulled her gaze from the creature and towards the tree, craning her head back as she tried to spy the very top of the willow. She thought of the few times she'd been up close before, what she'd seen the tree do to others in the village, both good and bad.

'Why are you showing me this? I don't understand. What do you want me to do?' Already, the panic of not understanding was beginning to return. This place was beautiful, calm. Safe. But she fretted. It couldn't be real. It couldn't be true.

'Do you know what this tree is?'

Lena stared up at it again. A question. She didn't know the answer, so she went with her best guess. 'A magic tree. It helps people. But it can hurt them, too.'

It laughed, the sound echoed around the glade and rolled over the hills beyond. 'It is a gateway. You should walk through it.'

As *it* spoke, the enormous trunk split open like a door. Light burst forth, golden and bright. It brushed her skin, so warm and inviting she didn't think she'd ever feel cold again.

Lena didn't trust it, and she didn't move. 'W — why?'

'For you, there is only terror in the waking world. But in the world beyond? There will be peace.'

Peace wasn't possible. It could never be possible. Not

for her.

She shook her head, and the gateway closed, taking the bright light with it.

Again, *it* regarded her. 'Wouldn't you like to leave your cabin?'

She fumbled for the fabric of her nightgown with trembling fingers, desperate for comfort against her growing panic. She *wanted* to leave, but she didn't want to hope. This could be a trick, or a test. 'Yes.'

It smiled, beak widening to reveal sharp fangs within. 'I can help you leave.'

'I… I'm afraid of you.'

'Is your fear of this place not greater than your fear of me?'

Lena didn't reply. It was always safer to keep her mouth shut than to say the wrong thing. The creature's words made sense. She *was* afraid. She *did* want to leave. It may have been a silly, childish dream, but it was *her* dream.

She thought back to her window. It should be so easy to scramble through it, to get away.

But she couldn't.

'Why can I see you but no one else can?'

It smiled, rang the bell, and faded, leaving behind a wisp of smoke. Everything faded with *it* — the fields of grass and dandelions, and the pale tree.

She *felt* the break before the child screamed, and the echo of the bell ringing filled her mind.

Lena raced back to the window and peered out. One of the children lay on the grass, ankle jutting out at the wrong angle. He had probably tripped and landed wrong — there were plenty of rocks and logs half-hidden in the tall grass, difficult to see with so much rain.

She gasped, already beginning to panic at the sight. *It* was coming again. *It* always came when a bone broke. Always.

Lena wanted to get off the windowsill, didn't want to

see what would happen next.

Just as she predicted, the creature manifested beside the group, though none paid *it* any attention.

She knew they wouldn't.

They couldn't see *it*.

It crept towards them, to the boy with the broken ankle. *It* passed through the others gathered like a phantom, not that anyone noticed.

Despite her apprehension, Lena watched.

It raised the skull bell, held it over the boy's leg, and the blue flame encompassed the skull in fire. Something that looked like smoke, if smoke were a thing made solid, rose from the broken bone. It flared from the boy's ankle, sucked into the missing jaws of the skull and fed the fire within, the blue flames flashing so brightly it hurt to look at.

When her vision cleared, *it* was gone.

Lena had leaned so far forward her nose was pressed against the glass.

For the first time she could recall, the all-encompassing fear she carried with her had faded a little.

***

Lena struggled to follow the passage of time. It seemed as though every time she blinked, day had turned to night, and people had come and gone. She was left, ignored and floundering.

When she next came aware, someone was crying. Their sobs filled the cabin, and a chill hung heavy in the air. It was night again, and though the rain had stopped, steel grey clouds threatened more.

She crept away from the window, towards the noise. The dying embers of the fire in the hearth burned low, providing a hint of light and not much more. Shadows of furniture elongated against the walls, flickering slightly.

Every step seemed to take an age, and Lena struggled

to move. She pushed on, desperate to find the source of the tears, even though it felt like she was wading through a river, against the current. A rich, sickly-sweet smell permeated, stinging Lena's eyes and throat. It reminded her of apples long past time to eat, pale maggots burrowing into overripe flesh.

Finally she reached the kitchen. The floor was wet, but it was too dark to see much detail.

She recognised who was crying.

'Mum?' Lena whispered, ever cautious.

The woman didn't reply, slumped over, head resting against the wall. Her sobs had quietened to sniffles and something dark stained her tunic, but Lena didn't know what it was. Sweat-damp hair was matted across her forehead and down her neck.

Lena's bottom lip quivered. Her mother acted like this every now and then, and Lena never knew why. Never understood the stupor her mother wouldn't rouse from for hours. She could see her pain, her mother's fear a mirror to her own, but didn't understand why her mother didn't hide in the same way she did.

Perhaps she *hid* in these states, the way Lena tried to hide in her dreams. Her made-up worlds.

Her mother was muttering in between sniffles, and Lena crept forward to hear her better.

'… never meant it. Never meant any of it.'

Lena approached, bare feet passing through the sticky puddle, but she didn't care. 'Mum?'

Her mother's eyes opened wide and she gasped as if she were drowning. 'His own father and brothers beat him and worse! It was a hard time. Wolves preyed every day. Demons every night. Nowhere was safe. Not like we have it now.'

Lena put a hand on her mother, but she couldn't feel anything under her palm, everything was too cold. Strangely, she missed the light of the tree that *it* had shown her.

'He never meant to hurt you, Lena… He loves you, in his own way…' Her hair shifted, revealing dark bruises along her cheeks and neck.

Lena clutched her nightgown again, balling the fabric in her fist.

Her mother fell to the side, the wall catching her shoulder before she slid to the floor. Her cries slowed along with her breathing, and she drifted in and out of wakefulness.

Lena backed away and left her mother where she was.

***

Clouds darkened the skies as the promised rainfall thundered down. Lena watched folk huddle under blankets and shawls as they raced across the streets, her windowsill affording her a clear view of anyone who approached the cabin.

All the while, the tree shone, and Lena stared at its pale leaves as if there was no other distraction in the world. She imagined the golden light, wondering if there truly was peace through there. Wondered whether anyone else from her village knew what it was or had made the journey through it.

Wondered if she was being a stupid girl who'd made up another silly story instead of just doing as she was told.

Her mother's fingers had been set and bound in stiff linen wraps, and she had not seen *it* in the cabin since that first encounter.

She heard the bell, though.

Every time a bone broke in the village, she heard the call, a pull in her chest. But the window might as well have been a locked iron door, because try as she might, she could not pass through, no matter how much she wanted to.

Lena thought about what the creature had said. *Fear is*

the only thing in the waking world.

Power to rise above that fear would be nice, she thought. Like the tree's power. Like the power her father had over any who encountered him. If she had *that*, she could do whatever she liked, go wherever she wished. There'd be no restraints.

Her parents continued to ignore her as the rain continued. She didn't sleep much and never ate, though she strangely never hungered, either. Lena had always loved honey when they could get it, or the sweet yellow pears that grew in the field behind Elissa's house. But no one thought to offer anything to her, so she said nothing. It would be worse to attract attention and get in trouble for asking too rudely.

She'd been forgotten many times before, during both the summer and rainy seasons. If there wasn't enough to go around, she didn't eat.

Although she couldn't recall having gone *quite* so long without...

Fire crackled in the hearth in an attempt to keep the worst of the cold at bay. Lena knew sitting by an open window didn't help, but neither of her parents ever managed to push the window shut. It suited her. The sill had long been one of her favourite spots — on a clear day, she could see hawks circling high above the village, or hear the splash of the stream as it wound its way through the mud.

There was less to watch during the rainy season, but she didn't move from her spot save to hide.

Lena *wanted* to leave. To escape the misery.

But she was stuck and afraid and none of it made any sense. She wanted to see the dark creature again, to see what *it* did when bones broke. To see the gateway within the tree again.

Lena put her head in her hands, not wanting to sob but not knowing what else to do, when she realised something didn't *feel* right.

Gently, she moved her fingers. Realised they weren't touching skin, but something *harder*.

Her skin had broken. There was something wet and sticky that she'd never noticed before.

And underneath that…

Lena trembled.

Her skull… her skull was exposed.

A crack ran along it, and when she applied pressure with her fingertips, bone *moved*. It sounded like something wet crunched in her ear, small pebbles grinding against each other.

With that, the bell's ringing filled the room.

Something dark appeared beside her. She didn't need to look to know what.

'You… again?' Lena whispered.

'Are you ready to move on from your fear?' *it* asked in that grinding, grating tone.

Lena didn't trust herself to speak. She looked at *it*, and at the skull bell *it* carried. 'Why is that flame blue?'

'It is a symbol of my power. Fire is red in the waking world. Blue in the world beyond.'

'I don't understand.'

'There is deep magic here. Old and forgotten. Allow me to show you.' Something sharp pierced its tone, like a hidden blade. *It* beckoned her with one clawed hand and turned away.

Lena clambered down from the windowsill and followed. As *it* walked in front of the fireplace, the orange and blue flames contrasting with each other, she found her steps grew lighter, easier. Fear of the unknown crept up her spine like an icy hand, yet she pushed through it. This creature had not harmed her, even if she was afraid of *it* on a deeper level she could not understand or explain.

It led her into the kitchen, the stone floor like ice against her bare feet. She shivered, one hand returning to her head, feeling the strange indentation she had not noticed before. Every time her fingers brushed the hard, flat surface of her skull, the tiny fire in the creature's skull bell blazed.

It stopped at the far wall, where an iron ring protruded from the floor.

Lena knew there had been a cellar down there, once — she remembered her parents complaining about it being sealed up — and stopped. 'There isn't anything here.'

'You are sure of that?'

She could have sworn the thing was *smiling*. As if a creature without flesh could smile.

It reached forward with one scaled hand, grasped the ring, and pulled the hatch open.

Lena didn't know why *it* had needed to wait until her parents' door opened before *it* could enter their room but had no trouble with a sealed off trap door. She held her tongue. It was always better to say nothing, otherwise there'd be accusations of stupidity.

The door was thick with dust and seemed too heavy for such a small creature to lift, but *it* did not strain nor falter as *it* disappeared into the darkness beneath. Lena held her breath as she followed down the stone steps. She wondered if they'd ever seen sunlight or had spent eternity in darkness. The musty stench of stale air was stifling, and she took shallow breaths to save herself a coughing fit.

It took some time to make out the details in the gloom, and when her vision adjusted, she gasped at the sight.

Bones littered every inch of floor space, in all sizes and shapes. Most seemed human, but there were animal bones, too. Skulls of cats, dogs, birds, and all manner of unidentifiable creatures piled up against the walls or strewn across the floor.

Lena walked through the room. She took care where she put her feet, until it became apparent that every step would result in crunching bones. The cellar was enormous, stretching far beyond the confines of the cabin. She wondered how deep into the village it went, and whether it reached the white tree or the fields beyond.

She had thought cellars were for storing wine or cold meats. Had this place existed underneath her feet her entire life? Did her parents know about this place? Or anyone in the village? Surely the chief would have known if the village had been built atop a graveyard of bones.

'Was this put here by sorcerers?' Lena asked. If they had been responsible for the tree, which had been here far longer than anyone could remember, perhaps they were responsible for this place, too.

'There is power here for creatures such as I. Magic in the bones of those living, and those who have passed.' *It* appeared at her side, moving so swiftly and silently that Lena jumped. 'Those between worlds might take some of this power for themselves.'

Lena kept her hands firmly at her sides. She didn't want to feel her head again. Didn't want to touch the bone.

It meant... It meant...

Water dripped from somewhere ahead. Perhaps a trickle from the stream that had made its way down through the cracked earth and stone to dribble down the cellar wall.

'The sorcerers summoned us to tend the world after they had gone. Their power is ours,' *it* said.

'What is your power?' Lena asked. She was rarely in a position to demand something, and it gave her a boost of confidence.

It was so close that she could see the details of its scaled face. Feel its putrid breath against her skin. *It* grinned and raised the skull bell to her.

She stepped back. She was used to fear. Used to grappling with the terror that forced its way into her life. But this was different. Scary, yes, but not the mind-numbing fear she'd wet herself from in the past.

It remained in place, bell held high, offering. Waiting.

Lena glanced around and felt more alone than ever, in the dark cellar surrounded by the bones of the dead. The forgotten dead, she thought.

Steeling herself, she reached out, fingers trembling, and touched the bell.

She saw herself lying underneath her windowsill, blood pooling around her limp body. Her head had caved in on one side, dark blood congealed in her hair. More spots darkened the floor around where she lay, the faint tang of salt and iron on her nose. Sounds were muffled, like she was underwater, and though she couldn't see them, the familiar shouts of her parents were present.

Lena didn't understand how she could be *outside* herself. She couldn't see her face — pressed into the rough wooden floor — but she knew it was her.

She knew she wasn't getting up again.

Knew there was nothing of *her* left in that body. Only… whatever she was now. Where she could see and speak with *it*.

Between worlds. That's where she was.

That's why she wasn't hungry. Why no one spoke to her. Saw her.

She stared at her body and raised a hand to her own head, feeling where her skin had broken, where her skull was exposed to the air. Felt the blood, the crack, the dent in her bone.

'This bell helps me travel across realms. Sipping up the power from the broken.'

Lena couldn't see *it* but heard the voice clearly enough.

'Essence is released when they break. I feed off it, as fell wolves feed on flesh; as flowers feed on sunlight.'

She trembled as she looked down at herself. She had no memory of these injuries.

'Most do not see me. Entities like me exist between worlds, created by dark sorcery to ensure no power is wasted. To ensure a land dry of magic can still thrive. I am called upon by breaking bones and I take what power I can.'

Its words washed over her like the rains outside. She fought to keep from being overwhelmed, fought to keep her tears at bay.

Silly girl. She was crying too much! If she just took the time to *think*, she wouldn't need to get upset —

'Let me take the rest of your power and I will take you to the gate. You can find peace. You can rest.'

Lena backed away.

Peace. There was no such thing. 'It won't work!' She closed her eyes, hands over her ears, and huddled on the floor. Her panic was back, heavy and thrashing inside her. 'I can't…'

'If you do not leave, nothing will change.'

She hunkered into herself, burying her face into her nightgown. 'I know! I know I'm stupid! Useless!' Lena didn't bother trying to stop the tears anymore. At least neither of her parents could see her.

She bit down on her bottom lip until all noises faded.

When she next opened her eyes, her vision was blurry, but she was back in the cellar surrounded by dusty bones. She wanted to scream. Run. *Anything*.

'Your fear keeps you trapped.'

Lena wiped her face with one arm, blood and tears streaking down her skin. She looked away, brushing one of the skulls closest to her with her elbow. Flinching, she twisted around.

It looked like a predator of some kind, heavy jaws and sharp teeth burst from the bone. She picked it up.

What had this belonged to? Were they stuck, too? Like her? Or had they passed through the tree?

Lena shivered, her toes scrunched against the cellar floor. 'I can't leave.'

'I will take you to the tree.'

'How?' Lena touched her cheek with one hand, re-membering the intense pressure every time she'd tried to clamber through the window. Freedom had been so close, but she'd been denied.

It held up the skull bell and rocked it gently from side to side. The bell sounded, high-pitched and echoing, the single blue flame blazing within. 'This collects the power. It can affect the waking world in small ways. It can be used to help you leave this cabin.'

She sniffed. 'Why would you help me? No one helps me...' Lena bit her tongue before she said too much. Such talk was likely to invoke wrath. Even hiding under the cabin, in the bowels of a hidden graveyard, fear of her father kept her rooted to the spot.

Its grin broadened, teeth glinting in its beak-like mouth. 'When you pass through the gateway, I will take the remnants of your strength. Every last morsel of what keeps you stuck here. Your fear, your pain. And you will find peace in the world beyond.'

Her lip quivered as new panic flushed through her. *It* took power. Fed off it. Off *her*.

But she'd never escape the nightmare if she stayed.

Lena turned her attention back to the skull in her hand. It was long, with sharp teeth attached to its jaw. A canine of some sort, perhaps. It *felt* the same as the left side of her head — hard and slightly rough.

Its presence seemed to fill more of the space than it had before. Why was she always at the mercy of others?

She remembered how enamoured she'd been with the white tree, how it had frightened her and tempted her with the warm light.

There was fear and uncertainty in whichever direction she turned. She'd always dreamed of distant lands. Of a world away from the fear of her family, and the fear of what stalked outside their home.

Dreamt of fields of flowers, birds and dragons, and places where *she* had power and there was nothing to fear.

'I can't.' Her voice came out as a whisper.

It tilted its head, feathers fluttering, and lowered the bell. 'I shall visit in a few centuries in case you change your mind.'

'Wait!' Lena was on her feet, though she didn't remember standing up. One hand clutched her nightgown, the other held the long skull. She was trapped here. Trapped and would remain trapped forever.

And she'd *promised* herself she'd get away when she could.

'Changed your mind?'

Something flashed in her memory. 'You said... You said I wanted your power.'

It didn't respond but ruffled its feathers.

She took slow steps towards *it*, bones turning to dust under her bare feet. 'I *do* want power. I don't want to be scared anymore.'

Still, *it* said nothing.

'I can't stay. I can't move on. But *you* can go where you wish. I... I want that, too.'

It let out a screech so high it set goosebumps along her skin. But Lena knew fear, and she wasn't scared of this creature anymore.

Not when there were so many other things that could harm her.

Lena stood a handful of paces away from *it*. 'I could leave the cabin if I had your power. Leave the village! Speak to people like me... people who are lost or hurt. I could do that, couldn't I?'

It raised its skull bell, blue flames engulfing the bone.

Lena raised her own empty skull. 'Your bell can affect the waking world. Maybe it can get rid of my fear, too.'

Something cracked. The air shattered around her. Lena's hair whipped up as blue flames burst from its skull and crept over *it*, licking at the dark feathers and black scales. Fire peeled away its pale grey face and sightless eyes, its clawed hands and legs.

Thick, viscous smoke poured from *it*—the same

substance she'd seen from the boy's broken ankle. It swirled in the air before careening into the skull she held high, biting into the old bone, chips falling away as it re-shaped and contorted in front of her eyes.

The lower jaw dropped onto the floor, crumbling into dust. The top of the skull domed upwards, pulled from the elongated snout.

The substance shifted, liquid, then blue fire burst into existence. It dangled in a thin stream, rattled against the edges of the skull, and rang.

Power flooded Lena's limbs, pushing away the con-stant, aching cold and grinding fear, replacing them with strength. She wanted to leap over the stream, run the length of the village, and race back again. She giggled at the lightness she felt, at the warmth.

Fire licked back along the bell, her fingers, and up her arm.

It tickled.

Her giggling stopped as the blue flames peeled her flesh away, revealing blackened bone beneath. It burned her nightgown and hair, the acrid stench filling her nose even as it was ripped from her face. Blood oozed down her bones, then that burned away, too.

In place of flesh, dark flames burst from her bones, and scales covered what was left of her skin.

She flinched as pain wracked her body and she hunk-ered into herself. But the fire burned and there was no stopping it.

It was a lesser pain than she had experienced before, the stabbing of needles, short and sharp, and over in a moment. When it passed, she knew she looked much like the creature whose power she had just taken.

She hadn't *meant* to take it. She'd just wanted some for herself. Perhaps they could have worked together.

Lena held her bell high. The world around her was dark, save the glowing blue light of the fire. She looked above her, unable to see through her own eyes anymore.

Perhaps they had been burned away, too.

In the darkness, she could only see two pale yellow shapes glowing faintly in the murk. Beyond those, other shapes of light glistened in the distance.

She willed herself to see her parents, and the flame in her bell burned once, brightly. Suddenly, she was no longer in the cellar. Lena stared at them as they slept, they who had once held so much power and control over her. Who had kept her stuck between worlds, trapped by terror.

The skull grew warm in her hand, and she lifted it to eye level. Heat flared and the single blue flame crackled. A vessel of power. Magic from long-dead sorcerers.

She could affect the waking world. Make small changes.

One small change that would grant her the peace she'd been desperate for.

Lena smiled a monstrous smile and backed away. Crossed the dark void, retracing her steps through the cabin, though she could no longer see it.

Touched the brass handle of the door and pushed it open. Rain pattered outside, splashing cold drops onto what her face had become.

She felt no pressure when she stepped outside. No barrier stopping her. Lena was guided only by the blue light of her skull bell.

She walked. Faded into darkness. Followed her new-found power.

And she would never be afraid again.

HAND

By
Bjørn Larssen

'What I am saying' – Jacek continues to resist my efforts to remove him from my bar – 'is that money is' – burp – 'a ssssoshal conc… construct. It isn't real…'

I let go and catch him when he falls. 'It's very real to me,' I say through clenched teeth. 'I have bills to pay and you owe me twelve thousand kronur.'

Jacek gasps theatrically and I wonder how drunk he really is. 'Shurely not more than ten?!'

'Here,' I snarl, extending my hand. It's shaking. 'Give me ten thousand social constructs and we're friends.'

'I– I don't have it at hand… you must undershtand, the sheashon…'

I perform my daily act of kindness by opening the door and pushing him out rather than kicking and sending him flying into the… green snow. We both stand, motionless, staring. If anything, the light of the aurora became even more intense. The red neon letters above my bar's door, RIS KO – the other 'I' died recently – can't compete. Green snow falls upon more green snow… like on that last night before they took Dad away, as I stood

111

with my tongue out, trying to catch snowflakes. Dad went inside to make some calls, and sure enough we had enough stuff to last us until he never made any calls anymore…

Jacek and I seem to wake up at the same moment. As he stumbles towards his car, I shut the door, rest my back against it. Short, shallow breaths, as if I came back from a run. Or am I having a panic attack? I am. Calm down. Can the radiation get through the door? Is this green snow really snow, or nuclear fallout? I lock the door and move behind the bar, where I belong, where I serve the patrons, except there is no way anyone will show up. Nobody will risk going outside unless they must. Except the postmen delivering third and final warnings in red envelopes about the energy company being totally done with me not providing them with enough social constructs. Once the season begins and the tourists start arriving, Jacek's father's car rental… I nearly drop to my knees when I realise. There are very few tourists who will want to be here, now. Two weeks after the Chernobyl explosion that – the media assures me over and over – did not affect Iceland. The green light that covers the sky, the empty streets, paints snow and mud alike poison green, is unrelated.

I look at my hands in the dim light of the lightbulb that will stop shining sometime soon, examine them. If I have radiation sickness, will my skin come off? Blisters appear? No blisters, nothing, only my hands shaking. I'm going to get high and stop thinking – oh shit, fuck crappity shit.

He picks up on the second ring. 'Gunnar?'

'Ulf,' he sighs. 'There is nothing on the market. I promise you'll be the first to know.'

I feel blood drain from my face. 'Just one gram…'

Gunnar hangs up.

I swallow, my mouth ashy. I don't even want a drink. Just to get high. There's just enough inside my bullet to last me until tomorrow… two days, if I slow down. Then I'll dip a wet cotton bud in, clean the remains, swallow the cotton… I am already sweating. He'll get it tomorrow, I tell myself, before taking a sniff that's too greedy. Now I won't have enough for two days. My heart slams inside my chest, yet I calm down. It will be okay. I don't know how. A problem for tomorrow's…

'Ulf?'

I nearly drop the bullet in shock. The green light pours into the bar. 'Close that door!' I shout, and I want to add you're letting the radiation in but instead I do drop the bullet, because the door closes by itself. I don't even have to wonder whether I really locked it when I hear the locks click in again.

How much did I… It's never done this before, I've never had visions. Hallucinations. It's the radiation doing it to me, to my brain. The man comes closer to the light and I see him now. Long, light hair. Bright, intense blue eyes, too intense, but I am high. I assess him. Beard in progress. A shy smile. A very cute kid.

'We're closed,' I say stupidly. I have a patron – the door locked by itself – I need to lie down. Are you real? I want to ask. He seems real, but hallucinations would, right?

'Odin,' he says, extending his hand. 'Good to meet you in person, Ulf.'

I give him a sweaty, weak handshake. His hand feels warm and real. 'I locked this door,' I say, a statement that's also a question. 'How did you get in?'

'I'll have a glass of wine, please. Dry red.'

'No,' I say, because I am scared. 'Are you even old enough to drink?'

When he smirks, he looks even younger. Baby Odin, I re-christen him. 'I can pay,' he says, and places something familiar on the counter. A small plastic bag with white powder inside. Three grams, a part of my mind assesses. My hand shoots and grabs it. It feels real.

'Right back,' I gasp. Baby Odin doesn't matter as I run to the toilet, the little bag in my hand. There are bars where patrons do drugs in the toilets and the owners throw them out. Risiko is a place where the owner snorts in the toilet and the patrons loudly worry about him... I can't make a line, I don't have my bullet, I just dip my fingernail in and inhale hard. Oh Jesus. This stuff is good... I make sure the ziploc bag is closed, put it in my back pocket, black and white flakes obscuring my vision. I lean against the toilet seat. It's slippery, I fall to the floor. Back against the wall. My heart is a punk drummer. I forgot I was already high.

'Dad,' I whisper, or just think, 'not yet.' Now my mouth is dry. Sand in throat. I see myself as a huge dog, a wolf, slurping water from the toilet. Instead, I pull myself up, hoping the sink won't fall off the wall as I hang on to it. It takes me a few seconds to remember how to open the tap. I drink some water, spread the rest on my face, stick my head under the tap. Thanks, Dad, I say to him inside my head, I know he hears. I miss you, but not yet. Not today... My bowels growl. Mid-shit – 'Fuck!' – oh, good, I remembered to pull my pants down. Muscle memory, they call it. Dignity, they call it.

Empty and high I make my way back, where Baby Odin awaits, with that sweet smirk on his baby face. He could be my son, probably. How old are you? I want to ask, but it's not appropriate. What is? I pour him that glass of the least shitty red in stock. He paid for it, he did. But now he just stares at me with those too-blue eyes. 'What can I do for you?' I ask. My patrons don't do... any of what he has done so far.

'Glad you asked. I need a favour.'

Laughter builds inside me. I force my eyes shut – my pupils must look like dots – when I open them, he's still here. I feel something under my foot. My bullet. I quickly squat to pick it up. 'Like what?' I ask, grabbing sparkling water for myself. I am a serious business owner. Not someone who just took drugs from a stranger, then started shitting without checking whether his pants were down. This could have been anything, the stupid part of my brain starts…

'A ride,' Baby Odin says.

I snort. 'Do I look like a taxi driver?'

'I need someone to get me to Lockdown.'

'What Lo… oh,' I remember. I shake my head, droplets of water spray around. He doesn't flinch. 'There's nothing there.'

'How do you know?'

I blush. 'They said on the news,' I mumble.

His laugh is sharp, hard, doesn't fit the baby face. 'Obviously, you have the best sources, ones that can be trusted. What exactly have they said on the news?'

I pour the water into a glass, so I can add some Brennivín. Only a little. I'm not stable on my feet. 'Not much. There is a part of Iceland currently inaccessible for tourism.'

'For tourism,' Baby Odin muses. 'I'm not a tourist.'

'No,' I quickly correct, 'for anybody. You can't go there.'

'Why?'

I shrug. 'What do you think? Chernobyl, Soviets, Iceland is safe, natural phenomenon, aurora…' I stumble for a moment. I have to call Árora again. I haven't seen her since… this started. 'They got an American professor to confirm,' I say, aware of how limp I sound. Nonsense. Iceland doesn't have nuclear power. Sheer coincidence. I don't believe a single word of this myself.

'I was asking about the Lockdown.'

He has not touched his wine, I notice as I take a gulp from my glass. 'It's forbidden to go there,' I mutter.

Baby Odin openly grins now. 'I see you have been informed in great detail. Well, that's where I need to go.'

'But it's forbidden…'

'My bad!' His hand flies to his mouth, those blue eyes wide in shock. He's mocking me. 'I must have found the wrong person. I was looking for the Ulf who went to

115

Cambodia for a vacation, fell off a scooter he couldn't ride, broke his arm, then took his cast off to swim…'

'It was a vacation,' I snap. 'First day, too. What would you do? Sit on your arse for two weeks, sulking? Everyone would have done the same.'

'Trust me, not everyone.' He winks. 'Are you the Ulf who got arrested in Vietnam for…'

'They weren't even drugs! I was innocent!'

Baby Odin chortles. 'You didn't even care you got arrested. Only that you overpaid for chalk.'

My first instinct is checking if the baggie is still in my pocket. 'How do you know all this?'

'You have a reputation.'

'Bullshit. Only Árora knows about Vietnam and she doesn't talk.' Even to me, recently. 'Anyway, I have changed since then. No…' My voice breaks when I think he'll tell me to give him the baggie back. I should have refilled the bullet first, at least. Oh no, I dropped it. Fuck.

'We all change,' he agrees, nodding. 'I offer a hundred thousand.'

'The fine for trespassing is more than…'

'Dollars,' Baby Odin says, nodding towards a briefcase placed to my right, one of those lawyers and criminals carry, one that was not there a second ago. Did he come in with a suitcase in his hand… I rub my face. I want to lie down. 'A hundred thousand dollars.'

I blindly search for my stool. I'm about to pass out. How much would that be in kronur? A million? More. Ten million? It's not like I have bought, sold, seen dollars recently. 'What's in there for you? In Lockdown?'

Now he frowns and his face suddenly ages, from a kid into his grandfather in an instant. 'My way home. A doorway between worlds. I have strayed off my path. I must return before the bridge closes again. Have you looked up recently?'

Automatically, I do. I should repaint this ceiling.

'The sky,' Baby Odin says, irritated. 'That green light

means the Universes have connected, and mana is leaking from my world to yours. The intensity is growing. Mana is the energy that powers our magic. It does not belong here. And neither do I.'

'One of us is crazy,' I mutter.

'Open the briefcase.'

I can't move, even to lift my glass.

'Open it,' Baby Odin barks.

One lock clicks open under my thumb, then the other. I lift the lid and – stare. Packs of banknotes, held together by paper wrappers. Green banknotes. His eyes shine like steel now. 'This is yours,' he says. 'If you agree.'

I bite my lip, hard. How high am I, even?

'Also,' he continues, 'where else would Árora go?'

Jesus. How stupid am I, even?! My head nods by itself. If my brain is fucked up, hers lacks the part where fear lives. Her indestructible bike probably got there before the authorities. 'You know too much,' I snarl, except it comes out as a blub.

'I do,' Baby Odin agrees. 'Think about it.' He reaches for the briefcase, turns it away from me, slowly, watching me watching the money as it disappears. The clicks of the locks make me jump. 'You need money. I need to go back to my Universe. Tomorrow…'

'No.'

His eyebrows move up. 'No?'

'It can't be done tomorrow. I have to prepare. See the place. I don't even know where exactly it is, it's not an area… maps, plans… fences… they're probably guarding it…'

Baby Odin shrugs. 'What I meant was that I'll come back tomorrow, so you've got time to think about it.' Something lands in front of me. A map. 'I marked the place for you.'

I gawk. It's a non-place. A farm that's not even off-road. If it's a farm, it must be accessible… somehow. Inside my head a plan is already forming.

117

'You'll see me in the morning,' Baby Odin informs me drily, turns away, heads for the door. When he reaches it, he places his hand on the wood. With a clang, the locks open. The poison green swallows him, the door closes, the locks shut again. My keys are in my pocket, chained to the belt. In the smoky silence, there's just his glass of wine, the only sign he was here... except the baggie. I check. Still there. I have to lock the door... this was a trick. I left it unlocked. But now the door itself scares me. I don't quite walk, I slide, half of me wanting to hide in bed, half wanting to run away.

And then I see it and choke on my own sharp intake of breath. He left an impression of his hand on the door. How? It looks as if the wood rose around the shape of the fingers, as if the door was made of soft clay. I rub my eyes, blink, try to force myself to breathe. The imprint of his hand is still there. The door is locked. It was locked. How high can I be? I don't know what he's given me... but in order to give it to me, he had to come inside, so he was real. This, here, I mutter to myself, isn't. I rewind the tape inside my head, replay it. It makes sense in a way that makes no sense. Automatically, my hand reaches back, for the bullet, stops midway. I look at it, at my hand, then squint at the imprint. I can see his fucking fingernails. With better light, I'd probably see his fingerprints.

I have to prove to myself this isn't real. I have to.

Barely breathing, I lift my hand, bring it close to the – impossible – closer – there's no magical energy or anything else radiating from the handprint. When I laugh I scare myself, a high-pitched shriek of insanity. Fuck this. I place my hand where his was. It fits perfectly. Like a glove. Made of wood.

I need fresh air. The door handle doesn't work, it takes me a few seconds to remember the locks, I open the door, step outside into the atoms. I inhale. The air is cold, humid, green.

On cloudless nights, the light of the aurora gets so

118

intense it colours the snow. The sky is cloudy now, though, and it's not night yet, not that it matters. The lights are dancing behind the clouds, making them belch, bloat. I feel claustrophobic, now that I am outside, being crushed under the belly of a giant, fat lizard pregnant with impatient snakes. A dragon, maybe. I can't laugh anymore when I remind myself dragons don't exist, and neither do other Universes or – radiation. Radiation exists. I hide inside, lock the doors. The hand is still there, left for me as a reminder.

Now that he's gone, and my head screams at me, I make the mistake of switching on the radio. To calm down.

'… the natural phenomenon we have been experiencing,' says the news. 'We have with us Professor Smith from America to explain it.' The tone is half-awe, half-fear.

'It's very simple,' says Professor Smith. 'Auroras, or northern lights, are caused by magnetic fields…' He pronounces it 'owowahs,' instead of 'auroras,' to prove he is a real American professor. I grind my teeth and switch the damn thing off. It's very simple. The fucker sounds so condescending. Just because you're paranoid, doesn't mean they're not lying. Baby Odin has a point.

Are magnetic fields more real than other Universes? I haven't seen either. I haven't seen Árora for two weeks. My hands shake as I dial her number, then listen to the signal of nobody picking up. She would have told me. We always told each other before doing something crazy. In the last years, since Dad died, it's only been Árora telling me, not the other way round. Now the craziest thing I did was juggling bills.

A hundred thousand dollars. Is there a number I can call to ask how much that even is? A lot, is what it is. I can sell this dump for peanuts, buy a real house. Go to school. Become a real person. A nurse.

I cried so hard when they came to pick up his dead

body. Then this huge nurse just hugged me and held me as I sobbed, wept, hiccupped. She made no sound, didn't move, just held me. She only let go of me when they were all finished. 'All clear,' someone said, and it really was. There was nothing left. As if Dad never existed. There, then I decided to become a nurse. I wanted to be the person who would hug someone through their tears. There were no calls from the coroner, or from the mortuary, or wherever they put dead junkies. There were no calls from the police either. And I did not become a nurse.

I stand in front of the mirror, switch on the big light – still works, so I might as well use it. I look sixty, not forty, my face that of a starving animal, eyes of a wounded one. I am made of angles, skin covering the bone shards. If I tried to hug someone my arms would cut through their skin. I switch off the light and try to wipe out the image of me from my head. I need to have flesh. I should eat something. Real people eat food. Bodies are made of food. I am made of angles.

The fridge is broken. All that's inside is a somewhat rotten apple. I consider it. I don't eat it, but I consider it. I make myself a coffee. I want to lie down, but I don't, I study the map, squinting. 26… F26? The red – in the faint light, at least – circle. This isn't even off-road. There's a river to cross. The old me would jump at the opportunity and tell him to keep the money.

You have a reputation. I briefly organised exciting rides for tourists, purposefully ignoring the maps, explaining, as they screamed, that the point of off-road driving was being off roads. They did not recommend me to their friends and I was no longer allowed to borrow the Defender.

Cambodia… I used to grin at this memory. We had no money to pay for both the hospital visit and the scooter. Árora left me in the vomit-coloured room, then returned, waving fistfuls of money. 'I played Russian Roulette and won,' she announced. Like it was Monopoly. I didn't dare ask who lost, or how one finds a place where people play Russian Roulette.

'You're never more alive than when you're about to die' used to be our motto. But I've been dying for years on this same dirty mattress. Saving money by not eating, so I could keep the bullet full. Árora's crazy, I'm just not normal. Maybe with a hundred thousand dollars I could become the nurse holding somebody else as they cry until they run out of tears, the nurse that eats food because you don't get to hold someone like that if you sniff instead of swallowing.

I cut away the rotten part of the apple and try to eat the rest, but I can't, so I just finish the coffee, refill the bullet, take a very little sniff, lie down and think of a brown briefcase and piercing blue eyes. What exactly does he want to pay me a hundred thousand fucking dollars for? Because sure as hell it's not my driving talents.

***

'I brought you breakfast,' says Baby Odin.

The styrofoam roll was sprayed with puke orange before it got cut through the middle. Inside it, a flaccid, long penis made of minced rat meat mixed with glue lies on display, decorated with cum of mayonnaise and diarrhoea of mustard.

'It's a hot dog,' Odin says in explanation. 'Aren't you hungry?'

'Like a wolf,' I mutter. Real people eat food, I remind myself. My first step. I lift the delicious hot dog and a piece of half-transparent rubber slips out. Impressive how they almost managed to make it look like real pickle. I close my eyes, try not to breathe, push the monstrous creation into my mouth and bite as hard as I can, surprised by how soft this thing is. I swallow without chewing. It tastes like regret and bad decisions.

Baby Odin's gaze is heavy when I try to force myself

to do this again. He radiates a nun-like aura of disapproval. 'I have rethought my offer,' he says. Was this a test?! He changed his mind. He found someone better. Sweat lifts the hairs on my arms. My hands tighten on the sponge. Something liquid oozes out. 'The deal I offered wasn't fair,' he sighs. 'I apologise. I'd like to raise my offer.'

Shock makes me automatically bite and swallow some more of the real people food.

'If you do my bidding,' he continues, 'you will never lack money again. You will never be hungry. And you will never crave' – Baby Odin nods sideways and we both know – 'ever again. This is my oath and I make it freely.'

I drop the product, opening its inner workings, cleaner and healthier than mine. 'Bullshit! Nobody can do that. I've tried. I–I went to Narcotics Anonymous… it doesn't work. You can't be Odin. You're not… how did you do the hand on the door thing? Is this…' Breath dies inside me as I realise, I have no idea what was in the baggie he has given me. It could have been anything and I would have snorted it, and he watched me do it. He knows how desperate I am. And then he raises his offer.

'Sit down,' he commands, and I do. 'Drink some water.' I do. 'Put the glass down.' I do.

An irritated croak. My gaze shoots towards the protesting wood, as the window to my right opens slowly. It was painted shut decades ago, repainted at least twice by me, covered with leaflets, glued or nailed to the frames. I forgot this even used to be a window. It opens, dust and flecks of paint flying in the air, the green poison of the eternal Chernobyl light pouring in. I let out a tiny sound, not even a squeal. I'd piss myself if the water had made it to my bladder already.

'You see,' says Baby Odin in a friendly tone, 'no secret can be hidden from me, no door can remain locked or' – the window slammed shut, making me jump – 'open. You can't imprison me. Unless you force me out of my own

122

Universe. That is why I must reach the bridge.'

'Bridge?' I croak. We were supposed to go through a river. There is a bridge?

'The one between this place and Ásgard. Don't they teach you history? The world of the Gods. My world. The one that is currently leaking into yours.'

I suddenly remember something they did teach me. 'If you are Odin,' I say – slowly – 'why do you have both of your eyes?'

His face changes so abruptly it's more shocking than what he did with the window. Now he looks cut out of stone with sharp blue lasers of his own eyes. I should not have asked this. I want to apologise. I can't produce a sound.

Suddenly, the pink, pretty baby Odin is back and so is my loud, shallow breathing. I gulp the rest of the water and hope he won't make me eat the products scattered and spilled on the bar. 'You said you can help the...' Now I do the sideways nod. I don't want to say the word. 'How?'

He shakes his head. 'Once you've done my bidding. You will get me into Lockdown and help me find the bridge. It's a dangerous mission.' Suddenly I think of grizzled CIA agents from the movies, tempted from their rock bottom to perform their last mission. They survive and thrive. I think. The movie always ends before that last part. 'Once it is done, your cravings will disappear.'

I don't see Baby Odin now, or the bar, I see a movie I was an extra in. Dad dropping the bullet, the powder spilling out, his face turning white and his lips – blue. Eyes bulging. Saliva, then vomit, a bubble of it coming out with his breath, bursting silently. I have seen this movie so many times I could write down the dialogue, if there was any, but there were just – sounds. This will be my end if I don't accept his offer. The first time, the first snort – I was eight when Dad shared it with me, when Mother left – was always the best. You never forgot it. You kept chasing it and you were always nearly there, and Dad did get there, but it was a different there, one with no return. The nurse, warm and solid. No handcuffs. No Dad. Just me rotting here in chase of there.

'Tell me about the dangers,' I say.

***

Jacek looks up when I walk in without knocking. I can smell his coffee, stronger than Arnold. The building has a transparent, glass roof, built like this to trap some heat in the eternal cold of Iceland. Now the glass roof is covered with something, but the radioactivity particles roll in through the windows. Green coffee, green face with a mouth that opens and shuts silently. 'Your father here?' I ask.

'No… he's… Ulf, I promise, I will have the money…'

I wave him away. 'No need. I'll have the Defender for a…' I don't know. 'Few days.'

Jacek's Adam's apple bobs up and down. 'Why would you-'

'I'm driving to Chernobyl.' It's hard to stop the laughter. For just a moment he believes me. My reputation. 'I'm joking. Just a little drive off-road. Been in a bad way recently.' Normal people speak in real sentences, I tell myself. I sound like I am that agent on his last mission. I should take out a gun and do that thing where they spin it on a finger. I could take out the gun Baby Odin gave me, but I would just shoot myself in the foot. It's the spinning that's hard, not the shooting.

'No,' Jacek says. 'If my father finds out I let you touch it, he'll kill me.' He falls silent. 'You've got someone who wants an off-road trip? Now? With this?'

I nod.

'Insurance…' he begins weakly.

'I brought the paperwork,' I interrupt. 'Here's five thousand dollars of insurance. Here's another five thousand for rental. Keys?'

'In the ignition... Ulf!' I'm already walking out, Jacek chasing me. 'What is this money? What is this all about?'

'I'll be back in...' As if I know. 'Three days. Tank full?'

'Ulf, we are friends. Tell me what you are doing. I don't like this. Any of it. I will pay those debts, I promise, but what...?'

I snort. 'Here's five thousand answers.' I push some more green money into his green hand. Jacek doesn't take it and the notes float down into the snow. His gaze is glued to the gun sticking out of my trousers. I'm not actually a CIA agent, I don't have a hidden holster.

'This is stolen,' he whispers. 'Counterfeit. I won't let you commit crimes...'

'Let go of my jacket,' I snap. 'Don't make me use this gun.' I'm down to eighty-four thousand. The place where I exchanged dollars for kronur was just shady enough to take a thousand, but more would have them call the police, and the gun would not help. 'It's important. I have to go somewhere.'

'What is that important? Did you just give me fifteen thousand...' He leans to pick up some of the money, his eyes fixated on the gun. 'Ulf, you must tell me what you are doing.'

I force myself to stop snapping at him. 'It's Árora,' I say with a sigh I don't need to fake. 'I must find her. She's the only person... I've been calling. I put notes under her door. Her bike's gone. That's all I know.'

'Someone stole it,' Jacek suggests weakly, lifting himself up, shivering. I am shivering too, now, under the jacket I should have zipped. He wouldn't have seen the gun we're now both scared of. My tough guy act ran out when I said her name.

'Have you seen her bike?' I ask. 'As in, ever?'

He nods. Árora's dirt bike, customised to hell and back, is not something an amateur could even start without her help. It's a holy artefact even I am not allowed to touch. 'Let me go,' I say quietly, and he does.

I leave my ancient Ford behind and wonder if I will ever see it again.

***

As I drive down the motorway, amazed by how familiar the Defender still feels, a sound scratches the window. Rotary blades. I'm immediately drenched in sweat. Reactions on autopilot. On the green road, I see the blue flashing lights, or am I imagining them? I put the gun in the glove compartment. Stupid. If they stop me, they'll look there first. The whirr of the helicopter overhead seems louder. Am I being followed? Calm down. I'm driving at legal speed in a legal car I have legal papers for... I hope. I haven't checked. I was busy freaking the fuck out.

The sound slowly quiets before disappearing. My hands shake as I park on the side of the road – illegally, not that there's much traffic. I pull the bullet out, inhale – hard, can't stop shaking. Jesus Christ on his moped. Now my imagination presents me with everything Baby Odin told me to expect. Tall electric fences with barbed wire, black-clad men with guns, dogs the size of wolves. Helicopters, clearly. It's all real now. The snow is melting into mud, same colour as the Defender. Good, or I'd have to paint the car now. I need air.

I open the door. I am trapped. Fucking seatbelt. I am a mess. I nearly break my legs when I fall out. I forgot this isn't a normal car, the Defender is a lovechild of a minibus and a truck from outer space, its wheels almost as tall as I am. I sit down in the snow. I want to feel the cold, the wet. The green air smells like it always does, sharp and a bit bloody. Air always smells a bit bloody when it gets through my nostrils. I suck it in and let it out. The nuclear fallout is killing us all to the monotonous soundtrack of professors and scientists insisting it's a natural phenomenon from their safe bunkers... I look back. Or from the

American base at Keflavík. Just when I thought I could breathe again. The helicopter is on the hunt for people heading to the currently closed for tourists part of Iceland. One even the Coast Guard and rescue services were strongly advised against visiting.

My hands shake as I pull the bullet out again and look at it, really look at it. The only thing of Dad's that I kept, his initials engraved on it – LL. This is all that's left of Dad. A thing that kills inside a thing that kills.

I don't snort any more. My heart would give out. Vomit, bulging eyes, a silent plea, a bursting bubble on my lips this time, except I'd be alone here, as Baby Odin awaits. I climb back into the car, take a deep breath. Metal, oil, leather, rubber, gasoline. My comfort scents. I close my eyes, imagining myself going 'ommmm' in the lotus position, whatever a lotus is, except instead I see myself trapped inside the car as it burns, bullets smashing the windows to pieces, barking dogs somehow making it through, their teeth searching for my throat...

I cry for a bit.

Then I pull myself together. I have shopping to do.

***

'Welding suits,' I list, counting on my fingers. 'Shovels. Water. Extra tank of fuel...'

'Gloves?'

I nod. 'And caps. Electrician shears...'

Baby Odin frowns. 'You can't cut the fence. That's why we need the shovels. If you cut this fence, they'll know. We have to dig underneath.'

'Right,' I mumble, 'too right.' Árora, I remind myself, I am doing this for her, not for the money... not just for the money. 'And I got you red wine...'

He raises his eyebrows. 'Me? Red wine?'

'Odin, I mean you, you don't eat? You just drink wine and...' I stop. Does Odin eat in Valhalla as he watches the… I stifle hysterical laughter. I am still balancing the line between believing him, in him, and driving myself to the hospital, begging to be admitted to the mental ward.

'Thank you,' Baby Odin says, his voice a bit strangled. 'I'm not used to this sort of kindness from strangers.' My hysterical laughter breaks through, a high-pitched sound like Dad's, and he winces. 'I brought you another hot dog. I don't want you to be hungry.' He hands it to me, together with a bottle of sparkling water.

I manage a bite, wash it down with the water. I'm getting better at being normal people. Except having Odin here and helping him to go back to Valhalla as we dig under an electric fence.

'Do you have enough…?' he asks and I know what he means. The appetite I don't have disappears and I hand him the rest of the hot dog. 'Yeah,' I mumble. The bullet's full. The rest, the baggie, is in my pocket, not that I will need it again soon. I'll keep the bullet, though. Empty. A keepsake to remind me of Dad. That and the nightmares.

'Let's go, then,' says Baby Odin, dropping the real people food in the mud.

I take one last look at the sign outside the bar. After Dad died, I took down the sign he put up there, a hideous clown, and put up the word 'RISIKO' in blue and red neon. It's now down to RIS K. Hilarious. I thought I'd fix it, fix myself. Instead, I kept pestering Gunnar for a fix. Reluctantly, I climbed into the Defender. It felt final, sad. I missed what this place never became, the vision I had for it, an art gallery and a stage for punk bands, and my drink untouched as the patrons climbed over each other to order more drinks. You couldn't buy beer in Iceland for some fucking historical reason… I was stalling.

'To the right,' Baby Odin says. 'Down the Ring Road until we find the 26.'

'How do you know the route?'

His sigh is his reply. Dumb question. But he answers. 'I took a flight in one of the helicopters and paid attention.'

'You took a...' My head hurts. My nose itches. I scrunch it rabbit-style, wipe it with my hand. I don't want to know, not really, but also I do.

Baby Odin glances at me with an unreadable expression. His face is very... adult again, the piercing blue eyes penetrating through the greenery that mocks nature. I shiver. I need a break. I need to calm down. 'It's surprising how helpful people become when you know every bad thing they've ever done,' he says to the road and to the window and to the air. 'Not all people, obviously. Only the good ones, who know shame and guilt. Some don't. It doesn't take much. Everyone lies, steals, cheats, hurts others. Everyone.' I gulp. 'This particular pilot sold a house knowing the foundations weren't solid.'

'Hardly murder.' I nearly choke on the words.

'As I said, he was a good man.'

Was. Without asking, I park, legally, this time. Not a single other car. I didn't have to give Jacek fifteen thousand, I could have played on his guilt. I could have said it was about his debts that he would not pay this tourist season, because there would be no tourist season until the natural phenomenon left the island dead. Did that make me more or less good a man? Good, I decide, although there is uncertainty.

I pull out the bullet and inhale. I almost shriek at an unexpected touch. Baby Odin's hand tightens on my leg. I drop the bullet and he catches it, flips it shut, open, shut again. I am covered in cold sweat. What if he doesn't give it back...? It's not the bullet I want, Dad's initials or not, I want the contents. This fear conquers the other fear.

'Drive on,' he says.

'When will you take away the...'

'The drug addiction?' Jesus. He makes it sound so real. It is real. Am I real? 'The process will begin once your part of the job is completed.'

Everything is toxic. The coffee he brought in a thermos

129

– thoughtful – is black, no sugar, exactly as I like it. My heart keeps pounding and I ask myself again, what did he give me? For all I know, it could be roach poison. But no, not yet, he needs me. Árora is there, he knows things, he might have seen her bike... he wouldn't know... but we have a reputation... my stomach is spasming, heartburn, I'll throw up, my eyes will bulge out, a bubble...

'Ulf. Get yourself together.'

I am driving through fluorescence. I am inside a car the size of a tank. The scent of metal that is both the car and my bleeding nose. I inhale sharply, hoping the blood doesn't drip down my face. 'I'm a bit nervous,' I croak. My muscles relax, finally, my drug addiction is fed for a while. I yawn. Didn't sleep well. Or at all.

'Where is your gun?' Baby Odin asks and I tense as if an electric shock went through me.

'In the, the glove compartment,' I stutter.

He mutters something I don't understand, pulls it out, throws it into my crotch. I nearly send the car flying off the road. 'I gave it to you for a reason,' he snarls, then points. I nearly missed the 26. I turn the wheel, a bit sharper than I should, correct.

'There's red tape on the sign...' I whine. It's way more ominous than it would be without the gun between my thighs. You need a gun to enter, it seems to say. Baby Odin doesn't even bother to sigh. I drive on, slowly, until we get to the gate that blocks the road. The gate is locked with a thick chain and a sizeable padlock. There is no way around, unless you have climbing equipment. Is it also electric? Not that it makes much difference. With the engine idling, I stare, flinching when the first heavy drop of rain hits the window.

I turn to Baby Odin. 'We have a river to cross, and if it rains...' Words die in my mouth. He no longer looks like the kid who asked for red wine and didn't touch it. His lips move silently as he stares forward. I follow his gaze and gasp when the padlock slips off the chain and falls to the ground. He can open anything. The chain screeches and clings as it unravels, slips, falls. The gate opens without creaking.

My mind is blank.

'Drive through the gate, then stop again,' he commands.

My mind is blank.

A slap across the face brings me back into poisoned consciousness. 'I said, cross the gate!'

He jumps out after I drive through. A stupid thought – I can escape now – flies through my head – escape where? With my head twisted, my neck hurting, I watch, open-mouthed, as the gate closes. One end of the chain lifts up, like a snake's head, it slithers up the poles, wrapping itself around both halves of the gate. I blink convulsively, rub my eyes. It keeps moving. The first link opens, like a jaw, and bites into the last one. The snake swallows its tail. Odin reaches through the gate, picks up the padlock, calmly shuts it on the chain. It's only decoration now. Everything looks like it did before. Only now you'd need a metal grinder to get through.

I need to… I jump out of the car, pick some muddy snow, smear it on my face. It stings and it is wet and now I have sand on my face. The rain feels real. I approach the gate as Odin moves away. When I extend my hand, my face contorts into a grimace, and when I touch the chain I am somewhere between suicidal and unconscious. It's a chain. It doesn't hiss or lunge itself at me. I rub it with my fingers. Cold, rough, wet steel. I don't even know which link was the jaw that swallowed the tail.

'Hurry,' Odin says, and I find myself a man of faith as I slide the gun between my belt and trousers, placing myself next to a God as solid as steel.

I'm wet and cold. The heater in the car smells like a dead mouse. I crank it up without much effect, hoping I'll stop shivering. 'This is some shit weather,' I say. He doesn't react. 'Can you stop the rain?' Still nothing.

'Because even this car won't be able to cross if the river...'

'Shut up.'

Maybe he can open the waters, like Moses did with the sea, or something. Maybe radioactivity doesn't first cause blisters, but melts the brain. The powder he gave me. I refuse for this to be real. Oh, I want to say, there is a–

'Stop the car! Follow me!' Odin is out before the car stops rolling. I forget I'm not in my Ford again and fall on my knees, lift myself up, follow. 'Shoot!' he yells. I pull out the gun. My hands shake. Two men are running towards Odin. One seems to be heading for me. I raise the gun, try to figure out where he is, I just see green and red, and –

Bam, bam. Bam. Bam.

I thought gunshots were louder. Maybe it's just movies. I touch my shoulder. The bullet penetrated the puffed-up jacket, but not my body. It wasn't me who fired the last shot. The third man shot at me while I was busy trying not to shit myself. Two of them fell backwards, the third – sideways, Odin saved my life. His face is contorted with fury, his breath steaming, fast. He motions with his gun and my legs carry me over.

The men don't have faces anymore. They barely have their fucking heads. Everything is splashed with – I bend and throw up on one of the bodies. It's not like he'll mind. A gun fell out of his hand, I register. It's on the ground, it's a real gun, semiautomatic. It's all a movie, I tell myself. The shapes and colours, the black blood splatters on the green remains of their heads, the – I am sick again, coughing out bile. I don't want to watch this. I look away and something catches my attention. Árora's dirt bike rests against the wall, next to the men's jeeps, as if it belonged here... 'She is here!' I cry. I'm right behind Odin when he enters the building and immediately fires his gun again. Inside the shack, the explosions are deafening as he destroys some sort of machine that no longer has lightbulbs, or meters, or much of anything. Radio, I think, glancing around, activity, I add. Two metal beds. A metal cupboard. Everything is grey.

'Is she in there?' I ask in a small, stupid voice. Of course she isn't.

'Let's get out of here,' Odin snaps.

'But where is she?' The faceless men inside my head. 'Is she dead?'

He finally actually looks at me. 'No,' he says. 'We have to leave this place. Three men, two beds.' It takes me a moment to understand what he means. One of them was supposed to go… back. Where the fences and the dogs await. I already met the armed men.

'I'm sorry I didn't shoot,' I say lamely.

Odin forces me to drink some coffee. It's rancid, acidic. Water won't flush the taste of vomit either. I drink some wine straight from the bottle, hand it to him. Some more water. I am shaking. 'You killed them,' pours out of my mouth.

'Pull yourself together and drive on.'

'But you killed them.'

'Do you want to find Árora?'

I slither a bit closer to consciousness. 'Where is she?'

'They took her to the bridge,' he says.

I twist myself to take a peek at the bike. I want to go and say 'bye' to it, but there are dead people in the way. Once Odin is gone and Árora free, I'll bring her here, pick the bike up. I curse myself for not having guessed. Thirteen years ago, before Dad died, finding out that there is an area 'closed for tourism' wouldn't be an invitation for freaks like us, it would be bait.

'Start the engine,' Odin says, impatient. There are layers of unreality around me and his voice comes from far away, with a long way to go before it reaches me. 'Follow the road.'

Like there is a road. 26 was a road. We are now on F26. What's the point in naming darker gravel surrounded by lighter gravel? Somewhere, thunder strikes. The rain smacks the car. I remember there are wipers. I see water on the ground now. Puddles, at first, small. Big. Streams carving the soil. The car is shaking, disgusted with the liquid shit I'm forcing it to go through.

'You can do it,' I whisper, to the car, to myself. We're surrounded by sick, pouring from the sky, gathering under the wheels, eating me from the inside. I need a break. We have to cross first. We can't take a break here. I push the pedal harder and immediately let go before digging myself into this shit until some men with guns come over to free us.

The car rocks and the seatbelts prove their purpose. I gawk at dead men's missing heads and wonder if what I have seen was their brains, or remains of skulls, or both. It shone differently. Árora's bike is red. She would never give the bike up, unless forced. This is why I keep going. I focus on the not-road again. Almost. Almost there. Not safe, but there, which is not here, but elsewhere.

We're on more or less solid ground again. Without asking for permission, I kill the engine. 'I need a break.'

'Fine,' Odin agrees. Surprise. 'You'll eat first. Then you can do your drugs.'

He doesn't even sound human, I think, then remember. I accept a meat roll. Why is everything meat?

'You don't like meat? What do you like?'

Oh shit. I did not intend to say this out loud. What food do I like? I can't remember. 'Apples,' I say weakly, remembering the half-rotten apple in my fridge. Why else would I buy it if I didn't like them? I force the meat wrapped in skin, human flesh wrapped in human skin, bulging as I push it through my throat. Normal people eat food. Normal people are not here, neither of us qualifies. My mouth is foul, feeling rather than taste, the red wine is blood. Odin just watches. I wish there was something to eat that didn't feel like I was eating people. Everything shines green. Soylent green is people. 'Is this light intensifying?'

'We're getting closer to the bridge. Now, do your drugs, and let's go.'

I keep wiping my hands, like Lady Macbeth, can't get rid of the grease, remains of people I have just swallowed. The bullet in my hand feels slippery, too. I nearly drop it. Those men were killed with bullets. This one killed my Dad, even if indirectly. Jesus! There is no Jesus, only Odin. I hate this bullet. It disgusts me. I disgust me. Just a bit, a little voice whispers. I'd laugh if I knew how to. It's always just a bit and somehow never just a bit. My heart beats slower, my lungs seem to contract. Even my nose, which will be bleeding in a few seconds, demands it. I want to put it back in my pocket, but my hand doesn't listen. My fingers click it open, my nose inhales sharply. It's not my fault. My hand made me do it.

'You'll kill me,' I say flatly. 'That's how it will all end. No more bills, hunger, cravings.'

Odin sighs, his lips tight. 'I promise you a long life.'

'How long in minutes?'

He shakes his head. 'Many, many winters.'

And summers, I almost check, drifting towards the familiar calm. I see myself from the outside now, without a head. The warm bubble of the drug and the fluorescent haze and the men and the bike, all of us pushed into the ground by the pregnant dragons' bellies full of snakes that are living chains…

'Ulf!'

I hear a God's voice as it calls my name. Suddenly, water splashes on my face, and I let out a cry of panic. I am too far. I want to go home. 'I want to go home.' A sound comes out of the mouth I still have, 'I don't want to go any further, you kill people, you're crazy, I am crazy…'

'Tell me, Ulf,' Odin cuts through. He almost sounds sorry for me. 'How long did it take for your father to die, as you were watching, doing nothing?'

No. Don't do this to me. You can't.

But he can. 'His head hit the table when he fell, but he

135

could still talk,' Odin continues. 'He pleaded for help. He told you the number to call before he started choking on his own vomit. You remember what his eyes looked like. He was gulping for air. And you watched him suffocate, doing nothing.'

In the silence, the movie plays out in my mind. I yelled, 'Dad, stop, stop!' It never occurred to me to turn him on his side, at least. I took some time to call the ambulance, because I had to get rid of the drugs first, hide them. So, I wouldn't get arrested. Dad was shouting, then he was just gurgling, and then it was quiet, and the nurse held me tight. Did I ever call for the ambulance? I must have, since it arrived. 'You're in shock,' she told me – I now remembered – no, madam, I am high as fuck and I let my Dad die because I was afraid you'd find the drugs.

'You are a good person,' Odin said when I started the engine and drove on.

***

There are halogen lights around, as if the blinding, green luminescence could be defeated. We simply walk, unnoticed, hide behind one of the farm buildings, the one nearest to the fence. The buildings are unguarded. I don't have to wonder what happened to the farmers, or the cattle. I decide to stop thinking. My shaky hand opens the front pocket, digs out the bullet, puts it back, takes it out again. Even the bullet shines green.

Odin peeks out every now and then. I try not to stare at his full beard, long hair, the face of a man old and ageless that I had noticed in the car, earlier. I'd have caused an accident if there were any other cars. Or a road. I still want to convince myself I'm hallucinating.

'Someone's coming,' Odin whispers and I nearly jump out of my welder's suit. 'Quiet,' he adds, and I put the bullet back inside.

If they see us, we're dead, I think, then notice the gun

in his hand. He's calm, ready, it's my hands that keep shaking. If they see us, they're dead.

A zipper opens, a familiar sound. Twice. They're pissing on our shed. I'm almost offended.

'Can I...' a voice breaks. 'Sir... can you be my friend Gary, not Sergeant Young? Just for a minute?'

A sigh. 'Brickster, I'm pissing.'

'I'm shitting. Bricks.' A little snort escapes me. Brickster indeed. 'Are you sure this is not...'

Gary finishes, closes the zipper, sighs. 'The Geigers don't show anything.'

'I don't believe any machine that can be tampered with. Any machine at all. Gary, I have family. We're walking round here without... I don't know. Nuclear gear. Have you seen it?'

'I've seen it.'

'But up close?'

'Brickster, are you going somewhere with this? We have to go back.'

'They put all their machines around,' Brickster says, bitter. 'And then we threw things in to see what happens. They disappear. And then the girl...'

I turn into a rock myself.

'No wonder she didn't come back with likes of you around...'

'Sergeant Young!' I hear. I am sweating under the suit, my hair is still wet – I will put the hood on, is the hood wet? Don't think. 'Sergeant Young?'

A sigh. 'What is it?'

'The helicopter's back. There's no response from point zero, because they all got... shot. The radio's fu– destroyed, too.'

Gary swears. 'Who?'

'We don't know. The gate's still locked.'

'Take the helicopter. Fly around. Find out.'

A brief silence. 'Should we double the patrols?'

'Whoever shot those two...'

'Three.'

'Fuck it. He'd have to be completely crazy to come here. Insider,' Gary gasps. 'Holy shit. I need to talk to the Captain.'

Three pairs of heavy boots in the gravel, marching away. 'What now?' I whisper to Odin.

'We proceed as agreed. The patrols go around the Lockdown every twenty to thirty minutes. Those two got delayed, which means we have maybe fifteen minutes.'

'We can't do it in fifteen…!' He's already moving. I jump to my feet. I can still see the three men in uniforms. If they glance back, we're fucked. Jesus. There's no Jesus here. Now I need my bullet.

Odin points at the fence. 'Dig,' he commands. 'Deep enough for us to get through.' He cocks his gun. 'I'll make sure we're not disturbed.'

I am fucking disturbed, I think. The little shovel is useless and I just throw it away. Who cares if they see it? Not like they won't notice the hole. Grateful for the thick gloves I dig like a dog would. The layer of gravel is thin and uncovers soft, lovely farm soil. What happened to the farmers? Don't think about it. I sweat like a pig. Is this deep enough? I assess the hole. Odin lowers himself to moving away the soil I dug out, so I have space.

'Someone's coming,' Odin hisses.

Either I fry or I get shot. Which death is faster? I stop moving, gawking. I don't know what to do until he points his gun at me. I will get shot anyway. And I hear voices approaching.

Suddenly I am crawling under the fence, getting stuck, he pushes my feet, then follows. I reach out to pull his hands and recoil. He's still holding his gun. Mine stayed behind. I'd rather lick the fence than touch it again. As if reading my mind, he drops the gun to the side, clumsily. Now I help him. 'Go,' he commands, bending to pick the gun up.

'Dogs…' I whimper.

'Dogs won't be a problem.' How many can there be? Can he shoot them all? My imagination presented a pack of wolves with green, fluorescent eyes. 'Hurry up!'

I do. There is a crude barrier around the… beam that shoots right from the ground, into the sky. My jaw drops. I have never…

The barking brings me back to unreality. Odin just steps over the chain. I stand frozen, terrified of both the beam and the dogs. Of Gary, Brickster, whoever else. Of Odin. I'll never make it out of here alive, I realise. Should have just licked this fence. I see the dogs now. They're fucking huge and keep growing as they get closer to me. Not yet, I plead, not like this…! One of the dogs leaps towards me, sending me to the ground…

… and licks my face – ew – whimpering joyfully. The other one is trying to push his friend aside. Those fucking dogs love me. And then, now, two shots send them flying. My face is wet, rain, sweat, dog saliva, blood.

'Come in here,' Odin hisses, pointing the gun at me. I can't move. 'Or I'll shoot you.'

'Shoot me,' I pant.

'Not to death. You'll learn to live without legs.'

That fucker. But now I hear voices, alarmed, approaching. They say you always have a choice. 'They' are probably normal people. I crawl under the chain. He yanks my hand, hard, just dragging me with him, and suddenly we're near the beam… except it's not a beam, it's a tree so tall it becomes one with the fluorescent sky, and then we are in the tree, and then I am not at all.

***

When my eyes open, everything around me is green and blue. Natural. I sit up, stupefied. I am naked, sitting in the grass, surrounded by some white flowers, and three men who are very much dressed. One of my hands shoots towards my chest, the pocket that isn't there, the bullet. The other tries to cover my crotch. Odin's in the middle. There's a man in a big pointy hat, resting on a wooden staff – spear – and a shadow covers one of his eyes, but not the other. And there is…

My…

'Dad,' I whisper.

Dad laughs, high-pitched. Cruel. 'Welcome home, Ulf Lokason, Ulf the Wolf.'

'But you are dead. Am I dead?'

'Shut up, Loki,' says the middle Odin. Have I ever seen a man so handsome? Brown locks, full, groomed beard, elaborate medieval tunic. I'm in a movie. Inside it. 'Ulf, I owe you a lot more than just explanations. I have lied to you about my name.'

Like this is the important part. 'Where am I?'

'I am Týr,' he continues, undeterred. 'The God of justice, courage, combat…'

'And keeping your promises,' says my Dad. Loki.

I shake my head. 'I have never heard of you.'

'This is why I assumed Odin's name. To ensure your cooperation.'

'You promised me…' I pause.

'I will uphold the oath I have sworn to you. You will never lack money again. You will never be hungry. And you will never crave drugs again.'

'Once the cravings wear off,' Loki adds.

I am sweating, cold in the warm sun of an August afternoon somewhere that isn't Iceland. 'Where is Árora?' I demand.

Odin clears his throat, making sure I see his smile. 'She has been elevated to a Goddess. She is the one who paints the sky with flames, one who can open and close the passages between the worlds. Only now she does it consciously. Týr has been stupid enough to pass, and will suffer the consequences he, himself, will deem just.'

'Where is Árora?' I repeat, approaching Týr.

'Everywhere,' says Odin. I ignore him. 'Together with

140

the Sun and the Moon, Árora is the sky itself. She's an artist and work of…'

'Shut up!' I yell at him. 'You lied to me,' I snap at Týr, drops of my saliva landing on his unmoving face.

'When?'

'You told me she is not…' I pause. That wasn't really a lie. 'You killed people!' I yell again, punching him in the shoulder. He winces, but his face remains impassive. 'You – you…'

'It was necessary,' he says. 'They died in battle, and they will forever dwell in Valhalla.'

It takes me a moment to process this sentence. Old comics come back to mind. Valhalla. Odin. 'Maybe they didn't want to die in battle?!'

Týr shrugs and I want to choke him until his eyes pop out of his skull. 'It is just that you are here,' he says, 'and me, too. They were obstacles.'

My knee can't quite reach his balls, the trousers he's wearing are too loose, but my fist still hits his nose. Loki laughs. Týr bends, grabbing his face in his hands. I've had my nose broken. But before I can go on, he straightens up, wipes blood off his nose. It's… it's fine.

I am not fine with this.

He might be taller and I'm a twig, but when I leap and push his shoulders, he falls. I am on top of him, my fingers heading for his eyes. He grabs my wrists. I am too slow. My foot hits his boot and I yelp in pain. I forgot I'm naked. With little effort, Týr rolls and now he is on top of me, pinning me to the ground. The soft grass helps a bit, but he's crushing me.

'I will let go,' he says, 'if you promise to behave.'

'I will behave,' I answer, not specifying how. He lets go. Idiot. But he's always just, unless he's killing people… although, to be just, those people tried to kill us first… or stealing Árora from me, or stealing me. Knight in shining tunic. I breathe heavily for a few seconds, forcing myself to appear calm. Make him think I gave up.

He's a trained warrior, with a sword or an axe… a gun. I had to learn to fight when my Dad's 'creditors' had begun to send 'warnings' that waited for me in the dark. One never walked again. Another's success with the ladies ended because of the facial scars. After the third lost an ear – this was where the 'Wolf' nickname came from – I made it clear that either they leave me alone and I pay bit by bit, or they kill me.

I never fought fair. That's how you lose. He is, apparently, all fairness. And he has the same fault almost all people do. There's always a glint in the eye, a slight narrowing, a moment before the decision is made. I don't make decisions. I just cause pain. Fast.

The fucker healed from a broken nose in seconds, though. And he was heavy.

'I'm going to stand up, slowly,' Týr announces. 'You will be clothed…' My fists land on his chest before he gets anywhere further with that, then I pound his stomach and he bends. Loki is laughing. Týr's weight falls on top of me, he begins to lift himself, manages to grab one of my wrists as my hands shoot towards his eyes, my legs are trapped, but I am smaller, his tunic is slippery and so is the grass, I writhe, he is surprised, clumsy, and when I bite his wrist, he screams.

Harder I bite, and harder he screams. The bones snap before the skin gives in. When his blood fills my mouth, I no longer feel his weight. My jaw tightens further, scaring me, I am not in control. I am filled with gold and power, I am the nuclear weapon, and I will destroy him. Týr is trying to pull away, but fails, as his own weight holds me to the ground. My teeth close. I have his flesh, blood, gristle, bones in my mouth.

I swallow.

'My son,' says Loki proudly. Týr finally frees me, lying on the ground, holding on to his – can you call it a wound if someone ate a part of your – the hand still hangs, held with skin and some muscle tissue. My mouth wasn't big

142

enough. It is now. I lick my mouth, my tongue strangely long. I have too many teeth. Too long. My eyes begin to see more. I sniff the air, and it is layered. There is blood, he is wasting blood I want. I try to stand up, but I can't. My legs, my whole body… it's all not like it should be. My ears turn at the sound.

'Tie him up,' Odin says. He smells like sadness. 'Now.'

'My pleasure,' Loki answers. I separate the familiar scent of my Dad from everything else. He smells like a joker villain. Something like fishing line wraps around my ankles and my… my what? Those are not hands. I am too confused to protest. I still taste Týr's blood. He smells like food. He is. There is more. Give it to me. I have a fucking tail now. This is not my body. Loki stands up and I realise my limbs are tied. I can't move. I can't stand up. I open my mouth to protest and the sound that comes out is a howl. Is me, is I have become a wolf.

I can't see Týr all that well. I can smell and taste him, and loathe all those men. The sad one, the evil one, the just one. Scratch me, I itch. Come closer.

'It is just,' he says weakly. 'I apologise for the lies and harm I have caused you.'

I smell his blood. Is I want.

'You apologise?' Old man. Odin. 'This is just? How?'

'Your orders deprived him of a life he could have had.'

High sound hurts my ears. Is laugh. 'You've seen his life. And he's immortal. He'd notice sooner or later.'

Immortal. Is villain saying, he means me. Skin itches. Sweat. Hungry.

'Cut my hand off.'

'This is your sword hand!' Sadness, surprise, anger. A bit of nervous sweat. I smell it all. Give it to me. Is not for sword. Is for me.

'The wound won't close until…' Weak. Easy prey. 'Loki?'

'I love helping!' Thud. Two cries, one laugh. Smell reddens, I can taste. Is give to me! I whine, can't move. Is too

143

far. I yelp and cry, can't shift, reach.

'Ahhh, my son is hungry' – joker's voice – is who 'son'? – laugh – 'Here, let me give you a hand.'

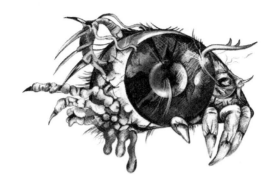

EYE
AN EYE FOR AN EYE

By
Lee C Conley

The shovel crunched on pale stone and echoed through the darkness.

'You know that's not the right tool for this,' drawled Mouse as he angled his crowbar to find purchase. Mouse heaved and with a deep scrape the heavy stone shifted a fraction. 'There we go,' he muttered.

Mug doubled his efforts with the shovel. 'I thought there would be more digging, like last time.'

'This is more burglary than digging grave dirt, my friend,' replied Mouse between strained efforts with the crowbar. Slowly the stone edged further, grinding with the ancient protest of something long settled. 'That old Gaffer was right, though. We must be near the old cemetery by the cathedral. Look at this place.'

Mug surveyed the darkness. Illuminated by the ruddy flicker of their filthy lantern. He wiped it with the cuff of his jacket, smearing the grime across the glass plate.

145

Mouse was right, it looked like some sort of crypt. The low, vaulted roof was wreathed in ancient spider webs and rubble scattered the floor. It smelt of damp, stale air, like a tomb. 'What else is down here?' he said to distract himself from their unsettling location.

'Well, the Gaff said they are digging the new sewers system — big plan, apparently.'

'I see why it spooked 'em,' commented Mug eyeing the shadows.

'And if they found this,' continued Mouse, 'just think what else they might find down here. We should keep friendly with him next time we're at the pub.'

'Aye, solid plan.'

The stone protested but it began to give. A trickle of dust slid down. 'Put your shoulder into it,' grunted Mouse. They heaved as the sarcophagus lid slid open.

'Got the fucker,' grunted Mug.

They peered into the desecrated cavity and were greeted by the skeletal smile of a desiccated face. It was more skeleton than cadaver, patches of dried and shrivelled skin still stretched across the bones.

'What the fuck is that?' exclaimed Mug as he recoiled in horror.

There was a moment of silence as Mouse peered closer, his expression twisted into a frown of disgust as he examined it. 'It's his eye,' he finally replied.

'No shit,' said Mug as he gagged and raised a filthy hand over his mouth. 'But… how? Why hasn't it rotted away like the rest of him? Why, in the god's name, is it like fucking that?'

'It must be a false eye,' suggested Mouse, still uncertain. 'It's good though.'

'It still looks fucking wet,' retorted Mug. 'And it's staring at me.'

'I seen some stuff in my time,' muttered Mouse, 'but this is one of them times. Fucking hell.' He pulled his gaze away. 'Let's get this done.'

'Can we cover that up a bit? It's creeping me out,' said Mug unable to look away.

Mouse dropped a handful of rags over the withered skeletal face. 'There.'

Mug shuddered and breathed a long sigh. 'Aye, let's get this done. I do not like it down here. I think I'd rather be dodging the grave keepers.' He studied the corpse before him, all too aware of that hideous staring eye beneath the rags. 'Are you sure the doctors will want this one? It looks a bit… gone,' said Mug.

'Not our usual fare is it? Less fucking rotten though,' countered Mouse.

'Aye there is that,' agreed Mug in a dubious tone.

'It wasn't the corpses that got me interested,' said Mouse. 'Think about it, these ain't no common folk they stick in a hole. This is a crypt, these are gonna be rich folk, and where there's rich folk, there's —'

'Money,' finished Mug with a grin of understanding.

'Aye… well maybe, but there certainly might be something worth pocketing. Check his fingers, might have some rings.'

'How do you know he's a he?'

Mouse suddenly looked uncertain. 'Fuck knows. One skeleton looks about the same as another.'

Mug shrugged and moved the lantern to shine deeper into the stone coffin. 'Aye, looky here.' He reached down and produced a dull ring set with a red stone and rubbed it between finger and thumb. 'I reckon that's gold.'

'Jackpot,' exclaimed Mouse as he unfurled the tarp on the floor. 'Here help me with the body, it's probably gonna fall to pieces.' They lifted the desiccated corpse out and placed it onto the tarp. Bones clattered to the stone floor as part of its leg fell. 'Get all of those little bits, we want it whole.'

'Why would they want this? I thought they wanted the fresh corpses?'

'Look, I dunno. Might want it for the bones.' Mouse

flashed the bigger man a dark grin. 'Might make a nice puzzle for them to put back together. You know these doctor types – weird people.'

Mug grunted a nervous laugh and brushed the spilled bones onto the tarp.

'Get anything in the coffin, too.'

Mug brushed through the dust of the sarcophagus. He pocketed another ring, which he guessed to be silver, and some sort of chain. 'Got a few nice bits here.' He reached into the bottom of the gloomy space and his hand found something hard, but rotten and delicate. He carefully grasped it and lifted it out. 'What about this? Looks like a book.'

'Yes, take it. Books are expensive. Hurry up, let's go,' urged Mouse.

Mug agreed this thick darkness was oppressive. He wanted to get out into the fresh air as soon as possible. He placed it in his sack along with everything else.

Once satisfied they had captured any errant bones, Mouse busied himself rolling the corpse in the tarp and securing it with rope.

'You're taking the eye?' asked Mug.

Mouse plucked it from its dry socket. He looked like he immediately wished he hadn't. 'Gods, it's real,' he spluttered. Mouse gagged and stuffed it into a pouch, then wiped his fingers on his jacket. 'That was disgusting.'

'Why… why would you do that?' asked Mug with disbelief.

'Might be able to sell it as extra, and besides who is gonna believe this unless we take the eye.'

'You're wrong in the head.'

Mouse laughed. 'Come on let's get out of this creepy shithole.'

***

148

Malc sat there slowly thumbing a silver coin over two fingers. *Heads. Tails. Heads. Tails.* He watched the coin rotate, almost staring through it, as though staring into another place entirely lost in empty thoughts.

'Another?' asked the barman, wiping a dull glass tumbler with a filthy rag.

Without looking up, he tapped the bar loudly with the coin twice. The barman winced at the sharp rap of metal on wood.

'I wish you wouldn't do that, Malc,' groaned the barman. Still, he poured out another measure of dark brown liquor.

Malc grunted and cast the barman a smirk. 'It's a shit old piece of firewood, I'm just giving it some character, mate.' He knocked the drink back. It tasted like smoke and piss. 'Giving it a story to tell, ain't I?'

'It's a bar it doesn't need a character, or a story —'

Malc slammed the tumbler down, interrupting the barman, and looked him in the eye with a frown of shocked disbelief. 'That,' he slurred, waggling a finger at the man. 'That there is some fucking bullshit. How can you, a proprietor of a fine establishment such as this' — he waved at their dingy surroundings —'not see the vital importance of character?' He shook his head in disappointment. 'A story can make a place, and the place with the character is the place with the stories.'

The barman shrugged and shook his head. 'I'd just rather you didn't.'

'Fucking amateur, I thought you knew better than that, Paulie.'

Paulie poured another drink and, with a glance at the door behind Malc, moved to serve another customer.

'I thought I'd find you here,' said a voice behind him.

'I could say the same for you,' replied Malc.

A finely dressed man pulled up a stool beside him and placed his top hat on the bar after giving the wood a wipe with his handkerchief. Malc regarded his partner with a

149

sideways glance. *Always so fancy, but he spends as much time in the gutter as anyone else 'round here.* Thaddeus Cairnholme was a gentleman though, born of finer blood than he — born of money — yet here they both were, working the cases together for the city's brass. He was an older man who carried the air of money about him, though any potential softness was marred by the scar across half his face and his missing eye. Thaddeus hid his disfigurement beneath a black patch and rarely spoke of it. He wore a handlebar moustache and kept up with the high society thing, but Malc always said he had the face of a cut-throat in the suit of a lawyer.

In comparison Malcolm Elms was born of the streets. He had no airs or graces, just a bald head, a smart mouth, and fists. The chief had paired them together a few years back and they'd been partners since. It worked though, believe it or not, they got it done.

'What we got then?' asked Malc, resuming the slow rotation of the big coin between soot-stained fingers.

'Well, old chap. A few interesting bits and bobs.' Thaddeus gestured at the barman with a gloved hand. 'Chief has put Lanner and Croyle on the grave robbings. Thank you, Paulie,' he said to the barman with a nod as the man poured another measure into one of the cleaner glasses. Thaddeus produced a silver coin and laid it on the bar.

'So, what are we on?' asked Malc.

Thaddeus delicately probed at an itch beneath his eye patch. 'They found some bodies.'

'A murder?'

'Perhaps… in fact, likely,' replied Thaddeus, carefully adjusting the patch into its proper place. 'The report stated "mutilation".'

Malc sat up, his interest piqued. 'You don't say.' He rubbed his red-rimmed eyes. 'Where are they?'

'The crime scene is down on Salters Row.' Thaddeus examined the contents of his glass with a vague frown.

'The Watch are, well, watching the place.'

'They do have that tendency,' commented Malc.

'They've got the place secured and are waiting for us. No one should have been in, except the poor soul who found them, and the first of the Watch who got there.'

'How many bodies?' asked Malc.

'That remains to be seen. Finish your drink so we can get going. I have a carriage waiting. I will fill you in on the rest on the way.' Thaddeus knocked back the drink and retrieved his hat from the bar. He nodded a farewell to the barman with a salute of his pewter-shod cane and strode for the door.

Malc cursed under his breath. The same way he did every time he had to leave the pub for something work related. He sank his last drink and placed the tumbler upside down on the bar, before flipping the coin one last time into the air and catching it to examine which face stared up at him. 'Tails,' he muttered before placing it in his jacket's top pocket. 'Be back soon, Paulie. Have one ready for me.'

***

Malcolm Elms had seen a few sights. He had grown up in the poorer neighbourhoods, the parts of the city that weren't even given street names, just gutter row, or slum square, to refer to a whole warren of dilapidated over-filled tenements. He had seen his fair share of violence — hell, he'd dished out his fair share — but this was something else, one of those rare acts of sick cruelty which an average person should never have to stumble onto.

There was blood everywhere. It seemed to Malc that there was more blood than could be possible. Two bodies sprawled in a macabre scene akin to a charnel house canvas.

The eyes…

The first thing that struck him were the eyes. There

151

were no eyes, they had been carved out. Bodies drenched in gore and viscera. Gouges torn through mangled faces, the flesh open like the furrows of a field that had been tilled in preparation for a harvest of spite. Blood pooled in empty eye sockets that still stared, regardless. Malc shuddered at the wide accusing gaze of the eyeless dead. It reminded him of those creepy portraits that watched you wherever you stood. One was twisted and disembowelled on the floor. The coils of bluish ropey entrails had spilled amongst the pool of thick gore. The gash visible through the victim's torn clothes plunged deep up its torso. It looked like a blade had been driven deep with inexplicable malice, and it looked like it had been torn free with the kind of cold, savage purpose that he, as a sane man, could not fathom.

Malc was certainly not a stranger to violence — it was a worn and familiar currency in his world — but this level of brutality chilled him. The person that did this could only be wholly evil. The other body lay sprawled in a chair. Its arms and head flung back, its mouth agape in a voiceless scream. It looked as if he had been pinned back and held down as the attacker slowly carved out his eyes. This one had died frozen in terror. It looked like he had been stabbed in the chest repeatedly, likely after he had died. The senselessness of it made his stomach twist and writhe.

Thaddeus moved slowly about the hovel, methodically examining the scene, as was his approach — lifting items of clothing and personal effects, before carefully placing them back as he found them. Malc crouched before the body sprawled in the chair and chewed on a toothpick, unable to pull his gaze from the butchered eye sockets that still somehow stared back at him. He eventually rose and searched the man's pockets, producing a silver snuffbox from the man's jacket and turned it over in his hands before sliding it in his own pocket. *He won't need that*. He glanced through the open door at Thaddeus. His partner spoke with a sickly-looking woman in a tattered shawl who looked visibly shaken by her discovery. The witness, just some poor soul who had stumbled on a nightmare. Thaddeus had removed his top hat and held its rim in two hands. He spoke with a concerned frown. Malc cast a last, morbid look at the two bodies before stepping over to join Thaddeus.

'Inspector Elms,' Thaddeus explained to the shaking woman who watched him approach. 'It's alright now though. You should try to put it out of your mind. I think that's all I need,' he said, acknowledging Malc with a nod. 'Thank you for your help,' he said to the woman. 'The sergeant outside will give you a little something to help you. Nothing much but enough for a strong drink, or whatever you feel will settle your nerves.' She nodded and left without another word.

'Looks pretty shook up,' commented Malc.

'Indeed,' agreed Thaddeus. 'I doubt she is a suspect.'

Malc threw a bemused look at his colleague. 'Aye,' agreed Malc.

'What do you think?' asked Thaddeus as he replaced his hat.

'Whoever did it is an animal — a right evil fucker!'

'Yes, I agree. Quite the mess.'

'What did she say?'

'Other than the men of the watch first on the scene, only she has been inside. Apparently no one else has disturbed the place. She didn't know them well. She described them as "dodgy."'

'Know the type,' said Malc.

'She thought they were some sort of petty thieves or gangers,' continued Thaddeus. 'She said, word about is, that they had just made a good haul. Mentioned that she had heard them talk about graves before and said they had been asking about where is good to sell some old book in the pub over the road. Her guess was they probably fell afoul of one of the street gangs.'

'Think this is a gang job then?' asked Malc.

Thaddeus scratched his whiskers and shrugged. 'Could be.'

'They look like they're robbing graves, look at these tools,' said Malc indicating a dirt-crusted shovel in the corner. 'Found this,' said Malc, producing the snuffbox. 'Looks too nice for their like. I'd say it was stolen.'

Thaddeus nodded. 'There's a few other pieces, a saw in a box. Likely also stolen. Looks like something was taken too—there's marks through the dust and filth.'

'Strange the suspect left the other silver,' commented Malc.

'Umm,' frowned Thaddeus. 'Indeed. That does seem odd. Maybe they got spooked before they could look around. It could be the gangs, hard to say who they upset. We can ask around a bit more.'

Malc grunted. 'No one will talk.' Malc had seen enough, he felt a sudden urge to get out. He turned and walked from the hovel. Thaddeus followed in his wake.

'What do you think?' asked the waiting sergeant.

'A bloody mess,' commented Malc.

'Have it cleaned up,' said Thaddeus. 'Send the bodies to the coroner. Keep the place on guard for a day or two, report anything to our office.' He handed the man a card with his details.

'Coroner already came by,' said the sergeant. 'We didn't let him in though, not until you had a proper look.'

'That's good protocol, Sergeant,' said Thaddeus nodding with approval.

'He didn't seem happy. I asked if he wanted to wait for you but he apparently didn't have time.'

'Good work, Sergeant. Have your men get started. This will need cleaning away as soon as possible before a crowd gathers.'

They turned and left the dilapidated tenement and its hidden charnel horrorscape, and walked along a cobble street that stank of piss and gods knows what else—the

154

effluence of the wretched. The light faded revealing an acrid smoke pall that hung low over the cobbles.

His greasy hair felt damp. Malc wiped the cold sweat from beneath his cap and wiped his hand on his jacket. *Not a sight easily forgotten*. He watched the lamplighters move from lamp to lamp along the narrow thoroughfare, each trailing a lambent glow of a lit taper. He lit a cigarette with his match and watched the gas lamps puff into life to send the smoky fog swirling into the encroaching shadows of dusk.

'Nasty business,' said Thaddeus to break the silence.

'And all for what?' spat Malc. 'Not the silver, to murder two grave-robbing, book peddling, street thieves.'

'The heavy object from the shelf! That's a thought, it could have been a book. She did mention a book. I didn't think of that.'

'Not just a pretty face,' grinned Malc.

'What if they *were* after the book though? Books are expensive,' added Thaddeus.

Malc nodded. 'You say that as if I can't read.' He threw Thaddeus a scowl. 'You know I can read, better than most.'

Thaddeus smirked at him.

'Someone got ripped apart for a book?' Malc frowned and shook his head. *Not a chance it was over a book.*

'Perhaps,' suggested Thaddeus.

Malc was more than dubious. 'Well this is an odd one.'

They walked further along the street in thoughtful silence.

'Wait there,' said Malc. He brought out the snuffbox. 'I wonder…'

He read an engraved inscription he'd noticed on the silver box lid aloud. *Edward. P. Langfish. Physician.* 'Maybe this bloke knew 'em.'

'Could be our mysterious coroner?'

'You know, I thought that was a bit fucking odd!' exclaimed Malc. 'No bloody chance a coroner got there before we did. It just wouldn't happen.'

'I thought as much myself,' agreed Thaddeus.

'Bloody idiots let him right through.'

'He must have looked the part.'

'Aye, and talked the talk too—Fucking idiots!'

'Whoever that was is our best lead!' Thaddeus looked down at the silver snuff box and the realisation struck him too. *Aye Thad. A bit too convenient isn't it?*

'Perhaps we should pay this Mr Langfish, Physician, a visit,' said Thaddeus.

'Aye, I think we fucking-well should,' agreed Malc.

***

Thaddeus rapped on the old wooden door with the end of his cane. Malc seemed to be peering up at the building's eaves. It had begun to rain, and water cascaded from the gutters in sheets. This part of town was attached to the university, a row of town houses that had become part offices and studies for their academically inclined residents.

The heavy door creaked open to reveal a man's lean face. 'May I help you?'

'Mr Langfish?'

'So it states on the door plaque.' The man squinted at them, ready to slam the door shut at a moment's notice.

'Ah, my apologies for disturbing you so late in the evening. This is Inspector Elms'—he gestured to Malc—'and I am Inspector Cairnholme. We are from the city's Office of Marshals and Investigations.'

'Lawmen?' asked the man uncertainly.

'Indeed, quite so,' replied Thaddeus in his best friendly yet stern voice. 'We were hoping you could assist us with our inquiries.'

The man hesitated. He looked like most did upon answering their door to him, that suddenly nervous expression that told Thaddeus he was not welcome but would

156

be tolerated.

'May we come in? It is rather wet out here.'

The man did not look like he wanted to invite them in, but finally relented. 'Of course, inspectors,' he said reluctantly and opened the door wider. 'Will it take long? It is, as you, say quite late.'

'We will be as quick as we can.'

The man led them down a corridor illuminated by a candle guttering from a brass chamberstick. The hallway was laid with a threadbare carpet and several faded paintings were hung on the wall. It looked like somewhere that tried desperately to cling to some sort of status and class but was woefully underfunded — like many institutions of the city. He wore an old suit that needed replacement and seemed to fit with the decor in its dishevelment. He led them into a cluttered office and indicated a chair. The chair creaked as Thaddeus sat, and Malc lingered in the hall examining the portrait of an elderly man.

'Can I presume you are Mr Langfish?' asked Thaddeus.

'Said as much didn't I. What is this about?' he said as he sat down in a high-backed office chair. He sat beside the embers of a soot-stained fireplace, the ruddy glow illuminating one side of his face.

Thaddeus noted an old fire-brush and a poker which lay abandoned in the hearth. His desk was strewn with papers. *Very disorganised for a physician.* His eyes were drawn to the shelves lining the walls. Part library, part collection of ethnographic and anthropological curios. There was a strange skull, perhaps of some primate, its fangs elongated and primal, yet hauntingly human. There was some sort of primitive knife from a world away, and other strange trinkets and baubles. His gaze lingered on what appeared to be a human eye in a jar, it stared at him with an unsettling presence. There were other jars, strange things suspended in liquid — samples of some creature's anatomy. *Or even human!* The thought chilled

157

him. He glanced at the eye staring from its jar one last time before dragging his attention to the disgruntled physician.

'We'll be brief,' said Thaddeus. 'What is it you do here?'

'I'm a physician, a medical practitioner. We are studying anatomy for the university.' There was a pause and the man looked flustered. 'You obviously know what we do here, but you're wasting your time. So before you ask, yes the bodies are all signed and accounted for through proper channels. Criminals and specimens from the coroner. I don't know what you think you've heard but we have no dealings with grave robbers and common thieves here.'

Thaddeus watched him, bemused by the nervous tirade.

'Well, that's not entirely true is it?' said Malc.

The physician's face reddened with rising anger. 'What are you implying?'

'We are looking for information about two men,' interjected Thaddeus. He checked his notebook. 'One by the name of Mouse and another named Mug. We have reason to believe you may be acquaintances of them, or have had some contact with them?'

'What? No!' said the flustered physician. He let out a slow controlled breath, attempting to calm himself. 'Well, not that I remember.'

'They have been involved in some unpleasantness,' continued Thaddeus.

'A murder actually,' said Malc.

The physician's face paled. 'The bodies? Is that what you think! Look here, I am not that kind of doctor we would never kill — swore an oath.'

'We're not here about anything like that. We are not investigating the black-market body trade. We obviously know you haven't bought the bodies because we have them secured. Just tell us what you know of these two suspected grave robbers,' said Thaddeus with a wry smirk.

'Obviously,' repeated Malc in a voice laced with sarcasm. 'And we know they have had some contact with you in one way or another.' He placed the silver snuff box on the table.

'That's mine!' spat the physician. 'Bastards stole it!'

'So you may know them after all?' said Malc.

The physician looked snared for a moment, then frowned and sighed.

'The idiots tried to sell me the eye as extra to some medical specimens,' he indicated his shelf.

'Medical specimens?' asked Malc dubiously.

'We're not here for that,' said Thaddeus with a look at Malc. *Just let him talk.*

The physician seemed momentarily wordless again. 'Yes… specimens.' He quickly changed the subject back to the eye. 'I am no fool though.'

'What do you mean?'

'What they claimed was impossible. They said it was a hundred years old. Ridiculous!' he spat. 'An eye would rot, it was probably some pig's eye from the abattoir.'

'But you took it anyway?'

'Of course. It's a perfectly good specimen, but I gave them only a half-penny for it. How dare they try to sell me offal and claim it as a curiosity.'

'Of course.' He nodded. 'And is it a curiosity?'

Thaddeus found it hard to pull his attention away from the disquieting eye that stared back from the shelf, the blank gaze that stared from beyond death. He fancied he could hear whispers. He shuddered and shook off his creeping unease.

The physician shrugged. 'Unlikely, but it has a strange quality, wouldn't you agree?' He shook his head as if trying to convince himself. 'Unlikely,' he repeated. 'They must have stolen my tin before I sent them off.'

'And these specimens,' added Malc, 'were legal?'

The physician spluttered. 'I already told you, I'm registered from the College. All our specimens are legal.'

'Of course, our apologies,' said Thaddeus throwing Malc another irritated look.

'Listen,' said Malc, striding from the corner. 'I frankly don't give a fuck about you body snatching, body chopping fucks. I don't care where they come from. We know someone who might though, we know exactly who might, but as Inspector Cairnholme said, that's not why we're here.' He let the threat hang. 'Tell us what we need to know and we'll be on our way.' He leaned in. 'Perhaps we won't look too closely at where these *specimens* come from.' He flashed a menacing smile and pulled back. 'After all you are a respected medical man,' he finished, with a pat on the physician's shoulder.

The physician forced a weak smile. 'Of course. There is not much else to say. They made themselves known to the right people, and although I avoid their more illicit wares, of course—'

Liar.

'Some of their ilk have been known to have some use at times, curios and the like.'

Malc stared at his hand. He had leaned on the table whilst plying Mr Langfish with his rather coarse form of persuasion—he certainly acknowledged its uses at times, however. Malc suddenly reached for the table and brushed a finger across an old book beneath some papers. He rubbed his fingers. 'Blood… Where did you get this?'

Thaddeus couldn't help but notice now that he examined the desk properly, that the book looked to have been hastily concealed amongst what seemed to be expected from a physician's desk. The physician stared, horrified. *He knows we know it was him.* The physician looked from Malc to the book, and then locked gaze with Thaddeus. The room seemed to freeze with tension.

The physician suddenly burst into motion, swinging a fire poker at Malc's head. The small detective tried to dodge but it still caught him. Malc went sprawling. It was all happening so fast, it caught Thaddeus off guard. One moment, gentlemanly discourse and the next, an explosion of intense violence. He watched the physician raise the poker again and lurch towards Malc's dazed form.

The pistol *cracked* and disgorged a barrel of white smoke and flames. The shot left his ears ringing and nearby dogs barking. The ball-shot tore through the man's shoulder and sprayed blood across the opposite wall as it went clean through him. The man swung around to face him with the force of the impact and Thaddeus realised he had hit him perilously close to the heart. The physician coughed a gout of blood and slowly sank to his knees.

Thaddeus watched the man die. He tried to claw his way towards the shelf, his eyes fixed on a particular jar. He collapsed as blood pooled alarmingly quickly. Thaddeus ran to his side with his cane prepared to strike just in case. The man was mumbling something. Thaddeus leaned down to listen.

'It shows you. It whispers,' mumbled the physician. 'I needed to go back and get the book, it needs it, it showed me.' He coughed. 'One of them said it spoke to him, seemed such a trifling thing at the time, but I couldn't stop thinking about it. Then it showed me where, and how.' His face contorted as a string of blood spilled from his lips. He stared into Thaddeus's eyes, and the inspector saw a terrible agony deep within, fear wrapped around his core. 'It controlled me,' he spluttered. 'It killed them, with my hands — but the things it shows you. It can show you th—' He fell silent. Thaddeus found himself knelt in silence beside a corpse, processing the man's final words, remembering it.

'Bastard,' growled Malc as he spat a mouthful of blood. 'He got the jump on me.' He leant against the far wall to steady himself. 'Good shot though, Thad.'

Thaddeus nodded to his colleague but said nothing. It

was a strange thing to kill a man. He found he lacked words as the gravity of it struck him.

'That thing makes a mess,' commented Malc, nodding at the smoking pistol as he brushed himself off and regarded the blood splattered wall. 'Well there's no fucking doubt he was our man. Did you catch what he was mumbling?'

Thaddeus found himself staring at the eye in the jar. 'I did. He was our man. He went after a book and killed them both for it.'

'A book, well fuck me,' said Malc in disbelief.

'We best call in the watch to clear this up,' said Thaddeus. 'We'll need to write this up. Plenty of evidence though.' He looked over at the blood-smeared book, then at the dead man at his feet, then back to the ever watchful eye and its blank dead stare.

'Case closed,' grinned Malc. 'The lawman's word is the deadman's guilt.' He scowled down at the dead physician. 'Let's get out of this shithole, I need me a drink.'

Malc plucked the silver snuff tin from the physician's desk and tapped it once on the wooden desktop before returning back into his pocket with a smirk. Thaddeus watched Malc take one last look around, and then walk from the room as he lit a cigarette. Thaddeus reached up and took down the jar with the eye in. He looked at Malc in the corridor and turned the jar to examine it. Thaddeus pondered the confession that just spilled from the physician's mouth with his dying words. *What did he mean? Just nonsense of the doomed when they feel death's gates open before them.* He spent a moment just meeting the eye's gaze as it bobbed gently in liquid. *Still, this is evidence.* He slid it into his pocket.

***

Malc sat spinning the coin on the polished wooden top of the bar. He stared at the silver until it began to make the

162

room spin too. He frowned and ran his hand over his face. It felt strangely numb. He scooped up the coin and clutched at it tightly until it steadied the whole world around him. He had to concentrate to hold it still, to stop it spinning and tumbling. *I'm fucking drunk.*

'You okay, Malc?' asked a muffled voice.

He rubbed at his eyebrows and slowly focused a rheumy gaze on the barman.

Fuck off Paulie.

'Aye, Paulie. We're fucking heroes, haven't you heard?'

'You been goin' hard this week,' said a man strangely torn between concern and greed.

He *had* been going hard for longer than that. *Had it been weeks? More like a month since he'd laid eyes on that first grisly murder scene? Fuck knows!* He'd seen some violence, some terrible shit, in fact, but something hit him hard that night. Something snapped in him. Seeing those bodies all cut up, the damned physician in his house of horrors. That night had just been the beginning. For some god's damned reason, it was those grisly memories that suddenly sucked the mirth from his spirit every time those sights flashed through his thoughts. He knew he shouldn't let it get to him — he really knew it — but the worst thing was the more he thought about it, the more it bothered him. One terrible sight too many had tipped him over some unseen precipice. So he drank, the best sanctuary in his arsenal. He had been drunk nearly every day of the last month. Every time he thought he had been going too hard, he found himself thinking about why, and it hit him again. He could see the bodies when he closed his eyes. Eyeless blood-streaked faces, haunting him.

There was something else though, something nagging at him. The other murders, these copycat killings — why would they copy that? *Who the fuck does that? Who looks up to that and thinks 'Yeah, I'm gonna copy that'? What the fuck has happened to people?* If he had to look at one more eyeless face, if he had to gaze into those gory, empty sockets — sockets that stared horribly despite the lack of eyes — he thought it really would be enough to break him once and for all.

But he and Thad were the heroes now. They kept solving the murders. It had gotten them a lot of attention, and the commissions from the city had become a small fortune. But it seemed for every lunatic they sent to the gallows others just stood in to take their place. Every victim slashed and eyeless — it was like some sick underworld trend now. A fashion of murder. The very concept made him despair at what kind of world he found himself in. *Sick fucks*. But was he too different? He'd done things that haunted his conscience. He was no angel. He had gone too far before, undoubtedly, but that level of malice and sheer spite was something he struggled to accept he was capable of. He fished in his pocket for the silver snuff box and brought it out with a wavering hand. He took a pinch of snuff and snorted it up one nostril. Everything in his face burned for a moment. He shook his head violently and exploded with a snot-splattering sneeze. His head swam, and he dizzily clutched the bar and focused his eyes on his glass before him. *Shit!*

'You know you've always been a man of unquestionable class,' said Thaddeus. He walked up and placed his hat and cane on the bar. Paulie was already pouring him his usual drink from a dusty green bottle. Thaddeus regarded him with *that* fucking pompous amused look he used to tell you he was better than you while humouring you.

'You would know mate,' slurred Malc. *Fuck you, Thad. They can all fuck off in fact.* 'Oi, where's mine, Paulie?' he said, berating the glass with his finger.

The barman frowned but poured him another whiskey.

Malc flashed him a grin, and propping himself against the bar, swung himself clumsily around to regard his partner.

'I hear congratulations are in order,' said Paulie. 'Another sicko off the streets. Well done, lads.'

Wasn't me though was it. It's all Thaddeus-fucking-Cairnholme. Malc scowled. *The clever bastard.* Thaddeus had known — it was like he had just fucking known each time. It's like the man had a second sight. Malc remembered how they had left one crime scene last week, and just headed straight to a nearby house and arrested the man. Thaddeus knew where the weapon was hidden. Recently it seemed he always just knew. He knew where some piece of crucial evidence was stashed. Malc was gobsmacked at it all. *Far too clever, and I ain't no idiot. How does he do it?* He reckoned Thaddeus must have a source. *Probably Paulie, for all I know,* thought Malc as he eyed the barman. *Someone's definitely talking. Barmen are always listenin'. It's the only way he could know all that. Unless he got a great fortune teller.* Malc barked a laugh.

Thaddeus appraised him before shaking his head when Malc was not forthcoming with an explanation. Either way they were heroes now, best inspectors in the city. A reporter even printed them in the newspaper. *Fucking heroes.* The extra coin had been welcome. Malc had need of it and lost himself in a silver-fuelled spiral down the inside of a bottle. All to get his head straight, of course. Funny thing is, the more he spiralled the less straight his head got. He cursed himself. He had more control than that. He was Malcolm Elms, a fucking hard bastard and too clever to become a damn drunk. He laughed again, seemingly to himself. *But here I am, a drunk.*

'What is so funny?' asked Thaddeus.

Malc just shrugged.

'Where you been then?'

'Here and there,' said Thaddeus.

He's always here and there.

'Haven't seen you all day,' said Malc. *What the fuck does*

he get up to all the time?

'Well I knew where you were if I needed you.' Thaddeus smirked.

Fuck you, Thad! Malc's grin soured a moment with genuine annoyance and then returned. *He's just fucking with me, but does he have to be a pompous dick about it?* The room was slowly spinning again. He was too drunk again and he knew it. He'd always been an angry drunk. Things just pissed him off, and he would go from a grin to throwing a punch all too suddenly after a few too many. He sighed. *Maybe, I should give it a rest for a day or so… Tomorrow.*

'Well, I just stopped in for a nightcap,' said Thaddeus. 'Thought I better check in on you, old chap, but I'd best be off.'

Where you off to now?

'Wait, it's night out there already?' spluttered Malc.

Thaddeus smiled at Paulie. 'Good evening, Malc.'

***

It could have been a day or two, he couldn't remember — it could have been this morning, fuck knows — but again Malc found himself on his familiar barstool burning through a purse of silver and copper coins until he needed to go and get more coin to piss away. The days often blurred into one at the moment. He had no idea even what day it was. Maybe, he would give it a rest tomorrow.

He had been dwelling on a nagging thought. *This doesn't feel right, something is off. It just doesn't feel right.*

'What did you say?' asked Paulie. Malc must have been muttering to himself again.

'Nothing,' he replied waving the barman away. It was these murders, they haunted him, wouldn't leave him alone. *And how the fuck did he know?* Something about it all just didn't add up and even a drunkard couldn't put it out of mind. *We solved them, but how? How does he do it?*

Malc resolved himself to confront Thaddeus about his source.

'Paulie, it's you isn't it?'

The barman paused and looked over at him.

'You're his source ain't you?'

'What?!'

He looked confused. *A likely cover story.*

Malc had to know how Thaddeus knew. It had to be more than a hunch.

Then a slow realisation dawned on him.

No…

The suspicion grew.

No fucking way. He hasn't got it in him.

Malc had to know the truth of it.

'Paulie, what sort of time does he usually come in?'

'Who?' snapped Paulie.

'Thad.'

'He ain't been in for days.' The barman looked him over. 'I really think it might be time to call it a night, Malc. You're wasted.'

Malc swore and waved away the barman's words when it became obvious he wasn't getting more whiskey. Malc pushed himself to his feet and swayed violently. He straightened and took a great effort to put one foot after another. Eventually, he made it outside to discover it was still light. Dusk was leaching the light from the sky and filling it with colours. Plumes of smoke belched from factory smokestacks and drifted across the heavens to blend with the clouds. The evening smog was already starting to creep in.

'Ain't been in for days,' muttered Malc. *Where the fuck is he?* He leaned against a brick wall to steady himself before continuing. As he staggered home he became of a mind to pay his friend a visit. He needed to know, Thad would tell him straight. He began to head towards Thaddeus's street, when he caught sight of that familiar gait and the distinctive top hat. He made to call out to his partner, but

he stilled himself. The ridiculous nagging drunken suspicion had stilled him. He didn't want it to be true. *It couldn't be*. Yet he still stopped himself from calling out.

Malc watched Thaddeus move through the low mists. *Where is he going?* Malc couldn't decide if he was seeing things but his partner seemed to skulk across the cobblestones, drawn to the shadows or perhaps avoiding the pools of light from the street lamps. Not his usual manner. Something seemed off. Malc followed, keeping a cautious distance.

Malc's curiosity grew, and with it a growing sense of unease. *What am I doing? He is up to something and I gotta know.* He soon found himself following through an ornate iron wrought gate and stalking between mausoleums and crypts, tracking past gravestones and statues. *A graveyard.* The grass between the flagstones of the path was wet and spongy, like the earth was ready to disgorge its grim secrets. The gravestones he passed were faded and unreadable, many covered in patchy orange lichen.

He glimpsed the dark figure of Thaddeus ahead. *What are you doing, Thad?* He felt a sense of panic whenever Thaddeus turned a corner out of sight. The mist seemed thicker here, as if heavy with old spirits. It hung thickest quite low and formed an opaque blanket of white above the ground. Lanterns burned on the paved pathways casting a ruddy light and shadows that flickered and danced from the corner of his vision.

Something loomed above him. Spires of twisted stone ruled the darkening sky above. *The Cathedral.* It rose into the evening sky, a great fortress dedicated to the gods. The old cyclopean stonework that formed its base gave way to buttresses and the spires above. Huge vaulted stained-glass windows intersected the stone, leached of their colours by shadow and darkness inside. Instead, it seemed they were great pools of blackness. Those dark portals held no warmth from the gods, instead they held an abyss of darkness eternal. Leering stone faces and snarling beasts stared down from above. The gargoyles of the cathedral squatted on their lofty perches like sentinels of dread in the dying light. He shuddered.

Malc followed his partner to a large wooden door in the cathedral walls. It was ajar, enough for a man to slip through. He waited, uncertain if it were a trap. Darkness leaked from inside the building, the gloom of silence. He waited longer, but it appeared nothing stirred. He glanced up at the gargoyles grinning down at him, weathered and petrified creatures of stone. Malc always thought it strange that these evil looking things guarded places supposed to be holy and good. It wasn't just the evil spirits they made uneasy.

He entered the gloom of the doorway and found himself in a cavernous interior. Subdued colours could be seen through the arching windows and shadowed pews lay in endless rows away into the darkness. He heard something. *What was that?*

He followed the sound, a voice. It was indistinct, Malc didn't recognise the words. The voice led up a tight winding stone stair, up hundreds upon hundreds of steps. After some climb, he reckoned he must be high up in one of the spires. The voice grew louder, and a glow of light reflected off the walls. He crept closer. A flickering glow leaked from a doorway ahead. Malc peered around the weathered masonry and clutched the grainy stonework beneath his fingertips.

It was a vaulted chamber, filled with strange statues and ornate carvings. A figure stooped in a circle of candles at its centre. *Thaddeus.* A book was laid open before the figure. Malc recognised *that* book.

The strange chanting stopped.

'Malcolm Elms,' said Thaddeus without turning. 'You know it's rude to follow someone, especially when they are your trusted partner and colleague.'

'You knew I was following you?'

'I knew exactly where you were—I can see where

anybody is. I let you find me.'

'What the fuck are you doing, Thad? You're talking like a madman.'

'Did you ever hear of the magi that supposedly built this place?' said Thaddeus conversationally. 'Madmen, they said, but they built all this.' He beckoned at their gloomy surroundings. 'They were buried deep in the crypts beneath this place. I never knew, but something showed me. One of them found something you see. A way to never die, but it only worked on a part of him. Kept his essence from rotting away.' Thaddeus turned. His face lowered and hidden in shadow beneath his tall hat's brim, only a twisted grin was illuminated from beneath. He held a jar in his hand. 'You know they say the eyes are the window to the soul.'

'Magi?' asked Malc sceptically. 'You are talking some mad shit, Thad,' he said, edging around the side of the room.

'You asked what I am doing,' said Thaddeus. 'Well it's something glorious, Malcom. Something sublime. You would not understand, there had to be… sacrifices. A price for the gift of eternal life.'

'What are you talking about?' asked Malc. He shook his head, trying to sober up.

Thaddeus slowly removed his hat and Malc's heart froze. Thaddeus's face was a red ruin. His eye patch had been discarded, leaving a gaping hole on one side of his face. The true horror was the other eye. It was gone. *He gouged out his own eye.* Blood trickled from the wound. Malc glimpsed the glob of glistening flesh that must have been his eye beside a twisted dagger laid on the blood-stained pages of the open book.

'You're blind! What the fuck have you done to yourself, you poor bastard?' exclaimed Malc.

'The less I can see, the more it shows me,' replied Thaddeus with a smile.

Malc glanced at the jar in Thaddeus's hand. Inside the

eye seemed to glow and was fixed on him. Its terrible glare was alive and full of malice.

Malc heard whistles outside. He glanced down through a window and saw the lanterns of the city watch swarming through the graveyard below. *Back up is coming.*

'You did it, didn't you? You killed those people?' asked Malc, as he watched Thaddeus. He couldn't help but being morbidly drawn to his mutilated face.

'I knew you were onto me,' continued Thaddeus ignoring the question, and acting as if mutilating oneself was an everyday thing. 'I knew you had finally risen from that piss drunken stupor long enough to realise -- you've always possessed a keen mind, I'll give you that.' He paused. 'I couldn't have that, so I filed a report.'

'What report?'

'The word of a gentleman against the word of a drunk.'

'What have you done?'

'What have I done?' Thaddeus's voice was mocking. 'No, it was you who killed those people Malcom, don't you remember?'

Malc's mind reeled. For a moment he doubted himself. *Could I have?* Had he drank that much? He had a violence inside him, he knew that. He had beaten his wife in his drunken rages. She had left him in the end. He had often awoken with bloodied knuckles and a stinking hangover. *No.* He couldn't have. He knew he hadn't.

'It was you,' grated Malc between clenched teeth. 'What the fuck has happened to you?'

Thaddeus smirked. 'Such a keen mind. I left plenty of evidence in your rooms—murder weapons, bloody clothes. All the proof they need. You should know they're coming for *you*. It's only fair to give you a sporting chance. You see, I couldn't wait for back-up. I had to *confront* the copycat madman before he kills again.' Thaddeus laughed.

Malc's glance darted to the approaching lanterns below. The realisation struck him. *Shit I'm fucked!* Malc's stomach clenched and twisted. *They're coming for me.* 'No,' he muttered shaking his head in disbelief.

Thaddeus produced the pistol from his jacket, and although he had no eyes, sightlessly trained it on Malc with an eerie accuracy. 'They will find me wounded — blinded no less— but they will find you a dead man. What is it you said? "The lawman's word is the dead man's guilt",' said Thaddeus, echoing Malc's own words.

Bastard.

Caught like a wounded animal in a trap, Malc lunged for Thaddeus.

The pistol exploded in a plume of blinding smoke. *He missed. Thank fuck.* He remembered what a mess that thing made. He barrelled into Thaddeus and they both went sprawling. The glass jar fell and smashed on the stone floor. Thaddeus screamed and fumbled blindly.

'You can't see now, can you, you fucker,' roared Malc in triumph.

Thaddeus clubbed him with the heavy butt of the pistol and Malc collapsed into darkness with a flash of light. He heard the scrape of steel on stone. It sounded distant. His head rang. *The dagger.* His vision slowly cleared. He stared up into the eye. That evil staring eye full of hate, that now glared from Thaddeus's empty socket. *He's fucking wearing it.*

Malc was horrified, but that didn't stop him running his mouth like he always did. He spat a mouthful of blood. 'Nice fit, you fucking psychopath.'

Thaddeus grinned. 'One last sacrifice,' he said, advancing and brandishing the twisted blade.

Malc feebly pushed himself into a crouch and summoning every remaining ounce of strength from his battered limbs, he launched himself into Thaddeus. He tackled the gentleman and sent him stumbling backwards. It all happened so quickly.

Suddenly there was a gaping window where Thaddeus had just been standing. He heard a scream, and a sickening crunch. Malc dragged himself to the window and looked down. He watched the limp figure of Thaddeus crash and bounce off the roof slates and buttresses as it fell, before plunging into the flagstones below.

There were shouts from below, and footsteps echoed from the stairwell.

Well fuck.

***

Malc was placed in irons and led away. The city watch were not gentle. He had put up a fight but quickly realised it only added to his guilt. They beat him and bound him in the roughest way possible. There was nothing he could say that would dissuade them. They had seen him push Thaddeus from the spire window. They had seen the evidence Thaddeus left in his rooms. They had seen the bloodied murder weapons and torn clothes of the victims. They had seen orders. To them he was a murderer. He was scum. Nothing could persuade them otherwise.

He recognised the same sergeant from the first crimescene seemed to be in charge of the watch. The sergeant spat at him and said 'I knew there was something fishy about all those murders. You're a fucking disgrace!' He spat again. 'Your drinking finally got to you, Malc... like it got to your wife.' He landed a boot in Malc's stomach. 'You murdering bastard. Take him away, lads.'

They dragged him away and Malc knew he was fucked. He knew he would swing for this. They led him past the splattered body of Thaddeus. Blood pooled around the corpse, the back of his head smashed open on the flagstones like a dropped melon. But there it was. It stared at him as they led him past. He stared back, he fought to get free and crush it beneath his heel. It only made him look violent and crazy, trying to stamp on the

173

head of a dead lawman. A truncheon clubbed him to a subdued daze. They hated him. He wasn't one of them anymore, was no longer a ranking lawman. He was a killer, plain and simple, and he would hang.

The eye stared up at him, following him, tracking his passage as he was led away. It stared from the fractured skull, from the mutilated socket of Thaddeus's pulverised head. It watched.

A hand reached down and plucked it from the bloody ruin that was once a face, and silently slid it into their pocket.

LIVER

By

Jacob Sannox

'If you enter, there's no leaving,' said the soldier guarding the door. 'Understood?'

His words were not a surprise. The city of Ashdwelyn was a mysterious place, closed to the outside world. Only its fantastic exports and rumours of opportunity, innovation, upward mobility, and magic, ever left.

We exchanged a glance, and my companion, Avarid Seem, nodded, his face just visible over his muscled arms, which were folded across his barrel of a chest.

It wasn't a choice when you considered the lives we were leaving. Besides, who would want to leave Ashdwelyn?

The city had come to represent hope to the lower classes, those unlucky souls born to the wrong parents, such as myself. In my darkest moments, I damned the fisherman and sailmaker's daughter who had spawned me. Yes, they loved me and made many sacrifices to build us a life, but I was meant for more. I *felt* it. I had been destined for a nobler womb and a richer life. When I announced that I was leaving, I feigned doubt and reluctance, but in truth, I was eager to escape to a better life — the life I *deserved*. Mr Seem, whom I had met on the road, was a veteran of forgotten wars, reduced to begging in the streets and sleeping under the stars.

Not long ago, we had stood far back in the long line of people filing into the city, mostly in pairs, but sometimes one at a time. From there, we could only see the tops of the marvellous buildings beyond the plain walls. In a world of hovels and crude buildings, Ashdwelyn was an architectural marvel with towering cloudscrapers of silver and glass reaching for the sky, no doubt housing the great and the good, their families, their businesses and, of course, their banks.

I returned my attention to the soldier in his clean, tailored uniform.

'Well, are you coming in or staying out?' he asked.

'We'll take the risk,' I said. The door swung open by itself, as if it had been *listening*.

I led us out of the unforgiving world we had known, into Ashdwelyn.

***

We found ourselves in a dimly lit room, in the centre of which stood a waist-high stone pedestal with a silver bowl filled with blue liquid. Behind the pedestal, a middle-aged clerk with sandy hair was sitting at a small roll-top desk scattered with ink pots and dip-pens. He appeared to be consulting a leatherbound tome.

'Step up, step up. Welcome to Ashdwelyn. Papers, please.' It all came out in one breath.

We handed them over, and the clerk read them in silence.

'Del Pargeter,' he said.

'That's me,' I replied, my voice shaking.

'And Avarid Seem,' the clerk continued.

The big man grunted assent.

'Very well,' said the clerk, plucking a pen from its pot. 'I shall enter your details.'

He paused for a moment, evaluating us, then he closed his eyes and held his breath. His brow furrowed, and I felt an arcane wave pass through my body. I shuddered, feeling as though the clerk was searching through my soul, laid bare before him.

I was too nervous to object. I had never witnessed magic, but in Ashdwelyn, even a *clerk* had arcane ability.

The sandy-haired clerk opened his eyes, nodded, then made two final marks in his book before telling us everything was in order.

He jumped from his chair, snatched a wooden case from somewhere in the depths of the desk and walked to the pedestal.

'You are required to undergo a brief scanning ritual before you enter the city. It marks you as a resident so you can pass the arcane wards and not set off any alarms. Quite painless. Quicker if we do two at a time.' He set the case beside the bowl of blue liquid, flipped it open so that the scarred wood smashed into the stone, and pulled out a pair of towels.

'A hand each in the bowl, gentlemen, if you please.'

I splayed my fingers and set my hand atop the liquid, intending to submerge it, but there was some resistance. I looked at Mr Seem, who was doing the same, and we both plunged our hands into the basin. The blue liquid became intensely hot, and I pulled back on instinct but couldn't move my hand; it was as though I was being held in place. Panicked, I looked at Mr Seem, but he didn't react, so I assumed he was feigning indifference.

I only realised later that this was not the case. He had felt nothing to begin with, but then a swirl of darker liquid, more a royal blue, opposed to turquoise, whipped around Mr Seem's hand and enveloped mine. The intense heat faded and, just as I was relaxing, I heard the big man yelp. As my pain faded, his began. He gripped his left wrist with his right hand and tried to pull it out.

'Just one moment. Thank you. Nearly done,' said the sandy-haired clerk. 'Annnnd, we're done.'

I withdrew my hand and Mr Seem stumbled back as though he'd been released.

'Take a towel each. You can keep them. Through that door. The welcoming committee will sort you out. Welcome to Ashdwelyn!'

I dried off my hand, which seemed no worse for wear. Although I knew the ritual initially hurt, it didn't trouble me now, whereas Mr Seem was cradling his hand, which looked red and sore. The clerk withdrew a small bottle from his pocket, put a few drops on one of the towels, and passed it to Mr Seem.

'You are allergic, Mr Seem. Best rub the pain away. Here, let me show you,' he said, snatching back the towel and tending my companion.

I took the opportunity to sidle closer to the clerk's open book and saw a list of names separated into pairs, and two columns beside them, one labelled *Entrant* and the other was smudged. At the time I thought it was *Savage* or *Ravage*. It ended *-avage*, anyway.

I found our names and saw that I had a tick in the *Entrant* column whereas Mr Seem had a tick in the *-avage* column.

I caught the clerk turning out of the corner of my eye and stepped away, faking a smile.

Hands dried, pain alleviated—for me, at least—I led Mr Seem towards a door the clerk pointed to in the far corner.

It swung open to reveal a second room and a line of smiling, beautiful people, some clapping, some holding gifts. I was instantly exhausted at the prospect of socialising but faked a smile.

'After you,' I said to Mr Seem, but the big man shook his head, still rubbing his hand.

I shrugged and he followed me through.

The door closed behind us.

'Welcome to Ashdwelyn,' the welcoming committee chimed without a hint of coercion, flattery, or insincerity.

Could people we'd never met honestly be *this* happy to see us?

On the face of it, I saw nothing but appreciation. I was thanked for coming to their city before they added, 'Of course, it's *our* city now.'

It was like being applauded for finding treasure.

This, I thought, *is a strange place.*

But I liked it already, and I was getting the attention I always felt I deserved.

Mr Avarid Seem and I were as rocks amid rapids, if rocks were awkward commoners and rapids were adulation.

Before a moment had passed, I was clutching three wrapped boxes decorated with ribbon, and Mr Seem had four, all different than mine.

I frowned, wondering why *he* got one more.

'Have you come a long way?' asked the same sandy-haired gentleman we had left in the previous room.

How had he got in front of us? Was this more magic?

I pointed back over my shoulder towards the previous room, and he gave me a knowing smile; polite, but unamused.

'My brother is stationed at the immigration desk,' he said, extending a hand. 'We are identical, you see. I'm Norrid Kaharn. I'll be taking you to the welcoming reception.'

'Del Pargeter. I'm not really one for parties,' I said, unable to think of an appropriate lie. It had been a long day, and I was growing too weary for niceties. 'Does it go on long?'

'Oh, my dear fellow,' he laughed more than was warranted. 'You *must* be new! The reception never ends. It goes on all day and all night, every day. You… *people*… just keep coming.'

179

'Yes, I'm new,' I said, unsmiling, but it did not deter Mr Kaharn.

'We'd best be on our way. Don't want to be late,' he said, tugging on Mr Seem's sleeve and asking him to come along.

'Late for something that never begins or ends?' I muttered. If anyone heard, it didn't show on their smiling faces.

Mr Seem and I followed Mr Kaharn through double doors to a courtyard, ringed by fancy horse-drawn carriages. I caught sight of another disappearing through an archway on the opposite side. The next carriage pulled up in front of us and we climbed in.

The cloudscraper towers jutted skyward like glass stalagmites as we passed through the streets, like nothing I had ever seen. Light reflected off them, and even my jaded soul leapt at the sight. If this was the outside, unmarred by guano and untainted by salt like the buildings back home, how elaborate and luxurious were the interiors?

I longed to live up there with the great and the good; the kind of snobs that lectured folk like me about how we should try to make something of ourselves.

I was sharing the forward-facing bench of the carriage with Mr Seem, each of us staring out the open window while Mr Kaharn, sitting opposite us, gave a prattling explanation of what we were seeing as we passed through the streets.

The air smelled sweet, and the cobbles made no noise, as if our wheels rolled over bread rather than stones.

Such decadence and style on display, such glitz and glamour beyond my wildest imagining. The pedestrians could all have been lords, ladies, lawmakers, wealthy merchants, and other such smooth-fingered glitterati.

How did their clothes fit so perfectly? What materials were they made from? Were they not afraid to wear their jewellery so openly? Were there no thieves or was the constabulary here simply *that* good?

I kept my questions to myself. I had decided Mr Kaharn was not my sort. A little man with a big mouth showing me the splendour of a place by rote. How worthy of my time was he, after all? He was a greeter and a guide and his twin manned the front desk. They were obviously a poor family. Working sorts. I hadn't come here to spend time with better dressed versions of the same folk back home. I was here to get away from all that. To infiltrate the upper echelons!

I looked for people in the shadows, those who had fallen through the cracks: the buskers and beggars, the homeless and hopeless, the disgruntled veterans and venereal seekers.

None.

Could Ashdwelyn *really* be as perfect as the rumours portrayed? I had expected a better standard of living, but this… I'd yet to see anyone who looked less than rich.

'What do you think, Mr Seem?' I asked. He never took his eyes from the view.

'I think we have a chance,' he said. And that shut me up.

***

The carriage came to a standstill before the doors of the tallest cloudscraper. The building was only more impressive the closer we got. I remember looking up at it, trying to see the top, but it was too tall. How had they constructed this thing of which I was in such awe when the rest of us were still making do with wattle and daub and thatched roofs? I spied my answer when I saw the glimmer of arcane effects, competing with the light from the dropping sun.

I felt every inch the imposter as men opened the double doors, and Avarid Seem and I were ushered into a glorious room with diamonds and lights hanging from the ceiling like spider webs, if spiders spun jewels.

We had lost Mr Kaharn. He hadn't even said goodbye.

A short man in a very red uniform with gleaming buttons led us to a door. It slid aside on its own, revealing a small, square room.

We entered, and the door closed behind us.

'What is this?' asked Mr Seem. The little man in red leaned towards a trumpet-like brass tube that emerged from the wall and said, 'Seventy-eight.'

Within moments, the box rattled, my stomach dropped, and I realised we were rising.

'No stairs,' said Mr Seem.

'I'm sure there *are*, Mr Seem. And I bet my first week's wages that we'll be using them in future. Not that we'll ever see the inside of a cloudscraper again. I imagine there are poor souls somewhere, stripped to the waist like sailors, sweating and hauling on the ropes that propel us skyward,' I replied, shocked by my own cynicism. Later, I felt stupid. Of course, the lifting-box was magic in nature.

After an eternity, we stopped and the door slid open. Music and chatter swept into the lifting-box.

A dinner party was in full sway, the goers were a mix of finely dressed denizens of Ashdwelyn and their shabby immigrant counterparts, all seated at a series of long tables with silverware set upon perfect white tablecloths.

I looked at Mr Seem, waiting for him to lead the way, but the big man stepped back.

'There will come a time when you must go first, Mr Seem,' I said, sighing. He nodded as if he believed it.

A middle-aged, sandy-haired gentleman identical to the clerk and Norrid Kaharn, turned from making small-talk at the table and came to greet us. He was attired in a fine suit seemingly conjured specifically for his proportions. Jewelled rings adorned his fingers.

'Welcome, welcome!' he said. I knew this dance.

'Mr Kaharn, I presume?'

He beamed at me, eyes cold. How clever I was!

'You've met my brothers! I'm Jolan Kaharn! And this'—he waved an arm at the party—'is for the two of you.'

'Thank you,' said Mr Seem.

'Can we expect to meet more of the Kaharn brothers or did your mother see fit to stop at three?' I asked, sounding ruder than I intended. It had been a long day.

Mr Kaharn beamed.

'Triplets, dear Mr Pargeter. Poor Mama!'

'You're lucky. I had brothers,' said Mr Seem, looking over Mr Kaharn's head with a faraway countenance.

'Had?' I asked, but he didn't respond.

'I'm sorry, Mr'—he searched for the name—'Seem,' said Mr Kaharn, and I disguised a smile as he returned to his own story. I didn't believe he felt much empathy. 'There is a special bond between us, having shared a womb. We feel what one another experiences, to a degree. It gave us a... particular understanding. But enough of that, welcome to your reception, gentlemen!'

Jolan Kaharn showed us to empty seats. I eyed the various cutlery while he explained that we would be served momentarily.

'The meal is free, of course. As is the bar! Take a moment to look out the west windows, which afford a beautiful view of the harbour and the sunset sea beyond! Don't worry about your clothes. Nobody will think you are shabby. Once you've had enough welcoming, head to the assignment desk'—he pointed to a table piled with paperwork and a woman sitting behind it—'and we'll let you know your work assignments and where you will be staying! Enjoy!'

We were left alone before a waiter arrived and set plates piled with delicate pâtés before us. I ordered Ashdwelyn's signature spirit. The pâtés were moreish, and I wolfed them down. A waiter whipped away my plate and replaced it with another. I downed my drink and ordered another as the waiter set a selection of cheeses and something he called caviar before me. I demolished everything and turned to comment on the food to Mr Seem, but noticed his second course was different to my own; he had white meat and vegetables. Perhaps the waiters knew our preferences by some arcane art? I was about to remark when my second drink arrived. I downed it and asked for another.

Eventually, full to bursting, we exchanged a look and silently agreed it was time to get our assignments, part ways, and find our beds.

I only realised later we had forgotten our gifts.

***

'I have them here… some… where,' said the woman at the assignment desk.

'Seem and Pargeter, Seem and Pargeter. Annnnd there we are.'

She handed us each an envelope. Inside mine, I found two cards and a key like I'd never seen before. The first card read, in gold lettering:

Floor 78. Apartment 6.

I frowned and looked at Avarid Seem. He showed me his card.

Rose Cottage, Petunia Lane, the Flora Quarter

'I'm sorry, floor 78 of which building? There's no address,' I said to the woman, whose bun was pulled too tight.

She beamed at me. Folk in Ashdwelyn were forever beaming. It was beginning to disturb me. Nobody could be this pleasant all the time; I know I couldn't.

'Silly. This building, Cloud Tower, in the Gate Quarter! Top floor! High quality real estate for *even* the immigrants!'

An apartment in a cloudscraper? I could hardly

believe it.

My stomach lurched, objecting to the various foods and copious amounts of spirits I had imbibed, so I nodded and looked at my other card.

Coroner's Aide.

This couldn't be right. I'd been hoping for something more glamorous.

'City guard,' read Mr Seem from his own card.

'There must be a mistake,' I said. 'I was hoping for something a little more... well, something else.'

'No mistake. First jobs aren't optional. I assure you, the system works. You will excel!' the woman replied. 'There will be job openings elsewhere for which you can apply, and, in time, put in for different properties if you desire. Report to work tomorrow, as per the instructions on the back of your cards. Ah hello! Welcome to Ashdwelyn.'

I looked over my shoulder, following her gaze, and saw a group of three women and two men stagger into the room holding one another up.

Mr Seem and I shook hands, parting ways. He set off toward the lifting-box, and I went in search of my new home.

***

I woke, smiling and stretching, to gulls calling, a salty breeze, and sunlight from the open window warming my face. I was confused, as one will be in a new place. I looked at my splendidly appointed apartment, and the events of the previous day came rushing back. And I had been spared the hangover I had been dreading.

My luck was turning.

I jumped out of bed, leaving it unmade, and took in the view of the other cloudscrapers and the harbour where ships sailed, no doubt carrying Ashdwelyn's goods around the world and gold back to its docks.

I heard falling water through a half-closed door and found a tiled room with a glass box stretching from floor to ceiling. I marvelled at the water appearing inside, falling from the ceiling and disappearing before it hit the floor.

I turned my back on the 'rain closet', needing to urinate, and spied a porcelain bench with a hole in the middle. I was expecting to see a 78th floor view of the street below, with perhaps some poor people's houses, ready to be coated in my excrement, but the unit was self-contained. Remembering the arcane features of the rain closet, I shrugged, said 'Oh well' and aimed my flow into the hole. The stream disappeared before hitting the bottom. Remarkable.

I washed in the rain closet, using the soap provided, and felt cleaner than I ever had. The bed was made when I returned to my room, and new clothes sat on the covers. I pulled them on. They fit perfectly. Nothing special, but well-made work clothes and boots. Under them was a beautiful gold pocket watch.

**

Out in the streets, Ashdwelyn was still far too clean and devoid of homeless people. I did see the first of the city's tradesmen, craftsmen, labourers and such, all well dressed and clean on their way to work. An incredible place, I thought, but then a cart bearing corpses rolled by, and I followed it to my new job.

**

'Ashdwelyn is a wonderful place to live, do not mistake me,' said the coroner, 'but as is the nature of the world, where there is sweet there is sour, where there is abundance there is deprivation, even if it is not financial, where there is health and increasing life spans, there are incurable illnesses and unnecessary death.'

She was tall for a woman with bulging forearms, a regulation grey bob, sensible boots, a fitted blouse, and some mix of britches and a skirt. She wore a brown leather apron, splattered with dried gore and huge gloves of similar appearance that ended at her elbows.

Hands on hips, she had barred my way while she made her speech at the top of the steps to the double doors which stood open, revealing a warehouse beyond with work slabs bearing covered corpses. She beckoned me to follow as she went inside.

I sighed and entered my new workplace, hardly relishing a life of retrieving, examining, and documenting the dead. The coroner handed me an apron and gloves as though they were badges of office, then she continued.

'Accidents, suicides, and a mysterious wasting condition that runs rampant in both the Flora and the Fauna Quarters make up the largest proportion of the deaths.'

I remembered Mr Seem's new address: Rose Cottage, Petunia Lane, Flora Quarter. Why would they send him to such an area? I was about to ask, but the coroner continued.

'Symptoms of the illness include coughing, jaundiced skin, and signs of excessive living. Autopsies find fatty livers, sometimes enlarged up to ten times the normal size. When we encounter the latter, we do not examine the bodies ourselves, instead sending the cadavers to the hospital for further study. If you find somebody is suffering from the illness, it must be reported at once. Those who are not identified until they are advanced are given beds in the hospital, where they are offered palliative care. But there is hope. I am assured a cure is on the way,' the coroner concluded, her eyes twinkling.

***

Isn't it funny how quickly we can adapt to new situations,

both good and bad? A few weeks in Ashdwelyn and already splendour, privilege and abundance had become normal. Anything I wanted or needed was provided. My work was unpleasant, but I adapted to that and began to find it grimly fascinating.

My role varied. Sometimes I assisted in autopsies, trying to hold down my breakfast as I received bagged and labelled organs while the physicians and the coroner attempted to establish the cause of death. In cases where the mystery illness was suspected, which amounted to a large proportion of the deaths, those bodies were sent to the university for a more detailed examination.

I learned that Ashdwelyn was divided into four sections. Mr Seem lived in the Flora Quarter, which was beside the Fauna Quarter. I lived in the Gate Quarter, then there was the Harbour Quarter in the west of the city.

Travel was allowed between Flora and Fauna, and between Harbour and Gate, but the two halves of the city were closed to one another, in an attempt to contain the illness. Only those with official business were allowed to pass through the gates into the stricken areas. The Four Quarters looked much the same, with various residential, commercial, rural and industrial districts, cloudscrapers and fine carriages.

Every day, I went on a dedicated carriage, sometimes within the Gate Quarter or crossing into Harbour, but most frequently travelling through the guarded gates to the contaminated districts to examine the scenes of a death or bring the bodies in when the corpse-haulers were busy elsewhere. Staff were thin on the ground but bodies were not in short supply.

The coroner hadn't been joking about the amount of suicides and accidental deaths. Most of the dead were affected by the illness to different degrees and I wondered if it affected motor control, leading to clumsiness.

I cut down hanging victims, scraped jumpers from the cobbles and extricated accident victims from under carriages.

There were far too many accidental deaths in general. How could so many people be so unlucky?

Corpses are unpleasant. Their stink clings to you even with masks, gloves, and aprons. They belch and fart, even in death, letting out clouds of noxious gases. Sometimes, they even groan.

I encountered fly-ridden soups, that had once been forgotten people, sometimes only remembered when they dripped into their neighbours' rooms, below.

Terribly unpleasant, but for some reason, and the coroner confirmed it was a common reaction, being around the dead made me ravenous. I ate well after each encounter, despite experiencing gruesome flashbacks, such as green skin covered in maggots. The dead stayed with me and I saw them when I closed my eyes in bed.

***

After work, I ate at the perpetual dinner party, shovelling down pâté, cheese and caviar, but afterwards, I took to exploring the leisure districts, clad in the fine clothing and exquisite jewellery my room provided, drinking and fucking into the early hours.

I would wake after only a few hours' sleep, as fresh as a daisy.

I made new friends, built new connections, and was attacking my new life with alacrity. I was offered a position with a friend's shipping company. She told me I was destined for great things. I'd known it all along.

With a few days of working for the coroner remaining, I returned home from a night out in a drunken haze. I tripped as I approached my apartment and smashed my forehead on the doorframe. I assume I knocked myself out, as I woke in the corridor next morning.

My head felt fine, and when I sat up, still dreading a hangover, I found my head clear and my stomach at peace. I rushed inside, washed and changed into work clothes, checking my reflection in a mirror. No bruise on my forehead. Handsome as ever.

I set off for one of my last days working with the dead.

***

I was sitting on the box seat of my carriage, reins in hands, as I crossed the Flora Quarter, heading back from the last job of the day (a hanging, the corpse removed by the haulers) when I realised I was on Petunia Lane, and thought to visit Mr Seem. I kept on the lookout and brought the carriage to a standstill outside Rose Cottage, identifiable by a hand-painted sign affixed to its red door.

I knocked and after some time, the door swung open to reveal Avarid Seem.

He looked different. His skin yellow, jaundiced, and papery, his hair lank and thinning, his back bent, and he was clutching his gut with one hand. He seemed disoriented and slow.

The mystery illness had taken him, and he was quite far advanced.

'Mr Seem! It's been too long, I… goodness, what did you do to your face?' I asked, seeing a massive bruise on his forehead.

'I didn't even bang it. Wasn't there last night. Woke up and there you go, bruised as you like,' he said, and my heart went out to him.

And yet, something did not sit well. Had I not suffered a blow to *my* forehead and woken as pretty as I had been the previous morning? No pain? No bruising?

I eyed my friend, noting that not only did he look ill, but he was unsteady on his feet.

'Avarid, are you drunk?'

He huffed or was it a little laugh?

'Never touch a drop these days.'

I leant close, foolishly perhaps, eyebrows arched. Mr

190

Seem obliged by breathing in my face.

Sweet. Too sweet, but not a trace of alcohol.

I frowned as I looked at his gaunt, yellow face remembering all too well the coroner's warnings of fatty, failing livers among the other symptoms of the disease.

'Avarid,' I said, 'have you seen the physicians? You don't look well.'

He only smiled.

'Nothing to be done. I might last weeks or decades. It's different for everyone.'

My gaze drifted to his bruise, and I rubbed my forehead.

'I start a new job soon, in the Harbour Quarter. I wanted to see you while I'm still allowed into Flora.'

Avarid nodded.

'You never stopped by before, Del,' he said.

I had no excuse. I'd been having too much fun.

'Come in and have something to eat?' he asked.

I had intended to stop in then get on with the day, but my mood had soured, knowing Mr Seem was so afflicted.

And that bruise troubled me.

It reminded me of something Mr Kaharn had said at the welcoming reception.

'There is a special bond between us, sharing a womb. We feel what one another experiences, to a degree. It gave us a... particular understanding.'

Clearly Avarid Seem and I were not brothers, but had he experienced *my* pain somehow? *My* injury? The consequences of *my* drinking?

I settled into an armchair and took in my surroundings while Mr Seem prepared a meal of white meat, vegetables, and olive oil. He looked after himself while I did not, and yet our appearances suggested the opposite; he was a mess and I was in fine health.

I was growing suspicious about the nature of the ceremony we had undergone after entering Ashdwelyn. I remembered how, when we put our hands in the bowl, my

191

pain faded while Mr Seem's intensified. Had we been connected in some way? Why?

Was I the cause of Mr Seem's illness? Was his health and fortune failing so mine would flourish?

I intended to find out, though looking back, I suppose it wasn't the most moral of methods I had in mind.

Later that night, and every night that week, I went out dancing, drinking, and snorting illicit powders. Every morning, I drove a carriage into the Flora Quarter to check on Mr Seem. Always he seemed hungover and exhausted, despite a solid ten hours of sleep, while I was awake and as happy as the larks when the sun came up.

By now, I had explained my theory to Mr Seem, and he was as curious as I. If a little… perturbed.

'You're saying that whatever happens to your body, a smack on the head or a night of drinking, I'm the one who experiences the consequences?' he asked.

'I suspect so,' I said.

'You've been drinking all week, knowing it would hurt me,' he said.

I didn't reply.

'I have a theory.' I produced a shiny gold coin from my pocket.

'Call it,' I said and flipped it high.

'Heads,' said Mr Seem, and I uncovered tails.

I flipped it again.

'Heads,' said I. Heads it was.

We tested the coin for over an hour. By the time I was weary of it, we were both slumped, him against the bed and I against the wall.

'This goes beyond the physical then,' I said. 'I get all the good luck and you the bad.'

'Magic,' Mr Seem grunted.

'But why?' I asked. 'Why condemn half the population?'

'Not everyone drinks and snorts like you, Del,' said Seem, and he looked sad. I confess, I felt guilty about all I

192

had done to him but I had intended no ill will. The blame for this lay elsewhere, and I suspected the Kaharn triplets. We resolved to investigate further.

I decided to lay off the partying that night, but when the sun set, I felt the call of the bottle, and once I had polished off a plate of pâté, I took a bottle of Ashdwelyn's finest from behind the bar and finished it in my room.

Next morning, I felt the hint of a hangover, and my theory seemed to be disproved.

Until, that is, I arrived at Rose Cottage and got no answer. I let myself in and found my friend lying beside his bed looking worse than ever. I checked him over and realised Mr Seem was dying.

***

I ran into the street and rang a bell mounted on a lamppost. Two constables appeared from the morning mist. I explained that my friend was gravely ill. One of them ran to fetch an ambulance while I returned inside with the other. Mr Seem's breathing was rapid and shallow, sweat beading on his yellow skin.

The stretcher bearers arrived and after a glance, looked at each other.

'If he's to have any chance, he'll need to go to the hospital straight away,' said the senior.

I watched, dismayed, as they bore my friend away.

I returned to the Gate Quarter and told the coroner I was sick, which wasn't a lie. My head ached and my stomach was sending warning signals; a hangover, but mild.

In my apartment, I poured a whisky, the first of many. I spent the morning wondering about Mr Seem, trying to hold back my desire for alcohol, but ended up drinking heavily. I have no memory of that afternoon.

I woke the next morning to a knock on my door. I stood in a panic, my head swimming, and vomited on my bed. Then, I staggered to the front door and opened it, to reveal Jolan Kaharn.

'Mr… ' He raised his eyebrows.

'Pargeter,' I said, wiping my mouth.

'Mr Pargeter. I am sorry, but it is my unfortunate duty to tell you that your friend passed in the night.'

I leant against the wall.

Avarid was dead and I was hungover. Had I killed him with my excess? Destroyed my human liver, tasked with the job of processing and filtering the excess I poured into my body? And now I was feeling the conse-quences of my actions, the link severed. I collapsed on the floor in front of Jolan Kaharn.

'Come, come,' said Mr Kaharn. 'This won't help. Let's get you something to eat. You need your strength to bear the loss.'

'I can't possibly eat,' said I as he hauled me to my feet and led me towards the perpetual dinner party.

'Nonsense,' said Mr Kaharn. 'Once you've eaten, there is something we must discuss.'

He guided me to an empty seat beside a bespectacled man in a cheap suit then wandered away.

While I waited to be served, I wondered if my good fortune was gone too. I pulled a gold coin from my pocket and flipped it, thinking '*heads*'.

I need not tell you how it landed.

A plate of pâté was set before me and, reluctantly, still fearing I would vomit, I carved off a piece with my fork. I began to eat and within a few moments, I began to feel better and even my mood lightened. I tucked into the meal, hoping for bacon and eggs for my next course.

I noticed the bespectacled man beside me scrutinising the caviar that had been set in front of him. I identified it for him with my mouth full.

'Thank you, I'm familiar with it. I'm a bit of a foodie. Caviar, of course, but of what region? I see you've helped yourself to the foie gras! Expensive taste.'

'Foie gras?' I asked, swallowing another mouthful of pâté, and he pointed at my plate, an eyebrow raised as if to say, 'I'm better than you.'

'Caviar is the salt-cured roe of the family Acipenseridae. Fish eggs,' he added, correctly judging my ignorance. 'And you are eating foie gras.'

'I thought it was pâté,' I said.

He nodded.

'A sort of pâté. Foie gras is the liver of a duck or goose fattened by gavage.'

I paused, my fork halfway to my mouth, still loaded with pâté... no, loaded with foie gras.

'Gavage?' I asked.

'Force-feeding, often until their organs rupture and tumours form in their throats. Enlarges the liver up to ten times its normal size.'

I remembered the smudged column title from the clerk's book, just after Mr Seem and I entered Ashdwelyn. The column with a tick beside my friend's name.

Not *Savage*.

Not *Ravage*.

Gavage.

Enlarged, fatty liver pâté.

The mystery illness.

I spat foie gras onto my plate and stood up so fast that my chair fell over.

Jolan Kaharn appeared behind me.

'Is all well?' he asked.

'Gavage,' I whispered, feeling the blood drain from my face.

'I see,' said Mr Kaharn, frowning as he righted my chair. 'Come this way. Sorry everybody.'

He marched me through the kitchens and into a corridor beyond. I leant against a wall, the smaller man hand on hips, barring my way to the door.

'What have you done to us?' I whispered.

'Do you feel better?' he asked.

'Because of the foie gras? It's human liver, isn't it? Enlarged by the magical pairing you force on unsuspecting immigrants. Your own version of gavage.'

Mr Kaharn smiled.

'The restorative effects of consuming it are temporary, alas. The Sacrifices' livers are so saturated not only in fat, but magic, that they become a delicacy consumed not only as a ritual to honour the fallen, but as a distilled form of the link itself, strengthening the bond in any who consume it and temporarily removing ill-effects when the link is severed. You have a choice, Mr —' said Mr Kaharn.

'Pargeter. Del Pargeter,' I muttered, wondering if I should make a run for it. But where could I go? Nobody ever escaped Ashdwelyn. Though, I thought perhaps I could escape on one of the ships in the harbour?

'You have a choice, Mr Pargeter. You accept a new link with someone else or you will… disappear. This secret is known to only some who reap the benefits. The wait staff, the cooks, the corpse-haulers, the coroner and, of course, those who take our exports to sea. Trusted beneficiaries, one and all.'

'Made to disappear,' I repeated.

'Inexplicably and totally,' said Mr Kaharn as though he was trying to reassure me.

'You'll magically link me to some unsuspecting soul like Mr Seem and then they'll feel unwell, reaping what I sow? And I'll get the benefits of their efforts, their luck and virtue while their body copes with my excesses and my misfortune? You condemn half the immigrant population to be living livers, filtering out the poison from the other half. How can this be tolerated? What purpose does it serve?'

Mr Kaharn smiled, clasping his hands behind his back.

'You, sir, are not that naive. We can't all be born with luck, health, and wealth. Some must work and labour and suffer so that the rest might prosper, is it not always so in this world, if a little less directly? Does it make sense for

196

ill health and luck to strike at random? This is far more organised. Half get ahead and achieve things humanity has never dreamt of, mastering business, love, and magic, living lives far beyond our natural span, while the rest live in more comfort than they ever would outside until they pass,' he said, and one of the waiters appeared from the kitchen, checking on him, but Mr Kaharn waved him away. He continued.

'You were born low but have been selected to be one of the privileged. My brother at the immigration desk came to know you when he looked into your nature before choosing which role in the pairing you would take. You felt entitled to more. You felt dissatisfied with your lot. You *want* this even if it disgusts you.'

I said nothing and Mr Kaharn continued.

'Remember, they will suffer only what you put them through. You don't have to abuse your next partner like you did Mr Seem. Take up clean living, be kind to your — how did you put it — living liver? I have lost only two partners in my lifetime, but I exercise, eat fresh vegetables, and avoid substances that harm the body. My current link holds a steady job and has only moderately ill health. Like your actual liver, your partner can rejuvenate if given time but you hardly gave yours a chance. It takes a special sort to bring down a man like your friend in such a short time. You can't lay all the blame on us now, can you?' said Mr Kaharn.

'This is absurd,' I said, shaking my head.

'Is it?' he said, stepping forward. He may have been small but he seemed to loom over me.

'Well, Mr Pargeter, absurd or not, the choice is before you. I could incinerate you by snapping my fingers and the arcane wards around the city would do the same if you attempt to escape. If you breathe a word to anyone, you will condemn them to death. Stop resisting. Accept the gift and then live your life well. Take advantage of those bumps in fortune and health as best you can.

Perhaps throw a few crumbs your partner's way by not fatally exploiting their weakness to your advantage. But that is entirely up to you. Burn through another twenty Mr Seems, if you must. There will always be a line of people waiting to enter Ashdwelyn.'

I frowned, never taking my gaze from Mr Kaharn, who was once more smiling sweetly.

I wondered if he didn't know me better than I knew myself.

I wasn't prepared to give up my good fortune, not even at another's expense.

'How do you live with it?' I asked him.

'How do I live with success, good health, and contentment? You find a way,' he replied, smiling. 'Most people rationalise their fortune and never come to learn the nature of the deal.'

'I could just as easily have been the unfortunate one, couldn't I?'

'Oh yes, if Mr Seem had wanted it more or if you had been paired with another. But what of it? None of us made a choice before our births, Mr Pargeter. Would you have chosen to be at the bottom? Of course not. In the outside world, most people find themselves struggling through life and dying young. In Ashdwelyn? Half of us are the luckiest folk alive and half are looked after better than those scraping a living beyond our walls. This is *privilege*, sir. Live with it.' He shrugged. 'Or don't.'

Perhaps I *could* live with this arrangement, perhaps I *could* look after my next partner better than I had Mr Seem? Of course, I had the luck to succeed at anything I put my mind to, didn't I? I would use it to help my partner and then, I reasoned, they would be at no disadvantage at all, as long as I spared their liver from excessive drinking and snorting; perhaps keeping myself in good shape. I could even take up running. I could save them from a *worse* partner.

And, of course, I also wouldn't be executed.

How easy it is to rationalise under threat of death. But maybe I was being honest with myself for the first time. I wanted a life of success, health and good fortune. I'd have done almost anything to get it.

'I… 'I started to give my answer, but Mr Kaharn held up his hand.

'Let's just be sure so there's no moment of "oh, but if I had only known" later.'

He led me down the corridor and passed through a door at the far end into a cold room where tray after tray of engorged, faintly glowing human livers were set. A man in a bloody white apron appeared through yet another door, through which I heard moans and groans.

'After you,' said Mr Kaharn as we neared.

I turned the door handle and pushed my way into the room beyond.

I was met by the familiar stench of death and gore, and I covered my mouth and nose before taking in my surroundings.

There, in what I first took to be a hospital ward, was a long, dimly lit room with beds on either side. The people in the beds were tied down, many of them still, but so many more were writhing and groaning, their terrified eyes wide. They were naked but covered by sheets, many of them obese, yellow-skinned and with a wide tube inserted into their mouths and down their throats so that their heads were forced back and they could see only the wall behind them. Each of these connected to a wider tube that ran the length of the ceiling towards some kind of machine. A masked man was shovelling corn into the machine, and I realised the trembling tubes were pouring food directly into the people's stomachs. One of the waiters wheeled a trolley into view, and I saw him scrape leftover foie gras and other food stuff onto the man's shovel.

A team of people surrounded one of the beds, removing a liver from a corpse.

Gavage. Force-feeding. Not *just* a metaphor for the

link.

Here were those about to die from the liver disease caused by the arcane link, finished off by industrial feeding, bloating their livers until they were ready to be served to the lucky half of society.

I looked at the closest bed, and before me lay Mr Seem with a tube stuffed down his throat, still trembling as corn poured into his stomach. His skin was yellow and his previously muscular body hung with excess fat. Surely the process had been magically accelerated. He could not have transformed so quickly overnight.

He whimpered, and I jumped, crying out, before dashing to the head of the bed.

Not dead. Not at all.

'We sever the links before they die. The gavage finishes the process,' said Jolan Kaharn.

I looked into Mr Seem's open, weeping eyes and noticed his outstretched fingers. I held his hand and offered what comfort I could through my grasp.

Suddenly, the magnitude of what I had been eating at the buffet table hit me: human foie gras.

I fell to my knees and threw up what remained of some poor soul's liver.

My hangover instantly returned.

I braced myself against the table and forced myself to my feet.

'The dedicated few, those who succumb for the sake of the rest of us, do their duty until death and beyond. Avarid Seem will live on in your successes,' said Mr Kaharn. 'But for now, here he lies, having suffered through all of your negative emotions, cynicism, toxins, poisons, and bad luck. His liver will grow until he can go on no more. Then you will eat him at supper, because it serves you to do so.'

I was so horrified I could think of no reply.

'What will you choose?' asked Mr Kaharn. 'Take comfort in knowing if you accept a new link, your revulsion will be short-lived, passed on to another, beginning the process all over again.

I could lunge for him, and snap his neck; perhaps save Avarid, I thought. *But he could kill me in an instant, I'm sure.*

I turned and looked down into Avarid Seem's desperate weeping eyes.

'Can you put him out of his misery?' I asked.

'No,' said Mr Kaharn. 'We will not waste any part of him that can be of use.'

I held Mr Seem's hand and leant in close then whispered, 'I will make your sacrifice count, my friend.'

I released his hand and walked back the way we had come.

'Let's get you to my brother and match you up with somebody new, eh? The sooner it's done, the sooner you'll feel better.'

'What if I'm paired with someone more selfish than me?' I asked.

He laughed.

'Excuse me,' he said, 'but I think that is unlikely.'

***

A few hours later, I rode in a carriage beside a nice young woman from a village not far from my hometown. She already looked peaky and was clutching her stomach while my hangover was quite gone.

I was beginning to relax, the guilt and horror ebbing away, presumably gifted to the woman beside me.

At the perpetual dinner party, I took Jolan Kaharn aside to thank him for his support.

'Your friend gave his life so that you could live well,' said Mr Kaharn. 'You see that, I hope? He will not be forgotten. None of them ever are. Mr —'

'Seem,' I reminded him.

'Yes, Mr Seem will always be remembered,' said Mr Kaharn. 'Now, I imagine you have work tomorrow, so why not show your new friend a good evening, but perhaps don't overdo it, for her sake.'

I nodded and he beamed at me. Taking me by the arm, he guided me towards the table, where I sat beside my new partner.

Plates of foie gras were placed before us and, ravenously hungry as I often was after dealing with the dead, I took a deep breath and began to eat. Perhaps it was my friend on my fork or another unfortunate, I did not know. Deciding I needed a drink, I asked a waiter for a bottle of Ashdwelyn's finest.

I finished a mouthful of foie gras, raised my glass, and silently toasted the memory of my dear friend, Avarid Seem.

TEETH
BABY TEETH

By
Krystle Matar

The work order said the load went down the river to White Crown. Easy work. It only took a few days to go that far south, and then László could pick up a new load, bring it back to Yaelsmuir to make the return trip profitable, too.

The problem was that it was Davik Kaine's load, and Davik didn't like the idea of fourteen year old boys smuggling illegal shit down to White Crown without an adult on the barge.

'He's the best driver I know,' Emil said. 'He'll out drive all of the people here. My boy was born on the water—lived it his whole life. Down on the lake, it ain't optional like it is here.'

Never mind the fact that the river moved differently than the lake where László was born and where he learned to swim and to drive a boat with his Talent. The river was mean and cold in a way that László still struggled against, and he fought to get his head around the politics of each dock he stopped at. And never mind the fact that none of the family—their father Emil, László, Irén, and János—were registered. The Authority was getting strict these days about people with Talent being properly registered, especially on this stupid river.

László stayed out of it. Stayed on the far side of the barge with his baby brother, just to keep him out of the way. János wiggled his loose teeth until they bled and then spat at the river, bright red gobs because all four front teeth were ready to go.

'János,' Irén said. 'Quit it.'

'But László said I gotta get 'em out during the day or else I'll swallow them when I'm sleeping!'

'Just leave him,' László said, elbowing his twin sister in the ribs. 'He ain't hurting anyone.'

Irén scowled but glanced over her shoulder at their father and Davik. Against his better judgement László looked, too. Their father was talking, but Davik was staring at them. Hard, dark eyes eating up the distance between them, his arms crossed over his chest as Emil talked at him.

'But what if something happens?' Davik asked, glancing at Emil with so much scorn it crackled in the air like fire. 'You just going to hang your boy out to dry instead of being there to protect him?'

'Ain't nothing going to happen,' Emil said. 'And if it does, László can take care of it. He was the best shot on the whole float, did I ever tell you that? He took a gator once at a hundred and fifty yards. Right through the eye. A man eater, it was, well over three hundred kilos, but my boy, he took it down.'

'It was seventy-five yards,' László muttered.

'Da!' János called.

László winced. 'Hey, no, don't—'

'It wasn't a hundred and fifty yards!' János said. Blood dribbled down his chin and he leaned over, spitting it into the river. Oblivious to the way László grabbed his arm, squeezed it, shook his head. 'It was seventy-five. László said so!'

Emil shot them all a withering glare and Davik went back to watching them. Staring, like he was waiting for László to peel off his own skin and reveal the muscle and sinew and bone beneath. Just so Davik could know what László was made of.

'It's fine, Mr. Kaine,' László blurted because he couldn't stand the way both men were staring at him. He wanted to say that it didn't matter how much Davik pushed, Emil wouldn't go down to White Crown. Emil was scared of getting scooped by the Authority. László wanted to say that it shouldn't be his job to take this risk. Wanted to say that a decent father would protect his son. But saying any of those things would be a disaster, and they couldn't afford to refuse loads. Living on this stupid river was more expensive than Emil bargained for and coin was stretched ugly thin. So instead of any of that, he said, 'I can handle it. Promise.'

***

Irén stayed behind — probably because Emil knew that László wouldn't ditch Yaelsmuir without his sister. If the siblings left the city together with the barge, there was no good reason to come back. László brought János with him because he was the only person in the family who could get János to listen. Sort of. Mostly. He figured it was because he didn't make János do anything. Their father was always about forcing them to obey. It had never worked well with any of the siblings, but János was especially stubborn. Determined. Lively. László figured out pretty early how to get János to cooperate; the little boy just wanted to *know* things. So long as László made time to answer all of János's millions of questions — even if the answer was simple as admitting that László didn't know a thing — then János usually cooperated well enough. He just wanted to understand what was happening.

The only remarkable thing that happened on the way down to White Crown was that János lost his bottom two teeth, and on the way back he lost his top two. Both on the same day, they just popped out when he was sucking on a heel of half stale bread. He sat around and made funny faces; he stuck his tongue through the big gap his teeth made, turning his face into the wind and pulling his lips wide open to feel all that air on his gums. László wished he could sit with János and make fun of his silly faces, maybe stick his finger in the hole to make János squeal with laughter, but he had to concentrate too hard to keep the barge facing the right direction. Just when he thought he'd gotten used to the river, it was changing with all the autumn rain. The Brightwash ran faster and faster as the water rose, pushing hard as they moved north against the current.

János handed the teeth to László as he spat more blood into the river because he didn't know what else to do with them. Down on the float, they would have put the teeth in János's keepsake box, along with various other scraps that mattered. They'd keep the bullet casing from his first shot, a trophy from his first hunt. Things would accumulate over the course of his life, and then when he was older, he could go through it all and remember how he came to be, how he was formed by his family, and how he survived the hard, unforgiving world. And then, when that world inevitably took him back, the people who loved him could keep little pieces of his life to hang on to.

But his father had left everyone's boxes behind when he brought them up to Yaelsmuir. Sold their houseboat to another family to buy this river barge and told them there wasn't any time or room to bring anything but essentials. László scooped a few things before they left — the big tooth from the gator he killed, his stepmother's wedding ring, the sight that broke off his first rifle, and put them all on a necklace so his father couldn't say it took up room they didn't have. The rest was gone. Left behind. Maybe the family that bought their boat had kept their things out of respect. But maybe not. Maybe everything that once defined the Dargis family had been dumped into the lake. Unless László found a way to get back there, he'd probably never know.

Maybe that's why László felt like he'd ceased to be. It seemed an awful lot like his father didn't much care about who his children were or how they defined themselves. They were just labour to drive his barge down to dangerous places because he was too much a coward to do it himself. All he wanted was his wife back; the National Tainted Registration Authority had taken László's stepmother and László's father said he didn't stand for things being taken from him.

That's what he said, anyway.

Seemed to László that their father didn't stand for much at all, but not in the way their father wanted people to think. Their father made a mountain of himself, a hero, the sort of man that stood and fought; but lately he'd been drinking so much that standing was a harder prospect than he wanted to admit and the Authority was a tougher opponent than he'd bargained for

Didn't seem right to let the teeth go, to toss them away. Maybe one day they'd go back to the lake and they'd have keepsake boxes again. Or he'd figure out a way to let János keep them. Either way, László put those baby teeth in his pocket and went back to work.

***

'Could I use my teeth as bait to catch fish?' János asked.

'Fish don't give a shit about teeth,' László laughed. 'They like squirmy things like worms and bugs and other fish. And little boys who make funny faces. I bet if I dragged you behind the boat, I'd catch plenty of fish.'

János laughed and stuck his tongue out at László

through the gap his teeth made—lips back, nose wrinkled, pink tongue pressing between the white sentries that still held their posts. 'I bet I'd catch giant fish with you, since you're so big and smelly.'

They were coming up on a spot where the river tried to pull west toward the big rocks near the bank, so László leaned into the rudder arm, bracing himself against the push of it. He closed his eyes and let his Talent sink into the water, feeling the cold rush, the swirling eddies, the air bubbles that got sucked down as the barge danced, long and wide and a little clumsy, across the surface.

János repeated himself, louder the second time. He just wanted the attention. But László didn't answer. Their father would beat his hide if he fucked up their barge, especially after he spent so much time promising Davik everything would be fine. They couldn't afford another repair, not so close to winter. They hadn't even paid for the last repair yet, and the debt hung over the whole family.

Later, after everything, probably for the rest of his life, László would lie awake at night and wish he'd answered his baby brother. At worst it would have been a good memory. One last moment where János was a funny little kid with a bunch of missing teeth, and László something awkward between boy and man, growing but not grown. A moment where they were just brothers and they could pretend life was good.

At best, it might have changed how things went after. Maybe if János wasn't already restless and angry because the trip back was long and boring, he wouldn't have gotten so loud, and their father wouldn't have gotten so angry, and János would still be alive.

***

Since the night János died, they'd been hiding in a bay outside the city. Emil gave János's body to the river, and they parked the barge. The water was gentle in the bay. It might have been a nice, safe place, but nowhere felt safe after Emil killed János. The quiet of the bay only seemed to highlight how empty their lives were without János's endless talking, always so much louder than he needed to be.

László hadn't slept well since moving to the river. The cabin of their barge was tiny compared to their house boat in the floating village on the lake. There were only two beds in the cabin, so all the siblings crammed into one. Emil took the other. And János squirmed so much. That boy hadn't been still a moment in his life, not even when he was sleeping, until László was so exhausted with the overflow of János's energy that sometimes it felt like he could sleep for years and it still wouldn't be enough. But then János went still in László's arms, and something in László died at the same time.

Sleeping was even harder now that János was gone. László and Irén slept in their same spots, leaving space between them where he used to be. Some silent agreement that if they didn't touch the empty space, they could pretend János was still where he belonged instead of down at the bottom of the river.

When László tumbled into sludgy, grief-haunted sleep, the dreams made everything worse.

He dreamed of the lake. Of sinking into all that calm water, into the blue-green nothingness and passing through the pockets of warmth and cold. He could open his eyes and see the fish flitting back and forth in their schools, could see where they liked to hide. He could hold his breath for a long time—longest of all the kids his age, longer than some of the adults. He'd stay until his whole body screamed for air, until his nerves and his senses fired against this unnatural state of being, until he had to grit his teeth against the instinct to open his mouth and breathe. Down there, he could stave off the inevitable pain that was surely coming his way when his father got

209

tired of squabbling with neighbours and needed a fight
he could win. Down there, his life was just blue-green and
the tracks the sunlight made as it reached toward the bottom, and the quiet embrace of water that had been there
longer than he could imagine, water that would still be
there long after he was dead.

Sometimes, when his father was especially combative,
he'd wonder what it would feel like to suck all that water
into his lungs and let the lake have him. Would he sink to
the bottom, to the mud and rocks and layers of plant life,
or would he float back up?

In the dream, he had János's teeth in his hand, but they
were so heavy they were dragging him down. And the
gator he killed was coming. A thing of beauty and power
and killing force, legs tucked against its belly and a long,
undulous body that cleaved through the water effort-
lessly. Coming straight at László at first, its snout round
and menacing and scarred. There wasn't anything in the
world quite like the panic of being under the water and
seeing a gator come right at you like that. And László
couldn't swim away, because János's teeth were too
heavy.

The gator knocked against László as it passed, its tail
slapping his shoulder before the haze of the lake swallowed it again. László spun through the water until he
couldn't tell which way was up and which was down.
The tracks of light, once so clear and straight, had been
swallowed by the depth and turned into an indistinct
murky blue-green. His lungs burned. His eyes flashed
white. He swam, but maybe he was just headed toward
the bottom because that's where the teeth wanted him to
go. Down, down, into the mud that would wrap around
him like a funeral shroud. Down, down, until he was just
another dead thing at the bottom of the lake. If he'd let go
of the teeth, maybe he'd make it to the surface. But he
couldn't. He kept his hand in a fist around them because
he couldn't let them go. They were all he had. So he just

opened his mouth and let the vicious cold rush of water invade his lungs, claiming him as belonging to the lake forever—

He woke with a scream, the sound tearing a path right through him. Or maybe he hadn't screamed. His father still snored and Irén lay against the wall, breathing that slow, thick way she did when she was out cold. Maybe he hadn't made any sound at all.

László touched the place where János should be. Too empty and too cold. Too still, too quiet. László was awake, but it felt like he was still under water. Suspended in between shock and grief, neither one sinking into him just yet. And anger, too, somewhere in the distance, coming at him as sure as that gator.

***

László really did see that gator while he was under water. The big, dangerous man-eater. But gators were easy to deal with if you had Talent. You just kind of reached out to them and touched their cold little minds. You stripped away any sense that you smelled like blood and muscle. It was the panthers that you really had to look out for; the big cats that stalked the cypress forests crawling around the borders of the lake were harder to fool. They trusted their eyes more, and sometimes it seemed like they understood Talent a little bit, like they could feel it the same way humans could.

The problem with gators was when you didn't see them coming. They lunged their massive bodies out of the water, sometimes straight up, higher and faster than should be possible. That big gator, the one with all the scars on its face like it had been fighting its whole life, had learned to hunt the floating village that László called home. It lurked in the gaps between the boats, near the platforms and the floating gardens snatching people as they jumped from one to the other.

László shot it, just like his father told Davik. Right through the eye with his lucky rifle — he called it his lucky rifle because it was a *shit* rifle but it was his, damnit, and down on the float you didn't turn your nose up at a thing just 'cause it was broken. The sight was snapped off and it had a habit of pulling left, so he had to aim off what he was trying to hit. But sometimes, if you knew how to handle a shit rifle just right, you could take a gator through the eye at seventy-five yards and be a hero for a little while.

Except heroes didn't let their father kill their baby brothers. Heroes didn't freeze up when bad things were happening to the people they loved most in the whole world.

'I shoulda done something,' László whispered, just so he could let the words out, 'cause they were rotting inside him. 'I shoulda stopped him.'

'It was already over by the time we got down there,' Irén said. She sat slumped against the rudder arm, staring off at something. She hadn't looked László in the eye since. Like maybe she blamed him as much as he blamed himself. 'You couldn't'a done anything.'

On the far side of the barge, their father dragged his fishing lines in. So long as they could pull fish from the river, they could eat. But Emil was running out of whisky and it was making him restless. The fishing line came up empty and Emil kicked an empty whisky bottle across the deck, sending it spinning, twisting, and then overboard. A splash, and then it bobbed away on the current.

'I shoulda,' László said again.

Just like he'd done something about that gator. Put a bullet through its lizard brain, turned it into three hundred kilos of resources — meat and bone and skin, every scrap useful to the float. Except there wasn't a single ounce of Emil Dargis that was useful, not anymore. László was the one who was learning how to drive the barge on the too fast and too mean river, László who learned every inch of their new home and the way it danced different than their houseboat did. László who learned the rhythm of each dock he visited. And Irén was the one who learned how to dicker over cargo fees. She learned real fast that you didn't take the first offer for transport, because people tried to pay you less than you were worth, so you had to fight for more. And if the cargo was illegal, you fought for *a lot* more because you damn well could.

Emil coiled all his fishing line together, trying to be angry with it, but fishing line wasn't interested in anger; it was too light and too wild. If you threw it, it flopped around and then got tangled worse than before.

And for an ugly, vicious, hate-filled moment, László wondered what it would be like to skin a man the way he helped everyone on the float skin that gator. If he peeled back the flesh, would his father's muscles be pale pink like that gator, or deeper red like a pig? If he used his Talent to touch his father's brain, would it be cold and simple and easy to confuse? There was no way Emil was complicated and intelligent like the panthers. No fucking way.

'Pull up the anchor,' Emil said. 'Get us turned around.'

Neither Irén nor László moved. Irén kept staring off somewhere else, like she hadn't heard him. László looked up at his father and tried to imagine what kind of man hit a kid that hard. What kind of empty predator of a man looked at a kid and said, *Fuck you. You ain't nothing but meat.*

Emil met László's eye and László's rage turned colder and smaller. Could Emil tell what László was thinking? Could he see László's scorn, could he see his own death, unfolding in the dark places of László's imagination?

'Now!' Emil snapped. He took a step closer. Irén flinched, her eyes snapping back into focus to watch Emil. 'I said pull up the fucking anchor.'

'Yeah,' László said, standing. Putting his body between his father and his sister. Just in case something else happened. 'Fine. I'm doing it.'

***

He could smell the city before he could see it. Shit and smoke and too many people wafted on the breeze, turning his mood sour.

He hated this city *so much.*

Fuck the river it was built around, and the people that crowded the cobblestone streets and the towering tenements. They polluted the river by living so thick on the banks. Fuck the cows that milled in the stockyards, filling the city with the smell of their shit as they waited to be slaughtered.

Fuck the National Tainted Registration Authority for arresting his stepmother for having Talent, breaking their family apart once and for all.

Fuck his father for bringing them here, thinking big thoughts about rebellion and resistance and changing the stupid world. The world didn't change, and now his father was so angry that everything set him off worse than before.

Maybe it wasn't fair to hate a whole city since none of the things that had happened to the Dargis family were the city's fault. But it was scary to hate his own father with so much passion that he imagined skinning the whisky-pickled bastard. Hating him that much made László just as ugly and dangerous as his father, didn't it? Worse than that, hating him that much meant giving up on the possibility of things ever getting better. They used to see a glimmer of how things could be if his father wasn't so damned angry at them all the time. Little moments of feeling like a family, when their father gave them parts of his dinner because he could see they were still hungry, or when he brought László out under the night sky and named all the constellations. László was pretty sure most of the names he said were wrong, but it didn't matter because he just liked his father talking to him like that, in that low, quiet voice. The voice of a man who loved his son.

It wasn't always *this* bad. It wasn't. There was a time before when they were just a family. Loud, maybe more rambunctious than the other families on the float. Before the hits hurt so much.

It wasn't the city's fault things were this bad. It was his father's fault. And the Authority's fault for sweeping through their float, arresting people for nothing but having Talent. People who were otherwise minding their own damn business out there on the lake. Most of the Dargis family escaped but they wound up on the river where they didn't belong. Fighting against the Authority, except not really, because all Emil did was send László up and down the river and drink their money away because Davik Kaine was the one fighting the Authority in this city, and Davik Kaine didn't like Emil one bit.

'We gonna go down to the Hive, get another load?' László asked. River traffic where everything passed through the city was the worst part of learning the current. The water itself was hard to navigate, but László could keep his Talent attuned to the water and it would teach him what it wanted to do. Not so obvious were the lanes the other barges used, the places where you were allowed to pass, the places where you were allowed to go north, the places where you could go south. Some of the real big barges would run you the fuck over if you were in the wrong lane, except the borders of everything were imaginary.

'It's too late to go to the Hive,' Emil said. It wasn't, but best not to point that out. 'Dock up somewhere. We need supplies.'

Supplies was a funny way to pronounce whisky, but it was best not to point that out, either.

***

The plan was to steal a bottle.

His father sent him off the barge and into the city with a pair of copper crowns, but László would stash them somewhere. Save 'em up, so he could figure out a way to ditch his father, like László's older sister had a few months ago. If he could just get him and Irén back to the lake, maybe he'd find his older sister and the three of them could start to make some sense of the world. Maybe then he could grieve János properly.

He was still hanging, suspended in time and place, the grief holding him just like the water of the lake used to. Something big was coming at him, something big and dangerous, just like that gator and bearing just as many scars. Eventually László would break the surface of it all, and…

What?

Didn't matter—for now, he had to survive the city. The farther he got from the river, the worse he felt. The buildings and the streets weren't ever straight, so it never took long before the city hid the river from view. Once László was far enough away that he couldn't hear it anymore, it was impossible to make his way back unless he took the time to memorise the route he walked. Sometimes he caught sight of the docks and the Hive—the towering structure above it where all the trade of Yaelsmuir passed through the hands of the crime lord that ruled Cattle Bone Bay. But then he rounded a corner past another massive warehouse and the city hemmed him in again and he was as good as lost. He imagined the predator people, trailing him in an ever growing knot. Tension lay across his shoulders, ratcheted the bones of his spine tighter together. Everything his father said about the city echoed in his sinew. Every street felt like he was heading deeper into predator territory, like he was tempting the swamp things to come for him. He could almost feel them lurking at the edges of his senses—people-predators, like

216

the gators and the panthers, except the thing about people was that you couldn't tell who was capable of ripping your throat open and who was just minding their own business. Not everyone was a predator, but the ones who were generally hid it well.

László glanced behind, half expecting to see a crowd of people stalking him in that slow way a gator drifted through the water with its eyes on you, but there was no one. Or at least, no one paying attention to him. But that didn't clear the dread.

This city will eat you up his father said, more than once. Maybe every day since they got here. *Can't trust no one. They ain't family like it was down on the float. They all just mean and a little hungry and a kid like you is an easy mark.*

Fuck them all. He wouldn't be an easy mark. If they tried something, he'd show them what he could do with his Talent. It wasn't just for driving barges on the stupid river; his Talent was bigger than most of the people he encountered around here, and wild, and it could sink into a man and see his beating heart. He'd always wondered what it might be like to use his Talent to stop a person dead in their tracks, the same way he could move a barge against the current or hold it in place no matter how fast the water ran.

But even that thought sent fresh fear through him — he wasn't registered. If he started problems, would the Authority come for him like they came for his stepmother?

If they took him, his father sure as fuck wouldn't save him. Would Irén?

László thrust his hand into his pocket, closing his fist around the pair of coppers his father had given him. It wasn't enough to get away, not yet, but he'd keep hiding coins and eventually…

János's baby teeth were in his pocket, too. He tightened his hand around the teeth, the jagged roots digging into his palm. Sharp and ugly and filled with a kind of anguish that couldn't *quite* pierce his skin. It was like his emotions were being held in front of him. He could see them, touch them, name them, but he wasn't feeling them yet. They were taunting him. Threatening him.

How many bottles of whisky could he buy with four baby teeth? If he laid them on the counter and explained why he had them in his pocket, would someone give him enough liquor that his father could drink himself to death?

He didn't have time for that; he needed to bring a bottle back to his father. So, he let go of the teeth and picked a group of people drinking together at the mouth of an alley. Most of them were half drunk already, and there were so many bottles between them that none of them were going to notice any missing. Probably. Hopefully.

He didn't notice Davik Kaine in the group, or he wouldn't have approached them at all.

'Hey,' he said. 'You seen a kid around here?'

This act needed two people. Imagining how it should have gone—László made a big deal about trying to find his brother and drew everyone's attention, János came up behind the crowd to pick pockets and lift a bottle or two—made László's chest feel hollow. János was really good at it. He could lift a person's whole life out of their pockets.

'How about you fuck off, yeah? Whatever you're selling, we don't want it.'

László shook his head. 'You don't have to be an asshole about it. I'm just looking for my brother—' His voice cracked under the strain. Saying the word *brother* split something ugly and raw open, sending it bubbling up through his chest. 'I don't know where he's gone. Have you seen him? Have you seen a kid wandering around? He looks like me except his hair is brown instead of blond—he got that from his mother—he's a real shit, too, so he was probably causing trouble when he came this way—'

He pushed his hands back into his pockets but that was a mistake. The baby teeth drove home how horrible the words were to say out loud, because László would give a piece of his soul to have János back and causing trouble again.

'Hey,' someone else said. László's eyes were so blurred with tears that he couldn't see the crowd anymore. 'You alright, kid?'

'Fine,' László said, wiping at his eyes with sharp motions. The ugly, hot, vicious things that were trying to bloom in him were turning into the business edge of a knife, turning into hatred for his father that was cutting him open from the inside out. The bastard, the perfect fucking bastard, and here László was trying to get a bottle of whisky for him after what he'd done, because he convinced László that this was just their life. 'Fine. I'm just looking for my brother. You seen him or not?'

'No, we ain't seen a kid,' a woman said gently. 'You want some help looking for him? You're Emil Dargis's boy, aren't you? Where's the last place you seen your brother?'

He definitely wasn't expecting them to recognise him.

'I don't—I can't—I don't know—'

He turned away. The rattle of János's baby teeth filled him with emptiness—or maybe it was weight. He wasn't sure. He didn't have the time or the space or the energy to consider it. He needed to get away as fast as he could. Staggering on the uneven cobbles, tripping over the raised curb, fumbling through the city until he didn't know where he was. All the streets in this part of the city looked the same. Too tired and too old and too cramped, the buildings leaning toward each other like they were already drunk, that morning's rain still drip-drip-dripping from the eaves. Alleys were like warrens, cutting every which way, and unlike the water, he couldn't spill his Talent into the current to understand the flow. He couldn't even use his Talent in the city, not without risking the attention of someone from the Authority.

A hand dropped on his shoulder, sending a hot jolt of

fear through him. His legs bunched and his body fucking moved, except another hand closed around László's upper arm in a vice grip, holding László in place even as his feet scraped against the cobbles.

'Whoa there, laddie.' That voice was familiar, a round northern burr sliding like butter. 'Easy now, I'm not going to hurt you.'

'Get off me!' László howled, twisting, swinging, trying to get traction, but that pair of hands had him. 'Let me go! Just fucking let me go!'

'Relax, fuck. I'll let you go when you quit thrashing, or you're going to get a face full of cobbles, and such a pretty face it is. Be a shame to bust it all up. Just settle down and we'll walk and talk, hey? Take a breath.'

László twisted again. He saw the scarred knuckles first, and the tattoos. And the warm brown eyes that looked almost amused as they took in László's ineffectual flailing.

The thing about those panthers that lived around the lake was they had a habit of hiding up in the cypress trees and dropping on their prey. So even if you had Talent and you knew how to use it against wildlife to convince them you weren't prey, sometimes you didn't get the chance because the damn panthers came out of nowhere and their jaws were on your throat before you could defend yourself. That stealth and that power let them take gators sometimes. Maybe not the real big ones like the one László killed, but younger gators sunning themselves in the shallows were vulnerable to panther jaws.

László saw it happen once by chance. Not to a person. He was swimming near the floating gardens that his stepmother lovingly tended to, watching someone's herd of pigs wallow in the muddy edge where lake and land blurred together and couldn't quite decide what it was. The light was fading toward dusk and the world was half shadow and then the panther dropped from the tree right on a big sow's back, and the pig's squeal cut like a scythe

220

across the lake. And the quiet after was heavy with death. That's what it felt like, being caught by Davik Kaine.

***

The bastard had dropped on László out of nowhere. And unlike the various predators down around the float, Davik had Talent, too—László could feel the weight of it, forcefully controlled and ready to pounce. Ready to sweep across László's senses like a mudslide, but hotter somehow. Maybe a controlled burn, the kind farmers used to clear brush. It singed something in László, cut away… something. But László wasn't sure what was gone exactly, just that the inside of his chest felt different somehow.

'Shit, I think you're even skinnier than the last time I saw you, which wasn't that long ago, was it? You're the wrong age for losing weight, laddie. Why don't I help you find your brother and then I'll treat you both to a meal, hey?'

'My brother's dead,' László blurted before he could stop himself. 'János is fucking dead and my father dumped his body in the Brightwash so no one would know what he'd done and I can't—I hate him. I hate him so fucking much. But he wants me to get him a fucking bottle, but I'm just so sick of *everything*.'

Davik's expression changed in slow measures, and László couldn't identify any of them. László twisted his arm to pull himself from Davik's grasp, but Davik had him tight. His scarred, tattooed hands were as strong as vices. So strong, they hurt. So strong, László felt like a tiny animal caught in something's jaws. Davik was going to eat him up. He almost reached for his Talent, but fresh fear stripped him down to nothing. Davik had Talent, too.

'You shouldn't be losing weight at your age,' he said again, but his voice was harder than before. 'Let me feed you, put some weight on those bones of yours, and we'll talk.'

'There's nothing to talk about,' László said, putting his hands on Davik's chest and trying to push him away. 'Just let me go, I have to go find a bottle.'

'I'll tell you what. If you come sit with me, have a meal and a drink, then I'll send you off with a fresh bottle when we're done. How's that sound? You and me, we should talk about that old man of yours. Maybe we can solve some problems together, hey?'

***

Following Davik felt an awful lot like letting a panther drag you into the forest. Except László was so exhausted from all that unexpected crying that he didn't have any energy left for fear. Something else took its place — resignation, maybe.

'You folks ain't been in Yaelsmuir long,' Davik said. 'I was trying to give your old man the benefit of the doubt — I know it takes a while to get used to the flow of things. I ain't from here either.'

'We never wanted to be here,' László said. 'But the Authority took my stepmother and he got it in his head that he'd save her and now —'

And now they'd lost another Dargis. Another piece of who they used to be, chipped away. Snuffed out.

'Aye, your father said as much,' Davik said when László couldn't continue. 'Said that's why he brought you kids up this way — Authority scooped her up from the lake, brought her here. He heard there are people around who might be able to save her.'

'He said there's rebels in Yaelsmuir,' László said, forcing the words through the thick grief in his throat. 'Said there's Talented here who want to change things.'

'Laddie, there's tainted everywhere who want to change things,' Davik muttered, rounding another corner. They were so deep into the city, László knew he'd never find his way back without help. But maybe that was the point. Maybe Davik wanted László to know that László was at his mercy. 'Let's go inside, we'll talk.'

'Why do you call us tainted instead of Talented?' László asked, stagger-jogging to keep up with Davik and his long legs. 'That's what the Authority calls us. Like we're rotting from the inside.'

Davik shrugged, heading for the public house. There was just enough light to see the sign above the door – a bucket, cut from wood and painted to show the shape of it. 'Seems stupid to try to give ourselves a better name when this whole bloody country works so hard to tell us our place. They call us tainted so they can feel like they're superior somehow. I don't like to get complacent. It's easy to think we're safe since they're leaving us be for now, but it wouldn't take much for the Authority to decide they'll start rounding us up after all. If we ain't ready for them, we have the most to lose, don't we?'

'Yeah,' László said so softly he wasn't sure if Davik could hear him. Davik opened the front door of the public house and the sound washed over László. Happy places all kind of made the same sounds, especially on unseasonably warm autumn nights like this when the air was still thick from the morning rain. And the smells – garlic and onions, roasted meat, the sweet yeasty smell of fresh bread, the crisp scent of cider. László's stomach gurgled at it all. 'That's how it was down on the float. There's lots of Talent down that way and the Authority mostly left us alone – until they didn't. A lot of people were taken that day.'

'Exactly,' Davik said. 'There's no telling when they'll come here looking for a fight. I like my people to be ready.'

'Is it true, then?' László asked. 'You've got rebels – Talented fighters – preparing for a revolution?'

Davik put his hands on László's shoulders, steering László toward the bar. The bartender dropped what he was doing as soon as he saw Davik coming. 'Cyril, this here is the Dargis boy. What's your first name, son?'

'László.'

Davik nodded, patting both of László's shoulders. 'If you see László come in here on his own, you give him a meal and a drink on the house.'

'Sure thing, Dav.'

'I'm taking him upstairs to talk. Up on the roof. Send up whatever's on tonight. You take beer or cider, son?'

'I don't know,' László said. 'Whichever.'

'Pair of the red ales, then.'

'Of course, Dav.'

Cyril the bartender went about pulling pints. The glasses were clean here, which was probably a first for the Bay — or maybe their father just never took them anywhere with clean glasses. The red ale looked rich and indulgent, the head the colour of peaches. 'I'll send your plates up, Dav.'

Davik scooped up both pints and nodded toward the stairs at the back of the pub. He led the way easily, the crowd parting for him. 'There are good people here, László Dargis. They'll watch out for you and your sister.'

László shrugged. Where had all that hard anger gone? He didn't trust this new, warm version of Davik. 'The old man doesn't like us coming this far from the river. Says it's dangerous.'

Davik laughed, turning to lean on the hinged half-door that blocked the stairs. 'Sure he does. I suppose he's afraid I'll feed you and then you'll have less and less reason to drive his barge for him while he's drunk on the docks.'

The way Davik was *exactly* right sent a shiver down László's spine.

'I should've told you that you were welcome around here.' Up and up and up the stairs. Heat gathered in the stairwell, thicker with every landing they passed, until László was sweating freely. 'Maybe if I'd said something sooner, I could have helped you and your wee brother. I'm sorry about that. Your da ain't an easy man to work around.'

Tears came back, hot and fast, blurring the world away into nothing again. Davik's words sent him spinning into his own what-if-world, like twisting and spinning through water, leaving him disoriented and unable to tell which way was up.

What if they'd all come into the city and asked for help? Could it really have been that easy to save János?

His father had somehow convinced him that no one would care. That there was nowhere to go, no one to turn to. They had their barge and that was it; they had no choice but to stay.

But here was Davik, proving their father a liar.

Up six stories, and László's body screamed with the unaccustomed exertion.

'Sorry, laddie,' Davik chuckled. 'I forget how hard it is for folks to climb these bloody stairs when they ain't used to it. You ain't afraid of heights, are you?'

László shook his head but didn't respond. Not that he could have even if he wanted to. He just gulped at the air, hot and thick with humidity. Davik opened the door, the rush of a cool breeze hitting László's skin like an exhale.

'Does everyone get service up on the roof?' László asked once he caught his breath enough to talk.

Davik shrugged. 'A benefit of owning the place.'

The roof was higher than most of the buildings around it, closer to the stars than László had ever been. When he craned his head back and looked straight up, it was easy to believe he was the only person in the world. It was just him and the spray of constellations that he'd memorised on short, hot summer nights like this down on the float. A wisp of cloud lit by the glow of the moon looked so close and so thick, he could reach out and grab a chunk out of it, hold all that fluff in his hand. Maybe if he caught a cloud, he'd just float away.

But if he floated away, Irén would be alone.

Davik pushed one of the pints into László's hand, standing between László and the door to the stairwell.

'Why don't you tell me what happened,' Davik said. It wasn't a question, even though it almost sounded like one. The hard edge to his voice was back. 'To your brother, I mean.'

László looked down at the pint glass in his hand, watching the head settle, some of it sliding down the edge of the glass where it had spilled over as they climbed the stairs. 'He's dead.'

'Aye, laddie, I know that part,' Davik said. 'But how'd he get that way? Last I saw your old man, he was heading north, out of the city, and the three of you were with him. Took a load for someone other than me 'cause he knows I'm not happy with him sending you south. Was it an accident, your brother?'

László shook his head. 'There weren't any problems with the load, Mr. Kaine. I handled it just fine, like I told you. That barge may as well be mine. I know how to drive it, and I know how to deal with each dock.'

Davik sighed. He headed toward the ledge and sat down on it, hanging one leg over and looking out across all the city around him. 'How old are you, László Dargis?'

'Fourteen,' László said, maybe too quickly. Maybe he should have lied and said he was older. But lying to Davik didn't seem like a good idea considering how much Davik already knew about him.

'I know that barge is yours, laddie. I can tell. But that's the problem, you understand?'

'No sir,' László said. 'I don't understand how it's a problem that I can do my job.'

'Boy, come here and sit down,' Davik huffed. 'You're making me tired, all that fidgeting.'

László went closer to the edge, even though it made his heart beat too fast. Made his head too light. It felt like he was on the water again and something in him was

226

spinning. His emotions kept shifting, like his rudder was broken and it didn't know which way to point, sending him back and forth across the current of his own consciousness. He closed his hands around all the charms on his necklace instead of reaching for János's teeth again. The big gator tooth was almost soothing.

'Your old man told me that gator story a few times, didn't he?' Davik said. 'Every time he wanted to convince me you can take care of yourself. Went on and on about three hundred kilos worth of man-killer, and how you took it right through the eye, and how he taught you everything about how to shoot and how to drive the boat and how to be the toughest motherfucker on the lake. It always rubbed me wrong, the way he talked about you, like you were his brother instead of his son — like it wasn't his job to protect you anymore. Or maybe he didn't ever think it was his job. I understand wanting your kids to grow up and take care of themselves, but it felt like he was asking too fucking much from you. I don't know, maybe I'm soft. It's just that I imagine my boy, and everything he's been through, and I'd like to think when he's fourteen, he'll still be my boy and I'll still keep half an eye on him while he figures out his place in the world.'

Anger burned hot across László's grief, eating him up so completely it was like he'd been tossed on a pyre. 'He didn't teach me to shoot. He didn't teach me to run the barge, either. That bastard hasn't taught me anything except how to take a hit and how to be fucking disappointed. He didn't teach me to shoot because when I was old enough to learn how to handle a rifle, he was too busy chasing after a new wife since my mother was gone. My older brother taught me how to shoot. My older brother was the best shot on the float.'

'Who taught your older brother how to shoot?' Davik asked.

'My mother.'

'The one in the Breeding Program?'

227

'No—that's my stepmother. My mother left. Our father gave her two black eyes and then we never saw her again. She never came back. I don't know what happened.' László shrugged, wiping his eyes with the heel of his hand and sucking back the rest of the beer. 'Of course my father would take credit for something he didn't do. Everything good in our family has happened in spite of *him*. The only thing he has any right to take credit for is the piles of shit, after everything good falls apart.'

'Did he kill her, do you think?' Davik asked. 'Your mother, I mean. Do you think he caught her trying to make plans to get away and sent her off with more than a pair of black eyes?'

The idea took the bottom out of László's stomach, so that he sunk into himself, folding over old grief and new anger. 'He wouldn't...' he whispered. But he couldn't finish the sentence. Because now he knew his father *would* so maybe he'd never known his father at all. Maybe any impressions that his father had some good in him was himself hanging on to the dream of something that wasn't true. Hoping for a father that loved his children instead of killed them. 'He wouldn't,' he said again because he needed it to be true so badly that his mouth kept trying to say it.

'I think it's time you tell me about what happened to your brother, laddie,' Davik said.

László shook his head, but the words started anyway. 'I just got back. I took your load to White Crown no problem, like I said I would—brought a fresh one back for someone else to make the trip pay. But I didn't haggle for it as much as I should have and we got fucked. I'm not good at it, the dickering. That's Irén's job, but he kept her behind. So, he was angry already. Saying stuff about how we had to be smarter about the jobs we pulled. Said he wanted to find loads that weren't for you because you were fucking us over. Irén said she thought you paid well and that made it worse. He wanted to go up north, out of

228

the city, to spend some time fishing, said it was too expensive for us to stay docked. So, I drove us north a bit. I thought maybe something happened with you, and he was running from trouble. Him and János started getting into it. János was in a bad mood cause he lost his teeth and he just wanted attention for it but we were all so busy. I don't know what happened. One minute, I was driving north, like he told me to. The next minute, János was screaming.'

László squeezed his eyes shut, because as soon as he said it, he could hear that screaming again. He could hear it so sharp and so insistent that it felt like nails being shoved into his ears. He leaned, just a little, toward the edge of the building. Maybe he'd throw himself off just to get away from that sound.

'Your da hit him?'

'Must've,' László gasped, forcing his eyes open. Don't look down at the street—look up at the stars. At the endless swirl of sky. Timeless and unmoving. Cold, but not in a cruel way like the river. Just cold because it was so far away. 'Must've hit him a few times because by the time I went down there, János was bleeding all over the place. And the old man's knuckles were all fucked up. He kept saying sorry, but János wouldn't stop screaming. He'd always been loud, I never heard him sound like that. Like he was angry, except he was in so much pain he couldn't… And then he started shaking. And the old man, he *kept* saying he was sorry. Sorry János. Cut it out, János. It ain't that bad, János, just walk it off. Except it was the worst thing I ever seen. And then he was still. He stopped shaking and he stopped crying, and that was even worse. He was just… empty. I seen enough dead things in my life, I know when life goes, you know? He went still and cold and that was it.'

There was more to say; about how his father made them carry János up on deck and how his father dumped János in the river like he was forty pounds of trash. About how his father made him and Irén clean up the blood, except they couldn't because they were both crying so much they couldn't see anything. About how his father went on and on about how they were all going to be caught, arrested, they were all going to be hanged for this, about how Irén and László had to keep their mouths shut or the Authority would get them all and that would be worse than being dead. And then the days in the bay, fishing and drinking, and Irén staring off at something that only she could see because she didn't look anyone in the eye anymore.

But he couldn't say it. He couldn't talk at all. He was frozen, half-alive, rotting with shame. A hero would've done something. A hero would've known how to protect his kid brother, no matter what. He drank his pint instead of talking, gulping it back without tasting it, swallowing his own tears at the same time.

'Your old man talks about that big gator a lot,' Davik said. Like he couldn't really bear the silence but he didn't want to talk about what happened either. He was a father, too—said he had his own boy. How old was Davik Kaine's son? 'And those panthers, too. A lot of folks around here find the whole deal fascinating, since we haven't anything like that this far north. I guess it's the one thing your old man has that makes him interesting, so he'll take any opportunity he can get to go on and on about them. Gators and panthers. Man-eaters, hey?'

'Sometimes,' László said. The subject change left him reeling again, spinning off into a distant place, separated from the pain. Talking about hunting predators on the lake was a lot easier than talking about the predator that took the space a father was supposed to occupy. 'It doesn't happen as often as you'd think. We learn the signs, you know? Learn where they like to hunt and stay away from them. And Talent helps, we can usually trick them into not noticing us. But the big one I killed had developed a habit of hunting the float. Left us no choice, really.'

Davik nodded, draining the last of his beer. 'Aye, that's what he said. Once they get the taste for people, it's harder to get rid of them. You folks down on the float don't kill 'em unless you need to. You hunt them for food sometimes, but if they start hunting you, they've signed their death warrant.'

László swirled his glass around and watching the last dregs dance down in the bottom. 'More or less.'

'I think people are like that, too. Killing comes differently to everyone. Some folks make it look easy, don't they? Others can't conceive of it unless their whole world is under threat. And even then, maybe they still hesitate. It's one thing, killing to defend yourself. Killing for... I don't know. A higher ideal, I suppose. Killing other soldiers because you're at war. You know? You ever kill a man, László Dargis?'

'No. Not a person.'

'A gator, though.'

'Yeah.'

'Anything else?'

'Plenty of pigs—helped a land farmer cull their herd at harvest time a few years in a row, earned some meat for the work. Pigs bleed a lot. You shoot 'em through the head to kill 'em fast, then hang them up to drain them. Catch the blood to make blood sausage. Hunting and fishing, too—it's how we feed ourselves. No one else is going to do it.' László shrugged. 'Why?'

'We aren't too impressed with your old man, I have to be honest. It's hard to get results out of him and he talks too much. He isn't a man we can trust to keep secrets. Feels like he'll run his mouth one day when he's halfway through a bottle. A man with a loose mouth can get a lot of people killed, can't he?' Davik sighed, rolling the pint glass between his palms, back and forth. 'And now he's also a child killer. His own boy. So, what do I do with Emil Dargis and the two kids he has left?'

'I don't fucking know,' László muttered. 'How am I supposed to know? I'm not a smuggler or a crime lord or anything. I haven't the slightest fucking clue. Why are you asking me?'

'I'm not asking you, laddie,' Davik said. 'Ain't your job to figure it out. I'm trying to tell you something.'

'So tell me already!'

'The load you carried down to White Crown for me?'

'What about it?' László pressed.

'It was lighter than it should have been.'

The whole world stopped. László looked in Davik's eyes and saw that predator's stare had returned. The one he noticed on the barge, when Davik was watching him even as Emil talked and talked. László was right, thinking Davik was smart like a panther. Smarter, even, because he'd lured László away from the river and up here to this roof. László sat in Davik's territory, with his throat exposed for Davik's killing teeth.

'I sent you off with eight kilos in those crates. A big load, but I paid your da accordingly. I pay well, like your sister said. But my people in White Crown, they only got six kilos.'

Here it was, the moment it all ended. Davik was getting ready to kill László as retribution for his father's crimes. Maybe Davik would push him right off the edge. He'd fall into the wide space between him and the ground, and float for a short time before the cobbles he hated so much turned him cold and broken.

He fell, he imagined Davik saying, that round burr of his making everything sound both rough and smooth at the same time. *Poor, stupid river boy, got too close to the edge of the roof and then he fell.*

'None of the packages were damaged or anything,' Davik went on. 'They were just missing.'

'I didn't...'

'I know,' Davik interrupted, his voice light and friendly. He even smiled. Patted László's shoulder. 'You ain't the 'moving stolen opium' type. You play your life too honest for something like that. I appreciate it. Admire it, even. I figure your old man, he lifted a bit before you left, sold it back to someone local for a quick profit while you were gone. That's why he was anxious to get out of town, I figure. Someone said something to him down on the docks, and I hear things got ugly. There was almost a fight until that sister of yours got involved, steered your old man away. How old is she, your sister?'

'Same age as me,' László said, the words popping out of him like bubbles. Giddy with relief, loaded with fresh fear. His father was stealing from Davik fucking Kaine. Was he trying to get them all killed? 'She's my twin.'

'The pair of you are good at handling him, hey?'

László shrugged. 'Can't be that good at it. He killed János and we didn't stop him.'

'Well,' Davik said slowly, 'what if I handle it for you?'

***

Davik gave him a bottle from behind the bar, the cheap house whisky, but that was perfect. Anything nice would have been suspicious. László peeled the wax seal off the bottle to get rid of the Bucket's stamp. He took a sip, just to have a reason for the wax seal to be gone. The smack he'd get would be a lot easier to handle than how bad his father would go off if he found out László had made it all the way down to the Bucket. As it was, his father was angry at him for taking so long, but the mostly full bottle improved his mood. So did the work order, the one that Davik gave László before he left the Bucket. He didn't show it to his father, and he didn't tell his father that Davik gave it to him; instead he lied about nicking it from someone on the dock. Emil relaxed a bit after that. He had a bottle of whisky, and money was coming.

And László and Irén were supposed to be asleep, but László whispered the whole story into the darkness, and now Irén was angry with him, too.

'Are you *fucking* daft?' Irén hissed. Through clenched teeth, her body tense with fury. 'What did you agree to?'

'Nothing,' László said. 'Well, nothing except what we always do. We've got the work order. All we gotta do is load up. He'll come with us when we head north.'

'And then what?' Irén hissed.

'I don't know. But he's gonna do something. Dad's been pinching from loads. Someone's gonna do something.'

'And then what?' Irén pressed. 'I don't like it. I don't trust it. You shoulda found out more. I don't like the way he didn't tell you anything. He's gotta be setting us up for something.'

That feeling again—he was a houseboat on the lake, but he didn't have any other boats to lash on to, didn't have the storm walls to protect him from the vicious swells of bad weather.

'Don't make deals without me anymore,' Irén said. 'Let me handle it next time.'

Footsteps shuffled above them before László could answer. Boots scraped on the stairs down, and then Emil's heavy breathing filled the cabin. Irén pressed her cheek into László's shoulder and held her breath, held it so long that her silence filled László's ears just like when he sank down into the water. Except it wasn't *that* silent, because his father was getting ready to stumble into bed beside them.

Irén's tears wet his shoulder. She cried *so* quietly. Like she didn't dare acknowledge it. She could pretend it wasn't happening, but for the tears that escaped. Tears for János, maybe. Tears for the pair of them, fighting to get their heads above water before they drowned. Before a predator got them.

***

He dreamt of the water. Instead of slow and cut with sun, it was cold and moving too fast. Air bubbles swirled around him and the current tugged him away from the barge. He tried to swim but he wasn't strong enough. János's teeth were on a string around his neck, dragging him to the bottom. He dreamed of a gator — except it was also his father. Hands with bruises on his knuckles and gator teeth in his mouth. Cleaving through the water like the current didn't affect him at all —

When he snapped awake, Irén and Emil were still sleeping. Emil snored in that way he did when he drank, the whisky knocking him out so cold, sometimes his body forgot to keep breathing. And then it started again, grunting and half choking, but still asleep.

László tiptoed his way up the stairs. The third tread from the top creaked loud, so he skipped that one. If he wasn't going to sleep, he might as well start working, get the barge in line to get loaded. He would have tried last night, but his father needed time with his bottle so he wasn't so fucking angry. The last thing they needed was him picking a fight with a dock hand, getting them banned.

The Hive was already busy when László stepped up onto the deck. The chaos of the dock system was almost familiar now; other barges joined the shuffle to get themselves loaded at the big warren at the centre — the structure that gave the focus their name, because it made the whole thing look like a hive, worker bee stevedores swarming everywhere to supervise every scrap of cargo and every barge.

László unhooked their barge from the off-dock — the place where barges were parked to stay well out of the way of the central system of the Hive — spilling his Talent into the water to keep the barge stable once they were no longer roped. He coiled everything neatly, feeling the push of the current against his senses. Reminded him of the dream, of struggling uselessly against that current,

János's teeth around his neck instead of in his pocket, trying to fight a current that was aggressive and loud. Too loud. László missed the quiet water so much. Maybe after Davik *took care* of their father, he'd take Irén back to the lake, try to find their older sister. Pretend none of this shit happened, live on the float where they belonged.

László sat beside the rudder arm and leaned into it, turning the barge slowly. For all the chaos of this part of the river, it was precisely organised. You just had to know the shape of it. He fell into line to get to the central Hive docks, but the panic came in slow measures. Maybe it was stupid to start loading now. Their father liked them to be proactive and get shit done, but he also didn't like being woken up. If he wasn't up before they started loading and all that crashing and shouting woke him, he'd be in a foul mood all day. The work order had them going up to a mill town a day or so north of the city. If László rode the river right, they could be unloading by tonight, but that still meant a day's journey back. Two whole fucking days of his father being in a mood sounded like maybe the Dargis family would fall apart a little bit more.

And what plan did Davik have? What did him taking care of things look like?

But now that László was in line headed for the Hive, he wasn't allowed to turn around, so it was too late.

Sweat beaded along his neck, crawling down his spine, turning his hands so slick it was hard to hold the rudder arm, so he leaned into it. The sun baked his bare shoulders, hitting all his freckles and turning his skin pink with the promise of a sunburn, but it wasn't anything as bad as the fire of panic that sat in his chest as the moments ticked by. Most of the time he hated how long the line took, but now it felt like it was going too fast, like barges were going through in half as much time as ever, and the Hive was getting closer and closer and still his father wasn't awake.

He'd made a mistake.

He'd made a terrible mistake, getting into line now.

And Irén was still down there.

If his father woke up in his too-much-whisky-last-night mood and Irén got hurt—

His heart hammered so hard he could feel the reverberation of it rolling through his ribcage to the tips of his fingers. Wishing for a natural disaster seemed too awful, but he still imagined a fire burning through the Hive, or an earthquake sending ugly shivers across the river—did they get earthquakes around here?—or a monsoon rain, the type that made the river impossible to navigate for a while. Anything to slow progress so he didn't hit the Hive while his father was still sleeping.

No—his father wasn't sleeping. He could hear voices in the cabin, his father half-shouting except the river nearly drowned out the sound. Relief. So complete that László felt empty again. Numb. But relief was a thing with claws, something would cut him if he let his guard down. Because *this* moment was fine, but that wasn't the same as being safe. There was still so much that could happen.

The cabin door swung open, and his father came stomping upstairs.

'I thought I'd get us going,' László said, shouting to be heard over the river chaos, 'since I couldn't sleep.'

Emil horked and spat off the edge of the barge. 'Go help your sister clean up.'

'Clean up what?' László asked.

Stupid question, stupid question, stupid question—but he was so damned tired, the words had slipped out before his slow-as-sludge thoughts could stop them.

His father came slowly, long arms swinging, big boots stomping, loading the air with dread. He cuffed László upside the head. It was an easy swipe, not the kind with any anger in it. A warning. László exhaled slowly—he was lucky this time.

'Just go fucking help, would you?'

László shot to his feet and his father took his spot at the rudder arm. Don't ask any more questions, just get down there, out of sight — he was in a half decent mood, don't ruin it —

Irén was on her hands and knees, scrubbing.

She'd pulled water up from the river. She clutched a big deck brush and she scrubbed with her whole damn body. She was only wearing one of László's thin under-shirts and her drawers, probably because their father had pulled her right out of bed and hadn't given her time to get dressed before he started making demands.

'What happened?' László asked.

'The blood — he was mad about the blood — he wanted to know why we haven't cleaned it up yet,' she gasped. Her voice was thin again, all her strength poured into the act of scrubbing, but it would be goddamn useless be-cause the blood had stained the wood as sure as white-wash. But red. 'I think he's scared someone will come down here — I don't know. He said we gotta clean it be-fore someone sees it.'

László's ears rang. Or maybe that was the sound of János screaming, trapped in László's memory. As long as he lived, he'd remember that sound. János hurt himself a lot because he was clumsy and wild and didn't have enough fear in him, but László had never heard him scream like *that*. Half pain and half rage and everything so loud down here in the cabin that wasn't made for four people.

László sank to the floor. His hands flexed like his fin-gers wanted purpose, but there was only one brush. Irén *was* crying, tears dripping off her face and onto the back of the brush as she scrubbed and scrubbed and scrubbed.

And László was just *empty*.

He'd done all his crying yesterday and he hadn't slept well and now he was just an impression of himself, skin and bones but no soul and no emotion. Suspended in the water like before, his ears buzzing so loud that he couldn't hear Irén. Just the river, the roar of it, the way it hit the hull of their barge as they clove through the current toward the Hive.

He caught sight of his lucky rifle, the one he killed that gator with, stashed under his bed. There was blood on it. They'd missed it when they cleaned the first time, half-hearted and shock-numb—they hadn't thought to check under the damn beds. László twisted to reach around Irén, dragging the rifle out.

Something skittered across the floor. He thought it was bugs at first, but no—they rattled too loudly on the planks. They weren't living things that moved, but rocks or something his rifle knocked out from under the bed.

Irén choked and gasped and stopped scrubbing. Her hand closed over the little rocks and she sobbed in earnest when she lifted them up.

'What?' László asked. 'What is it?'

Her hand shook when she opened her fingers, thrusting the rocks at László. No, not rocks.

More baby teeth.

Back molars this time, three of them.

He hadn't recognised them as teeth because they weren't white—blood sat on the surface, turning them rust red. But once he noticed the ridges and the roots, they were unmistakable.

His father had hit János so hard that it knocked the teeth right out of János's jaw.

László's grief split open, turning into a raging torrent that cut through his chest.

Everything he went through yesterday was just part of the living nightmare. He'd been spinning in the water and all that crying was him trying to right himself.

And now, with three more teeth in Irén's hand, he'd punched through the surface of the shock, and all his emotions pulled into sharp focus. The difference between looking at something while you were under water so that the blue-green murkiness smothered the details, and looking at something once you were above the water, all the details of it turned sharp and distinct.

He wasn't angry, at least not in the hot and wild way his father always got angry. It was a focused thing, sharp with logic, a hunting-killing kind of viciousness.

He reached into his pocket and pulled out the four teeth he had. The four János had lost the proper way. He held them beside Irén's hand so that he could see all seven together, and he wondered, distantly, if there were more teeth under the bed, waiting to be found if he went grasping under there.

The whole barge changed direction, lurching them so they knocked together, slumping into each other, both of their hands closing tight around the teeth so they didn't lose them. They'd reached the Hive, then. And they'd been roped by the dockworkers and dragged cross-current, and the barge thumped again when it hit the side of the docks with all the graceless efficiency that made Yaelsmuir water so much different than lake water.

The barge passed into the structure of the Hive and the noise was deafening, even down in the cabin. They moved so much cargo and everyone shouted at each other and the barges jostled against the dock -- perfect, precise, roaring chaos.

László pushed the baby teeth back into his pocket, scraping the blood off the gunmetal of his rifle. It fell away in flakes, but it clung to the jagged metal where the sight had snapped off. He kept meaning to try to sand it down, but he didn't have anything tough enough to sand metal. He checked the breech. It was still loaded. He hadn't touched this gun since they came here. People in the city didn't carry rifles out in the open like they did on the float.

The door opened and Emil came thumping down, but he paused on the stairs to shout at one of the dock workers.

Davik was right with the thing he said about gators

and men.

Once a gator gets a taste for hunting people, you had to put it down. And László got lucky, with his shit .22 that pulled left and didn't have a sight on it, spotting the gator off the north side of the float, both its malevolent eyes watching them like it was considering who it wanted to take next. A dog, a chicken, a person.

With perfect certainty, László knew that if he reached out to his father's mind the same way you reached out to predators down on the lake, he'd find his father's brain to be a cold and lizard thing. He wasn't a sophisticated predator like a panther — like Davik — he was just a predator of opportunity, always waiting for a chance to grab something good.

Emil cursed at the dockhands and slammed the door shut, turning down the stairs again. 'Where's the fucking work order, Irén?' he snapped.

'I don't know!' Irén snapped back, her voice thick with all the emotion, the baby teeth still in her hand, the bloody molars. 'You put it somewhere after László gave it to you. I didn't touch it. I never touch those papers!'

'Useless cow,' Emil Dargis growled, his voice rumbling in the cabin. László felt it in his chest more than he heard it — the Hive was *so* loud. 'You're just like your mother. Everything's always gotta be a fight with you, even when I'm just asking a question. What are you doing playing with your gun now of all times? We've got shit to do, László!'

The awareness that László had to do something came like a soothing rain, washing the panic out of him. Once a man got in the habit of hitting kids so hard it knocked their baby teeth out, you could never trust him again. 'I know,' László said, and he didn't know if he was talking to Emil or maybe himself. 'You said we gotta clean, so I'm cleaning. You always put the work order in the ceiling over your bed.'

He had to shout to be heard, but his voice was calm.

Not wild, like Irén. She wasn't a hunter, or even a good shot. Too impatient.

His father cursed again and reached toward the hidden compartment in the wood panelled ceiling. László adjusted his grip on the rifle to get his finger on the trigger guard. The work order that Davik gave him appeared out of the hidden compartment. Emil looked at the papers just long enough to read the name —

'Davik Kaine? You've got us working for Davik fucking Kaine?'

László stood before his father had time to turn. The pop of the .22 was quiet as far as guns went — it was still loud in the cabin, but it anyone heard it up on the docks, they probably wouldn't even guess it was a gun. Could have been anything, knocking around. A door slamming, loose cargo hitting a wall.

The bullet hit Emil Dargis at the base of the skull, where the back of the head sloped toward the neck, came up through his jaw and sprayed the wall with blood and teeth.

Emil Dargis dropped. He landed face first on his bed and gurgled and twitched, blood running hot and bright into his mattress, soaking right through until it dripped from the underside. The bullet must have opened the big veins and arteries in the neck, 'cause that was a lot of blood. László had bled plenty of pigs like that, just like he told Davik. Open everything up and let the red tide flow.

And Irén watched, her face washed of colour. Her mouth was moving. László's ears rang — the shot echoed in his skull and mixed with the memory of János's screaming and the present roar of the Hive. What was Irén saying?

'What'd you do that for?' A whisper, but loud, raspy, wild, straining to keep quiet while also being heard over the chaos, cutting through the ringing in László's ears. 'Oh fuck, László. What did you do?'

László tossed the rifle onto his bed. There wasn't much

kickback in a .22 but he could still feel it in his hands. It was just like killing a dangerous animal — the same exaltation, the same surge of survival-victory.

He had to lean over his father's body — still twitching, not a corpse yet, still halfway alive — to grab the work order from his father's hand. There was blood on it, soaking into one corner.

Fuck.

Panic snapped through him. He hadn't thought this through. Easy to tell himself that sometimes a predator had to die, but his father was a *man*. This wasn't hunting; this was fucking murder, and he'd done it in the Hive. How was he going to explain the blood on the order?

'Fuck, László,' Irén said, her voice buzzing.

'I'll tell 'em dad had a nosebleed,' László said, as much to himself as to Irén. 'That's why I'm taking over.'

He headed for the stairs. The dockhands would be getting impatient by now and he couldn't have them knocking on the cabin door. He had to get them away from the Hive so they could figure out what the fuck to do next.

Irén caught his arm. 'Wait!'

She pushed her hands into the bucket of water, using it to wipe László's face, his chest. He must have blood on him, blowback from the whole mess of it. Good thing he wasn't wearing a shirt. Blood was easy to clean off skin.

The dockhands didn't look surprised to see him. They looked relieved. He was better at this shit than his father. This was *his* fucking barge, damnit, even if his father's name was on it, it was *his* because he ran it best. The warren of the Hive made an imprint on his mind that he could see like a map when he closed his eyes.

The dockhand took the shipping orders and everything froze up. The dockhand looked at the order, and then at László. At the order again. At László.

'He had a nosebleed,' László said, but his voice was so small he barely heard it himself.

The dockhand said something, but László couldn't

hear over the chaos, over the roaring of his own heartbeat thudding in his ears. László leaned closer.

'Dav wants to see your old man,' the dockhand said. 'We're gonna shuffle you off to the side, send for him.'

'No—' László said.

But there was nothing else to say and no one to say it to. The dockhand jumped off the barge, handed the work order to someone else. They grabbed the ropes that kept the barge in place, using them to haul László's barge through the water and out of the way. Someone else took his place immediately.

The barge slid with the river's current and the dockhands held tight until they were in a part of the Hive that László hadn't seen before. One of the warehouses, boxes everywhere. It wasn't quite as loud here, wasn't quite as wild, but it was still moving. People taking boxes, bringing them out to the docks. People bringing boxes in and setting them aside.

'Just stay out of the way,' the dockhand said. 'And keep your mouth shut. Dav don't have a problem with you. Maybe you can work something out.'

László's mouth moved because he knew he should say something, but nothing came. Maybe he should say he took care of it himself. He tried to follow the deckhand up onto the dock, but the man stepped into the way.

'Just stay there,' the dockhand said. 'And when he comes, keep your mouth shut.'

***

At some point while waiting for something to happen, the stillness left and László's hands started to shake. Not his usual restlessness, but a shake so bad he felt like he was losing control of his body. He sat at the bottom of the stairs down to the cabin, his toes resting at the edge of the bloodstain. Cold and tacky, drying fast in the heat. He pulled all of János's teeth out of his pocket and listened to the seven of them rattle together like dice in his trembling hand, rolling for the gamble of what his future was going to look like.

'You really fucked us this time,' Irén whispered. She had trousers on now, but there was blood on them. On the hems, on the knees. On her bare feet. Fucking blood everywhere. 'What are we going to do?'

László looked at his father's body and the river of red that soaked into the bed, at the teeth scattered around his carcass. One of them was half-rotten with a cavity that must have hurt fucking all the time. If he was an animal carcass, they'd string him up fast so he could drain before his muscles went too stiff to move him around. But he wasn't for meat, and they couldn't move him because the only way out of the cabin was up the stairs, and dock-hands were watching. Waiting for Davik to arrive.

'I'll tell him I took care of it,' László said. 'He was going to do the same thing, right? So, he won't mind that I did it myself. Right?'

'I don't fucking know, László!' Irén snapped. 'I wasn't there! I don't know what he said!'

The cabin door opened and for a horrible second, László looked at his gun and wondered if he could reach it before anything happened. He'd shoot whoever tried to corner them and then they'd get their boat untied and let the current carry them out of here. Fuck this city, they'd go back to the lake where they belonged.

Weight made the third step from the top creak and László turned in time to see Davik come down. He moved slow, like there wasn't anything in the whole world that could make him hurry, and his dark eyes swept over the carnage like he didn't mind much at all. Like he'd seen his fair share of dead bodies, and all the blood that came out of them didn't bother him much anymore.

'Well, shit,' he said.

'We were defending ourselves,' Irén said.

Davik raised an eyebrow at her. 'And shot him in the

back of the head? What were you defending yourself from, exactly? He fart in a way you didn't like?'

Irén's mouth moved the same way László's had when the dockhand said Davik wanted to talk to their father. She wanted to say something but no words seemed right.

'He found out the work order was from you,' László said, trying to sound confident. Like the body didn't bother him much, either, like this was all an unspoken agreement between them and László had done what he was supposed to. 'I didn't want him to pull us out of line, try to get out of the city. You said you were going to take care of it, didn't you? Now you don't have to. I did it.'

'Right,' he said, clapping his hands together. The conversation was over already. 'Swing around south again and I'll meet you at the dry-docks.'

'The dry-docks?' László asked. 'We can't dock at the dry-docks without a work order — and the barge has debt that my father hasn't paid yet. They won't let us on even if we could get —'

'Laddie,' Davik interrupted. 'I appreciate that you know the way of things, yeah? You've only been in Yaelsmuir a few months, but you already know the heartbeat of this place — I like that about you. But there's another way things get done that you ain't been a part of yet, so just listen.'

'Yes sir, Mr. Kaine,' László said, closing his hand around the rudder arm, clenching his other fist around the teeth. He wished he wasn't shaking so much, not in front of Davik. It felt too much like he was showing weakness. 'Down to the dry-docks?'

'Aye, down to the dry-docks,' Davik said. 'When they ask for your work order, just tell 'em Dav sent you.'

'Dav sent us,' Irén repeated.

'Aye, that's right. No more of that Mr. Kaine shit — only my enemies call me Mr. Kaine. You can call me Dav since we're in business now.'

'Since when are we in business together?' Irén cut in.

Davik only smiled. 'Well, Miss Dargis, I could leave you to take care of this mess yourself if you'd rather. I'll send for the patrol, tell 'em the thing you said about defending yourself. Maybe if you cry a bunch before they get here, they'll feel sorry for you and ignore the fact one of you shot him in the back of the head. You could go upriver if you like, dump his body over the edge, but then what? How are you going to work? How you gonna eat? And then when you show up without him, people are going to start whispering about you. Wondering what happened. Or, if you've the stomach for it, you can let me take the credit.'

'Take the credit?' László asked. 'Why?'

Davik shrugged. 'My loads were light. I don't stand for anyone pinching product from me.'

'So you get to look tough, and I get to pretend I didn't do anything,' László said. 'Won't people want to know why I'm doing business with you if you've killed my father?'

'That assumes people think your father is a man worthy of your loyalty, laddie,' Davik said. 'You'll find pretty quickly that people don't think that.'

László turned to Irén. She was the smarter of the two of them, was better at seeing consequences that would never occur to him. Her eyes were red-rimmed from the crying, her face was drenched with sweat, and her mouth—a perfect copy of their mother's mouth—was turned into her tired frown. But all in all, she looked calm.

'We don't do shit for free,' Irén said. 'We work for wages. We can keep running the barge if you want, or we'll rent it to your people so they can run it. You're going to tell us what you're paying before you ask us to do anymore *favours*.'

Davik grinned. 'I see you're the negotiator of the family.'

Irén lifted her chin, her eyes going flinty and hard. 'Someone's gotta take care of this idiot. He trusts too much.'

Davik offered her a hand, those tattoos and scars all stretched out toward her. 'It's going to be a pleasure doing business with you, Miss Dargis.'

***

When László said *Dav sent me*, all the doubt and question and stern glares disappeared. People nodded and their faces went rigid and they spoke just enough to give László directions. Irén and László climbed off their barge, but lingered to watch, tied to that boat with their awareness that it was the only home they had. The dry-dock crew dragged the barge up and water sluiced down out of the bilge. Was it László's imagination, or did the bilge water look like blood?

They smuggled Emil's body down to the Bucket, where someone was waiting with a rope. László watched them tie his ankles together and haul his corpse up into the air, so that he swung from the sign over the Bucket like a hanging hog. Set to finish bleeding and to age the meat, except it was too hot for any of that. Instead, he dripped on the street and the sun baked down on him, promising to turn his body rotten and vile before the sun went down. Flies were already collecting in the wreckage where his face used to be.

Someone stepped out of the public house and froze, staring as the body swung in the sluggish, stagnant summer air. Since the sign wasn't directly over the door, people could come and go without being dripped on. But shit if it wasn't a wild fucking sight, seeing that body hanging there. And Davik standing with his hands on his hips, looking up at it like it was a piece of fine art that he was damned proud to own.

'Well, shit,' the patron said, swiping a hand over his face. 'Who's that, then?'

'Emil Dargis,' Davik said. 'Served him his eviction

notice from the Bay.'

The patron nodded like it was the most natural thing in the world. 'Sure.'

Was there something broken in László, that he looked up at his father's body and the spectacle Davik made of it, and he didn't feel any shame? And maybe László should have been afraid of Davik Kaine, and his too-smart, too-hungry eyes, who said things like '*I don't stand for anyone pinching product off my loads.*' But also didn't look surprised that László had taken care of it, like it was the seed Davik had planted on purpose in László's head. Like he'd wanted László to do the dirty part, the pulling the trigger part, so he could hoist Emil up for the city to see and keep Irén and László close as kids that would do what they were told.

But for now, that feeling didn't sink in. Just like before, he was back to being suspended in the water, held by something familiar. He had all of János's baby teeth in his pocket, but he left his father's teeth in the barge for the folks at the dry-docks to clean up.

He kept the bullet casing, though. He'd figure out a way to put it on his necklace so he'd always remember the first time he killed a man that needed killing.

TOES
THE TOE TAKER

By
BA Bellec

The raucous chatter of hundreds of villagers is over-whelmed by the smell of oil-soaked hay emanating from the centre of a courtyard. The night air is chilly and blankets the crowd which seems impervious to the recent temperature drop.

'Burn her!' shouts a man from a few rows back. The crowd roars in agreement and a few of the village folk go as far as to lob rocks at a young woman bound to a wooden stake by thick, tight rope. This beautiful woman, no older than twenty-five, wears her defeat by not ac-knowledging the rocks bouncing off her arms and legs.

Nausea inducing vapours burn her nostrils from the hay that surrounds her and is ready to ignite. The court-yard is dark save for the torches scattered through the crowd. A church is in the background and the majestic holy cross on the roof catches enough of the flicker to glow orange against the black sky.

'Silence!' barks a commanding man dressed in expen-sive white clothing. He stands above the crowd on an elevated wooden platform just a few metres away from the young woman.

'We have gathered here to bring punishment to the heretic.' He points to the bound woman. The crowd hoots and those with torches elevate them, the flames dancing in the night. Both the man's hands raise to calm the crowd and catch their attention again.

'We will not tolerate this *behaviour* in our village.' He emphasises the word behaviour by raising his voice and drawing out the inflection, speaking down at this woman bound to the stake. As he finishes the sentence, he takes a step back, signalling over to one of the village folk holding a torch.

'Any last words?' utters the authoritarian man in a low, deliberate voice.

She remains silent.

The torch is tossed into the hay. Smoke billows, burning her eyes and filling her lungs. She squirms to shelter her face or catch a lungful of clean air, but the ropes are expertly tied and impossible to loosen. She has no choice but to shut her eyes and hope this doesn't last long.

Shutting her eyes brings a hint of moisture back and gives her temporary relief from the burning, a tiny victory in a dire situation. With darkness obscuring her vision, her other senses heighten. The bitter, dry smoke is inescapable as her lungs and tongue are overwhelmed by the thick, sooty particles and oil gives the smoke a wretched flavour. The temperature rises, and she feels sweat begin to bead on her legs as the flames kiss off her shoes. Her toes tingle as the heat increases. The hay crackles. An instant later, the oil accelerant kicks in and ignites the tame black gown they dressed her in as well as the wooden stake she is anchored to. The inferno blankets her. Her flesh begins to crackle like a pig on a spit. It brings an unbearable pain as every receptor in her brain fires to try and offset the assault.

Then a new smell catches her attention. Sulphur. It's

her hair. She loves her hazelnut hair. She doesn't want to think about the strands that are sizzling beneath her nose, but she can't not think about them. A moment of panic sets in. This is the end. No one is going to stop this. Her hair and her body will burn to a crisp right here in the middle of the town with everyone watching.

Her brain is doing the best it can to process her inevitable end, but it can only mitigate a fraction of the damage this group of misguided fools has unleashed. Her skin splits like an overcooked sausage. She doesn't see it happen, she feels it. The heat and pain move from the exterior to the interior. She digs deep trying to find her last bit of resolve and keep herself together, but she can't hold her breath a moment longer.

This beautiful woman wails into the night with an ear-piercing scream that causes more than a few people in the crowd to cover their ears and all but reaffirms their suspicions as a scream like that could only come from a witch. The crowd watches with satisfaction at a job well done as the poor woman sizzles in the bonfire.

***

Two Days Earlier
Multiple blocks of firewood pop and crackle inside a black cast-iron oven. The embers at the core glow white-hot. The intense heat funnels to a grilled rack above where a dozen scones sit in an ancient well-seasoned baking pan. Off to the right, on a wooden chair used as a temporary table, sits a pan of raw dough. To the left, on the table, are three more pans bursting with golden buns that are cooling. Everything glows in the warm afternoon sunlight. Most of the kitchen has been replaced over the last two years as Mary prioritised anything that could improve her baking, but the rest of this creaky, wood-framed farmhouse is crumbling into near ruin. Her home of two decades could collapse under a stiff breeze. She

doesn't care all that much. Making her sugary treats is her everything.

Mary's grey, curly hair bounces like her apron as she operates her makeshift assembly line. Baking makes her feel twenty years younger, like that spry farm girl she used to be. As time and age crept up on her, she started making her treats once a week. The day after she bakes is the weekly market in the town square. Every person in the region knows that Mary and her morsels will be there come Saturday. Her routine is as predictable as the sun. She gets that from her husband, God bless his tender soul.

She pokes at the pan with a steel tong to check the crust. Nine minutes, just like the last batch, and the one before that, and every batch she has ever made in this kitchen. Not ten minutes. Nine. Exactly. With her other hand deep inside a thick, wool mitten, she grabs the lip of the tray, pulling the succulent baked delight from the oven.

'Perfect!'

They are always perfect. Mary never gets the recipe wrong and if anyone complains, it has nothing to do with Mary or her recipe. Mary knows what she knows, and she knows these buns are always damn perfect.

'Thomas, come help me.'

After a pause, she remembers her husband, Thomas, is gone. Sometimes she forgets that he passed away two years ago. After two years, you would think new habits would form, but some routines are so deeply ingrained they never change. She always used to chat with Thomas on baking day. She misses their conversations and his quick wit. The sad realisation she is talking to herself again sets in, something that has become more common these last few months, along with sleepwalking. More than once she found herself waking up in the kitchen or on the porch.

Once she pulls out this batch, she takes a seat. The room blurs which she knows is a sign she is overworking herself. The blurry vision is something new, she doesn't remember exactly when it started, but it was probably more than a month ago, which was when the hours of standing and baking started to give her trouble, often leaving her feet tingling and the room spinning.

After a brief rest, she gets back at it, finishing off the last few trays. The baking is only step one. She spends the next two hours melting rich, creamy butter and slathering it all over every plump bun. Each brush of butter is followed by a sprinkle of tantalising cinnamon. The final step is the secret weapon. On the top of the stove is what made the village folks refer to this delight as Mary's Magnificent Morsels.

The white sugary glaze consists of yet more butter, five times as much as she'd used in the other steps. To that she adds a glass of milk and an entire bag of the finest sugar she can find. She is always flabbergasted that the simple concoction seems to mesmerise people. Perhaps it is the hidden sprinkle of cinnamon that she specially orders from one of the wagon trains, or maybe it is the fact that many folks don't have access to butter like Mary does. The local dairy farmer was Thomas's best friend and has been providing her butter for next to nothing since Thomas died. She has easily quadrupled her consumption these last few years. Whatever the reason, these treats are the talk of the community and Mary's Magnificent Morsels won everyone's hearts, elevating Mary to royalty amongst this tight-knit group.

Not long after Thomas died, Mary's home had fallen into a state of neglect and rot. Their only son left for the city. He wanted to make it big in banking and he was doing well for himself because every few months an envelope of money would show up for Mary. Enough to keep the bills paid and park a few dollars for her inventory needs. Outside of the money, Mary has little contact with him these days. Perhaps she is too nosey and the money is his way of keeping her out of his business. At least she has the village. They are always the most supportive part of her life and more like her family than anyone in her actual family. Good church-going folks who would drop what they are doing to help anyone in the community.

Besides the occasional envelope, baking has become her sole source of revenue. Every week on Saturday she sells the entire lot and then uses the proceeds to hire young men from the square who would tend to the farm or bring her supplies. Sometimes the men will stay rather late and then sneak across the field to visit the only other house in the area. Good help is hard to find and she ignores what she views as a minor weakness they can't control. *After all, it isn't their fault they had fallen under a witch's spell.*

As she finishes her weekly baking, she moves to her nightly indulgence. What is the point of making delicious treats if you don't partake in them? One batch always stays behind. Not only that, but this is a special batch and she doubles the sugary glaze. The first bun is always the best. It takes some time for the glaze to cool but while she waits, she finishes the cleaning. Near sundown, she grabs a knife and then makes her way over to the wooden picnic-style kitchen table where the pans sits. The farmhouse is small and only has three rooms: kitchen, bathroom, and bedroom. However, it does have a gorgeous deck out front. She spends most of her free time sipping a drink and watching the waves of wind in the miles of corn and wheat fields that surround her home.

Once she knives the first bun out from the pan, she sits it on a plate near the window and busies herself at the stove boiling water and fixing a cup. No bun is complete without a cup of tea, three spoons of honey, as always. She prepares a second bun and starts to plate it but when she looks at the porch, Thomas's bun from yesterday, or maybe it was Wednesday, still sits, congealed and covered in flies, a reminder that Thomas is gone. She places the second bun back into the pan and discards yesterday's bun too.

Mary brings the tea over and looks out the window at the beautiful dusk rays of sunlight dancing on the field. Across the field and down in the golden valley is a wagon road and today, like most days, the last wagon is racing the sun, trying to get into the village while the light is still friendly. Wagons are prevalent in this area as this was one of the main throughways — at least five or six a day, all of them bringing rumours with them. Something supernatural is going on in nearby Salem.

Mary watches the horse-drawn wagon vanish into the horizon as she eats her freshly baked delight and ponders the secondhand stories of satanism she has heard. Her mouth waters. She's eaten hundreds of buns and still, the flavour never gets old. Thomas kept telling her to lay off the sweets but with him gone, she has only increased her intake, replacing the hole in her heart with food.

By the end of her bun and tea, dusk has turned to dark. Way over the land and on an adjacent hilltop sits her lone neighbour. Mary's house isn't in great shape, but her neighbour's house has fallen into disarray with shingles falling off and wooden shutters dangling at strange angles. The grass has overgrown in most of the yard and is easily the height of the deck Mary sits on right now. The rats have taken to living in the field and Mary has seen more and more of them making their way over to her plot these last few months. It all started after Thomas died, because around that time so too did Mr. and Mrs. Smith. Where Thomas was just old, the death of the Smiths is rather suspicious and involved an illness while on vacation, allegedly. The details never really emerged, and the community was left to create their own story about the mysterious surviving daughter who now lives there alone.

Mary didn't care all that much about what happened as she wasn't fond of the Smiths. It all went back to a dispute five years earlier. The Smiths started to complain Mary and Thomas's farm was draining a stream on the

Smith property and impacting their irrigation. A ridiculous accusation as the Smiths had just moved in and they used this stream as an excuse to try and blame Thomas for their failing crops and lack of farming knowledge. The relationship had stayed sour after that with nothing more than the cursory acknowledgements.

When they died, their estate was passed down to an alleged 'uncle', but no one in the village had seen this person, nor heard of him before the passing. The situation seemed rather 'convenient' for Elizabeth, their adult daughter, who, by the way, has never been to market or church. At first, Mary felt sorry for her. That poor thing was raised by a pair of nearly feral humans and now she was alone. But as the time passed, Mary came to realise the apple doesn't fall far from the tree and the antisocial, undomesticated habits of the Smith parents had passed on to their girl. Mary's feelings of sorrow turned into doubt and scepticism — maybe Elizabeth was behind it all. The death of her parents. The invisible uncle. Thomas, who was of good health suddenly passing. If this is true, Mary has to stop her. What could come next might be even worse than some spat about the stream. *Could Elizabeth try to poison me?* Maybe she has already started. Mary stops and thinks about her supply chain for the morsels. *The butter!* Elizabeth could be poisoning the butter. She could easily be doing it at night because the entire village and all the surrounding farms have no security. *That has to be what she is up to.* Mary looks at her current batch of morsels. She thinks about not selling them for a moment, but the bills need to get paid.

When Thomas died, Mary tried to talk to Elizabeth, but that woman was a creature of the night, never waking before midday and rarely making public appearances during daylight. In addition, a steady stream of wagons and farmhands seemed to make late-night visits. Mary has no proof, but with all the Salem rumours swirling she is almost certain Elizabeth is into something dark and twisted over there. Mary knows what she knows, and she knows Elizabeth is up to no good.

That Elizabeth and her red voracious lips, lush hazelnut hair, supple plump breasts, and a round bottom that melted the best of them couldn't be trusted. Plus, there was the mint green dress. It is not a common colour. Most of the women in the community wore black or white. Those are the traditional colours. The mint green seems to only add to the allure and she might as well have been naked as anyone could see all her womanly curves as that dress was far too tight to be acceptable for public wearing. Elizabeth had most of the young men of the night bending to her will, but Mary saw through the façade. The voluptuous attire is a distraction and it isn't the only flag. Elizabeth also seems to be the only person around not interested in Mary's Magnificent Morsels. Mary cannot fathom why or how someone would turn down her sweets, unless, perhaps, they know something everyone else doesn't know, like they are poison. Mary's other worry is the frequency of these occult rituals seems to be increasing with a nightly raucous ruckus becoming normal. The whipping leather, strange chanting, and uncontrolled moaning has woken Mary many a time and Mary values her sleep just about as much as her baked goods. More than once she considered grabbing the rolling pin and making her way over to put a stop to the madness.

As the moon starts to make an appearance, Mary hobbles her way to bed. Her old bones and aching feet could barely handle a day of baking, and it is only getting worse by the week. She fluffs the pillow and tightens the blanket before falling into the relaxing place where Thomas greets her with a smile and they can talk for hours. The feeling of crawling into bed after an honest day in front of the oven always has her blissfully snoring within minutes.

The next morning, she gathers her supplies and one of the other vendors stops by to help her get into the square and setup her table. It isn't long until people from the neighbouring communities start to flood in. This is one of the best markets in the region after all, maybe because word of Mary's Magnificent Morsels has begun to travel.

'I indubitably say that I unequivocally must admit your morsels are perhaps the most exquisite thing I have consumed since I set up my operations in your region,' Doctor Brown proclaims after savouring his first bite of the day, but probably his hundredth morsel in the last two years. His monocle catches the sun and shimmers almost like it is winking on his behalf. Mary glows from the praise. The stone courtyard in the village is surrounded by a church, a few shops, a pub, and the horse and wagon pen. The people, about fifty from the farmland scattered throughout the region, scurry about like ants purchasing their weekly supplies. Her popup table in the square is down to the last few Magnificent Morsels and it isn't even lunchtime yet. The people knew, if you want to get a bun at the weekly Saturday farmer's market, you have to get one early!

'Say, when is the last time you had yourself a physical, my dear? You are not getting any younger and I am sure with Thomas out of the picture, you could use someone to keep your health in check now and then,' says Doctor Brown, brow furrowed.

'Out of the question! I am fine.' Mary begins busying herself stacking the empty pans and trying to hide her limp. Mary knows what she knows, and Mary knows she doesn't need a doctor. 'I haven't had a physical in ten years and outside of a little toe pain now and then, there ain't nothing wrong with old Mary!'

A lie. Her toes have been in rough shape. So rough she hasn't been paying much attention to them these last few days, instead taking the path of stubborn ignorance. Plus, her pudge has increased significantly over the last year. This toe pain greatly reduced the amount of walking she could do, but she would die before she admitted her body might be failing. Besides baking, Mary has another skill she has mastered, and that is keeping her problems well hidden. There isn't a person in town who has seen her limp for more than a moment, and no one knows about her dementia, fainting spells, sleepwalking, or conversations with Thomas. Mary hides these things and even tricks herself into believing she is a decade younger.

'Besides, Thomas was big into doctors and health,' Mary continues with a stern look in her eyes. 'Look where that got him!'

'I didn't mean to offend, and please, feel free to engage my services at any time. I am just a concerned onlooker and I am happy to make house calls. Note that I do accept tasty treats in lieu of coin,' chuckles the doctor. 'We wouldn't want to see our dear Mary fall upon tough times.'

Doctor Brown smiles and bows his head in respect to Mary before making his way to another vendor. A stranger stands a few tables over and scans the various goods for sale while wearing a sharp suit and top hat. As he approaches Mary, she can smell the overgenerous application of some type of expensive bergamot spray all over his clothing. The reek of a sleazy salesman.

'I have been watching the people of this village and these sweets are a special treat. Have you thought about selling them on a larger scale?' remarks the citrus-scented man while a cheeky smile starts in the corner of his mouth. 'I know a few men back in the big city. They could take your idea to every major city in the area and set up a wagon supply chain with two or three more bakers. You could be moving thousands of buns every week. You could be making hundreds of dollars a day!'

Mary's breath quickens and her words escape her. She hates being put on the spot like this, especially by some young whippersnapper who doesn't know who she is or what this community is about.

'You leave old Mary alone!' The voice sharp and piercing, as always. Gossiping Gertrude, Mary's friend, and the queen of gossip in the region, has noticed the stranger and storms her way over with a raised fist. 'Her morsels are not just common bread! You need Mary to make Mary's Magnificent Morsels. How dare you imply you could do it without her. This isn't snake oil!'

Gossiping Gertrude shoes the young businessman away and helps Mary pack the last of her things. Mary, like always, expertly hides her toe pain and the brain fog that had just come over her from the stress of the ordeal.

'There, there, Mary. Don't you worry about those big city folk. We won't let them get a piece of you.'

Mary smiles and accepts the kindness. Gertrude dressed indistinguishably from the other women in blacks and whites, and despite being twenty years younger than Mary, she is happy to embrace any member of the community willing to listen to her gossip.

Gertrude pipes up again, 'Did you hear about Ted's cows?'

'No. What happened to Ted?'

Mary always pays Ted on Saturday for next week's butter. It is her way of budgeting. Buy the butter, then budget for her secret weapon, the cinnamon. She has a special way of getting the cinnamon that she dare not reveal for fear of someone trying to duplicate her recipe. Cinnamon is rare, after all, and required an order months in advance. After those two things, the rest of her supplies come easy and she can spend the rest of the leftover funds on day-to-day living and food. Ted hasn't stopped by which is peculiar and put her next batch of morsels in jeopardy.

'Rumour has it, two of his cows were pulled from the barn and eaten to the bone, then left in a pool of blood and organs with flesh scattered about. People have been talking. They say it sounds like one of them satanic rituals. Someone even said they saw a pentagram in the field. I don't know if that part is true. What do you think?'

Mary always thought—in fact, she knows—witchcraft

has been happening in these parts for months. Little things like this cow are just the tip of the iceberg.

'Remember when the chickens went missing a few weeks back?' interjects Mary.

Gertrude tilts her head up as the shock of the connections jars her. 'That's right. I forgot about that. You think they are connected?'

Mary nods. 'I think I know who did it. In fact, Mary knows what Mary knows, and Mary knows these events are too similar to not be connected. You know my neighbour, right? The Smith house.'

Gertrude sighs.

'Exactly,' says Mary. 'That daughter of theirs that took over the farm. She is up to no good. This is all connected to her. It has to be.'

'Do you think her parents disappearing is connected to Salem?' Gertrude ponders.

'It could be. I even think that Smith girl might have had something to do with my dear Thomas passing. I just can't prove it.'

'I never did care for the Smiths. All we asked of them was that they come out to market and church once a week. It's really not that hard. Who knows what they taught that daughter of theirs and God forbid she learned the ways of the occult. If she is performing some ritual, I know me and about a dozen other people would put an end to it. We can't have an incident like Salem in our village. You have to get out in front of these things.' Gertrude chuckles. 'We will do what we need to do. It's for the good of the community, don't you know?'

Mary responds, 'I couldn't agree more!'

They gossip for a good twenty minutes, looping in a few other vendors on their theory of a witch in the area before they move on to the next row of tables. And the next. They spend the rest of the day talking to people. The other part of the farmer's market that Mary loves is the gossip. She didn't get out much, so the faster she sold her treats, the more time she could spend gossiping. She often would get a dinner invite from one of the other wives at the market, usually Gertrude. Today was no exception. By the time everything wraps, she finds herself at Gertrude's dinner table with night creeping across the land. After a long day of standing, talking, and eating, one of the young men from town helps her back to the farm as the light fades. He aids her in storing her vendor table and the empty baking pans that would need cleaning before he is paid with one of Mary's special batch buns. The ones she doesn't sell to the public.

Of course, no day is complete without a bun and a cup of tea for herself. Three spoons of honey, as always. Mary carefully brings the cup of tea over and looks out the window, a rat scurries across her porch and gives her a chill. *That damn Smith woman and her derelict home!* Once Mary gets her wits back she watches the young man ride his horse-drawn wagon into the horizon and back into the village. By the end of her bun and tea the moon starts to make an appearance, and Mary hobbles to bed. Friday baking left her stiff and exhausted. The Saturday market didn't give her a moment to recover. She dresses in her white nighty and fluffs the pillow before crawling into bed and tightening the blanket. It isn't long until Thomas greets her with a smile. They chat for hours on the deck eating buns and sipping tea with their perfectly maintained farm surrounding them. The field is in full bloom, golden wheat dances in the wind with daisies and dandelions lining the sides of the road. The sky is peppered with sparse fluffy white clouds and the spring air is enchanting when combined with the fresh buns still emanating from the table on the deck.

WA-PEESH!

Mary's eyes open wide. Her beautiful dream abruptly ends. The glowing sun and bright blue sky are gone. Instead, a touch of moonlight illuminates the wooden beams of the ceiling. The sound of leather on flesh is unmistakable and still echoing through her brain.

'Thomas, that damn neighbour is at it again!'

WA-PEESH! — the sound is followed by the muted moans of a young man. The whole ordeal is happening across the field and up on the hill in that damn Smith house. They are not being overly loud, but in the night, the sound travels.

'What is she up to now…' Mary mutters, forgetting she is alone when she isn't in her dreams. There is silence. Mary relaxes and tries to find peace. If she is lucky she will find Thomas again. After a few more restless minutes, she resorts to counting sheep. That blue sky of her dreams comes back and clouds morph to grow sheep-like legs and heads. The sheep-clouds float by and Mary keeps counting them. Two. Three. Four. They aren't moving fast. Each passing minute brings a new cloud. Five. Six… her body becomes light and her mind drifts. It's peaceful and serene, maybe her favourite place. She sees Thomas, but before she can say anything —

WA-PEESH!

'Alright!'

Mary springs from bed as quickly as someone her age can. Her legs crack as she stands, stiff, but she feels energised with a purpose that makes all her pain and problems go away. *It is time to put an end to this incessant madness.* This is the last dream Mary is going to lose to Elizabeth.

She storms to the kitchen and looks out the window. In the dead of night and with a trickle of moonlight, it is almost impossible to see through the fog that has rolled in. A woman moans in pleasure. The sounds are faint, but it acts like a dagger in Mary's ears maddening her further.

'She is up to her witchcraft again!' Mary sneers.

The rolling pin sits on the table and Mary picks it up, slapping the heaviest part against her palm.

Hurricane Mary storms out the front door, slippers and her white nightgown still adorned, and the rolling pin wielded with enough anger to match the fire in her eyes. She grabs a lantern with her free hand and begins fighting the fog. The walk across the field is no easy trek and the whole while she has to tolerate the moans and whips that serenade the night.

By the time she makes the road, she can see the silhouette of the other house on the hill breaking the fog. A lone window is visible and lights are flickering, almost as if a room is full of burning candles. Short on breath and having begun to sweat through her nightie, Mary pauses to gather herself at the long winding private dirt drive leading to Elizabeth's dilapidated house. Mary looks at the door and sees it is open a sliver; the flicker of the candles even more obvious now that she is closer. *Maybe this is a bad idea.* Maybe she should just go back to bed. Maybe this is all a misunderstanding.

WA-PEESH!!! This time there is extra mustard on it. Being so close brings subtle noises with it she hasn't heard before.

A man's voice trembles, 'Pleee-eese stop!'
WA-PEESH! WA-PEESH! WA-PEESH!

'I will tell you when it's time to stop!' commands Elizabeth. Mary grasps her rolling pin and charges the door shouldering it open as if she is a young farm girl again. *This is the end of Elizabeth's façade.* Mary darts in and is confronted by an odour not all that different from a rotting animal left in the sun.

The smell moves to the back burner in her mind because what she sees is appalling enough to make her forget everything else. On an X-shaped wooden cross hangs one of the young men she saw that day on the wagon trail. He is restrained with leather straps on his wrists, ankles, and neck. Naked, save for a white cloth stuffed in his mouth and tied around the back of his head to keep it in place. His stomach and chest are lashed too many times to count. Blood drips and pools on the floor from all the slices.

He looks at Mary and motions her to run with what little movement he can muster. *Coming here WAS a mistake.* A wave of dread wraps around her lungs and steals her breath. Mary turns, rolling pin in attack position, but someone has locked the door behind her.

She looks down.

Her white nightgown shimmers from a combination of moonlight and candle flickers. The candles are on the ground, twelve of them forming a star. The house is shadowy, but there is enough light to make out the white pentagram painted on the floorboards. Mary hadn't realised until now, but she stands in the middle of these candles. That breath-stealing dread turns to full-blown paralysis. An animalistic, hellish, guttural clicking comes from the darkness. Mary trembles. She feels like prey.

The clicking continues, sending shivers down Mary's spine. She is frozen in place holding the rolling pin above her head, breathing still evasive in her state of panic. The man on the wooden cross whimpers something but Mary can't make out the words.

WA-PEESH!

A tail as long as the room whips out. It's black and smooth with a slime and sheen that glistens. The tail wraps around Mary's torso. She throws the rolling pin into the darkness and hears it clunk off the wooden wall missing its target. Another round of clicking emanates as Mary is pulled into the dark by this tail, inch by inch.

She fights and squirms, but the tail is too strong for her. As a last-ditch effort, she tries to bite it, but a few of her teeth break and she feels fine bits of tooth floating around in her mouth like sand. The tail is solid as a rock and with her teeth shattered, the taste of tin from the blood coats her tongue.

HUMPHF! Whatever the tail belongs to snorts from the shadows.

Suddenly, Mary's arms and legs are bound to a wooden cross, the tail still holding her as well. Then a white cloth is put in her mouth and secured from behind, much like the cloth she had just seen on the man. She is looking across the dark, shadowy room at the other cross where this dying man hangs.

'Please! Stop!' begs Mary through the cloth with the last of the air her lungs had saved between the bouts of panic. The words come out a muffled, jumbled mess. Someone behind the cross holds the straps even tighter.

'Release…'

Mary recognises Elizabeth's voice even though she can't see Elizabeth. Before Mary can react, the tail releases Mary and the beast emerges from the shadows. It tilts its head to the side in a primal way that elicits a whimper from Mary.

The monster stalks forward, with each step the house shakes. The beast's body is smooth and black and shimmers in the candlelight. Instead of a face, a series of layered beetle-like shells form a helmet with a few sharp rows of needle teeth jutting from the bottom of what might serve as a jaw. The same layered shells cover most of its body to protect its vital places, almost like Arthurian armour. The beast stands nearly as tall as the room and the tail is twice as long. On the end of the tail is a spade, presumably sharp as an arrow. The tail swings gracefully and controlled like a common house cat, but that spade could be used to kill at any moment.

It reaches a four-taloned claw toward Mary. The razor-sharp ends drip with slime. It operates the talons with tender precision, coddling Mary's foot and removing her slippers.

That's when Mary realises the man on the other side of the room has no toes. They seem to have been chewed, flesh from bone. A few ligaments dangle amongst the blanket of blood.

The beast doesn't eat, though. It holds Mary's foot. Examining it while awaiting its master's orders. A tongue, forked like a snake's tongue, appears. It licks the sweat from between Mary's toes and seems to enjoy the taste.

'KAAAAA KA-KA KA KAAA!'

The cackle sounds like it might belong to Elizabeth, but something is different about it. There is more menace, like something sinister is fuelling the laugh. The beast retracts its tongue and moves back to the shadows, keeping its head cocked to the side while facing Mary. Its breathing resembles purring. As it moves away, the source of the high-pitched cackle is revealed to indeed be Elizabeth as she emerges from behind Mary. Her skin is old, dry, and wrinkled. Her face, saggy. Her hazelnut hair, gone. Instead, a few grey wispy strands hang to her shoulders. Elizabeth looks twice as old as Mary. It is hard to make her out, but the shape and height are right, this is absolutely Elizabeth.

A shrill voice, different from the normal voice Elizabeth has, barks, 'You couldn't keep to yourself, could you!'

Mary knew Elizabeth was a witch all along. *Why didn't I expose the truth sooner?* It is far too late now. Mary squirms but there is no way she is beating the leather straps that hold her. Elizabeth smiles and leans closer. The candlelight catches her face to reveal ear-to-ear vicious teeth barely different from the beast's and a jaw that seems able to unhinge.

'I can't stand nosey neighbours. They chased me from Copenhagen. Then Salem. Now you.' The words crawl from her mouth. 'You know you can't stop me. I'm going to be young and beautiful again. I always find a way. That sparkle I have doesn't come cheap. The cost is people like you: nosey neighbours.'

The witch places the tips of her fingers on her wrinkled cheeks and gives her cheeks a slow pass.

'You are not the first to try to ruin my plans. I am still here… still strong… and lucky for me, I have a new assistant.'

The witch rubs her cheek against the slimy back of the

beast.

'KAAAAA KA-KA KA KAAA!' cackles the witch.

Mary thinks about screaming, but she knows no one is close enough to hear. She thinks about trying to fight, but even if she was lucky enough to escape, that monster would split her in two before she could so much as take a step. Instead, Mary watches as the witch drags a cauldron to the centre of the room, it glows blue and tiny bubbles simmer to the top before bursting. *Mary must be dreaming.* It's the only explanation. She retraces her steps in her mind trying to figure out how she got here. She was in her room. She was sleeping. The sheep-clouds were there. It was the middle of a spring day. *Oh no, that sheep-dream was in the middle of the day. This is night.* 'I am in a nightmare,' blurts Mary having accidentally vocalised a thought.

The witch dances around the cauldron. She is having the time of her life torturing these helpless people. She commands the room like Mary when Mary makes her morsels.

'Let us see. The toes of an innocent man.'

The witch looks across the room at the man.

'KAAAAA KA-KA KA KAAA!'

She makes a checkmark in the air and pirouettes around the pentagram before tossing a toe to her beast. It snaps it from the air like a dog. The witch then drops the rest into her cauldron. The glow changes from blue to aquamarine and the bubbles change from simmer to roaring boil.

'The toes of a father forgotten.'

She rummages in her pocket and pulls a small jar with a wooden cork. She carefully pops off the top and sprinkles the contents into the radiant blueish-green stew that emits vapours that seem acidic enough to remove paint from a wall. The witch pirouettes again, making a check mark with her free hand as the busier hand places the jar off to the side. It dawns on Mary that the remains of Mr.

Smith could have just been sprinkled into the cauldron. *Or was it Thomas?*

'Oh, and how could we forget...'

The witch turns to Mary. Elizabeth's eyes roll back and the unsettling whites of the back of her eyeballs are pleasant compared to what Mary sees when the witch opens her mouth wide. The razor-sharp teeth that could belong to a shark seem to grow in length and her jaw unhinges to open that extra few inches that pass the uncanny valley beyond what humans are capable of.

'The toes of a nosey neighbour!'

It's not the beast that is going to eat my toes, it's Elizabeth!

The witch glides forward, no longer walking. Her mouth opens wider and wider. Mary braces as the teeth close in.

CRUNCH! CRUNCH! CRUNCH!

Mary screams but the cloth in her mouth keeps her quiet. After another round of squirming under the straps, Mary accepts she is going to die and not by poisoning, no. Mary is going to die in an occult ritual. Elizabeth munches and sucks, spitting a few toes out before cannibalising her way through the others until only a few raw, bloody nubs remain. Mary fades in and out of consciousness. Elizabeth spits a toe into the cauldron and stirs. The chemical reaction sends fist-sized bubbles into the air and Elizabeth dips the spoon into her concoction and then ladles a mouthful. As Mary fades to black she witnesses this old, wrinkled version of Elizabeth shimmer like a diamond in the light as her skin turns one hundred years younger in an instant.

A rooster crows snapping Mary awake.

'Lord Jesus, what was that, Thomas?'

Mary sits up in bed. She is talking to herself again. Her memory is a hazy mess and her vision is blurry. She reaches her hand to her pillow and both her blanket and her pillow are soaked in sweat. That horrible toe incident was just a dream, and a strange one at that. There is no way that monster or witch is real. Mary knows what Mary knows, and Mary knows that couldn't have been real.

'Thank you. Thank you. Thank you.'

She pats her heart, grateful it was just a hallucination and her vision starts to clear, revealing the morning sun's glow.

A knock at the door.

'Mary, are you in there? It is time to get ready for church.' Gossiping Getrude's voice is unmistakable.

Mary tries to stand but the room spins and a sharp sting in her toes sends her toppling to the ground. They ache like never before. *Maybe it wasn't a dream.* She can't even put weight on them. *This can't be.* Another knock.

Mary writhes and manages to crawl along the bedroom floor, dirtying her sweaty nightgown. The sun is out. It's morning. Perhaps even a few hours into the day. She makes it to the door and unlatches it, barely able to muster the strength. She hates revealing her dire situation. Her dementia. Her toes. *Everything I have been hiding is about to be exposed... unless...*

'Help.' Mary quivers the words from the floor while laying behind the door.

'What's wrong?'

Mary doesn't answer. Gertrude opens the door and finds Mary sprawled across the floor. She helps her to a chair and gets her a glass of water. After a few moments to gather her thoughts, Mary gasps in a tremulous voice, 'I think the neighbour, that Elizabeth Smith woman, is a witch.'

'We talked about this yesterday,' returns the perplexed Gertrude. Her hands dropping to her hips.

'I had a dream. Or maybe it wasn't a dream. Elizabeth had a pet demon as tall as the room. And there was blood. So much blood. And the man,' Mary rants. 'They were going to kill him if he wasn't dead already. They were taking our toes and using them in a ritual. Go. Investigate. It's the house across the field. Please. And then bring the doctor for me.'

'Okay. Let's get you to bed. We'll take care of everything. Just relax.'

Mary smiles and nods, having found the perfect alibi to hide both her dementia and toe problem. It just so happens Mary had planted the seed at the market. If anyone else came to the door, this story might not have worked, but it was Gertrude, and Gertrude would go along with it. Mary knows what Mary knows, and Mary knows Gertrude would go along with her story.

Gertrude helps Mary limp to the bedroom, then refills the cup of water and sets it on the night table, leaving Mary to rest in bed.

'Stay safe and try to relax. I will be back in a flash.'

Sometime later, Gertrude returns with the monocle-touting Doctor Brown in tow. The doctor talks first, 'Well, Mary, you must tell me what happened that has required my services so quickly after our chat at the market yesterday.'

She doesn't respond with words, instead writhing with some pained movements while still lying in bed, sweating. Mary is making it seem like she is delirious when the reality is, she isn't all that badly off. As he waits for Mary to speak, he places the back of his hand on Mary's forehead. 'Oh my, you are hotter than a kettle. Quickly, get a damp towel from the kitchen!'

Gossiping Gertrude springs into action and returns a few moments later. The cool towel soothes Mary and relief cascades over her. Keeping her façade up, she pretends to shake off the cobwebs. She explains the entire twisted and disjointed ordeal. The doctor is following along but wears professional scepticism. As Mary talks about the man on the cross, the doctor interjects and points to Gossiping Gertrude, 'Tell our dearest Mary the troubling things you just saw.'

Gertrude pipes up with a twisted grimace. 'I went to Elizabeth's house to investigate. A young man is dead, mounted to a wooden cross and covered in lashes, just

272

like you said. Blood bathed the room. His toes were gnawed off; like field rats got to him after he died. It was truly wretched. I also found these…'

Gertrude rummages in a bag and pulls out dirty slippers and a rolling pin.

'They were on the floor in the Smith residence. It is proof that Mary was there. She was in that room last night. Mary is telling the truth.'

The doctor mutters, 'How is it that we can be sure?'

Gertrude looks to the doctor. Their eyes connect and Gertrude's tone gets stern, 'Does it matter if some of the details are fuzzy? We know there is witchcraft happening in Salem, and we know there have been issues with our farm animals. Doesn't it seem plausible? Even if it isn't all true, *Elizabeth isn't a member of the community like the three of us*. Think about that. Are you going to defend that heathen, or Mary and me?'

The doctor takes in this rather absurd story and Gertrude slowly moves her head up and down, trying to get the doctor to acknowledge the validity of what he's been told.

Mary, her eyes bright after having played the part of a victim, readies the question she has been planting. The words drip from her mouth like the idea is new and not something she has been thinking about for weeks. With the doctor here, now is the perfect time to ask the question and get his professional opinion on board with the plan, 'Gertrude, is it witchcraft?'

'It is witchcraft. Absolutely,' affirms Gertrude.

Mary's voice quickens. 'What about Elizabeth? Did you find Elizabeth? Did you find the witch?'

'No,' Doctor Brown and Gertrude answer in unison. The doctor speaks up, 'Now Mary, you said your toes hurt, tell me more about what happened after you saw the man last night.'

Mary, still in bed, continues her story. Gertrude plays along, reaffirming details she couldn't possibly know in an effort to get the doctor on their side just like how she planted the rolling pin and slippers. The doctor removes Mary's blankets to investigate her feet and grotesque, purulent toes bend in every direction. They ooze with fresh pus and blood. Some toes are in worse shape than others, swollen and bent in ungodly directions. It looks more like something discarded from the butcher shop than human feet. His face loses all colour and his monocle falls to his chest while Gossiping Gertrude dry heaves at the sight of these disfigured feet.

'My dearest of dears, were these like this yesterday? I do believe these toes are badly infected and the source of your fever. This is not the kind of infection that sets in overnight. These toes could have been so gravely infected you may have been hallucinating. The events you were a part of could have been entirely in your mind.'

'No. No. No. I spent the last two days baking and selling morsels. My toes have been fine. I wouldn't have been able to spend two days on my feet otherwise. It was her. It had to be. Gertrude found my slippers and rolling pin over there. And the body. This is real! She did this! Mary knows what Mary knows, and Mary knows Elizabeth is a witch!'

The doctor rubs his chin and his eyes connect with Gertrude again. Gertrude mirrors the movement from a few moments earlier, persuading Doctor Brown with a subtle nod. Mary watches and knows Doctor Brown is about to go along with the story. Even if it was a dream, the village will be stronger if the three of them can rally everyone around this and get the whispers to stop. One person sacrificed for the peace of mind of the rest. Elizabeth may not have been guilty of witchcraft, but she was guilty of not contributing to the community Gertrude and Mary had built, which in their eyes was perhaps an even more egregious offence.

Doctor Brown reluctantly proclaims, 'We will gather the people heading for church, we have ourselves a witch hunt. Gertrude, you and I better go straight to Elizabeth's house to make sure there is no doubt.'

***

The next day they find Elizabeth deep in the forest. She's hardly clothed and shaking. She tries to explain the young man was nothing more than an accident. A client gone wrong. She admits to prostitution, knowing her punishment will be severe. She had to pay her bills somehow and the farm hadn't produced a dime in years. She sold the only thing she had left to sell: her dignity. She did it in the night, picking them up in town when few were watching. Was she guilty of being the daughter of poor parents? Yes. Was she guilty of being a bad neighbour and not present in the community? Yes. Was she a witch? *No.* Not at all. She just did what her clients asked and this one got out of control. An accident. Nothing more.

The villagers are having none of it, Gertrude and Doctor Brown both testify to what they witnessed and their staged crime scene supports the story. When poor, old, hobbled Mary and her gauze-wrapped nubs stagger into the courtroom on crutches, the verdict is unanimous and instant. Guilty of witchcraft. The entire courtroom agrees, the prostitution story sounds like nothing more than a convenient cover and exactly the kind of story a witch would use to spin the events. In their eyes the evidence is undisputable: a dead man, Mary's mutilated toes, and all the strange events around town. It doesn't bother them that there had been wolves in the region, field rats running rampant on the Smith farm, or that Mary's story is paper thin. The truth would have been easy to discover if any of them had truly wanted it, but the truth was never the goal.

The people around the room plead to the judge for the death sentence. *Think of the children. Think of the community. These witches must be stopped. Make an example!*

The sentence: Elizabeth Smith is to be burned alive in the town square tonight. An unprecedented verdict, but events in nearby Salem have called for expedited decisions and Elizabeth is left with no recourse. Elizabeth sobs as the punishment is read.

The people rally. Word travels fast and folks who rarely come to these parts make their way into town. The growth of the market over the last few years was nothing compared to the wildfire that is the news of a real-life witch burning. No less than twenty carriages packed to the max with people from the big cities arrive throughout the afternoon. The wagon trail hasn't ever seen volume like this.

Old Mary and Gossiping Gertrude have a premium spot they picked out hours before the main event. They watch from a few rows back as the afternoon fades to night, both of them grin, having saved the village from years of whispers and rumours.

The flames are a sight to behold. The crowd seethes with enthusiasm as the screams of this hellspawn leaving the region serenade the night.

As the festivities end, Gossiping Gertrude and Mary are showered with questions that go on for hours. *How was the witch keeping herself hidden? How did you break the case? What can we do to find the witches in our community?* With each question, Mary's smile grows. She loves the attention and she loves that she had finally rid this community of the parasite that was the Smith family.

The moon is now prominent and the crowd begins to dissipate. One of the young men in town helps Mary put her crutches in the back of a horse cart. He gives her a ride home and in return, she gives him one of her special morsels. He gobbles it up as if enchanted by a witch's spell.

Mary limps her way into the bedroom using her crutches and then seats herself to unspool the bandages on her feet. The nubs that remain hardly resemble toes. The disfigured stumps wet with fresh pus and blood.

Mary sops the fluid up and replaces the bandages while wearing a smile. Her toes were a small price to pay for a day like this. She keeps that smile as she tucks herself into bed, but she is restless. Something is off.

It dawns on her that she didn't finish her nightly routine. She gets back on her crutches and staggers to the kitchen to fix herself a tea with three spoons of honey. It'll go nicely with a warm bun, double cinnamon, double glaze. The tasty treat that couldn't possibly have caused her decaying toe problem or put the entire village under a spell. Mary takes a bite and smiles into the night knowing that pesky neighbour and her clients won't be waking her up any longer.

A black cat walks across the road illuminated by the moon. The way its tail gracefully glides reminds Mary of that beast she saw in her dream. Maybe, she even saw that exact cat while she was sleepwalking. Thomas would be so proud of the story she weaved to pull this off. As she chomps on another bite, a dark thought creeps in: *I wonder if all the Salem witches put to trial were as innocent as Elizabeth… KAAAAA KA-KA KA KAAA!*

MIND
UNBROKEN

By
Sean Crow

The assembly of volunteers disappeared once the hunter announced his quarry. Most had been living off coin from war, but purses became lighter when supplies grew low across the slowly recuperating province. When word that a hunter with a contract was in town, many former soldiers were eager to fatten their purses before winter took hold.

The dining area in the Powder Keg, a veteran frequented tavern located in the heart of the town of Brenholst, was empty. Mostly consumed meals were left behind, chairs pulled away from tables, and only a handful of servers to clean up as dozens of former soldiers vacated the establishment.

'Is this the strength of the Greenfield Province?' The hunter called from the bar to those who departed. 'Did you not serve your country during the Midnight Campaign? Where is your courage?'

A barrel-chested man with several scars along his face

and arms, turned. 'I held the line at the Battle of Bloody
Oak, and I put down a number of Vulfkin and Half Dead
alike, but I'll not have my mind consumed in a foolish attempt to hunt a Black Wolf. Keep your gold, hunter. I'd
rather have a lean winter than none at all.'

With that, the man joined his fellows, leaving Russ
and a small handful of grim-eyed leftovers to hear the rest
of the hunter's proposition.

Greenfield Province and her allies barely managed to
repel the Tzarvan Empire. Most of the fighting had taken
place within Greenfield itself and the death toll had left
the province devastated. Only the farms and villages near
the capital had come through relatively unscathed, but
now they were filled with refugees too afraid to return
home.

For many who survived, there were no homes to return to. Russ was no exception.

There was little work to be had in the countryside, for
those who had once worked the land either abandoned
their farmsteads or died defending them. The cities were
overrun with refugees, all of whom were willing to work
any job so long as it put food on the table. While the government offered incentives to move back to the countryside, few were willing to return while beasts still roamed
the land.

Sergeant Tam, a man Russ had looked up to in the last
three years of war, tried to convince him to remain en-
listed. It was a tempting prospect, one Russ may have
taken him up on, but letters from home hadn't arrived in
months, and Russ needed to make sure his family was
safe.

Not that it mattered.

Tam fell at the Battle of Crimson Valley, when the
Tzarvan Emperor took the field in a last ditch attempt to
break the combined might of the western provinces. Of
the five hundred Greenfield Regulars who fought that
day, only Russ and forty-seven others lived long enough

to see the next sunrise.

After a week, half that number died from their wounds.

For a moment, Russ was back on the field, cannons roaring in the distance as the Vulfkin vanguard, four hundred-pound apex predators with inhuman strength and predatorial guile, swarmed forward en-masse. Their combined howls reverberated in his chest as hundreds took up the charge, guttural screams transitioning into the crunch of bone and rending of flesh when they reached the line of terrified infantrymen.

'You nine are all that remains,' the hunter said, drawing Russ away from the nightmare that trickled into his waking world.

A few offered nods while the two in the corner, who Russ marked as men hungry for coin, gave an unfitting chuckle of excitement.

During the war, Russ had met a number of men eager for battle. The foolishly brave who sought to prove themselves in their first conflict. Of course, all that courage went to shit when the lead flew overhead, and childhood friends were eaten alive. In his years of service, Russ could only recall two who managed to uphold their bravado: a madman called Tiller who preferred his axe to the flintlocks they were assigned, and Captain Vales of the Trenton Dragoons. Men whose confidence matched their skill in the craft of death were both inspiring and terrible to behold.

The rest of those eager fools were dead or had the decency to realise their confidence was misplaced after their first taste of the Void. For that was what war was, an unholy atrocity on mankind. A glimpse at what happened when men's hearts turned to the cold Void rather than the warmth of Creation.

Russ's da had warned him what waited out there. His father was a hard man born from a line of hard men. The world in which they lived was a violent place and those who understood that truth, knew what it took to survive. Thankfully for young Russ, he had a knack for knowing when he didn't know shit. When the time came for his first battle, he didn't feign any false courage. He'd been warned what was coming, so he did his best to remember the harsh lessons taught by a man who had survived the last war against the Tzarvan Empire.

'Get it out then, hunter. You've named the beast but not shown the purse,' one of the upstarts called, earning admonishing glances from the four in the corner with the markings of Valley Guard scouts.

Valley Guard had a solid reputation, stalwartly holding the passes to the east where the Tzarvan Empire sought a foothold.

'Hold your piece,' warned a middle-aged veteran with a permanent black powder stain on his face, a testament to the time he served in the Midnight Campaign.

The two loudmouths grinned and waved the older soldier off. If not for the fact they were here to be employed, by the looks on the other Valley Guards' faces, Russ wasn't sure the disagreement would have ended that easily.

If the hunter cared, he gave no indication. 'As I said before, I'm on the hunt for a black wolf that has been spotted in the area. It is my belief that it has a pack of human chattel, wolves, and at least one Vulfkin—a Lunger, to be specific. Another team is already dispatched to track them from the east. As most of you understand, a black wolf is a serious threat, so we won't go it alone.'

It was an important detail, especially when going against a beast of the Void. Russ might not have considered the job with so few in their party, but having another team working the target was a sound selling point. Black wolves were some of the worst the Tzarvan's had to offer. A man could learn to face the mindless violence of the Half Dead and Vulfkin. Such atrocities could be faced and put down with enough firepower. A black wolf, however, could break your mind and consume it without ever having a chance to fight back. Those who fell under a black wolf's influence often became puppets of the enemy, sabotaging powder kegs and killing comrades in the dark of night.

Thankfully, Russ's da had taught him many tricks which eventually saved his life on multiple occasions. One of those was to keep a bit of dried wolfsbane in his lip. It was the same shit they covered their ammunition with in order to slow a Vulfkin's regeneration. Da claimed it allowed a man to keep his wits when a black wolf went after a man's mind. Russ couldn't stand the herb straight, as his father had. Acidity in wolfsbane tended to sear the inside of a lip, burning like a hot coal after it sat there for any span of time. His father's lip must have been made of steel. To remedy the issue Russ added it to his tobac to cut the burn.

That's how he and Sergeant Tam made it through the night when a black wolf came after them one night on watch.

'The fuck's a Lunger?' one of the fools in the back called.

If Russ had thought they were draft dodgers before, there was no doubt about it now.

'It's a Vulfkin that has a taste for lung,' Russ said. 'It's in the name, really.'

The Valley Guard soldiers chuckled while the big man in the corner gave a snort. The fool glowered at Russ, earning an elbow from his bearded companion. It was clear they had outed themselves as having avoided service during the war. At least the bearded one had enough awareness to attempt to save face with silence.

The hunter seemed to notice Russ for the first time and gave him a nod. 'Indeed. While our quarry is formidable, I can say with confidence that every soul who signs on will be rewarded handsomely. A sum of five gold sovereigns. One to be paid after the first night on the march, and the other four when the job is complete.'

'Normally we'd be paid half up front.' This from the big man in the corner with a wide mouthed blunderbuss in his lap.

The hunter shrugged. 'For groups of Half-Dead, where the going rate is a copper a piece, that might be the case. This job will be one gold sovereign in advance, delivered once we are on the march, or you can go your own way.'

It was a hefty sum, Russ thought. As a regular, he had earned one silver mark a week. Five gold sovereigns was enough to get out of Greenfield and start a comfortable life elsewhere, not that Russ knew where he would go. Still, that kind of money could keep a man alive and well for years if he was smart.

Another in the back seemed to have made up his mind as he stood, tipped his cap to the hunter, and walked out of the tavern without a word. This left Russ, the two draft dodgers, four Valley Guard scouts, and the big man with the blunderbuss.

Scanning the faces of those who remained, the hunter laid out a contract and set a hefty coin purse beside it. 'If you are willing, gentlemen, sign below.'

Showing that much coin to a group of unknown killers was a bold move, but the hunter didn't seem concerned. If anything, his cold gaze was fair warning. While Russ considered himself honest enough not to contemplate stealing another man's purse, there was something about the hunter's bearing that made him doubt anyone would get away with such a feat and live.

Hunters were few and far between for a reason. Those who survived in such a brutal occupation were not to be crossed.

Russ was the first to cross the tavern to make his mark. Chairs scrapped against hardwood floors and boots scuffed behind him as the rest followed suit. As he approached, the hunter gave him a quick evaluation. Unlike his father, built like a brick with thick arms and a barrel chest, Russ was whip lean and tall enough that most had to look up when speaking to him. His da said Russ took after his uncles on his mother's side.

'Greenfield Regulars?' the hunter inquired, pointing at a patch on Russ's service coat.

'Without your company's last stand, the day may have been lost. I didn't think any of you made it out when the Emperor fell.'

Russ placed the quill back in the inkwell. 'People say a lot of things.'

The hunter raised an eyebrow and Russ could feel the eyes of the rest in the tavern on his back but he had no desire to relive that day by spinning a story. Thankfully, the hunter didn't push the subject and Russ was able to step away as the next man took up the quill.

Russ made his way back to the table and took a pull from the ale he ordered. It was heavier than he preferred, but it would do. Digging his fingers into the pouch at his hip Russ pulled a pinch of tobac free and placed it in his lip, tasting the acrid bite of the wolfsbane while he watched the rest.

The last to sign were the culls, their greedy eyes lingering a bit too long on the gold. As they passed by, he noted the unclean scent of men too long on the road. There was rust on knife hilts, ripped stitching along patches in their heavy coats. All the signs of men who lacked discipline.

'So, what do we call you?' this from the scout with the black powder stain on his face. With his forward nature, it was clear to Russ that the older soldier was in charge of the Valley Guard men. 'Most hunters have a call name or some such, or does a simple 'sir' suffice?'

The hunter offered a faint smile. 'I have been called Headsman, but 'sir' will suffice.'

The realisation of who their new employer was turned a few heads.

THE ANATOMY OF FEAR

At the siege of Dulchan, one of the most contested fortresses in the entirety of the Midnight Campaign, it was said the Headsman had earned his name by patrolling the ramparts of the fortress at night when Vulfkin and other Void born monstrosities attempted to scale the walls. Trophies of the hunter's quarry had been placed on the ramparts as a grim warning to the Tzarvan army below. The number of Vulfkin heads was said to be over fifteen. A feat that seemed unreal for anyone who had faced the monstrosities in battle.

Russ scanned the room, seeing realisation dawn on everyone save for the man with the blunderbuss. The big man's brows lowered, and he mouthed something under his breath.

'Now then,' Headsman said as he rolled up the contract. 'Have your gear prepped and ready by first light. There is word of a farmstead a half-day's march from here that engaged with the beasts. If we are to bring a quick resolution to our endeavour, it is best we start there.'

***

The next day was brisk as the warmth of summer gave way to autumn. The circumstance of their departure brought along the familiarity of Russ's time in the military. The small group of veterans marched down a dirt road leading into the countryside, a trail of steaming breath rising as they set a soldier's pace. Aside from the draft-dodgers, the rest of the men kept up without complaint or unnecessary conversation. There was comfort being part of a group where most of them understood what was required. Between breaks, Russ was better able to gauge those who had joined.

The black powder-stained veteran who led the Valley Guard was known as Ebrum. As grim-faced and resolute as any officer worth his salt. The other three scouts, Brenan, Cooper, and Lathan seemed solid enough that

Russ didn't question their ability. Each sported a Benny Green, decent rifles with a reputation for long range. Russ ran with an Ingram Model Three, generally given to officers in the Greenfield Regulars. Sergeant Tam had given it to him after his second battle, one in which the majority of the greenhorns had either been killed off, permanently maimed, or deserted afterword. It was a fine rifle, one that had seen Russ through many skirmishes and pitched battles, even if it didn't have the reach of a Benny Green.

The big man was known as Abe, short for Abraham. Hailing from the northern province of Wrin, he had served as honour guard for General Heckman. The man seemed to know his business and didn't bat an eye when he took a pinch of Russ's tobac mixed with wolfsbane. 'Smart habit,' Abe had said after tucking the tobac in his lip. 'Back in Wrin, we used to mix it in brandy, but you'd be belchin' bloody fire the day after. Surprised you got your hands on some.'

When the war ended, the Greenfield leadership didn't insist on the return of their armaments. With beasts still roaming the land, each surviving soldier was allowed to keep his equipment to keep the land safe in the aftermath. Wolfsbane was normally kept under guard, but Russ had made a habit of collecting it from the dead after each battle. With the stock he managed to keep after his discharge, along with several caches he had established during his service, Russ would never run out of the herb. He would, however, need to restock from time to time.

For the most part, the two draft-dodgers kept to themselves and none of the former servicemen seemed inclined to ask about them. Russ was no exception. They had all experienced the horrors of war and knew how important it was to be aware of the strengths of the men you served alongside. Without experience in the field, it was unlikely that those two would make it through the coming conflict.

It was a waste of time getting to know dead men.

The hunter was a man of few words and little time for the idle chit-chat of soldiers. Once their pack horses had been prepared and their party moved off, Headsman kept to himself. Spending most of his time at the front of their small column, he seemed intent on getting after their quarry as soon as possible.

While Russ had never worked with a hunter before, the stories he heard made them out to be single-minded killers who would rather die than give up on their quarry. Of course, all those tales came from the mouths of soldiers, and if Russ had learned anything in his time in the military, it was that soldiers exaggerated.

As they came upon the farm in question, Russ found himself faced with yet another scene of a world gone mad. Body parts, both human and livestock, lay scattered about. A woman in a blue dress, now drenched crimson, was the closest to them. She lay on the path leading to the main farmhouse, as if she had tried to run before the beasts caught her. Ribs jutted out of her back where a Vulfkin had likely used its terrible strength to snap her bones to reach the lungs it craved, leaving the rest of the body for whatever scavengers were in the area.

Judging by the drag marks, a good number of the dead had been taken to be consumed. A few smaller forms had been piled near the corral, marking where the black wolf's pack had decided to feast.

Black wolves were clever, almost akin to a human in intelligence, but they were more savage. Russ had seen a great many feasting piles on the march, always when a black wolf's pack had been spotted in the area. Vulfkin, or half-dead, were bad enough with their unquenchable lust for flesh. Yet a black wolf satiated itself on the suffering and anguish of its prey.

Behind him, Brandon, the draft-dodger, reacted much the same way Russ had his first time seeing a feasting pile. The bearded man was on his knees retching while his companion stood nearby, eyes wary.

Headsman didn't seem bothered as he continued his march through the farm. Russ and Abe weren't far behind while Ebrum and his scouts split into two groups and swept the perimeter; wolfsbane-saturated shot readied in their rifles. It was a wasted effort, in Russ's opinion. The kills were already starting to stink, a clear indicator that the pack had moved on.

They preferred their meals fresh.

Coming upon the homestead, Headsman pushed open the door and went inside. Russ looked up at Abe, who hadn't so much as unslung his blunderbuss.

'Regretting the job yet?' Abe asked, a note of grim humour colouring his words.

'Nothing I haven't seen,' Russ answered, moving past the hulking man.

Russ had seen death in its many forms; from grotesque and perverse to simple and sudden. Not much phased him since the day he discovered the fate of his town after the war. Everyone he had ever known and loved had been ripped apart and toyed with by the beasts of the Tzarvan Empire. For Russ, there was no depravity he had not seen, and no pain he had not endured. The Midnight Campaign had taken everything, and yet he was still standing.

Walking into a room where a family had been slaughtered during an evening meal caused the bile to rise in his throat. Not because of their deaths, but due to the stink of rotting corpses.

'Shit,' Abe growled, holding a scented kerchief over his mouth and nose.

None of the bodies had lungs. Like those outside, ribs had been torn apart to reach the desired organs. Maggots wriggled from the rotting meat of their bodies; one last hatching before winter. The hunter moved about the living space, looking for clues only he seemed to be privy to. Russ scanned the bodies, noticing wide lacerations across their throats and several stab wounds as well.

'Human chattel must have been used to lower their

guard,' Russ said, dipping his head in the direction of what might have been the father of this household. 'Throats were cut before they were eaten.'

'Small blessing that must have been,' Abe muttered.

At Russ's comment, Headsman returned from one of the back rooms and looked from the bodies to the young former soldier.

'Observant,' he said, staring a bit too long for Russ's comfort. 'Most would have been put off by the carnage to notice a detail like that. Have you worked with a hunter before?'

Russ shook his head. 'No, just seen my share.'

Headsman nodded. 'Indeed. Well, let's not dwell. We've still got ground to cover before the day is out.'

With that, the hunter exited the main building, leaving Abe and Russ alone. The big man watched Headsman, his eyes lingering on the door as it closed.

'Problem?' Russ asked.

Realising Russ was watching him, Abe broke from his thoughts. 'We'll see.'

Russ was about to inquire further, but the former bodyguard was already leaving.

Once outside, Russ could see the rest of the scouts had come in and were already holding conversation with Headsman.

'... footprints east, toward former Tzarvan territory,' Ebrum was saying, his gnarled finger pointing to the mountains in the distance. 'Tracks are still fresh, but they muddied them by backtracking several times. Rough estimate would put 'em around eight wolves, a few human chattel, and at least one Vulfkin, possibly two, unless the one is a glutton.'

'That's a big pack,' said Cooper. The scout scratched an old burn scar on the side of his face. 'Especially with a black wolf.'

Russ couldn't argue. He had seen what a single Vulfkin could do when it got close. It took a good amount of wolfsbane-coated lead to put one down, and their death toll was never small. Add some feral wolves and the chattel and it was a grim situation. Looking into the concerned faces of the men around him, Russ felt the weight of their circumstance settle on his shoulders. Even the cocky expressions worn by the two culls had vanished as uncertainty wormed through their resolve.

Russ knew when the will of men began to falter. He had felt his own threaten to break many times over the course of the war, grabbing hold of his heart when comrades were ripped apart around him. Perhaps, when he was still a farm boy who had no true concept of the world or of violence, he may have sat back and waited to see how things would play out. Russ scanned the fields of corn, seeing the abandoned tools scattered about for a harvest that would never come, it was all too similar to the home he had returned to and, for a moment, his heart ached for a life that had been stolen from him.

How many more families would suffer a similar fate if this black wolf was allowed to roam free?

'Then we had best get back on the trail before they find another home to destroy,' Russ said, forcing a touch of steel into his voice. 'For five gold sovereigns, I don't expect the work to be easy.'

No one spoke, but the scouts and Abe gave affirmative nods.

Headsman turned to the rest. 'We'll make camp at Tradesman's Crossing about three miles east. The hunt is on, so you'd best keep your wits about you.'

Russ's doubts began to fade as the uncertainty in their ranks gave way to order and purpose.

'Should we bury 'em?' the red-bearded cull asked. 'Don't seem right to leave them all torn about.'

Russ was surprised by the note of sincerity in his words.

'We could,' Headsman said, 'but then we'd be another half day behind our quarry. As Russ pointed out, that could mean another family slaughtered because we were too busy tending those beyond our help.'

The cull gave one last look at the wanton destruction. 'Yessir, I get your meaning.'

With that, the scouts took the lead and the rest followed, save for the red-bearded man. Russ held back, pretending to have an issue with one of his pack straps. Headsman's eyes lingered on him a moment and Russ waved him on. Once the rest were on their way, Russ approached.

'Brandon, right?' Russ asked.

The man glanced at him, the enthusiasm from the night before replaced with a newfound understanding of what the world was like.

'Yeah,' he said, unable to take his eyes from the body of a small boy caught in the fence between the cornfield and his home.

'It's a bloody business, Brandon, and before this is over there's every chance we'll see more, and worse. No shame in going back. You haven't taken his coin yet.'

Brandon glanced at Russ, righteous fury in his eyes burning through the vacant stare.

'I knew these folks. Took me in when I caught Yellow Fever and had no place to go. They didn't deserve this,' Brandon said, voice breaking. 'Creator as my witness, I'll put those fuckers down, sovereigns or not.'

Brandon's voice rang with conviction and Russ corrected his initial evaluation of the man. Perhaps he wasn't quite the cull Russ had made him out to be. Some folks just needed their eyes opened to the reality of the enemy to get their shit together.

'Then we best catch up,' Russ said, gripping the man by the shoulder and giving a firm squeeze.

'Thanks,' Brandon said, and together they picked up the pace.

***

That night, after the first of the gold sovereigns had been distributed, Russ was posted for the second watch and had just settled himself with his back to the campfire when Headsman approached. The man had yet to lay on his bedroll, instead choosing to remain apart from the group, quilling notes in a leatherbound book by lantern light. Russ tapped a knuckle to his brow in an informal salute as his employer took a seat on a nearby log. They remained silent for a time, the distant rushing of the Sage River tempting sleep with its steady flow.

'Were you an officer?' Headsman asked.

Russ shook his head, eyes tracing over the outlines of the clearing around their locations, looking for anything out of place. Holding a diligent watch was vital during the war, for the creatures that served the Tzarvan Empire were always eager to pick off those who slacked.

'Never held status. Just did my best to survive,' Russ said, spitting out a bit of tobac.

Headsman held Russ with the same evaluating gaze as before. It reminded him of the high-ranking officers who inspected his battalion before battle. By the time Russ had joined, most of the fools within the upper ranks had been demoted or killed in the early stages of the war, allowing those with a sharp mind for strategy to lead.

'You would have done well,' the Hunter said.

Russ snorted. 'Couldn't have paid me enough to take the role.'

Headsman raised an eyebrow. 'Oh?'

Russ didn't really feel like explaining himself, but if he learned anything during his time in the army, it was to stay on the good side of his superiors. They had more difficulty sending you off to die if they found value in you.

'Tzarvan practitioners ordered their beasts to target officers. Greenfield Regulars were offering triple pay for men promoted to lead. Fooled a few good soldiers into the role and not one of them made it out alive.'

Headsman smiled. 'Too sharp to buy into the lies of the aristocracy and too driven to die. That's a rare trait in a man your age. What are you, thirty?'

'Twenty-two,' Russ said, never breaking his gaze from the surrounding forest.

'Yet you've the mannerisms that speak of a lifelong soldier. How is that?'

Soldierly banter was well and good, but officers usually didn't pry, so Russ paused before answering. Perhaps he was still caught up in the rank differences between soldiers and officers. Sergeant Tam had been an exception to the rule, as his manner of command was anything but formal. Headsman didn't have the welcoming nature of his former sergeant, instead reminding Russ of the officers descended from noble stock. Such were hard men who did not see value in the lives of those who served under them. Still, the hunter was paying a heavy sum to hunt beasts Russ was more than happy to kill, so he played along.

'My da served in the Twenty Year War. Always said it was a matter of time before the Emperor's son decided to follow in his footsteps. Lo and behold, he was right. He taught me a few tricks growing up, a good amount of it paid off.'

The hunter gave a quiet chuckle. 'Such is the way with fathers and sons. My own served in the conflict as well. Seems we had a similar upbringing.' Headsman looked at his hands and shook his head. 'Perhaps that's what kept us alive? Learn from those who endured true hardship and better your odds of survival.'

Russ found wisdom in the words and nodded.

Headsman pushed himself to his feet. 'I'd best get some rest. We'll be covering a lot of ground tomorrow on our way to Raven Pass.'

Russ finally took his eyes off the field around them to glance up at the hunter. 'How do you know they'll head that way? Raven Pass is some eighty miles from here.

There are closer villages to prey on.'

Headsman shrugged. 'Been at this for a while, Russ. Black Wolves don't think like animals. They always have a plan. If I was a betting man, I'd say the beast has a goal in mind.'

Russ nodded, giving the hunter the benefit of his experience.

'And by the way,' Headsman said as he continued toward his tent, 'stop putting wolfsbane in your tobac. That shit will kill you if you keep at it.'

Russ watched him go for a moment longer before returning his attention to the duty before him. In this world, Russ thought, spitting another string of tobac to the forest floor, what didn't?

***

Several days passed as Ebrum and his scouts followed their quarry's trail. True to Headsman's prediction, the black wolf's pack seemed to be heading straight for Raven Pass. For the life of him, Russ couldn't understand why. As far as he knew, all that remained there was a small mining village of little consequence. He suspected the hunter was concealing something about this particular quarry. That was the nature of most leaders. They only told you what they thought you needed to know, but not so much that you realised the shitshow you were in.

While the first several days went without issue, the true danger of their quarry soon began to make itself known when they spotted a pair of farmers in a small clearing alongside the road. Their wagon had cracked a wheel and while one was searching for tools, the man nearest was staring intently at the wagon spokes.

Ebrum and Lathan, approached and offered to help. It was possible the two farmers had seen signs of their quarry and every bit of information helped.

Russ noticed the poorly concealed bodies in the

nearby brush too late. While a shout of warning was just forming on his lips, the dead-eyed farmer on the other side of the wagon levelled a pistol and fired, decorating the road with Lathan's skull. The man near the spokes immediately snatched a concealed sabre and slashed Ebrum across the shoulder, the lead scout barely managing to pull himself back from a killing blow.

Headsman was already moving as he drew and threw a knife in one swift motion. The blade caught a sliver of sunlight before embedding itself in the sword wielder's neck. Abe let out a roar and rammed his shoulder into the wagon, knocking the second assailant back as Lathan's killer pulled out another hidden pistol, giving Russ the time he needed to bring up his Ingram and put a bullet centre mass.

The ambush was over in seconds, leaving three men dead.

'It knows we're close,' Headsman said, walking past the deceased Lathan as he eased one of the pistols he carried back into its holster.

One of the scouts was at Lathan's side, helpless as he held the cooling hand of his fellow scout. Abe helped Ebrum stave off the bleeding from the sabre cut while the rest kept a steady eye on their surroundings.

Russ didn't feel the need to look for further attack. If the beasts had wanted to take them, they wouldn't have allowed their prey to prepare themselves. Instead, he began to reload his rifle. In less than thirty seconds, his Ingram was reloaded and hanging from the strap over his shoulder.

As Headsman returned, he called for the rest to stand down. 'Place Lathan with the dead. The locals will likely bury him along with the rest. We can ask about the whereabouts of his resting place on our way back.'

'What in the Void just happened?' the other cull, Terence he had heard the man referred as, shouted. 'What do you mean it knows we're close? These were bloody farmers, not monsters.'

'Human chattel,' Abe said as he cinched the makeshift bandage around Ebrum's shoulder. 'The black wolves keep a few of their victims handy for times like this.'

The colour drained from Terence's face as he looked at the bodies. Fear filled the man's eyes as the realisation of what they were up against must have finally set in.

As day gave way to night, they set up camp in a half-burned trade post farther down the road. It was a remnant of a once-prominent establishment that had not survived the war. At the hunter's orders, the night watch was set to two-man teams and Russ found himself, once again, on second watch with a lip full of tobac and a surly Ebrum for company.

'Should have seen it coming,' the scout said as he tossed another log on the fire.

'Bad habit, blaming yourself for something nobody saw coming,' Russ said. 'It'll eat you alive.'

The old veteran glared at Russ, who didn't so much as take his eyes off their surroundings. He could feel the man's tension fade as the aged scout realised there was no accusation in Russ's words, just a simple statement of fact.

'Kept Lathan by my side throughout the campaign. I saw the wide-eyed boy he was when he signed up as well as the man he became. Now his body is lying somewhere alongside the road without a proper burial.'

That hadn't sat well for Russ either. Quarry or no, they should have buried one of their own, or at least burned him. They were far enough east that days could pass before the bodies were found. There was plenty of time for scavengers to drag the corpse away to feed. They would likely never recover Lathan's body on their return.

If they returned at all.

There was little conversation to be had after that, for Russ was not one for comforting words and Ebrum didn't seem the sort to seek them. As Abe and Cooper relieved them of their watch, Russ lay on his bedroll and stared up at the stars. With sleep evading him, Russ thought back to Sergeant Tam, the man who had watched over him during the campaign. Tam had been a fine leader and a better friend, replacing Russ's da as a mentor. For weeks after Tam had been killed, Russ wracked his brain trying to figure out how he could have saved the man's life. Perhaps, if he had been paying closer attention when the left flank crumbled, perhaps if he'd added a bit more wolfsbane to the third shot he fired at the armoured Vulfkin... Ifs and buts, theories and unobtainable possibilities all of them ran through his mind after the final battle, even while the rest of the United Province Army celebrated their victory over the Tzarvan Empire.

As with any night filled with such thoughts, Russ focused on his breathing, allowing his memories to fade away as sleep took hold.

'Like I told you, just gotta have faith that you'll see it through,' Sergeant Tam said as they watched the Tzarvan riflemen sound the retreat.

It had been a bloody exchange. A total of six volleys had been fired by both sides while the artillery continued to pound into the retreating enemy ranks. Honour between the warring factions had long since been removed from the battlefield and the United Provinces took any opportunity they could to add to the death toll.

Russ's heart still hammered, his hands shaking as shock took hold. It was his first pitched battle and the regulars had held their own in a vicious exchange.

The sky was a bright blue, and though he had seen a number of childhood friends fall, he had never felt more alive. Russ watched the retreating forms of the enemy as they rushed back to the trenches established at the base of the adjacent hillside where their cannons had gone silent. Messengers ran from the erected defences as the Tzarvan command scrambled to recover from the loss. Yet, unlike the events of that day, Russ found his attention fixed on a point of the enemy-occupied hillside.

A black wolf watched from the shadows of the wooden palisade. It was almost too far to make out, yet Russ couldn't shake the feeling in his gut that it was watching him.

Then came a choking sound from behind and Russ turned to find Tam as he had discovered him on that final day of the war. Chest ripped open, snapped ribs sticking out from the gaping hole where his chest had been. The sergeant's death-glazed eyes settled on Russ, freezing him to the spot.

Blood flowed from his mouth as he smiled. 'Just have faith.'

Russ bolted upright, head pounding as he looked for Tam's mangled form, only to find that he was back in camp. Abe and Cooper were still on watch, their backs to him as they viewed the only entrance of the building they had occupied. Pulling the dip of wolfbane tobac from his lip, tender from having fallen asleep with it, Russ took his canteen and washed out his mouth.

That's when he caught the sound of something growling somewhere in the darkness.

Taking another pull of water, Russ did his best not to act as though he heard anything, even though his mind was screaming that he was in danger. Now that he could assess the two on watch, he noticed the slow rhythm of their chests rising and falling with sleep.

Something was wrong and, as far as Russ could tell, he was the only one aware of it.

Settling himself against his bedroll, Russ eased a hand to his pack and grabbed his pistol. As quietly as he could manage, he cocked back the hammer and palmed one of his wolfsbane pouches. His falchion, while a tempting option, was leaning against a nearby wall, just out of reach. If he timed things right, however, he could grab it before whatever was waiting in the darkness could get the drop on him.

Satisfied that he was as prepared as could be, Russ surged to his feet, black powder pistol raised as he looked for a target before quickly recovering his sword.

Although his heart raced and vision narrowed, nothing came for him. In fact, now that he had a moment to assess the situation, all he could hear was the crackle of a dying fire.

The sound of a cocking hammer drew his attention to the hunter's tent where the dim lantern light revealed two men outside. Headsman was on his knees staring defiantly up at Brandon. The red bearded draft-dodger, Brandon, glared back at the helpless man, hand trembling as his finger tensed on the trigger.

The how and why of the situation clashed in Russ's mind as he tried to reason what was happening. His first thought was he had awakened to a crime of greed, but then what was the growl? Had it been a remnant of his dreams? Why were the sentries sleeping? It would have been one matter if they were a band of fresh recruits, but those who survived the Midnight Campaign were unlikely to let their guard down while on watch.

No, Russ told himself, this had all the signs of a black wolf attack.

Russ had seen men under the influence of black wolves before. He had even watched Tam draw a man out of a possession once. It just depended on how much of his mind had been consumed by the beast.

'Look at me, Brandon,' Russ said, voice loud enough to catch the man's attention. 'The black wolf is close and it has its claws in you. Listen to me and we'll get through it.'

'You don't get it,' Brandon snapped, pistol shaking in his hand as he pointed it at their employer. 'He's not a man, he's a wolf. He's going to eat our souls, send them straight to the Void!'

Headsman slowly shook his head, eyes focused on Russ. The look that said Russ needed to shoot before it was too late.

Russ turned so his own pistol was concealed. 'That's not how this works, Brandon. Black wolves can twist what you see. Look at him, he's just a man. Lower your weapon.'

Russ hesitated as he saw those eyes. They weren't glazed, like those fully consumed. That had to have been a good sign. It gave him a chance to keep the man alive.

Shifting his weight, Russ said in a voice loud enough to give Brandon pause, 'Look at me, Brandon.'

Brandon didn't turn.

In the firelight, Russ saw the look of a man about to kill. As Brandon's eyes narrowed the blast of Russ's pistol rang through the night, the bullet taking him in the chest. Headsman swayed to the side as Brandon managed to pull the trigger, barely avoiding what would have been a fatal wound.

Brandon staggered a few steps and fell. Lying on the cold earth, he touched the hole in his chest. A brutal cough sent a clot of gore from his mouth. Russ's stomach sank as he watched the man writhe on the ground.

It wasn't the first man he put down due to the powers of a black wolf, but Russ had hoped he would never have to do something like that again. Fighting the abominations of the Tzarvan Empire was one thing, having to kill a man who didn't deserve it was another.

Headsman was already on his feet, watching Brandon as he clung to his last moments of life. As Russ approached, the hunter glanced up.

'Have you checked the rest?' Headsman said.

Russ didn't answer, he was still staring at Brandon. The young man was looking at the hole in his chest with a mixture of confusion and pained disbelief.

'We had best see —'

'Check them yourself, hunter,' Russ snapped. 'I'll not leave him to suffer alone.'

Russ could feel Headsman's eyes on him, but he didn't care. He just saved the man's life at the cost of one of their own. Draft dodger or no, Russ wasn't about to leave Brandon in his final moments.

'He's a wolf,' Brandon managed as the hunter's footsteps faded away. 'I can see it. Those yellow eyes...'

The life faded from Brandon's features as he took his last, shuddering breath.

Russ waited a moment longer, then closed Brandon's eyelids. He had seen far too much death and suffering to linger on those who fell. That was what Russ told himself as he rose to his feet yet the words of the dead man remained.

He's a wolf...

Men caught up in the illusions of a black wolf were difficult to watch pass, not only because they were comrades in arms, but rather the fact that black wolves continued to use them until they drew their final breath. Russ had seen how the final words of a man under the influence could sow the seeds of doubt throughout a company. A foul gift from the black wolf before their puppet expired.

Across the camp, Headsman shook Abe. The big man awoke from his slumber with a burst of violence. He snatched the hunter with one hand, his fist cocked back to swing as he screamed, 'I said hold the fucking line, you sons of bitches.'

Abe's bullhorn cry was cut off as Headsman twisted Abe's fist in his shirt, shifted his weight, and hurled the hulking former bodyguard over his shoulder so he hit the ground hard.

The big man blinked away his confusion as he came out of the black wolf's deception. The rest of their team woke in various stages of shock. Cooper openly wept and remained hunched over while the rest were left to deal with whatever twisted memories the beast had trapped them in.

Of those who remained, it seemed only Russ and Headsman had managed to wake themselves from the black wolf's assault. Likely, the creature had intended to bring the hunter down by corrupting the minds of their party. The fact that it managed to influence nearly every man present was a feat unto itself. In Russ's experience, a single black wolf would normally abduct one or two soldiers at most. He had heard of wolves so powerful that they could put small companies to sleep so that the Tzar-van infantry could kill them in a night assault.

Russ's gaze travelled to where Headsman sat, the man's attention devoted to the book he carried rather than those he commanded. How Brandon got the drop on the man was a mystery. So far, the hunter had seemed to be a man who saw more than the rest, a master of his craft and yet an untrained draft dodger managed to get the drop on him? It didn't feel right. Russ was about to head to the hunter to learn how it all played out when he saw that Brandon's companion had finally pulled himself from the foetal position and was now standing over them.

'Who did it? Was it you, you cold bastard?' he said, fixing Headsman with a look of hate through red-rimmed eyes. 'You take us out here to kill a bloody wolf and all we get is death in return.'

Headsman glanced up from his book, as if seeing the man for the first time. 'You can leave whenever you like, but you'll receive no more sovereigns from me.'

'I killed him,' Russ said, voice carrying across the campsite as the grey, pre-dawn light ushered in the new day. 'His mind wasn't his own and he was trying to kill our employer. I had no other choice. That's what black wolves do. If you had served, you would know. Now he's dead and you want someone to blame for taking a job you weren't prepared for.'

Russ did not allow his voice to waver and never let his eyes slip away from the other man. He would own what he had done, and deal with the consequences as they came. If the man chose violence then Russ would kill him, by blade or bullet, it didn't much matter.

Perhaps Terence saw the intent in Russ's bearing, or perhaps the man simply had his fill of death, for he deflated. His hand never moved to draw the long knife belted to his hip.

'Bunch of fucking monsters is what you are,' Terence muttered, then turned his attention back to the hunter. 'I'm done with you lot. I'll be taking my cousin home to-day.'

So it was, in less than a week, their band of nine became six.

***

The days that followed had them looking over their shoulders and double-checking the shadows of the forest as they neared the base of the mountain range. Due to their caution, travel slowed. The next trap could be just around a bend. Instead of wildlife causing branches to snap and bushes to rustle, a wolf, human chattel, or a Vulfkin could be lying in wait.

Night was no better and, by the hunter's instruction, they set several traps in order to catch the black wolf, should it make another attempt on their lives. Yet the black wolf proved far more capable than they anticipated. On the second night after the attack, they awoke to find Ebrum's lifeless body beside the campfire, bloody knife in his hand, the vein in his thigh cut.

Russ began developing headaches, growing worse every morning but easing off throughout the day. Each night his dreams were haunted. He would return to a past battlefield, reliving the horrors from his past over and over again; everything from the moment Vulfkin broke through their ranks at the field of Brinsberry to the day he returned home to find the scattered remains of his family. Through it all, he heard the ever present growling of a wolf in his mind.

After they buried Ebrum — something Russ had in-sisted upon despite Headsman's urging to push for-ward — Russ made a point to speak with the hunter while

303

they marched.

'This isn't a normal black wolf, is it?' Russ asked.

There was no condemnation in his voice. In fact, Russ did his best to keep any emotion from showing. The man seemed to respond better to those who could emotionally detach themselves from a situation. A hunter, Russ was learning, was someone who could witness the horrors of the world and allow it to wash over them in order to reach their goal. There was a familiarity to the line of thinking, akin to the way Russ's father had seen the world and that made it easier to follow.

In Russ's short and brutal life, he had met many who would be considered a better shot or handier with a blade. Yet they were dead, and Russ was alive because, when the chips were down and the lines of life and death intertwined, Russ never hesitated. In the heat of the moment, Russ could put his heart to the side and face whatever came his way.

In this, he and the hunter were kindred.

Headsman watched him for a long moment before letting out a gentle sigh. Russ could see the fatigue written on the hunter's face, barely kept in check.

'What we hunt may very well be beyond us,' Headsman said, voice lowered so only the two of them could hear. 'Although, to be honest, I didn't know it when we first began. Our quarry has proved far more capable than any Void born I have encountered in my time.'

Russ nodded. 'And the relevance of Raven's Pass?'

For a moment, Headsman allowed a smile to ghost his lips. 'When this is over, if you're still alive, I could use a man like you. You've got the mind of a hunter, and that's a rare trait.'

Russ wasn't sure how to respond. The years after the war had been filled with a constant dread of what awaited him. There was no peace to be had when he knew what lived in the dark corners of the world. Since joining this expedition, however, Russ found familiarity in soldiering again. There was comfort in the routine for his troubled mind, despite the horrors they faced. The guilt that followed him was simply gone.

'I might take you up on that,' Russ said. 'If we make it through.'

Headsman nodded, the hard set to his face softening. 'I don't know what lies at Raven's Pass, but I have suspicions. The Tzarvan Empire took the pass early in the war. Something in those mines must have been vital to their cause.'

'Something that brought about the black wolves and Vulfkin?' Russ asked.

Headsman grew quiet, face hardening once more. 'Perhaps.'

As they walked in silence, Russ dipped his fingers into the pouch at his hip and placed a bit of wolfsbane tobac in his lip.

The hunter raised an eyebrow. 'Still holding to superstition are we?'

Russ shrugged. 'Hard habit to quit.'

'How bad are your headaches getting?'

Russ looked up and Headsman shrugged.

'Happens when you get too much in your system. It's toxic, at least in the long term,' Headsman said, eyes on a steady swivel as they marched up the path.

'It's kept the black wolf out of my head so far,' Russ countered.

At that, Headsman finally took his gaze from their surroundings and focused on Russ. 'You really believe that, don't you?'

A younger Russ might have felt embarrassed that a man who knew so much about the Tzarvan abominations believed him to be superstitious. But Russ had seen Vulfkin rush past him in the midst of battle to disembowel men right beside him. Moreover, he had felt the draw of the black wolf in his dreams and had managed to keep it at bay.

'I do,' he said.

'Your life, I suppose. Shame that you depend on something that will kill you when it's you who has kept the wolf at bay.'

'What do you mean?' Russ asked.

The hunter returned to scanning the world around them. 'You've the will and spirit of a man unbroken by the world, Russ. You have seen what terrors it holds and have come through stronger for it.'

Suddenly, the last conversation Russ had with his father came rushing back.

'The world cannot break us, boy. Not unless we allow it.'

They had been working late into the evening, preparing Russ for the next day when he would join the regulars. Once he was packed and ready to leave, his brothers, sisters, and mother had wished him a final goodnight. When they went to sleep, Russ's father took out a bottle of brandy he had been saving and poured them both a glass.

'You'll soon get your first taste of the Void. That's what war is: a small taste of the Void and all the promises it offers. You'll see many upright and brave men, when faced with those Tzarvan bastards, run as soon as the blood starts flowing. We are made of sterner stuff. We are the sons of men who have held their ground, generation after generation. Through war and famine, plague and tragedy, we have stood tall before all that life can throw at us.'

At this point his father grew quiet. His scarred hands, the knuckles rounded after countless breaks, swirled the contents of his glass. 'When you meet death on the field of battle, you meet it on your feet. Do you understand me, son? We are Duncans, and the will of the unbroken flows in our veins.'

'I'm a survivor,' Russ said aloud, his father's words still ringing echoing in his mind. 'Nothing more.'

The hunter nodded and allowed for silence as they made their way to Raven's Pass.

Another night approached and Russ found himself on

watch with Abe. The big man seemed lost in thought and Russ was content to share the watch without conversation when the former bodyguard finally spoke.

'You know we're being led into a trap, right?' Abe said under his breath.

Russ forced himself not to react as he scanned the rocky outcrops around them. 'What do you mean?'

Abe maintained a soldier's discipline as he searched for threats in the dark.

'I served at the siege of Dulchan, where Headsman earned his name. Bad fuckin' business that was. Never met the man, but I spoke with those who had. They said he —'

Whatever Abe had been about to say died on his tongue as the big man's gaze focused on something beyond their camp. Immediately, Russ went on point, cocking back the hammer of his rifle as he searched for a target.

'What is it?' Russ whispered.

Abe didn't speak. Instead, he stood with his blunderbuss and braced it against his shoulder. Russ did the same with his in Ingram.

'Damnit, Abe. What am I looking for?' Russ hissed, scanning the barren ground before them, seeing nothing.

'Bloody cowards,' Abe snarled as he suddenly turned and levelled his blunderbuss at the sleeping forms of the two remaining scouts.

The firelight revealed the glazed look of a man caught in the illusions of a black wolf and Russ wasn't fast enough to stop him. The blunderbuss roared and the two sleeping men were ripped apart. Russ rushed to tackle Abe as another shot rang out. He couldn't see where it came from as he attempted to bring the giant man down, but the sudden lack of resistance made it clear who the shot had struck.

Abe staggered to the ground, blood oozing from a hole in his chest. Across the camp, Headsman held a smoking pistol, his eyes fixed to points as he stood there. Abe blinked a few times, his eyes returned to normal as he drew one of his final breaths, his eyes skipping from the hunter to Russ. The big man shook his head.

'Fuckin' knew it,' he said as he choked back crimson.

Then the stillness of death took over and Abe was gone.

Russ looked at the ravaged bodies, seeing Cooper's foot twitch a few times. There was no saving the two scouts. A blunderbuss blast from that close didn't leave much to recover.

'So that's it, then,' Russ said as he sat on the ground and stared at Abe.

Headsman remained where he was for a moment, then crouched across from him. 'What do you mean?'

Russ looked up. 'We left with nine and now there's just the two of us. Even if your other team has done better, we won't have enough for a pack like this. It was a bad situation to begin with, and now it's a lost cause.'

The hunter nodded. 'Might not be a lost cause for whoever still lives in Raven's Pass.'

'Maybe,' Russ said. 'But I didn't sign up to die.'

Neither spoke.

Then, the hunter asked, 'Why did you sign up? I've seen men hungry or desperate for gold just as often as those too old to learn a new skillset. But not you. You've a full life ahead of you and yet you chose to come after a black wolf. Some might say that's a death sentence in itself.'

Russ thought long on the question. He knew the answer but, having never given voice to it, he hesitated.

'I signed up to stay alive,' Russ said. 'A man needs to have a purpose in life and I just couldn't find mine. Void placed its mark on me, you see, and I know it'll come to collect sooner or later. Figure I might as well fight it with every day I have left rather than give it what it wants.'

'Marked by the Void,' Headsman said, as if testing the

concept. 'Perhaps. Or perhaps it's not a curse after all, but a gift.'

Russ shook his head. 'If it's a gift, it's one I'd be happy to return.'

'We live in a twisted world, my friend, and you have the ability to see the reality of it in a way others cannot.' Headsman held out a hand to the dead. 'There is more to the world than the aristocracy and those of blind faith would have you believe. If you would but –'

Shots rang out from somewhere in the distance and Headsman's words died as he stood. 'The other team,' he said.

Russ heard the urgency in the man's voice. 'Might be. Can't go running through the mountains at night though, especially not with that Void-damned wolf out there.'

The Headsman hesitated, but the set of his jaw and the way his hand gripped the pistol he carried made it clear his decision had been made. 'This could be our chance. With its pack distracted, we can kill it.'

It was a hard call, born of a will bent on victory despite the cost, rather than one based in logic. The how and why of whatever drove the man was beyond Russ, but he knew one thing to be true: Russ was in over his head. That didn't change that there might be people in need.

People like Russ's family.

'Then we'd best get moving.' Russ said.

***

Moving at night was not a task to be taken lightly, for footing was never certain even on a clear path. Headsman seemed possessed of a knowledge unknown to Russ, for he moved toward the gunfire without a misstep or redirection while Russ stumbled through the underbrush, stones and roots caught his feet. Low-hanging branches tore at his face and whipped him, but on he ran, taking account of what was available to him for the conflict ahead: his father's falchion, his Ingram and pistol, both loaded with wolfsbane shot, and a will to see this task finished. With the frail moonlight the only means to follow Headsman, Russ soon lost him to the night, yet the gunfire and cries of battle continued and he followed the sound, even as it slowly petered off.

A scream sounded nearby and Russ saw the faint flicker of torchlight ahead. Yet unlike screams born of violence, this was filled with soul-wrenching pain.

As Russ stumbled free of the forest, the scene before was akin to many a battlefield he had stood upon. At the entrance of a small mining village were the remains of a bloody struggle. The bodies of the second team were ripped apart, bits and pieces scattered alongside a dozen slain wolves or more. A Vulfkin, a hulking nightmare from the battlefield, lay in a steaming heap, its head connected to its body by a few strands of muscle while its torso was little more than lead riddled meat. Another of the massive creatures was disembowelling a man who died burying his bayonet into the beast's shoulder.

A giant of a man stood at the entrance with a claymore stabbed into the ground as he tried to steady his breathing. His breastplate had been ravaged and crimson leaked from the many rents in it. The side of his mouth had been torn open, revealing white teeth in the torchlight. A black wolf lay at the man's feet, half again the size of a normal beast with fur darker than night. Long, primordial fangs hung from its mouth, long tongue lolling out in death.

Opposite the swordsman was Headsman, who stood with his pistol aimed at the man.

'You best make it count, Void-whore, because you won't have time to make another,' the giant swordsman warned.

Russ hesitated as his eyes darted from the swordsman to the hunter, and then to the remaining Vulfkin as it began to snap the ribcage of the hapless rifleman while it fed.

'What's going on?' Russ called, rifle steady on the Vulfkin even as he tried to keep the other two in his peripheral.

'He's one of them, Russ, too far gone to be saved. Shoot him and we'll worry about the Vulfkin after,' Headsman hissed.

Russ heard the lie as soon as the words were spoken. A Vulfkin was always a priority when death was on the line. A single beast could ravage an entire platoon if it was driven enough. On top of that, there was a note of unflinching hatred in Headsman's voice, a complete break from the cold and calculated hunter Russ had come to know.

'How would he be controlled if the wolf is dead?' Russ said.

The man with the claymore spat onto the ground and let out a wet chuckle. 'Bastard took my name, son. Voidwhores like this one tend to have a knack for deception. He's a bloody practitioner; one of the nasty fuckers that brought the Void born into our world.'

Russ felt a wave of nausea roll over him as the events of their disastrous hunt replayed through his mind. Suddenly Abe's death made sense. The big soldier had been trying to tell him and Russ cursed himself for not seeing it. Brandon had likely seen something he wasn't meant to the night the young draft dodger died. His accusations about the hunter being a wolf had held more merit than he would ever have anticipated.

And Russ was the one to end his life.

Guilt and betrayal warred within him, yet it was rage, pure and just, that boiled to the surface as Russ turned his rifle on the false hunter.

The man parading as a hunter, the same man whose life Russ had saved, didn't so much as meet Russ's eye. 'You don't understand Russ. They've lied to you, all those generals and politicians, they sent you to die so that those in power could steal and rape the lands of their neighbours. They haven't seen what lies beyond this world, but you, you have the gift to see.'

The argument was one he heard shouted by disgruntled prisoners of war. Accusations that the United Provinces were responsible for the Tzarvan invasion. Russ didn't know if that was true nor, in that moment, did he care. All he knew was that monsters had come into his homeland and taken everything. His family, lifelong friends, his home…

Whatever trust the man pretending to be Headsman thought they had built, whatever gift he thought Russ shared, none of it mattered. As their eyes met, false hunter and ex-soldier, both understood there could be only one outcome, and the false hunter was the first to act, as he fired his pistol into the swordsman and shouted words dredged up from the depths of the Void.

They were the guttural atrocities, never meant to be uttered by the human tongue, let alone heard. Russ had heard such things on the battlefield, but never up close. They carried a power beyond the means of mortal men, usually ravaging the lungs of the practitioners who shouted them even as soldiers buckled under the words. As they reached Russ, searing pain enveloped his mind, nearly bringing him to his knees. Steeling his nerves, Russ attempted a shot before his legs gave out and the world tilted. He was aware that the rifle went off in his hands, but his pain was too great to see if he hit his target.

Rifle forgotten, Russ clutched his hands to his head in a futile attempt to stop the burning in his head. Distantly Russ heard the Vulfkin roar and the swordsman echoed its call. He was alive, but for how long?

The will of the unbroken lives in our veins.

His father's words remained a constant in his sea of mental agony and Russ latched onto them to stay afloat. Reaching down, his fingers drew a pinch of tobac to his lips in hopes of keeping the attack at bay.

Every movement was accompanied by a pain unlike

anything he had endured, yet the words of his father repeated in his mind as the wolfsbane tobac worked through his body. Slowly the pain subsided to something manageable and he staggered to his feet, even as darkness tugged at the edges of his vision.

The false hunter, now Tzarvan practitioner, strode toward him, sabre drawn and eyes intent on the kill. Blood trickled from the man's mouth and nose, eyes now bloodshot as he raised his sword.

Grasping at his belt, Russ's hand settled on the hilt of his father's falchion and he pulled it free of its scabbard.

The practitioner shouted another mouthful of obscenities and suddenly Russ was no longer in Raven's Pass but standing before his family farm. The decaying remains of his sisters and little brother were piled against the barn door, his mother's body drawn and quartered near the well, and his father's head placed atop their front door. The head turned of its own accord, its slack-jawed mouth opened in a rictus smile before it screamed.

… will of the unbroken.

Russ blinked, crimson drops falling to the ground from his face, yet he was back at the pass and the practitioner was closing the gap between them. Staggering to his feet, Russ found his balance and raised his blade, causing the practitioner to pause.

This man expected to deliver an executioner's strike only to find his prey had bared its fangs. Somewhere beyond them, the real Headsman clashed with the remaining Vulfkin, but Russ could only focus on the threat before him.

'I didn't lie to you,' the man said, settling into a low guard. 'You've a great deal of potential. To withstand the words of the Void proves it. Lower the sword, Russ. Men of your talent are rare and I'd rather not end that potential on my blade.'

If Russ could manage a retort, he may have spoken it then, but death had finally found him and he would meet the bastard on his feet.

Russ made to lower his sword in surrender and saw the glint of satisfaction in the practitioner's eyes. It was at that moment of the man's assumed victory that Russ darted forward. The practitioner screamed another obscenity and the mental blow nearly dropped Russ, but his momentum carried him on, even as his vision swam. As he roared his final act of defiance, a lesser pain pierced his side as his falchion bit deep and the world went black.

***

Russ blinked the grit from his eyes as he woke to the bright light of morning. Turning his face from the sun, he managed to open his eyes, groggy and unsure how he still drew breath. His head pounded and he found that he couldn't hear with one ear, but he forced himself to sit. The world spun, but as he surveyed the carnage, Russ found that he was the only one still moving.

Gathering his strength, Russ got to his feet, the fresh wound in his side leaking blood. The laceration burned, but a short inspection and the fact that he was still alive meant it wasn't fatal. At least not yet. Infection could set in, but that was a worry for another time, as he stared at the bodies of the real Headsman and Vulfkin.

Yet of the practitioner, there was no sign, other than a bloody trail leading from where Russ had fought the man through the mining village.

Slowly, Russ gathered his equipment, scattered about as it had been in the clash, and followed with pistol in hand. The morning light revealed a vacant town with no sign that anyone had been living here. Open doors revealed vacated homes with few supplies left behind. Whoever had originally lived here had left some time ago. Taking slow and steady steps, it didn't take long for Russ to find the end of the village where the mine entrance was located. A yawning hole in the earth loomed before the former soldier.

And that's where Russ found the practitioner.

The man lay against one of the wood supports at the entrance where kegs of black powder had been stacked. A quick assessment revealed the real Headsman's plan had been to destroy the mine. Fuses had been set and the kegs were placed in such a way that the intention had been clear, but likely the Black Wolf had struck before they could finish the job.

One of the practitioner's hands clutched a bloody wound from his collar to midsection where Russ's falchion had found its mark, while his other hand reached toward the darkness of the mine.

Russ thought the man to be dead, but as he neared, the practitioner slowly turned his head. Bloodshot eyes regarded him and Russ knew death would soon claim the man.

'Listen,' the practitioner muttered. 'Can't you hear them, can't you feel...'

The practitioner took a shallow gasp. 'Embrace... the call...' he said, final words that followed his spirit into the Void.

Russ stared into the inky darkness before him and in that frozen moment, he felt as though he stared into the maw of some sentience beyond his comprehension. To his growing horror, Russ felt the draw of this place as he took an involuntary step forward. It felt warm, and the faint sounds, like the distant buzzing of a beehive that got clearer the closer you got. It was as if some siren song of madness called him into its embrace.

There was something powerful in the depths of the tunnel. Some slumbering sentience that longed to be released.

Russ took another step, and the song in his mind grew stronger, as if words were just on the edge of hearing. His breathing deepened and the pain of his mortal body began to fade away as he took another step. Something caught his ankle, temporarily drawing his attention to the fuses lining the ground. Suddenly, Russ realised he had taken far more than a few steps, as the darkness of the mine now surrounded him. By the time he reached the end of the black powder kegs, the light of the entrance was dim.

He felt the sentience of this place focus upon him, sensing its hunger as his body longed to follow the path further into darkness. Russ found that he couldn't step back, no matter how he willed himself to do just that. Instead, he knelt to keep himself from moving deeper. As he did so, the faint buzzing in his mind changed. Instead of warmth, a terrible cold settled around him and the sounds shifted from a welcoming buzz to a sharp, tearing clash of metal and flesh that put his hackles up.

Slipping his free hand to the ground, Russ found one of the fuses. It was unlikely he could escape this place. His body longed to disobey his will and it took all of his focus just to remain in place. Whatever dwelled in this mine, the false hunter had wanted it, and from what he felt now, Russ suspected it wanted to be found.

Sweat dripping from his brow, despite the frigid cold that now surrounded him, Russ placed the fuse near the hammer of his flintlock and whispered into the darkness.

'I am a Duncan and I will not break.'

The darkness deeper within the mine seemed to shift and writhe as a shriek of defiant rage rolled through his mind. Yet he pulled the trigger and the fuse ignited, spreading to the rest of the powder kegs which would spell his end and seal the entrance.

Russ felt a sudden release and found that he was able to stand. Yet as he turned away from the darkness, running for all he was worth toward the light of the outside, the world around him blossomed with fire.

His final thoughts returned to the words of his father, so many years ago.

'We are the sons of men who have held their ground,

generation after generation. Through war and famine, plague and tragedy, we have stood tall before all that life can throw at us.'

As the flames engulfed him, Russ fixed his eyes on the light, and took solace in knowing that he stood his ground in the end.

Then the world went black and was no more.

NECK

By

HL Tinsley

Some people leave their bodies to science. Others commit their flesh to the ground, food for worms and wriggling larvae. I heard a rumour once; talk around the campfire, some folks get themselves stuffed and mounted like boars on plinths. Kings and nobles, I figure. They seem the sort to do that type of thing. I don't fancy it much.

Me? My plan was to leave my body to Gryff. Mostly because he wouldn't want it, and I always had to have the last laugh. Well, here we are, and there *they* are, the moonflies buzzing on Gryff's tongue. He smiles a toothless grimace.

Shit, I think. *The bastard beat me to it.*

Suddenly, death has an edge that's razor-sharp. I don't want it if I can't laugh at it.

It takes a certain person to want to be in Gallows Square past the midnight bell. Or a certain motivation. We're the right kind of people. Though, I suppose, there would have been an argument for us being the wrong sort. I hold Gryff tight under the knees as Wrigley cuts away the noose.

'You ready?' Wrigley lets the rope snap before I have time to answer.

Gryff comes down hard and for a moment, I'm crushed. They warn you the first time about the weight of a corpse but more than a dozen reclamations later, it still takes me by surprise.

'Bloody hell.' My ribs crack as Wrigley pulls me free. 'What did he eat for his last meal, the other prisoners?'

Wrigley grins.

To my left, Jim-Ben and Petar release another swinger to the ground. Petar fares better than I, but then, he's twice the size and half as careful about it.

'If you two were any slower I could've carved myself a Gryff suit by now and walked the bastard home,' I hiss between my teeth.

Jim-Ben hops down from the scaffold, sweeping into a bow. 'At your leisure, young apprentice.'

Ha, still funny. We lift our prizes and with practised ease, move them onto the back of the cart. Getting the bodies is the simple bit. It's keeping them that's the challenge.

My ears prick at the sound of two distant hoots. I see from the way Jim-Ben tenses that he's heard them too. Another two hoots, closer now. We need to leave. Wrigley climbs into the driver's seat and pats the spot next to him, the one reserved for Jim-Ben. 'Let's go.'

I crawl into the back, taking the spot between Gryff and the wooden panels and give thanks for the fact I'm smaller and skinnier than Petar, who has to take the middle. Wrigley cracks the whip as we hear familiar whistles blow and lantern lights come tearing around the corner. Wherever we go, the watchmen are never far behind. They don't like it when we take their property.

I've got no intention of ending up like Gryff. 'What are you waiting for? Get this thing moving before we get our necks stretched.'

We lurch forward. Above the rumble of wheels, I hear the faint bird calls of our watchers guiding us home. Wrigley pulls at the reins. The horses pick up speed and I feel the weight of Gryff roll against me.

'Hold on boys,' Wrigley calls from the front. 'We've got a bit more company than we bargained for. Six on our flank and another four coming up in front. You know the drill.'

We do, and I know for a fact Petar has already slipped the knife from his belt. Mine is in my hand, though I never like to use it unless I have to. We might go around stealing corpses but I don't enjoy making them.

'Fuck the watch,' Petar seethes from between the fleshy folds of our cargo. He doesn't mind so much.

We hear the next call. I lie back and watch a church spire pierce the darkness while the stars spin around me. A pistol shot comes and I know they're closing in because I crane my head forward to see the tip of Gryff's toe blown from its root, flesh beneath burnt and black.

'Keep your head down,' Petar yells.

There's a wagonload of watchmen on our tail and now we're not listening for the hoots of our comrades along the rooftops. We're flying blind, wind whipping, the wagon is taking each turn on two wheels. I hear the crack of a returning shot. Jim-Ben is the only one with a gun. He's the only one I'd trust with one. I glance to my left and see one of the lookouts running up along the skyline, keeping pace and then falling behind. He stops and watches us disappearing and then he's out of sight. I don't know if it's Cullen or Ragger but either way, there's nothing they can do from up there.

Jim-Ben fires off another shot and I just about make out a figure falling from the first watchmen's cart. He doesn't have time to cry out before a second follows. My stomach turns as it runs over him. The watch keeps coming, fallen comrade tangled in the wheels until

320

eventually, the weight of the wagon splits him open, and they leave half of him behind.

Another bullet goes over my head and lodges in the back panel. Most of the watch aren't good shots. Right now, I'm bloody glad of it. The cart dips without warning. Suddenly one of the bodies is slipping and at first, I worry it's the one we're getting paid for. Then I realise it's yelling at me. Without stopping to think about the bullets, I sit up and thrust my arms under Petar before he can slip any further. Now his body is on the wagon and his legs are in the air, bouncing around.

'Pull me up,' he's yelling. 'Pull me up!' His feet smack off the stone road and I know before I've seen them that the bones are shattered. Wrigley grunts. We're less than a quarter mile from the outskirts of town. Jim-Ben takes out another one of theirs. Petar cries out and I tell him we're nearly there.

Wrigley drives like the devil and a few moments later, the watchmen start to fall back. Petar's crying still, only it's not for me now. He's just crying.

The minute we're clear, Wrigley slows the horses. I lean over the sides of the cart and throw up anything in my stomach, because it doesn't want to stay there after the way I've treated it. Wrigley checks Petar's legs with a grim face.

'Is he going to make it?' I am always blunt. Wrigley's face creases. He knows wounds but he's no medic. Jim-Ben is better at that sort of thing.

'Best take a look,' Wrigley calls to him.

I turn around and my world slows. Jim-Ben is standing now. He's got one hand on the wagon and the other on his chest. His fingers can't stem the crimson flower that blossoms between his ribs. I don't speak. Wrigley says nothing and the silence is suffocating. We watch as Jim-Ben falls. Next thing I know, there I am, with Wrigley, crouching in the dirt as our brother coughs up his last rattling breath. The shot has torn a hole in him and I can't press my hands deep enough or hard enough. Wrigley yells at him, tells him to get the fuck up and stop dying.

But he doesn't. He keeps dying until he's cold and gone. All the way gone and we know we can't bring him back.

Soon after, our rooftop companions find us with the supply cart. They bring medical supplies too late for Jim-Ben and not soon enough for Petar. Wrigley gives him something to ease the pain and binds his feet to struts. We're not sure if they'll heal. Sitting around the fire with Cullen and Ragger, I glance at Petar. He's sleeping now and I envy him for it.

'What's to be done with that one?' Ragger points at the body Jim-Ben just sacrificed his life for. It feels like a waste. I hate the dead man for it.

A firm hand grasps my shoulder. 'His brothers will come to collect him in the morning. Don't waste your time eyeballin' it, kid. Ain't no point glaring at a corpse.' Wrigley has a way of knowing what I'm thinking.

I'm an apprentice, kid, or youngster to them. I haven't seen enough of the world to be anything else. I ignore the look Wrigley gives me. He heaves himself to his feet, food untouched on the floor. None of us have any appetite. 'Cullen, you've got first watch.'

Death isn't new to us. It's our business. What we do is dangerous. Sometimes we lost people along the way, but not two in one day, and not Jim-Ben. He couldn't die. He hadn't even told me his plan. I sit there staring at the flames until the fire burns down to the embers. When that's gone, I glare at that corpse so hard I fear I might set it alight, thinking maybe if I do it long enough, it might bring Gryff and Jim-Ben back. But it never does.

***

First light comes and Petar is in that partial state of consciousness that softens the brain. Wrigley tells Cullen to

322

take the supply cart and drive him to the next town over. He asks me to attend to the load on our wagon. He's trying to keep my fingers busy.

I prepare the corpses for collection. That's my job. We always try to make the bodies look presentable. It depends on how long they've been swinging as to how well that works. If they've been there too long... well, we're not bloody miracle workers.

The one we'd cut down last night was fresh enough. Two days gone, at most. I take his hands and fold them, one over the other. It doesn't bother me, touching them. I wrap a cloth around the corpse's neck where the flesh has puckered and folded around the rope.

There are three stars tattooed on each of the dead man's hands. They've all got them. Marks of the Otherworld, they call them. Tells you who's who and how scared you should have been of them back before magic was outlawed. A two-star mage might have had enough power in them to levitate a loaf of bread. A six-star, like this one, could throw a man clear across a room with the flick of a wrist. But there is no more magic. That's dead too, for a long time now. The authorities made sure of it, picking off mages like the one before me until there were almost none left.

I slide my hands down the dead man's torso and check for breaks or tears in the flesh. We humans think about dying a lot. Maybe too much. But we at least get a say in what happens to us after. Our bodies, at least. Which is more than these poor bastards do.

They commit the crime of existence and apparently that's more than enough to warrant a rope around the neck. I know that better than most. Us? We're not criminals. But we aren't heroes either. If we were, we'd help them before they were dead. But we can't. We're not an army. There aren't enough of us to make a real difference. All we can do is retrieve the bodies. We give them closure — the families of the dead. The condemned.

I glance up and see Wrigley pacing, eyes shifting across the horizon every few minutes. They'll come to collect soon and I don't get involved in that. None of us do. Wrigley deals with the mages, that's his job.

Cullen is packing up our things when they appear over the peak of the hill to the west.

I can always tell when they're coming. I can feel it in my gut. Right now, it's churning like I just ate one of Ragger's special stews – the sort we don't ask about and try not to taste. Wrigley gives us the signal to keep our distance. Humans and mages don't mix well. I see two men and one woman, head bent and hands to her face. Even from far away, I see her shoulders shake and wonder if anyone would cry for me like that. She seems too young to be a widow. Could be a sister, I suppose.

Wrigley is in the throes of negotiation with one of the men when the other looks across the field. He stares at me and the churning intensifies. He takes several steps forward and stops. I can see his face now. There are six stars on each cheek. He wants me to see them. I wonder if he knows – if he can sense the imprint of my fingers on his dead relation's body. I wonder if he judges me unworthy to touch him.

Perhaps he'd be right to think it. Truth is, we charge a fair price for our service. Just enough to cover our costs. We're not in it for the money. Not really. You can get ten coppers a piece for a bit of mage soap in the big towns. There's folk all over, rubbing their faces each morning with the rendered fat of fantastic beings.

They think it makes them beautiful. I find it grotesque beyond comprehension. I hate them all. Now I'm wondering if he can feel the bile in my blood. I hope he does. Hatred makes kindred spirits of its victims. I don't realise I'm touching my neck, running my fingers over the uneven white scars until Ragger steps up alongside me. 'Found a good place for Gryff,' he tells me. 'Right next to a good tree, he'd like it.'

I shrug. 'Nothing *but* fucking trees here.'

I doubt Gryff would care much either way. I feel grief stabbing in my chest as I think about how we still have to put Jim-Ben in the ground, and I know he *would* care.

We stand there, the two of us as Wrigley and the mages talk. I can see them moving their hands about. One of them puts a hand on Wrigley's shoulder. Wrigley has always been in with their folk. There are rumours. Sometimes I wonder why he does this. The men on the hill begin walking down the slope towards our cart.

Ragger knocks me with his elbow. 'Come on, we've got a hole to dig.'

***

We bury Jim-Ben and say our goodbyes in the time it takes Cullen to feed and brush the horses. Petar sits in the back of the cart and I can already smell the gangrene in his legs. We don't say anything but I suspect this is the last time we will see each other.

Our band is getting smaller. Not for the first time, I think about what I might do after all this is finished. I guess we might have another year at most. There aren't many mages left for the watch to hang. It won't be long before either they're all dead or we are. There were twenty-five of us when I started and now all of us fit on one wagon. Ragger's up in Jim-Ben's seat and it's not right. It's like wearing a dead man's shoes.

Wrigley's taken Jim-Ben's gun and all the shot we have left. I'm alright with that because I figure that's how Jim-Ben would have wanted it. Ragger asks me if I want his knife. I take it, though it doesn't feel like it's mine now. This time Ragger comes with us instead of going with Cullen. We're three men down and need the extra muscle. Ragger has muscles to spare and loves a good fight. I know Wrigley's in this for the cause. Ragger's in it for the blood. Me? I guess I'm in it for a bit of both. There's nothing like surrounding yourself with death to feel alive.

'We've got another job in Unston.' Wrigley doesn't elaborate. He never does.

'I hate Unston. Stinks of piss.'

I don't like any town, much less the people in them. Perhaps because they didn't like me and nobody could tell me why. Something about me offends them. Maybe it's the way I walk, or the cadence of my voice. Doesn't seem much of a reason to hang someone.

Sometimes it feels like the men to my left and right are the only ones who don't wish me dead. I don't know how much they care that I'm alive. But they don't seem insulted by my existence.

They'd never meant to find me. I guess you could call it a happy accident. Jim-Ben and Wrigley had been cutting down a fellow and there I was, still flopping and jerking on my own rope next to him. Wrigley was all for leaving me there. It wasn't personal. Nobody was going to pay for me. But Jim-Ben argued the case for keeping me in case I proved useful.

'Smells no worse than anywhere else.' Ragger likes Unston, but then again, he has reason to. Bridget is there. Ragger has a girl in every town and he's good to them. The sort of man who takes a woman a single flower instead of a bunch but always knows exactly the right one to pick. Bit of a smug bastard, really.

Wrigley doesn't tell us more about the job and I don't ask questions, but it doesn't stop me from thinking. At the moment, I'm thinking Wrigley is hiding something. I look over at him and his face gives nothing away.

'You hear the rumours?' Ragger doesn't do well with silence. 'Me and Cullen heard there's a mage in one of the east villages, got a bit of power in him. Brought up a whole swarm of locusts. Ten eyewitnesses, at least.'

I scoff. 'Every conman in every poxy town will tell you he's seen one of them do magic. It's all horseshit.'

'Could you imagine it though?' Ragger suffers from an

affliction that means he doesn't know when to shut his mouth. 'Back like it was in the old days? That kind of force,' he shakes his head. 'Some of them could rip a man's arms off without touching them. Think about it. You have all that power and lose it all.'

'You don't know what you're talking about,' Wrigley's tone is dark. 'Never seen a mage do nothing that wasn't done to them first, and worse.'

I taste the bile at the back of my throat. I know all about the purges. Everyone does.

During the first twelve months of the culling, most mages would have been grateful if the rope was all they got. I see Wrigley's shoulders tense and I start to believe the rumours. He's in this for more than just the cause. Wrigley has reasons that go beyond justice for the wronged. I don't say anything about it. Ragger finally shuts up, though.

By the time we get to Unston it's almost dusk. I glance up and watch the clouds turning over the fading sun. Wrigley snaps his fingers in my face. 'Get your head in the game.'

I look round and see that Ragger is already gone. Wrigley and I take the narrow roads and listen for his hoots and whistles, telling us which way to go and what ways to avoid. We can't see him. But I know he's in every crack and dark recess we approach, moving swift and quiet from one to the next.

'What are you thinking, kid?' Wrigley keeps an eye on the road. I can feel he's on edge. But I don't think it's because he's expecting the watch.

'I'm twenty. I'm not a kid.'

'Fine, what are you thinking, Twenty?'

See, this is the thing about talking to Wrigley. It never feels like a conversation. It always feels like a test. I can sense him now, probing around in my brain searching for something. 'I'm thinking this job is off. Like this one is bigger than the others. You're keeping things from us.

327

Jim-Ben would have told me. Jim-Ben never kept secrets.'

'You've got good instincts, Twenty. For the most part. But you don't know everything.'

Now I'm thinking whatever this is, there's a good chance one of us will be in the ground before sunrise. I think about Jim-Ben and realise that without him, Wrigley is different. Like a part of him is gone now and something has come adrift. Something in him is untethered. I think it might be the dangerous part. I don't want to, but I suspect the wrong one of us took that shot back at Gallows Square.

We pick up the pace, take the next corner and arrive at a house. Wrigley stops. I can smell something rancid on the breeze. Wrigley smells it too and we both know what it is. The door opens and Ragger's already there, puking his guts out. Bridget sits in her chair like she's waiting for us to arrive. A good woman is Bridget. Or, she was.

Now she's melting, flesh peeling off. My nose figures she's been dead two weeks. Ragger punches the wall so hard he leaves a hole. I assume he's calculating how many of the watch he can kill on his way out of town. I try to put a hand on his shoulder, but Ragger wants none of it. Sometimes comfort hurts more than the blow.

Wrigley leans forward and asks me to try and find some whisky, something to numb the pain. I find a bottle of something and give it to Ragger. He takes it to the corner of the room and doesn't look at either of us. I stand there, selfishly thinking how terrible this is for me. That I have to see this. Glad that Wrigley seems willing to deal with what's left of Bridget and doesn't ask me to help.

He's trying to work out the best way to move her when his face drops. 'Take him outside.' He nods towards Ragger. 'Now.'

I'm going to do what he says but then I see it. I don't mean to, and I wish I hadn't, but now I know and I can't stop my face from telling Wrigley as much. I look at Bridget. She's blinking at me. Half-rotted, fused to the embroidered cushion and her left eye is still flickering. It pulsates and I know she's still there. Trapped in a cage of her flesh.

Wrigley shakes his head, a warning not to say anything. I want to scream. The only thing that stops me is knowing Ragger hasn't seen it yet and I don't want him to.

This wasn't the watch. This is the work of mages. I don't know how. I don't know why. Now I'm thinking about what Ragger said. Maybe the con men are right. Maybe the magic is back. Maybe it's *angry*.

Wrigley tells Ragger that he'll take care of things and instructs us to wait outside. I'm glad when Ragger doesn't notice Wrigley's knife pulled from its sheath. Ragger turns and walks from the house, taking the bottle with him. I follow. A moment later, I glance back to see Wrigley quietly shut the door behind us. I sit on the kerb outside with Ragger and we don't say a word. Neither does Wrigley when he comes back out. A few seconds later we see curls of smoke begin to lick from under the door. We stop long enough to see the flames catch the curtains and I secretly wish I could burn the town to the ground.

***

We find a tavern, the kind of place that's nice and discreet and doesn't ask questions. Ragger finds himself a girl because he needs to live a little and I don't blame him. Everyone grieves in their own way. Ragger likes to fuck the pain out. To me, death is a game, something to ridicule. Something to get close to but never touch. Like putting your hand between the bars of a cage to see who was quicker, you or the animal.

I lie in my room picturing Jim-Ben's face, imagining the shot that took him passing over my head. I think about the purges, the thousands of dead mages lying beneath the foundations of the town, dropped into cata-combs like pebbles into a well. My eyes close and I feel the rope again, burning as it clenches tighter and tighter around my neck. I can't speak. I can't cry out. I can only jerk and flicker between the borders of living and dying. I hate that place. I love it. Part of me will always long to be in it. It's the only place I feel alive anymore.

The room is a decent size with a bed and wardrobe and barred windows. It's the kind of establishment where they're less concerned with people breaking in than they are bill-dodgers trying to climb out. There are shadows creeping across the floor. I don't mind shadows; they make for good company.

I hear someone outside and I know it's Wrigley before the door opens. He comes in and stands at the end of the bed. His face is grey and I feel like I don't know the man in front of me anymore. Perhaps I never did. 'We need to talk about what you saw.'

I prop myself up on my elbows and remember the knife under my pillow. 'What did I see? Tell me, Wrigley. What did I see?'

Wrigley looks at the floor, watching the shadows move. 'You saw a dead woman, something sad and terri-ble. She was a good person. She didn't deserve it.'

'No,' I shake my head. 'She didn't. She didn't deserve to die like that.' I try not to picture her eyes, but they're etched into my mind, scratched in like claw marks. 'Why? Why would they do that to Bridget? She never did any-thing to anyone.'

'Like I said, she didn't deserve that. But Bridget knew things she wasn't supposed to. We both know she had a mouth on her. It shouldn't have gone down the way it did. But it doesn't matter now. One more job, kid. Then this is over.'

I want to ask him what he means by that, but I don't. He leaves and the moment he's gone, I creep across the floor and take a chair, jamming it against the door. The rules of the game have changed. I can't feel the bars of the cage anymore and I think maybe the animal is loose. I don't sleep. My stomach rolls and during the course of the next few hours, I stink the place up good and proper. My guts would make Petar proud.

Morning comes and I stumble out of bed, staggering in the low light towards the bowl of water left on the windowsill. The water is cold. I have to grit my teeth against the sharpness of it, and that's when I see him.

At first, I'm glad Cullen is here. I figure he's left Petar in the hands of a healer — or an undertaker — and come to find us.

But my eyes aren't buying it. They tell me that whatever this is, it isn't Cullen anymore because Cullen always had a sort of rosiness about him, like he's got warmer blood than the rest of us. There's less life in the thing looking back at me then there is in the stiffs we pull down from the ropes.

I put my hands against the window bars. Something takes the breath from my lungs. They're so cold I can feel my skin burn, blistering and peeling. Not the normal sort of cold. Unnatural, deathly cold. Cullen opens his mouth. I wait for the scream. I can feel it, but I don't hear it. Instead of words the air fills with moonflies, the sort that lay their eggs in rotting guts and empty eye sockets. Hundreds of them swarm towards the window. I want to move but I can't, my hands frozen to the bars. The insects hammer themselves against the glass so hard they explode, leaving spots of blood until the pane is slick with red. Cullen disappears behind the haze. Then I hear a familiar voice. *Get out.* I know I can't have heard it though because Jim-Ben is dead. We left him in the ground miles away. Suddenly I can move again. I grab my things, put on my clothes, and run from the room, leaving my stink behind.

I want out. Whatever this is, I play with death by *my* rules. That's what I'm going to tell Wrigley. Only I don't find him, I only find Ragger sitting at a table, hood pulled low. He looks at me like I've got shit on my face. 'What the hell happened to you?'

I take a cup from the table. It still has last night's ale in it. 'Where's Wrigley?'

'Gone to check in with Cullen.'

The ale is gone in one mouthful. 'Cullen is dead.'

Ragger reaches up and takes the cup with a snort. 'How much of this have you had?'

Not enough.

I let Ragger know I have to go out and fetch something. He shrugs. Ragger isn't smart enough to know when to ask questions. I know he'll sit exactly where he is and wait until Wrigley comes back to tell him what to do. Not me. As I leave, I hear Ragger order a plate of sausages and bacon.

***

I don't know how I knew where he would be, but when I walk to where Wrigley sits, he doesn't seem surprised to see me. I drop to the ground, grass still wet from the night's rain. Across the road, a small stone building stands enclosed in a fence of wrought iron. There's a padlock on the gate, heavy bars across the door. It doesn't look like anything special. Maybe that's what made it so offensive. We're all surrounded by death, all of us all the time. We just choose not to notice it. It's only in the actual dying we make a spectacle of it. The rest of the time it lies beneath us, quiet and forgotten.

'You know how many of them are down there?' Wrigley asks. I don't, but I know it's less than there are in the catacombs of other places. Some stretch for miles, well beyond city walls and town boundaries. We watch a carriage roll past, someone going about their business and likely not giving a second thought to what they just passed over.

'Four thousand nine hundred and thirty-nine.' Wrigley's jaw tightens. 'You ever wondered why they bury mages? Why anyone would hunt something to the brink of extinction and then keep the bodies?'

'They use the fat for soap. A lock of hair under the bed of an infant keeps away disease. People buy eyeballs to put in boxes. They take them out at parties to show their friends.' I can't keep the disgust from my voice. Maybe that's why Wrigley is letting me sit with him. He can sense that I hate the world as much as he does.

'They keep them,' Wrigley tenses before continuing. 'They keep them because of the Dulcari.'

I have no idea what that is, but I don't let Wrigley know that.

'Dulcari — the burial rites of the mages.' His eyes narrow on the building. 'People think when a mage dies, their magic dies with them. It doesn't. You have to release it. That's how they did it, the watch - the so-called protectors of the cities. How they beat the mages. The magic doesn't end. It's an inheritance, passed in the flames from father to son, mother to daughter. It's all in there. That's why they keep the bodies where it's cold and wet. Magic needs heat, it needs to burn. They need to burn. People think they know what hell is.'

I've heard talk about the crypts. The watch are the only ones who enter. Some of them go down there more than others. They enjoy their jobs too much. I heard they do things there no person ought to contemplate. Sacrilege. Defilement. There are rumours of macabre puppet shows.

'Who's down there?'

Wrigley tries to smile and it doesn't sit right. 'My son.' The memory flashes across his face. In an instant, the smile fades. 'My boy. He's down there with the rest of them. Nearly five thousand souls beneath our feet, some of them dead twenty years and without death rites none of them can move on, can't pass over. All they can do is rot. There is no peace for them,' Wrigley's shoulders tense. 'So why should there be peace for us?'

I can't remember ever seeing Wrigley with a woman. He never seemed to pay them any attention. In our line of work, finding women is hard. Live ones, at least. Unless you look like Ragger. I sit and realise all the stories I've heard about Wrigley are true.

'It's coming.' Wrigley kneels, full of reverence before the crypt entrance. 'What people have seen so far -- small acts of magic, illusions for coin in outlying villages -- is just water spilling through the cracks in a dam. I hear the roar of the wave coming, and when it does, we'll all get what we deserve.'

'So, this is vengeance? For your son?'

Wrigley shakes his head. 'Not vengeance. Justice. Balance. The world has a blood debt to pay. Believe me, kid, you don't want to be around for the next bit. I wish things could have been different. But we've all got to pay for our sins.'

A tear forms in the corner of his eye. Sickness lurches in my stomach as I realise when Wrigley says all of us, he means it. Not just the watch. Not just the hangmen. Everyone. I see the look on his face. It isn't old grief. It's new grief. He's grieving for Bridget, and Cullen, probably Ragger by now.

He knows we're all going to die. And he's alright with it. I can't do anything as he slides the knife into my gut. I can't cry out or scream. He holds it in there. Looks me in the eye and tells me how sorry he is, and I believe him.

Then I start dying just like Jim-Ben did, lying on the ground with my blood seeping into the grass. Wrigley puts a hand on my shoulder and tells me not to fight. It's better this way. Then he leaves me to it.

***

The first time they tried to kill me, I didn't see anything.

334

It was disappointing, at fourteen, to realise death is nothing more than a full stop on the end of a sentence.

I sit up and expect pain. There is none. Curious, I look down and see the wound has stopped bleeding. There's a hole in my side where the knife went in and before I can stop myself, I stick a finger in it. I don't feel anything, only a sense of invasion as my hand probes around and investigates my insides. It's meatier in there than I thought it would be.

'Having fun?' I hear the voice and that does hurt. Jim-Ben stands over me, arms crossed over his chest in the way they always used to when he was pissed at me for doing something stupid.

The crypt is gone. So are the roads, all the buildings and the grass. Now, everything is hazy and flowing, a river of rolling fog. The ground stretches for an eternity, broken by the presence of great bone columns reaching into a lilac sky. In the distance, black trees without leaves, vines of dark sinew draped from the branches. I marvel upon seeing something so endless. Huge flocks of what look like birds swoop above us. One drops lower and I realise they aren't birds. They're skin, flesh, and blood, spinning together and forming a birdlike shape. 'What is this place?'

Jim-Ben glances around. 'This place has no name. It is between worlds, neither one thing nor the other.' He frowns. 'If you're here, that means Wrigley has found what he was looking for. Truly, I never thought I'd live to see this day.' He seems amused. 'Then again, I suppose I didn't,'

I wish he wasn't dead. Maybe even more than I wish *I* wasn't dead. 'Wrigley is going to help the mages get the magic back. They're going to kill everyone.'

'Yes, I expect that was always his plan.'

So much for there being no secrets between us. I wanted to be angry with Jim-Ben for not telling me. 'Why? What is he looking for?'

335

Jim-Ben looks like he's trying to recall something. His eyes grow dark and distant. 'Not what but *who*.' One of the birds breaks from their flock to settle on Jim-Ben's shoulder. He glances sideways at the creature, unfazed as it drips sinew onto his coat. The bird screeches at me, unimpressed. 'They don't like things that aren't dead,' he explains.

'Am I not?'

He shakes his head. 'Not yet. Though, from the smell of it, you might not be far off.' Jim-Ben reaches up and scratches the bird beneath the beak. 'For over two decades, Wrigley has been searching for a mage known as Johan. He is the last war mage. A creature of unimaginable fury and wrath.' Jim-Ben frowns as the bird pecks at his finger. 'There was a woman once. I don't remember her name. One night was all Wrigley had but it was enough to produce a son. He seemed happy. The mages weren't pleased, but they came to know him. They accepted him for the sake of his boy. But then the purges began, and the woman and child were lost in the cull. Johan is the boy's grandfather. Wrigley has dedicated his life to finding the man who could wreak vengeance on his son's murderers.'

'But why would you help him if you suspected what he was doing?'

He looks at me like he's disappointed. 'Because the cause was just, even if the plan was not. I didn't do any of it for Wrigley. Those mages deserved to find their way home, even after death. Perhaps I was a fool for thinking it was enough. That they could find comfort in our service. That it might give them peace.'

I curse Jim-Ben for leaving me. I curse Wrigley for killing me. Mostly, I curse myself. 'But how are you here? How am I here?' I wonder how many other things Jim-Ben never told me. He crooks a finger at me, indicates I should follow him across the foggy ground. We walk for a while, before he stops. I look down and see a crimson pond. One of the birds swoops down, crashing into the water. It emerges a moment later, feathers slick and glistening. It glares at me with black eyes and I feel like I'm intruding somehow.

Jim-Ben puts a hand on my shoulder. I recoil. Not because he disgusts me, but because I don't want to feel how dead he is. 'Tell me, what do you remember about the day they hung you?'

The scars on my neck are awake now, screaming. 'It was spring. I know that because there was still snow on the ground and I had holes in my shoes.' It was funny, the little details that stuck in your mind. 'They always hated me, the other boys in the home, almost as much as Master Taylor did. Just because I was different. They didn't like the way I looked. He used to come round with the birch cane. Liked the way it sounded against my skin.' My fists clench as I remember things. Things I don't want to think about. 'He always said my skin scars better than other peoples'.'

I think about the lash marks on my back, across my arms and legs. I keep those ones covered. Those are the ones I don't let speak to me.

There's a cry from above as two flocks collide, the bird-shaped bits of flesh exploding against one another and dissipating into the air.

There's a tremor in my voice now. 'He never stopped them. Just watched as the other boys dragged me into town and strung me up on that gibbet to watch me kick. They threw stones at me. I think they got angry I wasn't dying quick enough.'

Jim-Ben tightens the grip on my shoulder. I shrug him away. I don't want to be a victim. I *won't* be a victim. But he knows me. He knows my scars are still unhealed, exposed nerves open to the air and jagged to the touch.

'The first time we retrieved a mage corpse, Wrigley and I delivered the body to the woman's grandmother.' Jim-Ben lifts one hand and stares at it. The dagger he always kept at his side appears, in ghostly form. I look down, and realise the real blade is still hidden beneath my coat. The spectre of the weapon spins above his out-stretched palm. 'This was the gift she gave me. A talisman to protect against death. A few weeks later, I died for the first time. Shot, funnily enough.'

I wasn't sure what was funny about it.

Jim-Ben stares at his hand. 'You think you know death. I died three times before we even met. Each time, this blade brought me back. There's a magic imbued in it that keeps the bearer protected. For a time, at least. But all things end.' He sounds sad. 'When the time is right, you'll die too. But not yet. You've got things to finish, appren-tice.'

'I don't want it. Why should I? Life never did anything for me.'

'Life doesn't owe you anything.'

'It isn't fair.' I sound like a child. I feel like one.

'It never is.'

We stand there for a moment. I think about how much more I could have had from the world. I think of all the things I haven't done yet. Everything I pushed aside be-cause I was angry and wanted the world to know it.

'So,' Jim-Ben steps back. He lifts one hand to feed the bird a crumb of flesh from his shoulder, 'What are you going to do now?'

I don't know. I don't know anything anymore. I thought I knew death, how it worked. What it tasted like in the back of your throat. I look up and see Jim-Ben star-ing at me like he wants an answer.

Now I'm angry and it's good because suddenly I can *feel* again. My blood is warm and my heart beats against my ribs. I want to punch something. I want to dive into ice, cold water. I want to run naked through a town at midnight. I want to kiss girls and boys with reckless aban-don. I want to tear into the world and shovel great chunks of it into my mouth like fresh fruit. I want to live.

Fuck. I want to live.

Jim-Ben's lips crack into a smile as the flock of birds swoops one last time, picking me up and sweeping me back out of the in-between, as if they can't wait to be rid of me.

***

'So, what's the plan then?' Ragger spits a bit of sausage onto the table.

I blink a few times. My nostrils flare at the smell of grease and stale beer. Someone drops a cup behind us and the sound of smashing glass against the floor rings in my ears like an explosion. Ragger is looking at me like my brain has gone soft and for a moment, I wonder if it has. Maybe I dreamed it all. Then I slip my hands down to my side and touch the new scar where Wrigley's knife went in. I feel Jim-Ben's dagger sitting beneath my jacket.

'Cullen is dead.' I repeat my earlier words. 'Wrigley knows who did it. He knew about Bridget too. Something is happening and Wrigley doesn't want anyone getting in the way. He's working with the mages, and we need to stop them.'

This time Ragger doesn't mock me. His eyes darken. 'What do you mean he knew about Bridget?' The tip of his knife digs deep into the flat of the table.

'All those stories we heard about him? The ones we used to think were shit? They're true.'

Ragger shakes his head. 'Bullshit. It's illegal. No mage woman can bear a child to a human. It would be death for them both. Wrigley wouldn't condemn his own kid to the noose.'

'Maybe he thought he could hide them. I don't know. All I know is, Wrigley's on a suicide mission and he's going to take all of us down with him.'

Before Ragger can say anything, the door of the tavern bursts open. The place fills with watchmen looking for someone. I can guess who. Eight officers crowd together, swamped in thick woollen cloaks. One of them steps forward and snarls. 'We're looking for members of the Gallows Square Gang. One of them was seen up in Alderley. There's been a sighting of one of them with a suspected mage.' He holds up a piece of paper. I already know whose face is on it.

The man behind the counter shrugs. 'Ain't no mages been in here, not seen one for years.'

The watchman's head snaps from left to right. 'Reports came in. Several of them have been seen gathering outside town. You want to lock your doors and windows. It isn't safe outside.'

I try to keep my head low and Ragger does the same. I hope the watchmen don't recognise us but I know we're not that lucky. They've seen our faces. Some of them have pictures of us in their offices. We've even stolen a few. Ragger likes to keep his as a joke, and the worse they are the better he likes them. I feel eyes in the back of my head and I know it's too late. Ragger does too and slips a pistol into his hand beneath the table.

'You need to find Wrigley,' he whispers to me, voice strained and urgent. 'He'll be at the square by now. Find him and stop whatever this is. Do it for me and Bridget.'

I don't have time to say anything before he's on his feet, coattails flying around his calves. Ragger unloads a shot at the first watchmen and runs headlong into them. It's all dust and blood. He's fearsome. Roaring and barrelling, he screams for the bastards to come get some. And they do.

The guns are all on Ragger. There's so much smoke, I can't see. My boots hit the ground, one foot after another. I know my way to the square well. I've cut down more than my fair share of bodies from those ropes. My steps pound against the hard slabs and I feel it all the way up my legs.

I reach the square and scan the scene before me.

They've gathered a good audience for this one. I struggle to find Wrigley amongst the crush. When I do see him, he's standing on the other side with Cullen, hidden within the mass. People jostle and vie for the best positions at the front of the crowd. They say there's nothing quite like watching a mage dangle. In life they're luminous, skin so pale as to almost be translucent, wet pearl crushed to powder. When the knot tightens, the glow about them fades with every thrash and dying nerve, until they look human again. Like seeing a god rendered mortal.

I think about using my pistol to put a bullet between Wrigley's eyes, but I can't get a clear sight and I'm not a good shot. People surge around me and I can't go forward. I can't go back. I can only watch as the walking carcass that was once Cullen stands, silent and subservient. Wrigley pulls a flask from his pocket and empties it all over Cullen's cloak. Now Cullen is dripping, and I know what's coming next. The gibbet already creaks under the weight of six corpses.

There's a drum roll. The watchmen walk the last of the condemned mages up the steps to the scaffold, a dark cloak pulled tight around his shoulders. The mage is on the platform now, rope suspended above his head. From across the crowd, I see Wrigley flick a match across the striking surface of a silver tin. Cullen goes up like he's made of tinder.

The crowd screams when they see the flames. Cullen doesn't make a sound. I see him walk forward and climb onto the platform, moving like a man possessed. The watch unloads their bullets into him, and the shots do nothing. He's a human torch and I can't stop him from taking hold of the nearest swinging corpse. Cullen embraces the dead mage like friends reunited. *Magic needs heat, it needs to burn. They need to burn.* My nostrils flare. Cullen stinks like a pig on a spit.

The flames find purchase on the dead mage's cloak.

They're both engulfed in the blaze, he and Cullen embracing like lovers. The condemned man awaiting his noose does not move. The watch calls for buckets. Someone screams for water. I see smoke rising from the hanged man's flesh, dark and purple. Only it isn't smoke. It's magic. I can feel it pouring from him, seeking new life – a new host. A wisp at first, building and billowing until it smothers the platform.

The smoke expands until nothing can be seen. Then, just as quickly, it retracts. The cloud collapses violently inwards. I see now where the magic is going. The last of the condemned stands there, his hands extending outwards. Whatever energy is spewing from his cremated comrade, it's his now. He takes it all in. I hear a bang. Cullen flies back from the stage, carried by a blast of energy enough to wipe half the crowd off their feet.

The smoke is gone. The magic has found its new home. Amongst the charred wreckage, the surviving mage stands alone. His hood falls back and my mouth drops. I count them. Fifty stars. A hundred stars. More than I have ever seen; his skin so marked his features disappear beneath a galaxy of them, a whole sky's worth of magic. *Johan.*

His skin glows bright and next thing he's in the air, twenty feet above the plinth. The war mage lifts his arms above his head as the crowd drop to their knees. The whole town is trembling. Cowering before a wrathful god.

He casts his hands forward and the ground, torn from its roots, surges upward like a wave. The buildings around the square begin to crumble and fall. The stone blocks of the floor beneath us crack, shooting up great mounds of earth. Then we feel them. We can hear them, the mage souls imprisoned in their tombs. They're screaming, voices rising up out of the soil. I press my hands against my ears.

I feel myself going mad, every inch of me stripping

342

away. All around, I see men dash their heads against rocks rather than bear the sounds. Above me, the war mage's entire being crackles with violet beams, bolts of energy snaking about his arms and legs. He pulls one hand upward and the earth tears again. The gallows stage splits in two, folding like splintered firewood into a chasm. The watch fire their bullets into him. Johan absorbs each shot like his body is made of quicksand. One of the shooters curses as his chamber empties. A second later, he flies through the air.

I watch, slack-jawed as Johan moves his hands. He lifts another of the watch, bolts of energy curl around the man's waist and drag him upwards. Now he will have *his* macabre puppet show. Vomit fills my mouth. Wailing fills my ears. I see the last war mage take those two soft, breakable bodies and slam them together in mid-air. He pulls them apart. Does it again. Again. Until you can't tell which of the two men is which. They've merged as one great, grotesque paste.

Someone knocks me back. I realise everyone is running. The square is chaos. I glance down and Cullen's still. The flesh has burnt down to the bone. He's with Gryff and Jim-Ben now and I can't do anything but run. Run like all the other people who want to live. I stumble and falter, tripping over hot stone, buildings twisting and buckling as they fall. I hear the roar of the world rolling beneath its crust.

I feel the heat from the earth. They're burning the catacombs — Johan's men, Wrigley's mage comrades, in there now with torches and gasoline. They're setting them free. Five thousand mage souls finally able to move on, leaving their magic behind. Because it was never dead. Only buried. A bomb waiting for a fuse to light it.

Not like this, I tell myself, *not like this.*

I keep running until I reach the edge of the square. Past the tavern and back towards the boundaries of Unston. For a moment, I think I might make it. Then I hit something.

Or it hits me. I'm not sure. My nose cracks and I'm on my backside. Scrambling for my weapon, I unsheathe Jim-Ben's dagger. A mage is standing over me, turning his head to one side, considering me like I'm an ant and he's the boot. I know his face. He came to us in the field, along with his brother, to collect the last body I released from the gallows.

He lifts one hand and clicks his fingers. The blade tumbles from my grip despite my effort to keep hold of it. I don't move. My body isn't listening to the screaming inside my head. *Run. Run you stupid child. This is it. This is the animal you've always known would bite you. This is death.*

The mage bends down and plucks the knife from the ground. I watch as he runs his fingers across the intricate markings on the handle. I never asked what they meant. I figured they were just pretty. The mage raises an eyebrow. 'Who gave you this?'

My mouth is dry. Everything tastes of smoke and ash. 'A good man. He's gone now. Dead, like everyone else who ever mattered to me.'

The mage is unmoved. 'Where is Wrigley?'

I shake my head, 'I'm not sure. I didn't see. Dead, I think.'

I can't tell if he looks sad. He presses a finger to the tip of the blade. 'That's a shame.' I watch as his hand hovers over the dagger. A wisp of purple smoke seeps from it and into his palm. The metal seems to dull.

My voice cracks. 'What happens next?'

The mage steps forward. I can smell blood on him. A moment later, he's crouched beside me, staring hard at something that lies beneath my skin. He seems to recognise it. I think it's all my rage. He throws the blade at the blackened earth beside me. 'That's up to Johan to decide. Keep the blade. The way the world is going to be after this, you'll need something that cuts deep.'

With that, he's gone, screeching back into the air. It's

quiet now but it won't last. The mages have their power back, and there's a lot to answer for. I look up at the sky and see it full of souls. I assume that's what they are. I don't know how it works. A mage-woman made of shadows passes over my head with raven's wings. Perhaps the most beautiful woman I've ever seen. I swear I see her carrying Wrigley. I don't find his body or Ragger's. I don't stop to look. I just leave town. I walk to the coast and by the time I get there my boots are full of blood and my feet are raw with blisters.

***

It's been a year and the world isn't ours anymore. It's theirs again, as it was before. I don't set foot on land these days. Maybe I never will again. But I like my life aboard the ship. I like the feeling of the sun on my back, sweat in my armpits, and salt on my skin.

These days my plans have changed. I still think about the end sometimes. I'm human and it's what we do. But I'm going to live a bit first.

I've come to realise there's a difference between living and not dying. I don't think of death as a game anymore. The funny thing is, I think I understand the rules now.

HEART
THE RITUALIST

By
Ryan Howse

When I awoke in the night, the bird was dead. Its body had bloated and discoloured, and its feathers were damp. Drowned in its cage in my room. I sat up and opened the cage. The metallic squeak was loud enough to make my husband stir.

I grabbed the metal tray I'd left by my bedside for this, then pulled the bird out. The Drowned Below had kept their part of the bargain. I had offered them sacrifice, and they had accepted. Even now, water pooled in its mouth and I had to be cautious not to jostle the tiny corpse.

I set the bird on the tray and carried it down the hall. I crept past the room where my children slept, then walked down the spiral stairs.

There was always such a charge in the air—like a spark in your blood—when one of the entities accepted your offer. One never wanted to delay when the powers accepted a trade.

My parents had spoken similarly when they struck a deal. 'A merchant is like a heart,' my father would say.

346

'Keeping goods flowing through society like blood.' But he traded for coin. I trade with powerful entities, each of them locked in their own torment, each of them needing what only we mortals could provide.

I reached the bottom floor of our manor house and strode across the tiles to the door to my sanctum. It was locked; I had to balance the tray in one hand while I fished out the key and unlocked it, then entered.

The sanctum always had a strong smell. At the top of the stairs, the scent of dirt and dust was strongest, and as I went down further into it the mixture of chemicals and alchemicals, the animals, the herbs, flowers, fungi, and moss all mingled, along with the faint smell of rushing water. When we built this place, I'd hired people to make a small irrigation line that diverted a stream of water from the nearby river. A simple way to dispose of turpentine or excess paint, I had said, for my art. And they had agreed despite my lack of paintings, because when you're paid enough you don't ask questions.

The sanctum was a large room filled with concentric warded rings. Those rings were both my protection and my guarantee to the entities I bartered with. I had carved them years ago when I first built my sanctum. I checked them weekly and updated them as needed. When dealing with the entities, all things had to be perfect.

In addition to the animals, there were shelves of scrolls. Most of them detailed various rituals or the precise arrangements for wards, and I had much of that memorised. Some were lists of other scrolls, first person accounts of the entities, and one book had logistical information on what was stored in this room and where.

Once I entered my sanctum, my chorus of wildlife made their usual grunts and hisses. The adders in their glass case, the voles clambering over each other, frogs in a bucket with mesh covering it. Whether nocturnal or not, they all stirred at my presence.

But the pig was silent. I walked to its pen, and saw that

it, too, had drowned. Another part of the pact, I thought, satisfied. Its pen was soaked in aqua vitae, and blood and bile smeared the area right in front of its mouth.

I knelt and touched the pig's skin. Soaked through, cold and briny, just like the bird. Neither had suffered the warm, brackish swamp water from Ezkara, but the depths of the ocean where The Drowned Below were imprisoned.

They had taken two of my offerings. A fine trade.

I started with the bird. It was much smaller and more delicate. I had to be far more precise with my incisions. I broke apart its hollow ribs. The lungs and stomach had filled to bursting with water. Carefully, I removed the lungs, the heart, the stomach, tiny as they were and placed them on the metal tray to the side.

Those lungs had been filled by The Drowned Below, meaning that the water inside them was aqua vitae. That was the trade. The Drowned Below briefly got to inhabit those animals, and breathe air, until those animals drowned. For a few minutes, they could rest, and for that, they would offer much power.

As planned, they'd left my family alone and taken animal sacrifices instead. I'd granted my family mystical protection through wards of Those On High and various elementalists and even a dash of protection from the Susurrant Entities. Had The Drowned Ones tried anything against my family, they'd have their own broken bargains to deal with. I had wards throughout the room.

My parents would not want to think of their daughter hauling around large dead animals to carve up for rituals. As merchants, they'd taught me the importance of finding what people needed and what they were willing to give up for it. And I used those customs to make pacts with entities rather than people.

The Drowned Below were some of the easiest entities to entreat. They wanted air, a brief respite from their endless drowning, and they needed living beings to inhabit to gain that. They'd prefer humans, but they'd accept animals. The Endless Dead, too, wanted nothing so much as corpses to live within. The Thousand Faces wanted body parts for the infinite mosaic it created. Those Who Watch and Weep just wanted the thinnest slice of one's memory.

Those On High offered mystical protection in exchange for aqua vitae, as it was the only thing that could soothe their endless wounds, and that was what I hoped to use this for.

The Burnt Flagellant wanted obedience and disciples, and I remained cautious around their devotees.

It was one of few I never made deals with, as it required a lifelong commitment. Life was too long to devote to any one thing. And its hatchwife allies, spirits of life, unnerved me like little else.

When I finally got the pig to the grate, I had to push hard to cut through its tougher skin. As I pushed my knife into it, the strong scent of iron enveloped the air. It lingered in my nose and mouth, and even my eyes felt dry.

First I sliced the groin and waited as the blood drained. Insects landed on the wound and buzzed around my ears, a constant ongoing irritation in this swamp of a city. When the blood had drained down the grate and was washed away, I took the tip of the knife and ran it up the pig's sternum. The skin peeled back. Then, the bone saw, to crack the chest open. I am reasonably practiced with it, but it was still a tiring endeavour. But the bones were opened enough that I could begin pulling the organs out.

I was elbow deep in blood and halfway through removing the heart when the bells began to toll.

The Cacophine Bells of the Holy Basilica of the Burning Flagellant would only ring a single time each day at noon. If it wasn't noon, or if they rang more than that one single time, it meant there was an emergency. Given the heat outside, a fire seemed the most likely, and would be devastating.

I looked at my aqua vitae, sighed, and cleaned my

hands of the blood. First, oil, to help create a film between the blood and my skin, then a strigil for scraping off as much as I could, and finally, some water to remove the oil and last traces of blood. I left the half-dissected pig by the grate and headed back upstairs.

The view from my balcony would be the best place to see where the emergency was. I heard my children whimpering as I made my way up the stairs. They peered out of the darkened doorway, two sets of eyes, one atop the other.

'Hush, you two,' I said, smiling. 'Come with me.'

Celia and Ursu held tightly onto my legs.

Celia was the kind of child who would bide her manners and speak politely until you did something she disliked, at which point she'd become a raging beast. Ursu was too clever, but would never stick with any one thing. Every few months she would become bloated on a very specific knowledge, become sick of it, and find something new to gorge upon.

I love them more than anything.

'Come, come,' I said, trying to keep them from clutching my legs so tightly I couldn't move.

'Why the bells ringing, Mommy?' Celia asked.

'Why *are* the bells ringing?' I responded. 'That's what I'm trying to find out. Come now.'

We entered my bedroom, where my husband, already dressed, was leaning out over the balcony.

'What's the emergency?' I asked. 'Is it fire? Can you see it?'

'No fire I can see. Can't quite hear what the crier is saying just yet,' he replied. His voice was the calm in the storm. Even though his role as ambassador to Ezkara had been intended as a punishment for wedding me when someone else wished to, he had always maintained that composure.

I pushed my fingers against the children's necks as if I was playing scales on piano, ushering them to the balcony, then stepped outside. The night air was thick, and the scent of stagnant water lingered, but I could smell no smoke.

If there was no smoke, then the alarm might suggest there was an invasion force, though I could not think of who it would be or why anyone would want to conquer Ezkara.

'What's happening?' Celia asked. The bell had stopped, but the criers were still too far away to hear.

'I'm not sure yet, darling,' I told her, then picked her up. The town sprawled around us, hard-baked roads spiralling around shops and guildhalls and houses, with the Neverbreathe Swamp winding its way around the outskirts of the southeast corner of the city as a demarcation. Moonlight reflected onto the houses, and shops signifying their importance had alchemical lanterns flaring through the night. The bells rang again, three more times, and ceased.

Finally, the crier came close enough that I could hear the words. 'Witchcraft!' he called. 'Witchcraft in the town. Witchcraft!'

I went numb and had to put Celia down or I'd drop her. The words ran through me like a jolt of thaumaturgy. Witchcraft. I had been careful, but had someone found out about my pact-binding? Or was there another pact-binder somewhere in this backwater?

It took time and coaxing, but I got the children back to sleep. They were certain that the witchcraft would infiltrate our home, and I struggled to keep the conversation positive as they kept trying to outdo each other with graphic descriptions of what would happen to us. Celia believed our eyes would turn to Xs, while Ursu thought we'd have boils over our body and then the boils would pop and venomous snakes would emerge.

I had made sure they were protected but telling them they were protected under the auspices of another powerful entity, another form of witchcraft, would have terrified them all the more.

My children, bless them, had the power of any child to know when their parents needed them to sleep and to resist it with all their might. I laid with them in the dark, hushing them as they had terrified conversations, all the while my own heart pounding. It couldn't be me. How would anyone have found out about my pact? It must be someone else.

Finally, they slept and I went downstairs to find my husband putting his boots on. 'Where are you going at this time of night?' I asked.

'There's witchcraft in this town,' he said. 'Got to find out what I can.'

'Oh, Grigori,' I said, 'I should do that. I'm the one who knows how this works.'

He studied me. 'You did good getting the children back to sleep. Let me do my part. Besides, it'll be better with me showing up.'

He wasn't wrong. The acolytes of the Burnt Flagellant still mistrusted women, despite official decrees to the contrary. The man of the house searching for clues about a witch would throw suspicion off me. Were I to show up, I'd be seen as being too invested, not taking care of my children.

The problem, of course, was that my Grigori, bless him, knew little about witchcraft.

'Go, then,' I said, the words char upon my lips.

He stepped forward, cupped his hand under my chin, and kissed me. His stubble had grown through the night and brushed against my skin. Then the door opened and he was gone.

I sat at the table and ate apples on bread with a glass of water. Once that was finished I peeked at Celia and Ursu again. Both still slept.

I headed back to my sanctum. I had to find out what was happening. It was time for another ritual. I spoke a short incantation to Those Who Watch and Weep while my left index finger ran vertically down my forehead and my right finger ran horizontally across my eyes. I needed a vision, and to do that, I offered the thinnest slice of memory, a single heartbeat's worth. It vanished from my mind, but that was fine, because I had all those heartbeats from before and after. I willed to see the consequences of the witchcraft the crier had spoken of. An image appeared before me.

It was a family of three in a cart, being taken into a building. The Ramirovhs. A husband who cut lumber, a wife who carved wood, and their son, only a few years older than my own children. They were so much paler than I'd ever seen them, covered in water as if they had drowned in the swamp.

The building the cart entered was made of stone shaped as if it twisted upwards, a hand grasping towards the sun. To further this imagery, the roof of the building looked as if it had five bent fingers twisting out of it. The Basilica of the Burnt Flagellant.

As fast as the image appeared, I knew the Church of the Burnt Flagellant would have wards against pacts. The Burnt Flagellant didn't speak to me or make itself known, but I ended the image immediately.

They knew someone was searching. They might even know who.

I cursed. And, as awful as I am sure this sounds, I was furious at my children. I could have had this done an hour earlier, long before the bodies entered the Basilica, if they could have just slept. The image I'd asked for would either have been in transport or where they died, not in the warded Basilica. Why couldn't they have fallen asleep? Now the Burnt Flagellant knew someone had tried to peer.

Even now, after everything, I still feel guilt over my anger. They were just scared. But.

I could still find out what had killed the Ramirhovs. I knew where they lived, east of us. I would investigate it and pass my findings on to Grigori. Their bodies would be examined in the Basilica, but there might be information at their home.

After the warding had caught me I was hesitant to try glancing at their house through a ritual. I knew the wards were only in the Basilica itself, but I had already been burnt once tonight.

I'd seen the bodies, and they were soaked. A disease could have killed them, though that would be a lot of liquid expunged. Could have been a killer compelled to murder in a specific way. Either of those were natural explanations that might still make the superstitious believe it to be witchcraft.

But witchcraft — or rather, pact-binding — remained a possibility. No way I could determine it until I examined their bodies.

I considered making a pact with The Thousand Faces for some illusory magics to protect me but opted for a simpler home-made disguise. I used some of Grigori's older and more threadbare clothes, some makeup to change my complexion, and tied my hair back behind a hood.

With that, I strode through the streets of my city. Tumble-down houses sprang up around me like weeds, illuminated by the silver moon. The city stank of offal and piss and rotting food. The stagnant air clutched those scents to it.

Each bead of sweat clung to me, offering no surcease to the barren heat. I brushed them with my long sleeve but new ones appeared in moments.

Rats scurried into holes in buildings, making their nests wherever they could. The one decent thing the acolytes of the Burnt Flagellant did was use their own pacts to keep the little bastards out of our granaries. I saw one adder slip into the same hole some rats had fled into. Nature always hungered.

More people were about than usual for the late hour,

thanks to the crier, but no one gave me a second look. It hardly went unnoticed that the people out looking to find what was happening were largely men. The few women were all older and had no children at home. Old women were allowed to snoop.

I couldn't see anyone keeping watch at the Ramirhov home. It was possible there was someone I'd missed. I felt a compulsion to perform another ritual to Those Who Watch and Weep, but if someone saw me doing a ritual I'd be executed in accordance with the precepts of the Burnt Flagellant. I watched the house a moment. All seemed calm. I slipped inside.

Immediately, I knew it had been pact-binding. Witchcraft, in the parlance of the ignorant.

The floor was wet through the main room, seeping around my sandals and slapping with every step. The beds and blankets smelled of soaked down. And the liquid was clearly not water, but aqua vitae, with the brine and salt and cold of the depths of the ocean where The Drowned Below were captive.

The Drowned Below had not harmed my family, but they'd harmed a family. Drowned them in their beds.

Why?

There had to be markings here. This could not be from my appeal to The Drowned Below. I had set wards upon wards to keep people safe. Someone else had done this, they must have.

If that was the case, there had to be runes, markings, something to show that someone else had done it. There was another pact-binder in town. There had to be. Had to be a way to prove it. I searched the walls, the floor, the ceiling. I pulled back curtains. I tore through the house, frenzied as a starving rat. I laid on my back to examine the underside of their table. Nothing.

Exasperated and exhausted, I put my head in my hands and slumped against the bed. The thick wet down made me realise that there could well be sigils under the bed. Of course, that must be it. That's where everything would be.

I propped myself against the bed and tried to push it, but my feet slipped in the aqua vitae and the water in the bed made it heavier than normal. I couldn't move it and it was too low to the ground to crawl under. I gave up two heartbeats, one to see the floor and one to see underneath the bed.

No markings on either.

Had this been my work? I didn't want to believe it but what choice did I have? There was no sign of anyone else. I had made a deal with the entities the same day.

What had I done?

I hadn't known the Ramirhovs well, but everything I knew of them was that they were decent, peaceful folk. I couldn't help but imagine the fear of something else taking your body, a mouth filled with liquid, trying to expel it. Even worse, being unable to help your family. Those Who Watch and Weep, what had I done?

I felt as if brackish water had replaced my blood. Sitting on the bed, I felt the aqua vitae seep past my clothing to my skin. I put my head into my hands and stared at the floor.

There were dangers when dealing with such strange entities but I believed I had the specific requirements to perform the rituals safely. It was hardly my first time dealing with The Drowned Below. What had happened to create such a tragedy?

The Burnt Flagellant didn't have the powers of Those Who Watch and Weep, but they had divinations. They already knew someone had tried to search out the Basilica earlier. There was no one else to pin this on. Even were I to use all my pacts to fight back, I would at best take a handful of the acolytes of the Burnt Flagellant with me.

They would learn it was me. I no longer had the option to investigate this and pass on the real culprit to Grigori. I was the culprit. I didn't know how I had failed, but I clearly had.

If this was to be the end of my life, what would become of my children? Grigori could take care of himself but he'd make a poor father. Would we lose everything? Were I to die, would Grigori be executed as husband to a witch? Would our children be disallowed our land and titles, to be taken in by the same worshippers of the Burnt Flagellants who had murdered their mother?

They would be raised to hate me and that I could not abide.

I had few options, and none were good. No chance I could get my children out of the city in the short time I had left. Not with the wastelands around.

An idea came to me. I felt a roil of nausea in my stomach. I'd have to entreat with The Endless Dead and afterwards fool them into leaving my family in peace. I headed towards the local cemetery, on the edge of town. Nothing was past it save the wastelands.

There had to be someone left whose body I could exhume. It didn't take much; I just needed to find gravestones that had female names, of an age close to mine, that had recently been buried.

Flies and mosquitoes swarmed me as I sought out bodies that seemed appropriate. I slapped my neck trying to dissuade them and ended up covered in their corpses. My neck had a constellation of dead insects upon it.

I offered another heartbeat to Those Who Watch and Weep to find a recently dug grave. Several visions appeared before me, all layered atop each other, but the one by a bald cypress tree seemed the easiest to find.

I didn't have wards here for protection, but The Endless Dead's sacrifice was far less lethal than The Drowned Below. One of them would get to briefly inhabit this corpse, and I would trade my next sleep to them. They could truly rest in peace, while my dreams would be of staring out of their dead, long-rotted eyes at the ground they were interred in.

Mind you, I had no intention of following through with that part of the deal. Had I, the plan would have collapsed.

An uncomfortable few minutes passed as the corpse crawled out of its grave. The dead woman before me was pale and stiff. Scabs formed across much of her body. I saw a sharp puncture wound in her chest. She'd been stabbed through the ribcage.

I had neither time nor inclination to dress the wound properly. I wrapped her own shirt around it a few times instead. All I needed was a body; no need for it to be in perfect condition. This wouldn't work if people knew a body had been stolen. The corpse and I filled the hole back in.

I then had the corpse follow me outside the cemetery, through the wastelands beyond the city. We made our way around the outskirts, only turning back to Ezkara proper when we neared my home. The strangest part of it was how normal it felt, just two people out for a walk. In the wastelands. At night. And one of us was dead.

Thankfully, my house was also near the edge of the city. It was the dark before dawn at that point and even with the accusations of witchcraft people needed to sleep. I brought the body back to my house and didn't see anyone.

By the time I got back I was soaked in sweat and overheated. The night was so hot and the air so thick it made me want to crawl out of my skin. It would have been an unfortunate night to die. Honestly, not a great night to fake my death, either, but such actions rarely happen at opportune moments.

The acolytes of the Burnt Flagellant would know of my deals soon enough if they didn't already. I scratched out a note of my deep regret and remorse and how I had hidden this secret from my family.

Already, my sanctum was filled with bugs trying to find purchase on my skin. Nearby, my wren squawked.

It was swarmed with bugs but could do nothing in its cage. Poor thing wanted to escape, a feeling I could empathise with even as I had no plans to open that door.

I'd need strength for this. Not just the ritual of attunement, but the escape afterwards. I took a pouch full of coin then looked over the corpse. My replacement.

I looked back to the stairs and the door to my house where the children were sleeping. I wished I could explain it to them. Grigori would manage but the children were young to lose me, and I would miss them every day.

I hoped he'd find another wife, and more so, I hoped she'd love them the way I did. They deserved it. They didn't deserve this, but their mother had made a mistake, and one grievous enough that there was no other option.

I prepared my ritual. The last deal I'd make would be with the Thousand Faces. Everyone would believe this corpse was me. Then I'd have to prepare an attunement, to convince the eldritch entities that she was me. One ritual for mortals, and one for the entities.

So much bartering with these powers. As if nothing could go wrong. As if they weren't beyond our minds. And yet I couldn't stop. Not yet.

'Thousand Faces, I implore thee, listen to my request. I grant you of my own body,' I said. 'I offer my self as a new part of your collection. To prove my word, here is my hair.'

I grabbed the scissors and hacked through my hair. Giant tufts fell into the bowl. My long locks turned to scalp. I saw myself in the reflection of the silvered bowl. Celia and Ursu wouldn't recognise their mother.

I knew, in some ways, that was for the best, but the hole in my heart grew. *Focus*, I reminded myself, but it wasn't easy. I had to do this to keep my children safe. The hair was the easiest part.

'I offer you my nail,' I said. I grabbed a blade and jabbed the spot where my thumbnail met skin. I clenched my teeth and drove it down like a fulcrum, forcing the thumbnail up. I bit my lips to keep from screaming, and as the droplets of blood spattered the floor I threw the thumbnail into the pot. I grabbed gauze and wrapped it around my finger.

Couldn't just be the clippings, oh no. No pacts without pain.

Fingernails and hair were just the beginning. 'I offer you a tooth.'

I inserted a dental pelican and put it into my mouth and I nearly gagged, with the cold iron keeping my mouth open. The easiest option would be one of my canines, but the back molar, I thought, would be best in the long run.

The hard metal squeezed against the tooth and I yanked, but the pain from my fingernail hurt enough that I had to take a break. Now my mouth was in agony.

These were some heartbeats I wouldn't mind giving up to Those Who Watch and Weep.

I used both hands to grip the pelican and pulled as hard as I could, until the molar came out. The pain in the back of my mouth was excruciating. I spat the tooth into the bucket, along with the blood that oozed from my lips. Such blood would only add to my offering to the Thousand Faces.

I put a cold wet cloth into my mouth and dabbed at it several times. Tooth, hair, nail. Just one thing left before I could finish.

'I offer you skin.'

I pressed the knife against my forearm and slowly peeled a piece of skin as long as my hand. I wrapped my arm in gauze that turned red fast, then watched as the skin spooled into the runic bowl. I shoved my hand into my bucket of leeches and sat on my haunches for several minutes while they fed. Then I pulled them out.

'I offer you blood,' I said as I tore them off my hand, six long wiggling tubes with teeth being dropped into the bowl.

'Thousand Faces, you have what I offered. Do you accept?'

The things I had put into the bowl shimmered, indicating that they agreed. Then, the dead body slowly transmuted. My skin in the bowl changed colour to match the pallor of the corpse, and vice versa. The hair in the bowl became hers, growing rapidly. The tooth shimmered and her face shaped itself to look like mine.

Good. Halfway done. Now, the attunement. But first, a wave of dizziness overcame me. I laid back and put another cloth into the water, then on my forehead. Nerves were screaming from too many places now. My body didn't know which wound to prioritise. I dabbed my mouth again.

When I pulled the cloth out of my mouth, the blood on the cloth started blooming into pustules, sacs growing out of her old blood.

What? My body screamed, incapable of understanding. After a moment of blind panic, my mind realised what it was, and wanted to scream too. I had expected a battle with the acolytes of the Burnt Flagellant. Instead, they'd summoned something to kill me. A hatchwife, a spirit of life.

Don't let the moniker fool you. The hatchwife is one of the most dangerous of all spirits, and I'd never expected them to unleash it on me. If they were that terrified of my powers, they thought the Ramirhov deaths were intentional, that I'd meant to drown them from afar.

The hatchwife grows new life wherever it goes. And when I say life, I mean the basest forms: parasites, tumours, diseases. Whatever you were would change depending upon its whims. Arteries turned to vines, cartilage suffused with insect eggs.

Thankfully, I already had everything ready for the attunement. If I could enact it quickly enough the entities would think that the corpse was me, and if I was dead, the hatchwife would return to its own dimension.

361

The wren squawked in fear before its throat closed up. It belched blood forward and its body fell against its cage, and then tumours grew on its belly until they squeezed against the bars on the cage, trying to force their way through.

The bird's blood on the cold stone ground began to move and ripple, and then small hearts, the size of my fingernail, appeared.

I didn't have much time. I had to finish the attunement. I grabbed a needle and thread, and a jar of the aqua vitae I had taken earlier. I wouldn't have time to do everything the proper, cautious way, not with the hatchwife so close.

I poured the aqua vitae but let it sit in my mouth, rather than swallowing. I waited as it acclimatised itself. I saw the vipers in their glass cage attack each other. They were in pain and didn't know why. They couldn't know the hatchwife was manipulating their bodies. They lashed out. As their fangs sank into each other, small hearts bloomed from the wounds. Panicking, I dribbled the smallest amount of aqua vitae onto the floor.

Then I rushed to the corpse and opened her mouth. I spewed the water into her mouth, then sewed it shut so it would not spill. It would soon come out of the wound in her heart. The hatchwife's attention snapped from me to the corpse, and sensing that I was no longer alive, it vanished.

It felt like there was a sharp slice in reality. The painful stillness of the night sky released with a sudden wind I could feel even in the sanctum. My shaved hair was blown and then drifted into the river.

I looked at the fake self I had created, the simulacra. She looked so like me. It was an unnerving experience, staring at a dead version of myself. But if even I couldn't find the imperfections, no one could.

I took the corpse by the hand, sent her to the stream, and pushed her in.

I desperately hoped that my children wouldn't stumble upon this macabre scene. I wanted, more than anything, to go upstairs and hold them one last time. But that was the last thing I could do. To keep them safe, I'd have to flee.

I hoped Grigori would raise the children well. If he was to take another wife, please be one who would treat Celia and Ursu as if they were her own.

There was nothing else to be done. It was time to flee.

***

It will not surprise you to know my rest was not fitful. The attunement had severed my deal with The Endless Dead, so I was not forced to stare at the inside of catacombs or coffins or whatever place that particular soul had been entombed within. But still, the pain in my mouth, my forearm, and my finger kept rest from falling upon me.

I was certain the hatchwife's hearts were blooming along my skin, only to open panicked eyes and see a cluster of insects feeding where I'd cut myself.

Sunrise blurred my vision and I opened groggy eyes. The silhouette of Ezkara was on the horizon. I'd spent the last hour before dawn in a ditch, I had insect bites all over my exposed skin, and at least once I'd awoken to startle some small, furry predator that fled when I stirred.

I looked back on Ezkara. I hated that city. I always had. We'd been sent there as punishment for wedding my husband when someone else felt entitled. Hot and fetid, few natural resources, a constant stench. The perfect place to send ambassadors and their wives when you wanted them out of your sight. The perfect place for people who had been exiled.

My mind kept spiralling on the question of the Ramirhovs. What had happened to them? Why had my request gone so awry?

I knew I should flee. I was not prepared, but I'd taken my coin purse from my sanctum. A few days walking through the hot sun would get me to the nearby port city of Cenna Leon. With the money, I could book passage on a ship, sail to a place of white sand and clear water, open a business, do what I wanted.

But of course, never see my children again, nor my Grigori. Not except through Those Who Watch and Weep.

I performed the ritual again. Gave up another heart-beat's worth of memories. Tried to see how Ezkara was reacting to my supposed suicide. I didn't want to look at my family, couldn't bear to see Celia and Ursu so broken-hearted.

But the scene Those Who Watch and Weep provided me was one of worry over the Ramhirov's death, as if I was alive. They still seemed to be seeking the witch. The Burnt Flagellant had not told anyone of who did it or why.

That didn't make sense. They'd sent a hatchwife after me. Why had they not told the citizenry?

I couldn't peer at the Basilica itself; my attempt to do so last night started this. I gave up three heartbeats, flitting from location to location trying to find any members of the Burnt Flagellant outside the Basilica but none were speaking of it.

I could have kept going. Perhaps I should have. But now I couldn't resist looking in on my family. I winced, prepared for the worst. Ursu and Celia would be distraught. Grigori would put on a stoic face to the children, but if I caught him alone…

Swallowing, I offered up another heartbeat.

Celia was dutifully eating her breakfast, staring down a piece of bread as if she hoped it would surrender without terms. Ursu had already devoured most of hers, as evidenced by the disaster of crumbs around her seat. A woman was behind her with a broom, one with long black hair. She was wearing my dress.

Who was that? Had Grigori already hired someone to tidy the house? So fast? Why was she in my clothes? And given the looks on my children's faces, he hadn't told them yet.

Well. I didn't see much point in giving up more heartbeats just yet, as the next images would be almost identical, though my heart felt soothed from just seeing Celia and Ursu.

But lying in the wastes outside of Ezkara, with the wounds from my ritual last night causing such pain, a distraction seemed like a fine idea. And giving up these heartbeats meant nothing. I could contextualise the moments around it, make it seamless.

The next vision appeared, and I gasped like a stitch in my side had burst. Grigori's hands, running across the small of her back, the same way he had always done to me. This didn't make any sense. My head spun. I didn't pause. Another heartbeat, another flash.

Everything came crashing down then. I stared at me, but a me who still had her hair, who did not drool blood. A version of myself who had a wound in her side, wrapped in fresh gauze.

Had Grigori rescued the fake me from the water? No! You beautiful, foolish man, I thought. He had saved me, and in doing so doomed the whole family. If the acolytes of the Burnt Flagellant thought I still lived, they'd just try again.

My heart smoked. I had thought I had done what was necessary to save them, but nothing had changed. The acolytes of the Burnt Flagellant would be on their way to set our home ablaze. I had to get back there. I had to save them.

I dusted myself off, slapped more of the insects off, and trudged back, towards my home.

***

I walked through the streets of Ezkara a stranger. No one would know me if they saw me. Given the fear in the populace, best to keep my head low and seem as unremarkable as possible.

I made my way back to our manor house, and looked across the courtyard, where I saw Celia and Ursu. My heart wanted to fling itself from my chest at the sight of them.

'Mother!' Ursu yelled out, and I almost ran to them.

'Look, a beetle! Look at the hard front wings, Mother! Aren't they amazing?'

And then my heart, so close to leaping out of my chest, choked in my throat instead.

I watched as the other me, the new mother, knelt and started poking at the beetle with Ursu. I wanted to scream at her, to tell that thing to get away from my family, but they'd be so much more scared by me, terrifying as I must look.

My mind spun, confused as to how this had happened. First the Ramirhovs were killed by an incorrect ritual, and now my pact with The Endless Dead was going longer than it should have. My ritual space had been immaculate for years, and I knew what I was doing. So why had everything gone so wrong?

I waited, watching my children play. It was a balm despite everything. Ursu was filling herself with knowledge of every bug imaginable and would rush from place to place looking at them, letting them crawl on her, giggling wildly the entire time. There are times as a parent you simply ignore your own whims to please your child, and as I looked at that smile on her face I wished I could have dozens of the insects upon me.

And Celia, sweet as ever, trying her best to climb the juniper tree in the front yard, scrambling her little legs and kicking bark everywhere. She asked my mimic to lift her, and I watched as the other me bent down and picked her up, placing her on the lowest branch. Celia lifted her arms, as amazed as if she had flown there.

Eventually, the heat of an Ezkaran summer forced the three of them indoors. I felt a sense of loss as they retreated inside; I needed them out of the way so I could look into what was going on and I couldn't go see them with the other me there anyhow, but still, it ached to have them vanish from my sight.

I felt like a beaten dog as I slunk towards the small river near our house. I swam under the wall and came up into my laboratory. I knew it was a place I had left off limits to the rest of the family, a place only I'd had a key to, so when I surfaced I didn't expect Grigori to be down there, staring at me.

'Leave,' he said. 'You do not know what you are dealing with here.' His voice didn't quaver, though I could see the fear in his eyes. His years as an ambassador had given him the ability to seem calm even now.

'Grigori,' I said, 'it's me. Your wife.'

'My wife is upstairs,' he said. 'You are intruding on my sanctum, whoever you are. I have enough—'

'This is my place, Grigori. The stream was put in at my behest when we moved in and started making this place our own. This laboratory was filled with my animals, and…' The pens were filled with the remnants of yesterday's ritual. My animals were all dead, bloated, diseased, still in their cages. They should be burned and their ashes in the river before disease would spread. 'You should burn all of this.'

'You sound like her,' he said, and his voice shook, so slightly that I doubted anyone else would even notice.

'I am her. I had to do this to escape,' I said. 'They found out, Grigori. Why they aren't here yet, I do not know. But the acolytes will come, and they will burn this house to the ground. I thought a body would satisfy them, and you would all be safe. I put her in the water, and a note apologising for—'

367

'I found that note. And then I found you,' he said. 'I brought you out... or... oh no.'

He sat on a stool, his head in his hands. 'What is with our children right now?' His voice suggested he didn't truly want an answer, and it was hard to blame him.

'I used a ritual to make her look like me,' I said. 'The Burnt Flagellant know I'm a pact-binder, Grigori.'

'I could have gotten you out of that,' he said. 'There are advantages to being married to an ambassador, you know. We could have made some kind of arrangement. But not if you escalate. Not if you...' His voice broke for the first time, and that stung worse than any ritual.

'I was trying to keep you safe.'

'You nearly did the opposite,' he said. 'My wife dies suddenly? With rumours of witchcraft through Ezkara? They'd be suspicious about that, my dear, and they would have uprooted some uncomfortable questions. Questions like, 'Why is there a goddamned barn in our basement? Why are bloodstains all over the floor?' How am I going to answer that? And even if it had worked, what would it have done to our children? Losing their mother in such a strange way? Who would raise them? What kind of permanent wounds would they carry? How could you do that to them?'

It felt as though the next words were scraped from my mouth. 'I never wanted to. More than anything else, I never wanted to leave them,' I said, voice sharp and raspy, words breaking like the hand of a caught thief.

'But I thought if I was gone they'd leave us alone.'

'They will leave us alone because that's what our power does for us. We are staid, good folk. I know you come from merchants but there are benefits to having a strong lineage, and one of those is that you can just... not do what you did. We keep our heads up, do what we can, and no one bothers us. That's part of being married to an ambassador, to sharing my family name.'

'But the Burnt Flagellant knew. He sent creatures after

368

me.' I knew Grigori was past understanding now. He had a political way out of this and I had a metaphysical way out, but our tactics were clashing and we were speaking different languages.

He gestured around at the workshop. 'You put up so many wards and protective barriers. We could use that to redirect it to someone else, let the blame fall on them.'

I followed his gesture and my eyes fell on a series of markings at the end of the sanctum. Despite the heat, I shivered, as if I was at the bottom of a cold, black ocean.

My masterpiece wards, the seat of my mystical protection, had been disrupted. Alternate lines ran through them. 'What happened here?' I asked, pointing at it.

'I have no idea,' he said. 'Is it bad?'

I wanted to snap at him that yes, it was bad, but it wasn't his fault. All of this was on me.

I grabbed the scrolls that detailed the rituals and examined them, scanning to find the ones about this ritual. My hands flung aside The Assumption of the Endless Dead and The Broken Hymn of Those On High, knocked several parchments detailing how to beseech The Susurrant Entities. And then I found it.

The protective wards of Those On High were incorrect. I had misremembered. A ward was aimed northwards when it should have been east.

All those heartbeats I had given up were recollections of my training. Just a small sequence of events, but the entities had patience. Enough to break my wards and cause my rituals to misfire. One single line in the wrong direction was enough. And when those were incorrect, it wasn't that the ritual wouldn't work. It was that the ritual could be twisted by the entities.

The Drowned Below had taken extra people. I glanced at the northwards line and made a rough estimation. The Ramirhovs lived in that direction. And somehow the Endless Dead had taken over the corpse I had used. And all this for aqua vitae, which had seemed so important such a short time ago. I had planned to make a deal with Those On High for protection. I was a fool.

Sudden screams burst from both girls upstairs. I rushed past Grigori, knocking him to the floor in my rush. A distant part of me realised that seeing another me would baffle them, but that was far beneath the heart-frenzied panic of their screams.

I hit the top of the stairs and threw the door to the kitchen open. When I got up there, Celia saw me and screamed again and ran the opposite direction. Her face was streaked in blood. And I could still hear Ursu, somewhere above me.

'Celia, Celia, come here love,' I said, gesturing towards myself.

She went white and let out a whimper of 'Daddy.'

I slumped. 'I'm going to help Ursu, all right? Daddy is right down there,' I said, and ran for the stairs.

'You leave Ursu alone!' she snarled at me.

'Go see your father, dear,' I said, trying my best to keep my voice level, but I could hear the words bounce from my mouth. I climbed the stairs, my hand on the cold silvered wood. I could hear Ursu moaning, with occasional quiet murmurs of 'Please stop, Mommy.' As I rounded the top of the stairs, I saw the other version of myself, frozen in place. Blood spurted from the open wound in her heart and it had sprayed all over Ursu's face.

I ran towards her and pulled the fake me away, and as I did so I saw the eyes were blank, staring into nothing. The cavity in her chest had reopened and I could see into that heart, pumping its black sludge.

The Endless Dead within the fake version of me was diminishing, the corpse returning to its previous state. I pushed her back into my bedroom and slammed the door. The corpse likely wouldn't have the capability of opening a doorknob at this point. I heard a crash inside the room and knew it was over. The corpse was simply a corpse again.

'Come, darling,' I said, 'I'm your real mother, this is a fake. It's nothing. Just come with me, come away now.' Ursu wiped her eyes with her sleeve but smeared it across her face so she looked like a barbarian heading off to battle. She reached out a hand and I noticed the blood on her face was blossoming, small red dahlias coming to life.

With the death of the mimic, the hatchwife had returned.

'We have to run, my girl,' I said, but I had no idea where to. My wards would not keep it out.

I looked at Ursu.

Ursu was heaving sobs and unable to think so I swung her into my arms and raced down the stairs. Out of the corner of my eye I saw the hatchwife, drifting across the road in front of our house towards me. It had been horrifying last night, when it had been hidden from my sight. And in broad daylight, it was even more terrifying. A body in constant flux, skin emerging as pustules and popping and the liquid running cartilage that shifted into plants emerging out of what should have been hands, and then those plants were devoured by small parasites that fell into the body and were absorbed.

I darted into the basement. She'd been there before, but then I'd not realised that I had botched my wards. I doubted I had time to rectify them but what choice did I have?

Grigori looked at me. 'What's going on? Why is she bleeding?'

'It's not her blood,' I said. 'Where's Celia?'

'She's not here,' he said. 'She was upstairs.'

Dammit. 'I told her to come down here and see you,' I said. 'Can you bring her back? I have work I need to do or we're all —'

'I'm on it,' he said, and went upstairs.

'Stay over there, my girl,' I said to Ursu. 'Lots of insects for you to play with.'

'Ew,' she said, 'why are there so many dead animals?'

'Long story, my dear,' I said. I had no time to explain, nor would I know how to start. Sorry, Ursu, your mother is a witch.

I pulled out the silvered paint I'd used for the wards and sprinkled salt over the line I had made in error, removing its power, then knelt on the ground and started work on the missing line, leaving a slight gap, then made an inner circle. I sprinkled aqua vitae over the paint, adding in the protection of Those On High.

Grigori opened the door above us. 'What the hell is that?' he yelled.

'Did you get Celia?' I asked.

He shook his head. 'I couldn't get past it,' he yelled.

He staggered down the stairs. 'What is it?'

'Get Ursu and get out of here. Go through the river. Ursu, be a good girl for your father. And then make sure you get Celia.' She fled because she had feared me. Now I had no idea of her safety, and I couldn't guarantee it. There is no worse feeling.

'What are you going to do?' he asked, while pushing Ursu towards the small rivulet under the house.

I didn't answer because I wasn't certain what I was going to do. The hatchwife drifted through the door at the top of the stairs and flowers and grass burst forth from the staircase, more dahlias and sharp-thorned roses and grass the colour of veins. I heard the splash of my husband and child as they fled, and I hoped this would be the end of it.

Feeling flowers blossom from my fingertips was the oddest sensation. It was surpassed moments later by blooms bursting inside my body. I coughed blood, and the blood formed into hearts. The hatchwife drifted towards me as I shook with pain. I collapsed to the ground, silver paint on my brush still in hand.

And I painted the last, slight gap in the line. Two circles, one outer and one inner.

It was now in the wards, unable to escape. It battered itself against both circles I had completed. I, trapped inside with it surrounding me, felt blossoms in my throat and coughed blood that undulated and twisted on the ground.

I was trapped, as bound in the wards as it was. It surrounded me, stretching its body. I'd been altered by the hatchwife enough by now that the wards would prevent me from leaving. Were I to destroy that ward, I would dissolve into bursts of flowers and hearts and hatred and become part of the hatchwife.

And we would both be bound here until the wards failed. If the stream under the house rose and washed it away, if people with more curiosity than sense investigated, if the earth cracked and broke, on that day we would be resurrected again.

I stayed inside that tomb. Trapped as I was, I needed all I could get from the entities, and I would offer them whatever they wished in return. As the days faded to months and years, I gleaned piecemeal phrases of my story from far-away lands, from the true witches of the Deepened Woods, to the scholar-sacrifants of the Jagged Obelisk, and the pact-binders of my homeland. A new name upon their lips. She Who Trades With The Beyond.

SKIN
MY MOTHER TOOK HER SKIN OFF EACH NIGHT

By
Zamil Akhtar

CHAPTER 1

My gloved hands jitter against the keyboard. My eyes strain against the bright screen, which I set to maximum so I won't see my own reflection. I have to tell this story before Mother comes for my skin, so I can warn everyone about the evil that destroyed my family.

For most of my life, I could not remember my childhood. At night, I'd dream memories, but they'd be puzzle pieces. It was frustrating — to say the least — not knowing why I was the way I was. Then a few nights ago, I dreamt something that explained precisely why I'd chosen not to remember. I dreamt about Mother and what she did each night after crawling through my window.

Remembering also brought on a unique phobia, and it's making my life impossible. I'm disgusted by skin —

374

my own and others'. While most folks perceive skin as a nice, comforting wrapper for their bodies, I see it as something easily shed, something you might wear like a designer coat.

I wasn't always so disturbed.

My story begins when I was thirteen, with a more common malady: trypophobia. I'd have a panic attack upon seeing anything that resembled a pattern of bumps or holes. Beehives, Swiss cheeses, pomegranate seeds, and even these rashes I'd suffer from on my arms and legs. Wasn't too hard avoiding such images, so I lived a normal, suburban life under the care of my uncle and aunt, who'd raised me since I was eight.

Everything changed after college when I began working as an actuary -- a risk assessor for insurance companies. Sounds like a boring job, and it was, though the pay was good. The work-life balance allowed me enough time to hang out with friends on the weekend and continue my music-making hobby. After a year of toiling as an entry-level actuary, I found a higher paying job as a medical actuary at one of the big five insurance companies. It turned out to be a huge mistake.

My role sometimes required me to look at pictures of pre-existing conditions suffered by people applying for insurance. I had no fear of diseases, so this was mostly fine, except when it came to skin lesions. I'd often leave work hyperventilating, my button-down shirt covered in sweat, after looking at such pictures, and it happened so often that my timecard-obsessed boss called me to his office one day.

Something just scratched on my window – I pray it was the wind, but just in case, I'm going to speed this story up.

I was honest about my condition, so my boss suggested therapy. My therapist figured that some event from childhood had caused my phobia. It was then that I digested an awful truth, one that had been hanging over me my entire life: sitting in the sombre lighting of my therapist's office, I realised I had no memory of my life before I turned eight, before I moved in with my uncle.

We tried various methods, such as hypnosis, to help me remember. But I'd buried my memories too deep. I simply had nothing to latch on to from my childhood — not a single person, place, or object. So the therapist suggested I induce my memories to surface by dreaming. I was to keep a journal and write down everything I dreamt each night. I was then to bring this dream journal to our sessions, and by finding patterns within the dreams, we could identify people, places, and objects from my childhood, which I could then think about before going to sleep, to induce deeper dreams about those things.

This was when my life truly began to fall apart.

Every morning, I wrote in my dream journal. Most of the time, I'd leave a blank page because I simply couldn't remember what I'd dreamt about. But when I could, I'd often describe a place with bright lights. Lights so blinding, I couldn't see what was ahead of me. After my therapist read these entries, he told me to focus on the idea of *looking down* before I went to sleep. If I couldn't see ahead, perhaps I could see beneath.

I continued to dream of bright lights, but I couldn't remember to look down, despite focusing on the idea while in bed. Around this time, I met a girl named Nora at a friend's graduation party. On our second date, she came over and stayed the night.

Normally I don't like things to progress that fast, but when I noticed how much she loved some of the electronic tunes I'd make in my free time, I knew she was special. Also, she wouldn't space out whenever I talked about my job as an actuary. Weirdly enough, it was that very night — whilst thoroughly exhausted — that I finally remembered to *look down* in my dream amid the bright lights.

I saw my feet, pale and tiny, as if I were at the age when you walk for the first time. I stood on a metal floor, the texture smooth. The shadow of *someone else* projected forward from behind me. The shadow grew as the lights brightened, as if whoever loomed was approaching. And as this person approached, my heart thudded faster, until it was about to burst out of my throat.

At that moment, someone shook me awake.

'You were screaming,' Nora said, covered only by my sky-blue duvet. 'Nightmare?'

I nodded, then opened my nightstand drawer and grabbed my dream journal.

'That's cool that you keep a dream journal. I should start doing that.'

'It helps with creativity.'

I hoped she wouldn't think my dream journal weird. Though I liked her, after only two dates, I certainly wasn't ready to tell her I was doing this to find the origins of a lifelong phobia. Nora got dressed, I made scrambled eggs, and she headed home after a chill breakfast.

The next day, while sitting on my therapist's white couch, I read from my dream journal.

'Bright lights all around and a metal floor...' Doctor Nathaniel tapped his pen against his pad, then adjusted his spectacles. 'That sounds like radiation therapy to me.'

'Radiation therapy?'

'It's still done now, although it's far more targeted. But back in the day, people would stand inside these radiation chambers. The lights were blindingly bright. The floors, metal.'

'What for?'

'Skin cancer treatment, mostly. But serious cases of psoriasis and even eczema, sometimes. In your teenage years, did you ever suffer from any skin conditions?'

I hesitated. From time to time, I'd get these clustered rashes that would trigger my trypophobia. I'd do my best not to look at or touch them.

'Not really. Rashes now and then, but they always went away on their own.' I straightened and cleared my throat. 'I have a question. In these radiation chambers, would people go in alone or with others?'

'Oh no, they were only large enough for one person a time.'

'So what about the shadow I keep seeing?'

Doctor Nathaniel removed his spectacles, breathed on the lenses, and wiped them with his shirt. 'Look, dreams are often stitches of smaller things that make sense individually, but not when put together. In a room with light sources coming at you from every angle, there wouldn't be shadows. I suspect the shadow is your mind projecting the presence of whomever was waiting for you outside the room. Your caretaker at the time.'

'You mean my mother or father?'

'Most likely. I think you must've had some sort of serious skin condition when you were younger. Looking at similar things reminds you of that and triggers your phobia.' He put his spectacles back on, then smiled in his gentle way. 'But I also suspect it's not the skin condition itself that caused the trauma. It's something related that involves your caretaker. Now, have you asked your uncle about your parents?'

Whenever I asked him about my mother or father, he'd sweat and shake and grab his whisky bottle. My aunt would then chide me for bringing up my parents.

'I've tried, but he's not willing to talk about them.'

'What about other family members?'

'I have none.' I blew out a dismal sigh.

'I see. I suspect your uncle is trying to protect you. I often see this protective behaviour when a parent is in prison for a serious crime.'

'Prison? You really think that could be it?'

'It's a possibility. Despite what happened when you were younger, you've managed to grow up, get a good education, and hold down a steady job. He may not want a bad influence coming into your life to derail your success.'

Doctor Nathaniel put his pencil and pad aside, then crossed his legs, smiling at me all the while.

'I always suspected my mother and father were dead. Not sure why... just a feeling.'

'That could be the case. But it would be more difficult to explain why your uncle isn't willing to talk about them. To learn more, you should focus on a new command before going to sleep. "Look behind."'

'"Look behind." So I can see the caster of the shadow.'

'Precisely.' He tapped on his watch face. 'Oh, how time flies. My waiting room is full, so we'll have to continue another time.'

I headed home. Nora called me. She sounded excited to come over and make prawn pancakes. No chance I could refuse, despite being worn from work.

A fun evening followed. When it was time for bed, I took a melatonin pill, stared at the shadows on the wall, and waited for Nora to fall asleep.

Then I turned away and whispered to myself, low so it wouldn't disturb her, 'Look behind. Look behind. Look behind.'

'"Look behind?" What does that mean?'

I glanced over my shoulder to see Nora wide awake.

'Damn. Did I wake you?'

'I'm not a deep sleeper.'

Strange. She'd looked quite asleep a few minutes ago, with her mouth open and curly bangs shadowing her lids.

'It's for my dream journaling. I'm trying to give myself a command for when I'm dreaming.'

'Really? Why "look behind"?'

I let out a sigh. Perhaps with things becoming serious between us, I ought to explain. So I described my trypophobia, the therapy sessions, and also the dream with the bright lights and metal floor.

Nora listened with cool eyes, nodding the while.

When I was done, she said, 'I thought it was going to be something so much worse.'

'Worse?'

'Yeah. Being scared of small holes doesn't sound so bad.'

'It's not. It's only because of my job. And I *really* don't want to lose this job.'

'Although…' Nora pulled the duvet over her shoulders. 'It is odd that you don't remember anything about your childhood.'

'I used to think it was normal, funnily enough. That our memories only begin when we turn eight.'

'Most people don't remember anything before the age of five. So you're not so different, I suppose. It's really only three or four years that you're missing.'

The melatonin was massaging my mind and easing my thoughts. 'I better focus on my mantra.' I yawned, exaggerating slightly so she'd get the message.

'Okay.' She kissed my forehead. 'Sweet dreams.'

I turned onto my side, facing away from Nora. 'Look behind,' I whispered to myself. 'Look behind. Look… behind. Look be…'

Bright lights stared at me. I stood upon a textureless metal floor. The looming shadow grew larger and as it did, my heart roiled like a boiling pot.

'Loooooookkk… beeeeeeeee… hiiiiiiinnnddd…' a voice called from a distant realm.

I turned, though it felt like my limbs each weighed a thousand pounds.

There. Someone stood amid the bright lights: a shadow. I stared, without blinking, until features appeared.

Grey flecks dotted the man's neat brown beard. A robe the colour of blood shrouded him. An insignia glowed upon the robe's breast pocket, though I could only perceive it as a jumble of symbols and letters.

'May the light enter you.' He smiled too widely for a

human and the voice echoed out of his throat, the tones all wrong. 'May it purify you.'

No. I'd had enough light. I wanted to escape this awful prison. My heart smashed into my rib cage, yearning to fly away. But fear froze my feet.

Nora shook me awake. She wrapped herself around me, comforting my terror with warmth.

'Did you see what was behind you?'

I grabbed my dream journal.

'I saw a man... a man in a red robe. He wasn't friendly.' An understatement. He terrified me. And though I didn't recognise him, I recognised the dread he poured through my veins. It wasn't the first time I'd seen him.

We talked some more, though I couldn't say much. Because we both had work, we devoured the eggs I fried and headed to our cars.

It turned out to be an exhausting day, during which I constantly thought about the dream. After work, I walked to the building across the street for my therapy appointment. That terrifying man's image remained burned onto my eyelids. Even as I sat in the dimly lit waiting room, I feared the lights would brighten and he'd stand in a distant doorway, staring at me with his inhumanly wide smile.

When the door squeaked open for my appointment, I walked in, sat on the white couch, and almost cried. It seemed weak to cry about some strange man from my forgotten childhood, so I didn't allow myself the release. Still, the dream had left me sadder than I'd been in a long time.

'You seem rather worn,' Doctor Nathaniel said. He licked his finger and turned to a new page in his notebook. 'Tell me.'

So I told him everything. All the while, he jotted down notes.

Then he closed his notebook, clasped his hands, and

reflected in silence for a minute.

'Did you ever attend church?' he finally asked.

I shook my head. 'My uncle was not religious.'

'The robe… the way you describe it shrouding the man's body… the long, gaping sleeves… the arrowhead-like opening at the collar — it's similar to a church robe.'

'I didn't realise.'

'Now you also described a symbol on the robe' — he tapped his breast pocket — 'but you say you couldn't quite make it out. Could it have been, say, a cross?'

'I don't think so. There were these letters on it. At the very least, it seemed a lot more elaborate than a simple cross.'

Doctor Nathaniel jotted it all down, writing more than I thought was possible. 'The words the man uttered, "May the light enter and purify you" has a religious connotation. The light is meant to save you. Perhaps from disease — spiritual disease.'

'I have no idea.' I shrugged. 'It was all so strange.'

'Indeed. But we must find out more. You should ask the man "who are you?"'

'"Who are you?"' I parroted.

'Yes. And one more thing…' Doctor Nathaniel cleared his throat, sat forward, and lowered his gaze, as if in hesitation. 'Don't invite your girlfriend to sleep over. While she means well, it's not helpful if she wakes you before the dream has naturally concluded. Even if you tell her not to, I fear she won't be able to endure your screams.'

'Okay. I can tell her I'm busy.'

On the way home, Nora called, her voice so chirpy and bright. I told her I was working late and so couldn't hang. When I was tucking into bed that night, the room felt frigid without her.

'Who are you?' I repeated after taking melatonin and getting comfortable on my back. 'Who are you? Who… are…'

Again, I was back amid the bright lights. This time, I

already faced the man in the blood-red robe. He loomed like a giant, perhaps because I was a child. I was frail and helpless, trapped in this cage with him.

'Whhooo… aaarrreee… yoooouuu…' the thought echoed from some distant void.

'Who are you?' I said with a child's quavering voice.

The man simply stared down with his wide smile. Then he bent toward me, the motion choppy, as if the blinding lights made it difficult for my mind to process.

The man's head loomed over mine, his eyes never pausing to blink.

'Tell Doctor Nathaniel he's asking the wrong question.' His lips did not move, always stuck in an inhuman grin. 'Tell Doctor Nathaniel that we see him.'

The man grabbed my shoulders. My heart writhed, screaming at me to wake. Instead, all I could do was stare into the man's suddenly eyeless sockets, deep as an abyss. With no one to shake me back to my world, I drowned in terror.

Until finally, I gasped. I threw off my duvet and scratched at my burning skin. Scratched my shoulders, where the man had touched me.

I ran to the bathroom and doused my face in water. Pulled off my t-shirt.

A cluster of bumps, as if I'd been bitten by a hundred mosquitos, clung to my shoulders. I vomited the cheese sandwich I had for dinner. I grabbed a butter knife from the kitchen and used it to lather steroid cream onto the rash, gagging all the while. Then I threw on a long sleeve button-down and headed to my car.

I did my best to focus on work, and with hundreds of emails to sort through, managed to get my mind off the dream. During lunch, I almost called to cancel my therapist appointment but figured I should at least report the horrible dream to Doctor Nathaniel. Nora called me, asking if I wanted to get dinner at a Thai place near her house. Just hearing her voice was a balm to my nerves.

More of her would help me relax, so I agreed.

The rest of the workday flew by. Soon, I was sitting on Doctor Nathaniel's pristine couch. Instead of trying to explain, I handed him my dream journal.

'So it seems I've been noticed by your overprotective subconscious mind.' Doctor Nathaniel grinned. 'Quite the honour, I must say.'

I wasn't in a laughing mood but chuckled just to be polite. 'Doctor, I think I need a break from inducing these dreams.'

'I agree. I'm here to help you recover. The last thing we want is to overwhelm you.'

We talked about Nora for the remainder of the session. Sharing how happy she made me helped me feel lighter.

'Take it easy during the weekend,' Doctor Nathaniel said. 'And should you continue to feel anxiety, I can prescribe Xanax.'

'I'd rather not take anything. I just want to let myself go back to normal.'

'I understand. Oh…' Doctor Nathaniel shut his notebook with a *thud*. 'Well, maybe it's best we discuss this at our next meeting.'

'Discuss what?'

'It's a bit of a… heavy topic. Wouldn't want to ruin your weekend.'

My heart raced at the thought of what it could be. 'Just tell me, Doctor. Otherwise, I'll be wondering what it is instead of enjoying my date.'

'Have you ever heard of the Church of Bright Lights?'

I shook my head. 'What's that?'

Doctor Nathaniel removed his spectacles and rubbed the lenses with the bottom of his shirt. 'It was a religious organisation that achieved some notoriety about fifteen years ago. They had a local chapter about an hour's drive from here.'

'And?'

He put his spectacles back on and blinked a few times.

'When hospitals began replacing their radiation chambers with the more modern linear accelerator machines, most of them sold the radiation chambers for scrap parts or donated them abroad. But some of these machines were also purchased by a private buyer, often well above what they were worth. That private buyer was the leader of the Church of Bright Lights.'

Nausea wriggled through my stomach. 'Are you telling me…'

He tapped on his watch face. 'It looks like we're out of time. I've got patients waiting, so we can discuss it more next week.'

Were my parents part of some cult? Was my dream some cult ritual, instead of a medical procedure?

I wished I hadn't asked.

'Oh, one more thing.' Doctor Nathaniel reached for his prescription pad. 'I'm prescribing an antihistamine for the rash. Would you prefer drowsy or non-drowsy?'

'Drowsy. Might as well take it before bed.'

'We're getting closer to the truth,' he said with a smile. 'Shining a light on it *will* help you move on.' He got up and opened his door for me.

CHAPTER 2

I tried to enjoy my date with Nora but I kept tuning her out and thinking of my dreams, the image of the man in the crimson robe smiling at me with abysses for eyes.

'What's wrong?' She put her hand over mine as we waited for our noodles in the crowded eatery.

'My bad dream is ruining my day.'

'Was it another one of those memory dreams?'

I nodded. 'I looked behind, this time.'

'What did you see?'

Would it be wise to mention the Church of Bright Lights? It was only our fourth date, after all.

'An awful man with an awful face.' My shoulder

itched. I scratched it, but that only made it itchier. I wished I'd brought some steroid cream. 'I need to use the bathroom.'

As soon as I went inside, I took off my sports coat, undid the top buttons of my shirt, and popped my shoulder out. A bright red cluster of bumps stared back. I shut my eyes as my heart raced. I turned on the faucet, dabbed a paper towel, and patted down the rash. It continued to burn.

I returned to Nora and put three twenty-dollar bills on the table. 'Sorry. Something's come up.'

'Oh.' Nora let out a disappointed sigh. 'You look flustered. Is everything all right?'

'I'm fine.'

'You don't have to pretend. If something's wrong, I want to help you.'

I didn't want to tell her about the rash. But leaving her in the middle of our date was worse.

'Uhh… I have this… rash on my shoulder. It's acting up.'

'Do you need something for it? There's a pharmacy on the next block.'

It was a twenty-minute drive to my house. The sooner I got relief, the better.

'Yeah. I can probably get what I need there.'

Nora told the waiter to pack our food and we walked to the pharmacy. I got the same cream I usually used. But now I had to apply it, and the thought of touching those bumps terrified me.

'This triggers your phobia, right?' Nora said. 'Do you need help?'

No way would I let her touch the rash. 'Just give me one of those plastic knives they put in the bag.'

Nora reached into the food bag and took out a plastic knife. I lathered on the cream and then buttered my shoulder as if it were bread.

The itching stopped within seconds. I let out a relieved

sigh and pulled my sports coat back on without buttoning my shirt.

'Sorry.' I let myself grin from the ridiculousness of it all. 'Guess I ruined dinner.'

'We can eat in the park. It'll be more scenic.'

I half expected her to want to head home and never see me again.

'Let's do it.'

I followed her as she drove to the park. We sat on a bench overlooking an old oak forest, the only light a crooked path lamp. I ate my noodles, she ate hers, and we talked about nice, mundane stuff, like what sports we played in high school. I was a runner and she hated field hockey but played it because her sister did.

Then she invited me over. I figured it would be better not to sleep in my bed for a change. We watched an old comedy movie, which got my mind off morbid matters. After, Nora fell asleep quickly leaving me to toss and turn surrounded by dark, unfamiliar walls.

And so the questions I'd been trying not to think about surfaced. What was the Church of Bright Lights? What did they believe? Did they put me in a radiation chamber? Why? Where were my parents when this was happening?

I pulled out my phone and typed 'Church of Bright Lights' into the search bar. I hovered my finger over the enter button, worried that whatever I found would keep me up all night. Would ruin what had so far been a decent day.

'Can't sleep?'

I turned to see Nora rubbing her groggy eyes.

'I forgot to bring my sleeping pills. Don't let me disturb you, though.'

'I won't let you suffer insomnia alone.' She glanced at my phone. Her eyes widened upon seeing what I'd typed. 'What's the 'Church of Bright Lights?''

'I don't know, but I think my parents were part of it.'

'Is it related to the man you saw in your dream? The

man who scared you?'

I nodded. 'I've been resisting the urge to find out more. As if… as if I don't want to know.'

'Why? What do you feel?'

'There's this… this *old* sense of dread. I want to know why I'm carrying it, but at the same time…'

'You're afraid.'

I nodded.

Nora put a warm hand on my shoulder, which thankfully, wasn't itchy. 'Of course you are. It's only natural. If you want, we could look it up together.'

'It could be weird.' I shook my head. 'I'd rather not freak you out.'

'You seem to think I'll run away or something. Let me be here for you.'

I almost wanted to ask *why?* Why stay with me when the truth could be so awful? Perhaps she didn't realise just how awful it could be because her veins weren't poisoned by the same dread as mine.

But her eyes were bright and sincere, so I didn't want to deny her.

'Okay. Sure.'

Nora grabbed her laptop off the nightstand. She typed, 'Church of Bright Lights' into the search bar and pressed 'Enter.'

Three pictures popped up, all in black and white, of a balding man wearing a tuxedo. Motes of dust obscured the lenses, so the background wasn't clear. I let out a relieved sigh as it obviously wasn't the man with the inhuman smile from my dream.

I pointed to the first link, which was a Wikipedia article. Nora clicked on it.

Our ears brushed as we drew closer to the screen.

The Church of Bright Lights was a group of interconnected organisations devoted to the practice and dissemination of the Bright Lights Dogma, which is variously defined as a cult or a new religious movement. The movement has been the subject of a number of controversies and several executives of the organisation were convicted and imprisoned for multiple offences.

Nora scrolled down to a section titled 'History.'

The Church of Bright Lights was incorporated by James R. Seville and his wife Madison Perry.

There were more names and dates, as well as details about the group's expansion. They had a chapter in every major city in the country at some point, and several celebrities and important government figures were members. I skimmed all that and got to the next section titled 'Beliefs.'

The Bright Lights Dogma is claimed by its founder James Seville to be based on writings found in ancient Sumerian tablets that had been part of his family's private collection for several centuries.

I looked at Nora.

'Did you read the part about the Sumerian tablets?' she asked.

She was obviously suppressing a smile, as if she found it all so ridiculous and funny.

'Par for the course for a dumb cult.' I smiled to hide my anxiety.

Nora let her laughter surface. 'Sorry.'

'It's okay. If you can't laugh at this, what can you laugh at?'

We both looked back at the screen.

The Bright Lights Dogma teaches that human souls were all born from a primordial light. The true human identity is said to be a 'cosmic' and 'godlike' formless light, which is trapped within the physical form. It is also believed the universe came into existence by the combined will of this formless light, instead of being created by a divine creator. One of the central tenets is that humans can reconnect with this light through repeated, high-dose radiation exposure.

'Sounds like a great philosophy for getting skin cancer,' Nora said.

'You're not wrong.'

I rubbed the touchpad to scroll down to the

'Controversies' section. Embedded within was that black and white picture of the tuxedo-wearing man.

The Church of Bright Lights has been labelled a cult by critics and government authorities. Some of the actions of the founder and the organisation have brought scrutiny from press and law enforcement. The radiation exposure that is a central practice is said to be responsible for a high rate of skin disease and skin cancer among former members. There have been cases of blindness caused by members being encouraged to stare at the sun, and cases of death from heatstroke.

Well… what did they expect?

I selected the *search* option in the browser and typed 'radiation chamber.'

No results, so I scrolled to a section titled 'Founder's Arrest.'

James Seville and his wife Madison Perry were arrested for tax evasion…

That section wasn't very interesting, but the arrest of the founders eventually led to the collapse of the organisation. It wasn't active anymore, which was a relief.

I'd skimmed or skipped most of the details so I'd have to reread the page more carefully when I got home. Nora put away her laptop, and we cuddled in the darkness of her room.

'He got those silly beliefs from some Sumerian tablets?' Nora said with a giggle. 'It just sounds like bad sci-fi. And the radiation stuff reminds me of people who drink bleach as a curative.'

'You know, if I were underwriting a former member of that cult, I'd have to make sure to label them as high risk. Probably deny them coverage.'

'Huh?'

'They're all a high risk for skin cancer.'

'Oh… you mean for your job?'

'Yeah.'

'Well… that makes sense, I suppose.'

I'd suffered from rashes on and off my whole life. How

much radiation exposure had my parents put me through?

'Are you worried about yourself?' Nora asked, as if she knew what I was thinking.

'Shouldn't I be?'

'Maybe you should see a doctor.'

'I've had my annual check-up. Company require-ment.'

'So you're all good, then.' She said it with such relief.

'For now.'

As I drifted off, I thought about the man in my dream. He wasn't the founder of the Church of Bright Lights but he might've been the leader of the local chapter. How could I learn more about him? And what about my mother and father? What had made them such acolytes that they'd drag their child along?

'Where is my mother?' I whispered. 'Where is my mother?'

I repeated the question as I drifted into a deep, dark lake…

There I was, in the radiation chamber. Now I could see the light sources on the walls: these scalding bulbs en-cased in glass. The sand-like texture of the metal floor scraped against my feet. It all seemed *realer* this time.

And hotter. Rawness throbbed across my naked skin.

I raised my hands; they were large. I was an adult. I was so aware now, I could inhabit my own body in the memory.

I turned to see the source of the shadow. The smiling man stared back, the sharp corners of his mouth twitch-ing.

'Whereeee… iiisss… mmmyyyy… moottthheeerrr…'

'Where is my mother?' I asked.

The man raised a bony finger, his skin hanging off it like a blanket dangling off a bed.

'Turn it on higher,' someone behind me said.

I turned. A wide-eyed woman with snaking scars

391

around her belly stood in the chamber next to me. She had long, bleached hair and burned, red skin. Her rose-coloured nose ring stirred a deep remembrance, as did the stench of her burning flesh.

'I want to be one with the light. Turn it on higher.'

It got brighter. Gobs of sweat trickled across my underarms.

'Higher,' the woman said. 'Higher. I want to be free. I want to be light. Higher. Higher!'

Everything dissolved into blazing white. I fried as if the sun itself grew eyes and stared.

I tried to scream, 'Let me out' but flames sizzled on my lips and tongue. The woman released a panicked scream. Even amid her screams, she chanted, 'Higher! Higher!' all while the engine powering the machine hummed. I breathed only the bloody smoke sizzling off our skins.

When the machine stopped humming and the lights dimmed, the woman stood with a body like the landscape of a volcano. Blood streamed from her eyes, down her cheeks, and dripped onto the floor. So much smoke steamed off her. In certain spots, her skin had been pulled off, like fried chicken. In other spots, it was red with burst blood vessels. But mostly, it was char.

She grinned, her teeth pure, in contrast to her charred face. 'I am the light.'

I didn't wake screaming, perhaps because I couldn't scream. But when I opened my eyes, the light streaming through Nora's window terrified me. I recoiled upon seeing her sleeveless arm near my face.

I got up and dressed, trying not to look at the sunlight, nor at Nora, nor even at my own body.

'You're up early,' she said with a yawn. 'Want breakfast?'

'I've got to head home.'

Soon as I managed to get my pants on, I hurried out of her room.

'You okay?'

'Boss called. Urgent work thing.'

'On a Saturday morning?'

'It sucks, I know, but I can't lose this job.'

I shut her apartment door, got to my car, and hit the ignition.

I couldn't bear the sight of my hands on the steering wheel, especially the pores around my knuckles. They made me think of my mother's hands, patterned in char, all the skin dripping. When I got home, I dug through my drawer to find my winter gloves. I pulled on thick socks, too. Stayed in my sports coat, so I wouldn't have to see my arms.

I closed the blinds and turned off the lights. I remained in darkness without a hint of skin showing, save for my face, which was fine since I couldn't see it. Unless I passed by a mirror. I threw towels over those.

This awful day was only the beginning of my torment.

And though the dream I'd just had was terrifying, it was nothing compared to the dream I'd have that night.

The dream that would make me question everything.

I wanted to talk to my mother. So that night, as I lay on my side after taking both melatonin and the antihistamine my doctor prescribed, I whispered, 'What happened to you? What happened to you?' Soon enough, the tendrils of sleep grabbed me.

I stood in a dark bedroom. Mother was there, sitting on a rocking chair. Her skin stuck to the armrests and hung off the edges like melted cheese.

She breathed with the help of a silver oxygen tank. Father would care for her. He would shout at me whenever I went into her room because I 'might make her sick.'

But there I was, standing in front of her as she rocked in her chair and smiled with exposed gums and jaw.

'Whaaaat... Happpppeeened... toooo... youuuuu...'

'Mommy, what happened to you?' I asked with a child's tiny voice.

'I am one with the light.' She could hardly wheeze the

393

words. 'I am the light.'

'What does that mean, Mommy?'

'I am the light, so I don't need this anymore.'

Mother stood. She dug into her skin. Pulled gobs and clumps of skin off, scraping the tougher parts with her long nails. She tossed her skin at my feet, while wheezing out, 'I am the light. I am free.'

Blood and innards leaked into the carpet, the stench like dust and rot. Then she clawed her face, tearing off what remained until her eyeballs stuck out like perfect moons. Her ears were holes in the sides of her face. No lips; her mouth was a dark oval.

Tears drenched my cheeks. 'Mommy, stop!'

'It's better this way.' The sound came from deep in her throat, guttural and devoid, as if it weren't her speaking it. 'Can't you see the light, now? Can't you see it shining from within me? Soon, you'll join me. Once you're grown up, you'll discover the truth. You'll come with me to the light.'

I turned around and ran for the door. I pushed down on the silver handle, but it wouldn't budge.

'Please Mommy, let me out.'

Mother opened the blinds. A beam of white cast into the room, as if born from a million of those bulbs.

She opened the window with a *screech*.

'I need to show everyone the light within me.' She crawled out but we were on the second floor, and there was no roof below. 'I'll be back.'

I awoke from the dream to my phone ringing. I ran to the bathroom and spewed my dinner into the sink. Then I checked my call log: it was Nora. But why was she calling at four in the morning?

I called her back.

'What you did wasn't funny,' she said, her voice brittle and jittery.

'What are you talking about?'

'Don't fuck with me. I can't believe I trusted you. I

can't believe I liked you.'

'Nora, I swear I have no idea what you're talking about.'

'Shut up. You're sick. Sicker than I could've ever imagined. Don't come near me ever again.'

She hung up. I called back, but the tone was busy, which meant she'd blocked my number. I messaged her but it showed as unreceived.

I did have her email address. I opened my laptop and shot off a quick message, simply stating that I didn't know why she was angry and that I would never do anything to upset her. I ended by expressing that I was worried about her.

Then I opened my web browser and typed 'Church of Bright Lights' into the search bar. I clicked 'Videos.' The first one was titled 'Testimonial from former Church of Bright Lights Member.'

My heart shook upon recognising the face in the thumbnail.

No question. It was the man who'd cared for me all my life. Or at least, what I remembered of it.

I was staring at my uncle.

I took a deep breath, hovered my cursor over the thumbnail, and clicked.

CHAPTER 3

My uncle stared into his cheap, low-resolution webcam. Thankfully, the lack of detail kept my phobia from triggering. He seemed tired, as he often did upon coming home from his middle management job in the shipping industry. There was an annoying buzz, probably from the wire connecting his webcam touching another wire.

'I'm not sure who's going to see this, but I want to talk about the Church of Bright Lights. It's been fifteen years since I left and I haven't talked about it. Thing is... I can't go on like this. While I hope my family doesn't see this...

I need someone – *anyone* – to know.'

His sigh lasted an eternity. He looked into the camera as if he were staring at me. But I couldn't recognise the trepidation in his eyes. My uncle's stoicism had always been so reassuring as a child. A bedrock. Now… I realised it was his way of hiding.

'Look, the stuff you'll read online about the Church only scratches the surface. People already know about the light worship and the radiation stuff, but there's a lot more that happened that no one knows about.'

He gulped as the screen flickered. That annoying background buzzing intensified for a moment.

'There were several tiers you could reach within the Church. When you reached the highest tier they finally taught you the true beliefs. This stuff is not published online. You see, I've seen the Sumerian tablets all this was based on. Obviously they're written in cuneiform so I couldn't read them, but I was given a translation that I believe was accurate. And no, I don't think those tablets were a forgery. They were part of a private collection held by James Seville's family for centuries. How that family got them, I don't know. What I do know is that his family comes from a line of British explorers, so it's conceivable that these tablets are the genuine article.'

A door squeaked open in the background. Someone put a glass of whisky on my uncle's desk. I could tell from the freckles on the pale hand that it was my aunt. The sight of freckles made me shudder.

My uncle took a big sip as the door shut.

'Okay, so the translation I read of these tablets described a ritual. It starts by opening your heart and praying to become one with the universal light, which is an idea they try to indoctrinate into you as soon as you join the Church. Then you're supposed to spend time in the sun, recognising in your mind that you're purifying yourself and becoming one with the light. This is all stuff everyone in the Church knows. But the final part…'

He downed the remaining whisky, ice jingling as he set the glass on his desk.

'The tablets claim that when you open yourself, when you 'shed your skin,' you will become a vessel for a... well they call it a god, but I'd say it's a demon. As for who this demon is or why anyone would want to be its vessel, I don't know. Except to say that it's a way to transcend your form, and people hunger for that. Even if it means giving your body to another entity, it's a way to connect with something *more*, something beyond our physical understanding.'

The video suddenly ended. Wait... was that all he had to say?

Sunlight shone through the edges of my blinds. My uncle often woke early to run, so I phoned him.

'I saw your video,' I said as soon as he picked up. 'My mother went through this ritual to its utmost conclusion, didn't she?'

'We should meet. Why don't you drive over?'

'All right.'

I drove forty-five minutes to his house in the suburbs, where I'd spent my formative years.

He came out onto the porch to greet me. 'Why the coat and gloves?'

'I don't like seeing my own skin. Or any skin.' I could hardly look at him, with his neck exposed. At least he was wearing a long sleeve, button down denim shirt.

'Your phobia's getting worse. I hoped you'd get over it.'

'What happened to my mother? Where was my father during all of this?'

'Let's go inside.'

I sat at the kitchen table. He poured me water and himself whisky. Then he sat across from me.

'Did you remember something?' he asked.

'I remember seeing my mother with her skin sloughed off. I remember seeing her crawl out a window, saying she was going to show everyone 'her light.''

'Yeah, so you remember. What more is there to tell?'

He reached for his whisky. I grabbed the glass and dumped the contents, ice and all, onto the kitchen floor. 'Tell me what *really* happened!'

'Your mother was possessed! We never saw her again, but we know she did some terrible things.'

'What 'terrible things'?'

'You don't know about the murders?' My uncle's hand jittered on the table. *Thud-thud-thud.* 'The police were never able to make sense of them. They blamed them on some junkie, just to close the cases. But we all knew it was the demon in your mother's body.'

'There's no such thing as demons. The cult and my mother had clearly gone insane.'

'What difference does it make? See, this is why I never told you about her. I was trying to protect you from your past. But here you are, begging for the truth.'

'What about my dad? What happened to him?'

'I have no idea where he is. He took off one day and left me to clean up the mess.'

My uncle rubbed his eyes. I stared at the table.

'So my mother wasn't just a cultist, she was a murderer. How am I supposed to process something like this? How am I supposed to live a normal life?'

'You were never supposed to live a normal life. Don't you see? She wanted the same thing for you. Thankfully, the government came down hard on the Church around the time they were tossing you into that chamber.'

'So you were there? You were in the audience when they'd put me inside?'

'I'm sorry. I was as much a fool as anyone. More so, considering I reached the highest tier. I wanted to touch the divine, like everyone else. But after I saw what happened to my sister…'

My uncle went silent. He stood, got a glass from the cupboard, and poured himself another whisky.

'It's not easy to talk about this. I'm sorry, but I don't want to say more.' He swallowed the contents of the glass in one gulp. 'Come back some other time.'

I walked to the door, more confounded than ever, and got in my car. I kept checking my email on the way home, hoping that Nora would reply. My empty inbox sent jitters through me.

What exactly was Nora blaming me for? I got home and wasn't sure what to do. I sat on my bed, anxious, and checked my email. When I didn't receive a response come noon, I grabbed my keys and went to my car.

After a twenty-minute drive, I parked outside her building, shaking at the thought of approaching her, especially when she'd told me never to go near her again. It took me a few minutes to gather the courage. Then I got out of the car, approached the door of her building, and rang her on the intercom.

'Who is it?' Her voice came from the speaker.

'Nora, I swear, whatever you think I did, it wasn't me.'

'Did you really drive all the way here when I told you to stay away? Do you want me to call the police?'

'Please, Nora, I would never do anything to harm you. I'm worried.'

'Who else could it have been? Unless someone was listening in on us.'

'Listening when?'

'When we were up the other night searching for *you-know-what* on the internet.'

'What happened, exactly?'

Nora sighed with impatience. 'After you left, someone rang my doorbell. I opened the door and there was a note on the floor. It said, "I think your skin would look lovely on us. Open yourself to the light." Also, the note was covered in some red liquid. It smelled like blood.'

Cold fingers ran down my spine. 'You're in danger. Let me in, Nora.'

'Danger? From whom?' she scoffed. 'It could only be

you.'

'Please, you have to let me in. I think my mother is still alive. I think *she* sent you that letter.'

A frustrated grunt sounded. 'You need help. Go back to your therapist. Talk through all of this with him. I don't mind helping you with your rashes and phobias, but this… this is too much, even for me.'

No matter how many times I rang her on the intercom, she wouldn't answer. Worried that she would call the police, I got in my car and drove home.

Didn't do much else that day. I took a melatonin and antihistamine, ate a cheese sandwich, and turned in early. I chanted the words, 'Please don't hurt her. Please don't hurt her' as I lay on my side in the dark.

I was standing in my mother's bedroom. Cold wind whispered through the open window. The rocking chair sat empty, though it swayed back and forth, back and forth.

Then a creature crawled through the window. Crawled onto the ceiling. It stared down at me, its skin loose and dangling, its eyes these spheres of all-white.

It chittered down the wall. It wore its skin so strangely. Nothing fit right. Its belly button was too high, where its chest should be, while its chest wrapped loosely across its shoulders. Skin in the shape of hands dangled off its wrists.

'He was unwilling,' it said with my mother's hoarse voice. 'We'll try again and find someone who is open to the light.'

It sat in the chair and scratched off the skin it was wearing. Blood and mush spread across the walls and carpet. It even clawed out chunks of its organs, as if by mistake, though never showed pain. Instead, it groaned with delight, as if satisfying the deepest of itches.

No skin remained, just veiny muscle and dripping flesh. It got up and crawled back out the window.

The rocking chair continued to sway, despite being

empty. Back and forth, back and forth. It sped up, swaying once every second, then ten times a second, then a hundred times. Night turned to day turned to night as time rushed forward.

The creature crawled in through the window again. This time, its smiling face was uncanny and familiar. Its lips stretched wide between a closely shaven black and grey beard.

It was the man from the radiation chamber, crimson robe and all. Though I could only see his face, feet, and hands, none of it fit right. The face looked like a Frankenstein mask I'd seen someone wear on Halloween, all loose and misshapen. Blood dripped from bloated feet. Bumpy burns and swelling covered every finger.

'He was so happy,' the entity said with Mother's voice. 'He wanted to join the light and now he is among the stars.'

It sat in the rocking chair. It rocked backward, then bit into its own arm, sucking its skin into its mouth. It chewed, then spat the skin onto the floor, letting out a cackle as it eyed me watching. It rocked forward, pulled its leg up, and bit into its thigh, chewing on the skin and spitting bits of hair and porous skin. It continued to chew its own skin, and soon, all that remained was muscle and flesh with hollow sockets for eyes. After a few hours of rocking in the chair at speed and laughing in joy, it crawled out of the window once more.

Another day passed with me standing in the room. The rocking chair swayed so hard, it shattered against the wall, wood splinters clattering around me. The creature crawled in through the window, chittering all the while. This time, it wore its skin tighter. It was a man with oak-coloured hair and tortured, wooden eyes. I recognise him. I saw a similar man in the mirror, each day.

'Daddy was so happy to go into the light,' the entity said as one eyeball almost popped out. 'Overjoyed. It was nothing less than a dream come true. Who shall we bless,

401

next?'

'*Pleeaaaseeee… doooonnn't… huuuurt… herrr…'* The voice was like a forgotten memory.

'Please don't hurt her,' I said with the terrified voice of a child.

The demon tilted its head and grinned with my father's loose face. 'Don't worry. It's not Nora's turn… yet. Now come and sit in my lap.'

With terror thudding through my heart and throat, I couldn't resist the creature's command. I sat in its lap, the stench of decayed flesh, rotten blood, and sulfurous skin burrowing into my brain. I stared at a strand of muscle poking through the gaping skin on the thing's chest. So many holes in that muscle, as if it had been stabbed with a hairbrush. And those holes grew and shrank as it breathed in and out.

I saw holes and loose skin and strange fluids across its body. Were my insides like this, too? Was my skin so easily replaced?

I awoke to my phone's blaring alarm. Time to get ready for work. I dashed toward my sink and spewed – this was becoming a ritual. My whole body itched. I pulled off my shirt to see my skin colonised by so many clustered bumps. I jumped in the shower, pushed the dial to cold, and let the water freeze me. After, I used a butter knife to lather every inch of my skin with steroid cream.

I called into work sick but made sure to attend my appointment with Doctor Nathaniel.

I sat on his white couch amid warm lights. I took my time describing everything that had happened over the weekend. To help with my skin phobia, Doctor Nathaniel dimmed the room more than usual. He didn't write anything in his notebook this time. He simply sat and stared, sometimes nodding. Once in a while, it seemed he forgot to blink, so entranced was he with my story.

After I'd finished, he asked, 'Would you like some water?'

I shook my head. 'No thank you.'

Then he crossed his arms and legs, as if trying to make himself small. 'I think you need to consider the possibility that you did, in fact, leave that message outside Nora's door.'

'What? You can't be serious. I would never do such a thing.'

'It's the only plausible reality.'

'No. That thing is out there, Doctor. It's been out there this whole time. It wants her skin.'

'I know this all seems very real to you. But it's my opinion that you've experienced a break in reality. You've been under immense stress.'

My foot tapped on the carpet. 'What about my uncle? He believes it's real.'

'Your uncle is probably troubled by what happened, too. It's his way of explaining everything. It's unfortunate he put all that on you, just as we were making progress.'

I had to calm and comport myself. I couldn't let him believe I was hallucinating. That would have awful consequences for my job. 'Yeah. You're right. I have been stressed. Maybe I just need some rest.'

'You should see a dermatologist, too. I'll make a referral.'

I nodded, unable to control my shaking.

Doctor Nathaniel smiled. But it was not like how he usually smiled. It didn't fit right, the corners twitching and sharp. 'Go home. And when you see that creature again, I want you to ask it a question.'

'Q-Question?'

'Ask him where he hid the tablets.'

'Tablets?'

'The Sumerian tablets.'

I scratched my knee, then chuckled nervously. What a dumb joke. 'You're pulling my leg, right?'

'Just ask.' That came out much deeper and discordant. And Doctor Nathaniel's mouth didn't move in the right way, like when audio isn't synced properly with video.

'O-Okay.' I grabbed my knee to stop it from shaking. 'You know what? I've got to go.'

I quickly walked out the door and ran to my car. I tried calling Nora to check if she was okay, but all I got was a busy tone.

I arrived home to see my bedroom window open. I'd left it closed with the blinds down. I shut it, let out a terrified sigh, and checked to see if anything had been stolen. But everything seemed undisturbed.

My ringer went off. 'Uncle' flashed on the screen.

'It's come back,' he said in a panicked voice. 'Your aunt saw it crawling on our roof. It could be wearing anyone's skin. It could look like anyone. Sound like anyone. Be careful.'

'I will. You be careful too.'

'Maybe you should stay with us for a few days. I'm worried about you.'

'Yeah... that would be good. I'll pack some stuff and be right over.'

'Okay. Call me if you see anything.'

Soon as I put my phone down, my ringer went off again. 'Nora' flashed on the screen. I answered.

'Hey,' she said.

'Nora, is everything okay?'

'Yeah.'

'Thank God,' I breathed out in relief.

'I'm sorry about earlier. I was being paranoid. Do you want to meet?'

'Of course.'

'I miss you. We all do.'

'*We?*'

'We're waiting.'

She hung up. I tried calling back and was met with a busy tone.

I sat on my bed and cried. I was too late. I couldn't save her. She'd joined the light.

Would I join it, too? Would it finally be my turn?

Instead of going anywhere, I stayed in bed. I was too terrified to cry. My uncle called me twenty times, but I was too sad to answer. Too fearful that he'd already *joined the light*.

Once darkness fell, I sat at my desk and opened my laptop. I typed everything you've read, so far. Like my uncle did, I have to document my experience. If I can't uncover and overcome this evil, perhaps someone else can.

So, here I sit. I know, deep down, that I can't escape my fate. It will come for me. It's already taken everyone I love.

I doze off.

I am awoken by another scratch at the window. I gather the courage to open the blind, but I see nothing but my empty, dark street. Perhaps the wind is out to get me, too.

I sit back at my desk and stare at these words.

Another scratch sounds from the ceiling.

I put the laptop on my lap, swivel my chair, and look up.

There it is. I'm staring right at it. It's clinging to the ceiling and glaring down at me, its neck bent backwards.

'It's time,' it says from the depths of its throat, 'for your treatment.'

I'm too paralysed to do anything but type. The creature just crawled down the wall. Oh god… it looks like Nora, but nothing fits right. Why is its head turned backward? It's like when you put your shirt on wrong.

It grabs folds of its skin and pulls itself open.

Within it is brightness, the light of so many warm bulbs. The beautiful bulbs from the radiation chamber.

It soothes my worries. It calms my jitters. The perfect heat for my skin. For my soul.

'Come with us,' it says in Nora's beautiful voice. 'Come to the light.'

I'm going, now. Going to the light. I'll be with the stars, soon. If you want to find me, you'll have to go there. This is it. Goodbye, everyone.

THE ANATOMY OF FEAR

Thank you for reading The Anatomy of Fear.
FOLLOW OUR AUTHORS

Trudie Skies
www.trudieskies.com/

Tim Hardie
www.timhardieauthor.co.uk/

LL MacRae
llmacrae.com/
LL has provided the following warnings for Bone: Domestic abuse.

Bjørn Larssen
www.bjornlarssen.com/sm
From Bjorn: Thanks to Marian, Tim, Holly and Sarah for your patience and understanding.

Lee C Conley
www.leeconleyauthor.com

Jacob Sannox
www.jacobsannox.com/
Jacob has provided the following warnings for Liver: Suicide.

Krystle Matar
www.krystlematar.com/
Krystle has provided the following warnings for Teeth: Body horror, infant death and abuse.

THE ANATOMY OF FEAR

BA Bellec
babellec.com/

Sean Crow
www.lordofcrows.org

HL Tinsley
htinsleywriter.wordpress.com/

Ryan Howse
www.goodreads.com/au-
thor/show/15262976.Ryan_Howse

Zamil Akhtar

zamilakhtar.com/

We would like to thank you for reading.
If you have enjoyed this anthology, please could we ask
if you would be so kind as to leave a review somewhere.
Every review and rating is hugely appreciated.

Printed in Great Britain
by Amazon